Claiming the Caribou

By Georgianna Green

© Copyright 2004 Georgianna Green. All rights reserved.

No part of this publication may be reproduced, stored in a retrieval system, or transmitted, in any form or by any means, electronic, mechanical, photocopying, recording, or otherwise, without the written prior permission of the author.

Printed in Victoria, Canada

A cataloguing record for this book that includes the U.S. Library of Congress Classification number, the Library of Congress Call number and the Dewey Decimal cataloguing code is available from the National Library of Canada. The complete cataloguing record can be obtained from the National Library's online database at: www.nlc-bnc.
ISBN: 1-4120-2803-5

TRAFFORD

This book was published *on-demand* in cooperation with Trafford Publishing.
On-demand publishing is a unique process and service of making a book available for retail sale to the public taking advantage of on-demand manufacturing and Internet marketing. **On-demand publishing** includes promotions, retail sales, manufacturing, order fulfilment, accounting and collecting royalties on behalf of the author.

Suite 6E, 2333 Government St., Victoria, B.C. V8T 4P4, CANADA
Phone   250-383-6864   Toll-free 1-888-232-4444 (Canada & US)
Fax   250-383-6804   E-mail   sales@trafford.com
Web site www.trafford.com   TRAFFORD PUBLISHING IS A DIVISION OF TRAFFORD HOLDINGS LTD.
Trafford Catalogue #04-0631   www.trafford.com/robots/04-0631.html

10   9   8   7   6   5   4   3   2

Thank you Mom, for teaching me to love books and for giving me that little nudge.... I love you. And Miss Estabrooks for showing me all those years ago how much fun writing can be

CHAPTER 1

It was just the sight of it, really, that did it. One glimpse of the old cabin and the tension drained from her muscles. That's all it took. The very first breath of fresh wilderness air to rush through her lungs relaxed a jaw she had been clenching for the last three months. The cheerful chirping of the songbirds overhead and the lazy sound of the waves lapping at the boards of the dock eased the constant, dull ache between her eyes.

"..a hand getting those boxes to the door?"

With a start, Shelley realized the old man had been talking for some time. "No, I'm fine," she said with a smile, a big honest one that felt new to her. It had been a long time. Thinking of the boat ride to the cabin, the smile became an irrepressible chuckle. He had taken the corners of the river so fast and sharp and close to the bank that she had been able to touch the cones that dangled from the dying boughs of the pine trees. Uprooted by the high water, they leaned precariously over the river in a slow but sure descent to their own watery grave. The wind had pulled tendrils of her hair loose and whipped them into wild little tangles, and she could still feel the droplets on her cheeks from the fine water spray; the same sparkling spray that made rainbows along the side of the boat. "I'll be just fine," she repeated. "But thank you so much for the ride up the river, Mr. Lewis. It was definitely an adventure."

"Murphy," he insisted. "Everyone calls me Murphy." Tilting his old head slightly, he squinted at her and passed one gnarled hand over his mouth, rubbing back and forth thoughtfully. "It's been a good, long while since your grandfather has been up this way. We all sort of suspected that he ...well ..." He cleared his throat uncomfortably. "Don't even know if the cabin is in working order. Sure you don't need a hand, seeing as you're by yourself and all?"

"No, really Murphy," Shelley said firmly. "That's sort of what this trip is about. I've never been anywhere like this before - never left Toronto actually, but it's like a challenge and I'm looking forward to it. I really am. Plus, Grandpa mentioned that there is a neighbour down the path and he has a radio if there's any emergencies."

Murphy grinned, showing only two tobacco stained teeth in a slightly undershot jaw. Shelley couldn't help but smile back at him again - he reminded her of a stuffed toy she'd had as a little girl. It was a wrinkled, tattered bulldog with two stubby teeth poking out the front. She had loved it to death. They both had that same 'so ugly it's cute' quality.

"You take care, Missy. Use the radio and call in if you need anything." He heaved the last box of groceries onto the dock, untied the boat and sped off with one final wave of his hand.

Deciding she would explore the cabin before unpacking the groceries, Shelley picked up her pack and ran up the hill. The dirt path was worn smooth, lined on both sides with a natural curved wall of pink granite and covered in places with lush green moss and reindeer lichen. Even small saplings were growing out of the cracks and hollows in the rock.

Someone, most likely her grandfather, had scratched

the family name McGraw in the lichen. The name was starting to fill back in, becoming more and more indistinct with each passing year. She traced the name with her finger, chipping away at the dry flakes growing over it. She thought of her grandfather in the Old Folks Home, and how he had hated it. He had hated it when she called it that, too. He would always puff up his chest in mock indignation and say, "I am not an OLD FOLK. I'm in my prime." After his stroke, the partial paralysis made it impossible for her to look after him on her own. He had insisted on the move to the Home - even though he knew he would hate it. He died less than three weeks later, two months ago now.

Oh, right, she thought bitterly. He didn't die - he just passed on. That's what the nurse had said. "People pass on," in that condescending tone nurses and doctors develop when they become immune to other people's sorrow. He had been the only person left in the world that she loved, that loved her. The only one who knew her when she had braces and pigtails, that knew her fears from childhood and dreams of the future.

She had just finished her last semester of University this spring, graduating with her Bachelor of Science, so she put her summer job on hold and went through his personal things; pictures and books, keepsakes and clothes, keeping only his favourite things for herself. This cabin and a small bank balance were her inheritance. So here she was, to grieve and then move on. It felt like a good place.

The golden logs were faded and stained black on the bottoms from years of splashing rain. Moss was crammed between them to keep the winter winds and summer rains from driving through the gaps. It gave the cabin a homey, rustic look that she found very comforting. Pushing on up the hill, she skipped up the steps to the porch and past the two home-hewn rocking chairs flanking the door. She was startled and a little frightened to find that the solid wooden door, carved beneath the beautiful stained glass window with the words 'welcome friends', was already ajar.

She pushed it open slightly to peer inside. It was dark, much too dark to see if anything was amiss. With vivid imaginings of fat black bears romping and ransacking the kitchen foremost in her mind, she pushed the door open all the way and stepped inside. It was then that she heard it. A deep, male laugh, then another. Shelley's fear intensified at the sound, for the laughter was at once malicious and without mirth.

Shelley had always considered herself fairly 'street smart', having grown up in the heart of one of Canada's largest, most violent cities. She couldn't deny that she had a powerful, instinctive urge to turn around and walk right back out the door and call for Murphy or her neighbour or simply walk back to town. Yet ...something propelled her forward; perhaps the sudden surge of anger that her grandfather's precious haven had been violated, perhaps the feeling, the naive surety that evil things didn't happen to people in the wilderness, perhaps simple curiosity. Thinking back, she was never sure what was going through her mind as she crossed that dark room, her sneakers never making a sound. She did remember how the sliver of light under the door beckoned her. She remembered the rough texture of the door. The cool touch of the knob.

She pulled the door open and stepped silently into the kitchen. The sight before her held her completely speechless with shock. Back against the far wall of the kitchen stood a man. His arms were raised above his head, hands duct taped together over one solid iron bar of an old fashioned pot rack. His head lolled suddenly to rest against the wall. She gasped, horrified at the condition of his face. It was covered with bruises and cuts, some already crusted with dried blood, some still oozing. The biggest gash, crossing over his left eye, ran from his forehead to just above his lip. The blood ran freely from it, down his cheek and the strong column of his neck.

One man was beating him with a solid, wooden stick. Shelley realized with a sick feeling in her stomach, that it was a chair leg, elegantly carved and now coated with blood. Red droplets sprayed across the room with every powerful blow. She could hear it - the sickening THWACK as it connected with flesh.

Another man just watched, but they were both laughing, having a good time. The kitchen was a shambles. Empty beer bottles and junk food wrappers were strewn across the table, piled so high at one end that some had fallen over the edge onto the floor. There was nothing else, no clue as to who they were or why they were in the cabin, except for the gun. It lay on the table flattening an empty Doritos bag, gleaming dully in a red wash of light from the setting sun.

The man doing the beating was tall and thin, spare but strong with flat, wiry muscles. Dirty blond hair poked out in all directions from the perimeter of his baseball cap. She could see when he turned his body slightly that his white T-shirt was now spattered with enough blood to cover part of the 'NO FEAR' logo on the front.

The other man was bald, his head shaved so closely that the tight skin reflected light like a mirror. He was shorter than the blond man but twice as big, with bulging, over-developed muscles that bragged of hours and hours at the gym. She couldn't see his face either, but noted with a shudder the hideous, black tattoo on the back of his neck. It was a spider, and the legs seemed to do a macabre dance every time he moved his head.

The bound man was silent, letting out only an occasional involuntary grunt of pain as the stick connected with his face and abdomen. Shelley felt sickened by the brutal beating, but she hovered helplessly at the door. She didn't know what to do. The blond man stopped long enough then, to twist the cap off a new bottle of beer and drink deeply from it.

The unexpected reprieve caused the injured man to open his eyes and his surprised gaze collided directly with her own. His eyes went from her to the door several times, with a look so intense, she knew he was telling her to leave. Still motionless with shock, she didn't even notice that her bag fell from her fingers to the floor with a noticeable thud.

The other two men spun around to face her at the sound, twin expressions of stunned surprise on their faces; expressions which rapidly twisted into leers at discovering she was just a woman, alone. She took the offensive with a bravado she did not feel.

"What's going on here?" Her voice shook. "What are you doing in my cabin?"

Both men started toward her. The fear twisted in her stomach.

"My boyfriend and his friends are just outside. They won't be a minute," she lied. "Get out." Thinking to make her lie more convincing, she called the first name that came to her. "Kevin!! Kevin, come in here!"

The blond looked doubtful, but instructed his partner

with a jerk of his head. "Go check it out, Mark. It doesn't make sense that she'd be here all alone. Keep watch out there just in case and we'll switch when I'm done."

Knowing she had only moments after Mark slipped outside through the kitchen door, Shelley felt her panic rise. Her eyes skidded once more to the bound man.

"Run!" He yelled, his voice hoarse. "Run, Goddamn it!"

Gratefully spurred into action, she ran to the door, only to have it slammed by a large hand reaching from behind her. Grabbing her arm, the man spun her around and flung her against it. He backhanded her across the face, causing her teeth to cut into her cheek from the blow. Her mouth filled with blood, warm and coppery tasting. Completely panicked, she turned once more to scrabble for the door handle, only to be hauled back and thrown to the floor. He let her get up before slamming his fist into her cheekbone, knocking her back down. He waited, laughing, as she pushed herself up.

"What do you want?" She cried, sobbing with a terror she couldn't control. "Oh, God. You can have the cabin," she offered desperately. "Just let us leave!"

His only answer was an evil, crooked smile. It fueled her anger, so foolishly perhaps, she thrust her arm straight out at the shoulder and slammed the heel of her hand into his nose. His own hands came up reflexively to cup it, but the blood seeped through his fingers anyway, to drip onto the floor.

"Bitch!" He roared. He took his hands away, gaping at them in disbelief, at the red smears on his fingers, and his sport turned to serious business.

Shelley had lunged desperately at the door after her lucky punch, but his distraction was only momentary. He wheeled her around and let his fist fly, again and again into her cheek, her mouth, her eyes. The pain exploded in her brain. The blows were so rapid and ruthless she could no longer coherently separate one from the next. Finally his left hand released the handful of sweater that had kept her upright, and she crumpled into a heap at his feet. Dazed and barely conscious, Shelley lay without moving, hoping, pleading in her mind as she never had before - to Fate, to God, to any and all powers that be, that this bizarre attack was over.

She still didn't move when she felt him bend over her. She felt him pull her right arm straight out in front of her. Confused, she managed to lift her head high enough to look at him. Their eyes met.

"For my nose," he said with obvious satisfaction, grabbing the hand on the floor. With a swift and brutal jerk he pulled up with enough force to snap both bones in her right forearm.

Shelley screamed in agony. Blinking away the tears that blurred her vision, she struggled to her knees with her good arm, but just as she braced herself to stand, a vicious kick to her stomach sent her sprawling to the floor once more. Another kick to her belly stole the breath from her body. Long moments passed as he continued to kick, before her lungs managed to pull in any air at all. Blackness edged her vision, growing and growing until one final strike of his booted foot against her temple sent her into the blessed oblivion of unconsciousness.

Michael had thought at first she was some kind of vision, induced perhaps by the haze of pain he found himself sinking into, or even as a sign of his approaching death. She was young and pretty in a shy, understated way. He had felt a kind of relieved calm come over him as he studied her, thinking crazily that she had come here to him, for him, so he wouldn't have to die alone. He took in everything he could about her in those brief seconds, as he tried to memorize her image. He didn't want his killers to be the last thing he ever saw.

It was her horrified, panicked look that finally cleared the fog from his brain, making him realize she was no angel. His disappointment was so crushing, so complete, that it took a moment for the full import of the situation to strike him. Surely they wouldn't …but they would. Of course they would. Then they would kill her too.

He had tried to make her leave with his eyes, but she just stood there, rooted to the spot and stared at him with those big dark eyes. Then she dropped her damn bag on the floor and the game was up. It was over for her then, he had thought despairingly. Events had begun to unfold before him after that, like some terrible movie scene. He had never witnessed anything so brutal or seen such insane rage. The man was wild-eyed with it, so out of control that spittle ran unchecked down his chin. His fist slammed savagely into the young woman over and over and over again.

Michael lunged at the bonds encircling his wrists, making them cut deeper into his skin. He tried frantically to twist or pull free or even to haul his battered body up to rip them with his teeth but as always, the thick bands of tape held fast. He started to scream at the blond man, hurling vicious insults and taunts at him, every vile curse and epithet he could think of but he didn't even spare him a glance.

When he heard her bones snap and her horrible scream, he began to plead with the man, begging as he had refused to do for himself, groveling with helpless desperation. He would have gotten on his knees if he was able, but still, the tall blond man ignored him, too far gone in his rage to even register his presence.

He fell back against the wall in defeat, trying not to cry as he watched the angel that wasn't really an angel huddle on the dirty floor of the kitchen. She was in a fetal position, curled protectively into herself except for the broken arm; it stuck out, exposed and vulnerable and bent awkwardly where a jagged piece of white bone protruded from an ugly tear in her flesh. She no longer made a sound as he kicked her ruthlessly in the back, stomach and face. Her eyes were wide open and for an endless moment, Michael was sure she was dead. It almost broke him, dragged him over that fine, wavering line that marked the boundaries of his own sanity. But at the same time, it kindled a small flame inside him that had been extinguished hours before. Though fueled by hate and the need for revenge, it was quite simply, the desire to live.

He held his breath, praying silently for help or strength, any kind of miracle, when her chest rose to take in a ragged gasp of air. He had never felt such an incredible array of intense emotion in his entire life; hatred, rage, frustration, guilt, pity for this innocent young woman; each eddied violently around inside him. Mostly though, he felt relief that she yet lived, a huge, swelling wave of relief. He closed his eyes with a shudder as it washed over him.

He opened his eyes in time to see the man's boot connect with her head. He watched those beautiful eyes, green and luminous, glassy with tears and glazed with pain, close as she finally lost consciousness. The man stopped the assault, letting his breath out through his teeth in a hiss, to slow it down. He braced his hands on his knees for a moment, studying the young woman's prone form. Then he looked right at Michael.

"What do you think?" He taunted in the sudden quiet of the room. "Enjoying yourself?" He tossed a smile of wicked, twisted pleasure over his shoulder at Michael, taking in at a glance his torn wrists, at the blood running in slow drips to his elbows where they fell to form a small, sticky pool at his feet.

Turning back to the woman, he grabbed the front of her light summer sweater and ripped it open. Tiny buttons skittered across the polished wooden planks of the floor. The lacy bra was also ripped off and tossed aside, exposing her breasts. He made short work of her jeans, pulling them down to shackle her ankles.

Michael was horrified, for the man's intent couldn't be more obvious. How could he watch this?

"Stop! Jesus Christ, stop!" He demanded. "I'll do anything, please, just leave her alone."

The man laughed, no doubt delighted that he had gotten him to plead. "You don't have anything I want. Ah, but this little one ..." He ran his hand over one exposed breast. "Watch carefully."

Grabbing a handful of her hair, which had come loose and now lay in a tangled fan around her body, he pulled her into a half sitting position.

"Darlin'," he breathed into her face. "Wake up, gorgeous." He found and poured the rest of his beer over her face, where it ran in rivulets into her hair and down her neck. He chuckled darkly when there was no response from her, lowering his head to run his tongue along her neck and over to the top of her shoulder, where he sank his teeth into her flesh.

Her body jerked with a moan, her lashes fluttered for a moment and then in pained surprise, finally opened. She shrieked to find herself face to face with him.

Apparently satisfied that she was conscious at least, he let her upper body fall back onto the floor. Michael watched in growing horror, unable to look away as the man's hands went to the buttons of his pants. Renewing his struggles to free himself, Michael once again began screaming, alternating curses with pleas. All went ignored. He had never felt so helpless.

"You sick bastard! Haven't you done enough?! Look at her, for Christ's sake!"

The man dropped to his knees between her ankles.

"You frigging coward, fight me. FIGHT ME!"

His hands roved over her breasts, pinching and kneading. She struggled weakly, trying to turn onto her side, cringing away from his touch. He ripped her underpants off.

"You goddamn sick bugger! I'll kill you for this - I swear it!"

He wrenched her bare thighs apart and thrust himself into her abused body with a groan of satisfaction. She screamed, a terrible, blood curdling sound that was cut off abruptly when he cuffed her in the side of the head.

Michael closed his eyes, defeated and sickened by the sounds of the rape, wishing they had killed him instead of forcing him to witness such a thing. He could hear her crying, begging the man to stop, his coarse grunts and the rhythmic sounds of two bodies coming together.

He forced himself to act, to ignore the weakness and agony in his own body. Shaking, with biceps flexing, he pulled himself up once more to chew at the tape around his wrists. It was an almost impossible task, for the tape was above the bar, out of reach of his teeth. After what seemed an eternity, sweating, with muscles trembling, he managed to catch a section on his inner wrist and jerked sharply, ripping it about halfway down its length. He sagged back down when the sounds of the rape stopped, affecting an air of defeat. The blond man got to his feet and swaggered towards him, crudely refastening his pants.

"Just enough of her left for Mark, eh?" He taunted, glancing over at the woman. She was still flat on her back, legs spread grotesquely, unconscious now and barely alive.

Michael took instant advantage of both the man's nearness and distraction. He grabbed the bar with his hands, hauled his legs up then launched them out for a true, solid blow to the head. The man toppled over like a felled tree. The pressure of his hands and the weight of his own body made it easy for Michael to rip the tape all the way and free himself from the bar. The sticky material that had held him for so long peeled off his wrists, taking the damaged pieces of skin with it and tearing the wounds open even further.

Only momentarily stunned, the man was already pushing himself to his feet, so Michael lunged desperately for the gun on the table. His fingers slid down the barrel, smooth and cool, as he struggled to get a firm grip on it. He was conscious of only two things in those brief, brief moments. One was basic, driven by a fierce jumble of raw emotion, primal and almost overwhelming. It was a need to put the gun down and beat this man to death. Shooting him would be too quick, too easy. He wanted to hear him cry and beg, to see the desperate fear in his eyes, but most of all, he wanted him to feel even a measure of the pain he had inflicted on others this day. Yet, warring with his yearning for revenge was the sure knowledge that he would lose. He was just so tired, so completely physically drained and neither he nor the woman could afford to lose this round.

He spun around to face his attacker and raised the gun, waving it in front of him.

The blond man froze in mid stride, rocking back on his heels to regain his balance. He stared back at Michael, eyes icy and totally devoid of emotion; no fear, no surprise, nor even any acknowledgment of this sudden shift in power. His lip actually curled in a sneer of contempt. "You don't have the balls."

Michael felt another rush of frustrated, tormented rage at the insult. His breath came fast and hard, as though he had been running for miles. His chest ached with it. He pulled the hammer back with his thumb. It was time for this all to end.

"I think I do." He raised the gun again and took careful aim, never losing contact with the challenge in those cold blue eyes. He let his finger squeeze the trigger. The recoil sent sharp waves of agony throughout his entire body and he staggered back against the table, reaching out to keep himself upright as he fought the dizzying blackness that spun around him.

When he became aware of things once more, the blond man was already on the floor, half laying on the contents of the upended trash basket. Michael watched the blood stain grow around the mortal chest wound with a strangely disconnected feeling. He stepped closer, gun in hand, needing to see it finished. Carefully leaning over, he nudged at the man's jaw with the muzzle of the gun, making his head roll back and then toward him. The eyes were open but barely aware, and still, even in these last moments of his life, completely empty. No tears, no remorse, no plea for pity; there was nothing as Michael hunched over the body, watching, waiting for the final light of life to fade from his eyes. The man dragged in one raspy breath after another, his body hungry for the oxygen his heart could no longer deliver. It felt like hours, minutes dragging into yet longer minutes as Michael watched, though in reality only a few short moments passed before the deep, ragged breaths ceased to come at all.

The odd suspended feeling popped like a bubble and Michael leaped to his feet, knowing the dead man's partner had no doubt started up the hill at the sound of the shot. He hid behind the door and waited, heart pounding a crazy rhythm against his chest. His mouth was dry as dust as he thought about what he had just done, and was about to do. His swollen lips mouthed a silent prayer. It was so close to being over…

"You ass!" Mark shouted as he burst through the door. "What the hell are you doing? I didn't even get-"

Before the man even registered the body on the floor, Michael slammed the butt of the gun into the back of his head with such force he heard a popping noise. He swung again, hitting him twice more and forcing him down. It was so completely satisfying. He wrapped his fingers around the thick neck then slammed the already stunned man's head repeatedly into the floor. He squeezed tighter and tighter, slammed harder, watching the man turn red, then purple before blacking out.

The adrenaline was rushing through him like quicksilver and it pushed him into action he might never have taken otherwise. He thought briefly of alternatives; this man was subdued, possibly dying. Certainly no longer a danger. He could radio in. The police would come and pick him up. The man would go to jail. It all made sense, but the only thought he could focus on was the one that made him raise the gun once more. He would never, ever feel safe again if he let this man live. Again he aimed and fired, this time firing one neat shot into the side of the big man's forehead, killing him instantly.

CHAPTER 2

Michael gently set his burden down upon the sofa bed and resting on one hip, perched beside her. He studied her thoughtfully, wondering how to proceed. First things first and go from there. That was his mother's favorite expression, he recalled with grim amusement. Barely able to move, he wanted nothing more than to lay his aching body beside her and sleep, to find a reprieve from the unrelenting pain. But, he couldn't yet, couldn't just leave the poor woman like this; naked and filthy and bleeding. Plus, he had the unsettling feeling that if he crawled onto that bed he would never get up again.

He went to his work room to radio the provincial police and order a plane in for morning. The sun was already starting to sink into the tree line, so it was too late to get one tonight. He had a small aircraft of his own, a Cessna Skyhawk, and was in fact a licensed pilot, but as his plane was still at the hangar in town for routine servicing, it wasn't going to do him much good. The blood pounded in his head, throbbing at his temples like a vengeful pulse. His vision blurred, and shadowy shapes skittered just beyond the edge of his vision; shapes that disappeared when he turned his head to catch them. Poking gingerly at the inner corners of his eyes, he shook his head ruefully. All things considered, he had no trouble admitting that he was in no condition to fly anyway.

Next, he set about gathering the items he would need;

clean towels and washcloths, clean clothes, a first aid kit, a large basin of water and various other odds and ends he thought he might need. Going back to the young woman, he began to remove what was left of her clothes. He wasn't sure if he was doing the right thing - he certainly didn't want to traumatize her further. They would clean her up at the hospital in the morning, and take good care of her there, he knew that. Waiting twelve hours to wash the blood and semen and saliva from her skin may not make much difference to the health of her body, but he knew it would to her spirit, her emotional well being. For that reason, he felt it was important to do it now. Her sweater was still on her arms, so he ripped at it, thinking it would be easier than trying to pull it off of her broken arm. The material gave with a jerk despite his efforts to be careful. A low wail, borne as much from fear as pain, he supposed, escaped from her at the sound of the tearing cloth. Only half conscious, but still caught in the throes of her waking nightmare, she began to fight him, to strike out at him with her uninjured hand, her teeth.

"Shh, baby, it's all right," he soothed, grappling with her flailing good arm. He caught it and held it firmly to her side, although he had to rest a good portion of his weight on her heaving chest to keep her still. "He's dead. I won't hurt you. Shh." He repeated that over and over, until her struggles stopped. "I'm not going to hurt you. I'm going to clean you up. Relax if you can," he suggested gently.

She looked at him finally, one eye bright in her bruised face, the other crusted shut with blood. "You ..." She tried, using the tip of her tongue to wet her cracked, swollen lips. "You saw ...it?"

At his nod of confirmation she closed her eye and turned her head away again. A fat, solitary tear squeezed out from the outer corner to roll down the side of her face. He was held transfixed, watching that tear. It rolled near a small cut, turning a deep red before skirting it to continue down the side of her jaw. Guilt for his part in her pain was a huge weight pressing down on his shoulders. That tear felt like an accusing finger pointing at him. If only he had done things differently when he found those men in the cabin, if only he hadn't *watched* her get beaten and raped. It made him feel ...less than a man. With his thoughts running along such a vein, he was startled by her next words.

"Don't look at me. Don't see me. Please." She began to cry quietly, trying to cover her nakedness. "I'm so ashamed," she whispered.

"Oh, no. No! You have no reason to be ashamed. This was done *to* you. You didn't ask for this!" With a grimace of pain, he eased himself into a sitting position behind her and folded her in his arms. Without thinking, soothing words and sounds of comfort poured from him, as he rocked her back and forth. His compassion, sincerely and openly given, seemed to open the floodgates to her misery. She clutched at the arm he had crossed in front of her and wept. Great, convulsive sobs wracked her body until finally, she fell into an exhausted sleep.

Michael felt completely shaken. He didn't know this woman, not even her name, but he was deeply affected by her anguish, and touched that she had shared with him that depth of emotion. Touching her cheek, he vowed to himself that he would do everything in his power to make her well and help her recover.

His first order of business would have to be her broken

arm, though he found it difficult to even look at. Although the bleeding had stopped, the wound was fairly large and ragged, with a sharp piece of bone poking through. He dug through the pile of supplies on the coffee table to find the washcloth, but hesitated over the basin, unsure and frustrated that he didn't know what to do.

Think! Think! He scolded himself silently. Instinct told him not to try to wash it out, despite the fact that there was a high risk of infection with this kind of fracture. He dipped the cloth into the warm water, swirling it around the basin. Goddamn it, why couldn't he remember? Finally, sheer determination pushed him past the moment of confusion, giving him the strength to shake the indecision and the kernel of panic budding inside his chest. This was something he had to do. Studying the nature of the break and the position of the open wound, he simply settled on keeping it covered and supported so the jagged bone didn't sever any more nerves or vessels than it already may have. Working carefully but efficiently, he cradled her forearm in a thick half roll of newspaper to keep it straight, placed a pad of bandages over the wound then wrapped it all in place with gauze. Lastly, he fashioned a sling from an old pillowcase and secured the arm against her chest.

Once again Michael dipped the cloth into the basin of hot water, wrung it out and began to clean her other wounds, first with the soapy water, then a mild antiseptic. He started on her face, working his way down to her waist, stopping only to rinse the cloth or change the bloody water. Her face was discolored and grossly swollen, but the wounds were not life threatening. The gashes from the blond man's ring and the force of his fist were not deep and should heal, if not without scars, at least without complication. The swelling lump on her temple could be more serious, he knew. However, he didn't really know what to do for it, so simply wrapped some ice in a towel and placed it over the lump to reduce the swelling.

She had more than a dozen puncture wounds, small tears on her torso, front and back, each surrounded by vivid red welts that were already darkening into bruises. His cowboy boots must have had some kind of metal tip to do so much damage. He washed them out carefully and felt around her ribs to see if any were broken. They all felt like they were in the right place; no lumps or jagged pieces, so he judged them to be all right.

The nasty bite on her shoulder was still oozing. Bites, he knew too, often festered, so he washed it out thoroughly. Mercifully, she slept through his clumsy ministrations with slow and even breathing.

When he got to her waist he hesitated, uncomfortable and unsure how to proceed. Gently, he parted her legs enough to wash the blood and stickiness from her inner thighs. She still had some bleeding there and for that he was at a loss. He had no way of knowing how badly the assault had damaged her inside. Her legs were uninjured, save a few bruises. He couldn't help but notice as he ran the cloth down one limb, that she had beautiful legs. They weren't long, as she couldn't be more than five foot two, but they were shapely and slender, the skin lightly tanned and satiny smooth. Feeling like a pervert, he quickly finished up and covered her with a blanket.

Next, he struggled to dress her in a pair of his old sweat pants and an oversize T-shirt. Easing the soft cotton shirt over her head, he pulled it down her body and tucked the sling neatly underneath. Once he had her dressed, complete with a pair of grey wool work socks, he started the arduous task of combing her hair. The heavy mass, which almost reached her waist, was matted with blood and beer and caught up in what seemed to his mind an impossible collection of snarls. He worked at it for a long time, long after the tangles had been teased out. The steady rhythm was calming and he could actually feel more and more tension leave his body with each pull of the comb.

He could have stopped there, and probably should have, for physically at least, he was feeling worse and worse with every passing hour. His head felt like it was going to explode, the pounding and the pressure worse than he had ever imagined a headache could be. His empty stomach heaved with swell after swell of nausea, making him gag repeatedly as he tried to swallow the feeling down. His thirst was almost unbearable, but he knew with certainty that anything he tried to drink would instantly come back up. He settled for a couple of ice cubes, letting them melt inside his mouth, giving him temporary relief at least. Running his hand over the young woman's hair, he debated. He had done what first aid he could manage and made her as comfortable as possible, but he was quite sure she would feel better if her hair was clean as well. He would finish this one last thing and then rest.

The decision to wash her hair was one he regretted almost immediately, since he greatly underestimated the complications of washing all that hair. But wash it he did. He pulled her over to the edge of the bed just far enough to drape her hair over the side. After filling a pitcher with warm water, he carefully poured it, guiding the water with his hands through her hair and into the basin on the floor. He massaged her scalp gently to work up a lather, then rinsed the suds out. By the time he was finished, he was so sore and exhausted he could barely move, and his shirt and pants were soaked from kneeling in the spilt water. Despite all that, he felt absurdly pleased with himself. He toweled the excess water from her hair and set to combing it once more before plaiting it into a rough braid. It took him three tries to get the braid to resemble something more than a twisted mess, since he hadn't braided anything since he made rope in cadets more than fifteen years ago. Still on his knees, he rolled her back from the edge of the bed, arranged her limbs into a comfortable position and covered her once more with the blanket.

Bracing his forearms on the bed, he studied her, concerned that she was still sleeping. Her breathing wasn't shallow or rapid and her pulse was steady so he was fairly certain she wasn't going into shock or anything. But he was no doctor. She barely resembled the woman he had first seen a few short hours ago but he had done his best.

Michael's gaze fell to his own clothes, wrinkled, smelly and caked with dark brown stains. Blood had also dried on his face, tightening to a tight mask, and it pulled painfully at the cuts there. He wanted to at least clean that off before he went to bed. More than anything he wanted to have a long shower, to stand there and let the hot, cleansing power of the spray wash everything away. But he just didn't have the strength and it was getting harder to focus his thoughts on any one thing.

He fetched one more basin of clean water from the kitchen and set it once again on the small table. Pulling the table and an ottoman to sit on closer to the cabinet against the wall, Michael wet a new cloth in the fresh water and leaned over to flick the cabinet door open. He tried to brace himself for what he might see in the mirror inlaid there but the cloth dangled from his hand, forgotten, as he stared into the reflection that couldn't possibly be his own. There wasn't one feature he recognized under all that blood. Everything was so swollen and distorted. He brought the cloth up to his face, determined to find himself in the strange reflection, but the hand only hovered there for a moment, frozen, before it began to shake uncontrollably. He dropped the cloth into the basin with a soft curse and pushed it away, causing water to slosh over the lip of the basin and onto the table.

He slumped over in despair, glancing just by chance at the young woman on the bed, and straightened immediately in surprise. Her eyes were open as far as the swelling would allow, her gaze clear and direct. He couldn't read her expression.

"What's your name?" She asked softly.

"Michael," he murmured. "My name is Michael."

"I'm Shelley. You are a very sweet man, Michael."

"No." He denied, shaking his head back and forth. "You don't know. This ..." He gestured weakly toward her, "this is my fault. He did this to you because of me."

"Your fault? You weren't with them, were you?" Her voice rose as though she had never considered the possibility until now.

Michael chewed at his lower lip, not wanting to say anymore, but feeling that he should. "No," he denied finally. "No. I wasn't with them." He cleared his throat. Twice. "I wasn't with them but I made him angry ...and I just ...watched. I'm so sorry ...I ..." He ran his hands through his hair, frustrated that he didn't know what to say. "I didn't know how to stop him, Shelley." He held his breath and looked into her eyes, expecting what, he wasn't sure. Certainly not the compassion he saw there.

She reached out for his hand and he gave it. Her fingers were gentle on the mangled skin of his wrist. "I can see what he has done to you, Michael. I don't blame you, how could I?" She closed her eye for a moment as the force of the memory knocked right into her. "I ...I could hear you, screaming at him ..." She managed a tremulous smile with one corner of her mouth. "You can't blame yourself - it's not like you could leave the room. Just ...just don't tell anyone, okay? I don't want anyone to know that he ...that, well, there's no point. I don't want that to be the first thing everyone here knows about me. Please?" She beseeched, noting his hesitation.

He gave a reluctant nod then squeezed her hand in reassurance. "I won't."

Shelley pulled her hand away, avoiding his gaze. She had actually woken while he was braiding her hair, but had lain quietly in fear and confusion with her eyes closed, trying to piece together her memories of what happened, puzzling over the fate and whereabouts of her attackers and how this gentle man fit into all of it. She had watched him surreptitiously as he moved about the room, noting his obvious exhaustion and pain. She had seen much of his reaction in the mirror as he took stock of his own wounds for the first time and her heart had gone out to him as she observed his attempt to wash.

He needed help, but she wasn't sure if she was capable of giving it. She didn't know anything about wounds and dressings and internal injuries. But mostly she was just afraid.

And uncomfortable. People in general made her feel uncomfortable, but mostly men. The thought made her want to laugh wildly because she had never really had a reason to feel that way before …before today. She didn't want to have to touch this man, and make stilted, comforting conversation. She wanted to feign sleep forever. She had felt a rush of shame at her own selfish behaviour when she saw his despair. He had been so kind and selfless in his treatment of her that she would never forgive herself if she didn't at least try to return the favor. Coming to a decision, Shelley tossed the blanket back and pushed herself up to swing her legs over the side.

Michael protested instantly, obviously alarmed. "What do you think you're doing?" He questioned incredulously. "You need to rest."

Ignoring his protests, she stood, a little shaky, very, very sore, but determined to do her best for him. "Sit down." Her voice was quiet but firm. "What is it you said to me?" She teased weakly, patting the bed, "I'm not going to hurt you, I'm going to clean you up. Relax if you can."

He threw back his head and laughed; great, honest, warm laughter that lightened her own spirits and changed the entire mood of the room. When his laughter died down, he looked at her with a grateful half smile, but shook his head. "It can probably wait until morning now, Shelley. It's not really going to make much difference."

"No." She patted the bed again. "You'll feel better. I promise."

He rubbed the back of his neck, looking into her eyes, trying to determine if she really meant it perhaps, but finally heaved himself off the chair to the space on the bed.

Settling the ottoman comfortably between the bed and table, she debated over where to begin, but finally decided to start with the shirt. It was stiff with blood, lots of blood, and she couldn't stop herself from asking. "Is this all yours?"

He shook his head slightly, jerkily. "No. Some. Some is yours. Some is theirs."

Resolving to ask about the details later, Shelly reached for the buttons, but to her surprise he leaned away, clutching the collar like some outraged maiden.

"What's the problem, Michael?" She asked, surprised and just a teeny bit amused. "Afraid I'm going to strip *you* naked?"

His eyes flew to hers, horrified. He began to stammer. "I didn't know where … I thought you might …well, your clothes were …ripped." He finished lamely. "I'm sorry."

She would have bet her good arm at that moment that he was blushing, though she could hardly tell, his face being battered as it was. "It's okay," she assured him, although privately, her mortification was almost unbearable. "I know you meant well," she added in an attempt to ease the embarrassment for both of them. Pushing his hands aside she worked at the buttons of his shirt one handed, deftly slipping them through the holes until his shirt hung open. He slipped it off with a grimace and dropped it on the floor.

"I did." He affirmed softly, meeting her eyes. "I didn't mean to embarrass you, really I didn't. I just wanted to make you feel …safe and clean and …cared for."

She was touched by his concern; it seemed so sincere. "I really do feel better. Thank you." She desperately hoped he would leave it at that so they could both avoid any more embarrassing questions or comments. She examined him critically in the ensuing silence and the tiny, fragile spark of good humor his laughter had lit up inside her flickered and went out. He was a mess. Awkwardly wringing the cloth, she began to wash around the gashes on his face. "Ooh," she fussed, dabbing at the cut crossing his eye, "this one is bad. Maybe I should leave it. I don't want to hurt you."

"I guess you're not a nurse then," he tried to joke. "I think their motto is 'if it didn't hurt, let me try again'."

She didn't laugh. "You must be in so much pain already."

He lifted one shoulder in a shrug. "I've felt better," he admitted wryly, "but it's okay, Shelley. It needs to be done and I'd rather have you do it."

She bolstered her flagging courage and continued with her task, scrubbing in places where the blood had crusted. If he had so much as winced in pain, she would have dropped the rag from her shaking hand and given up. But he didn't show any sign of his discomfort and for that she was grateful.

It took a long time to wash the layers of blood and filth away but his features eventually began to emerge, even under the bruising, swelling and several days growth of beard. His eyes were brown, a deep velvety shade of brown. Thickly lashed, the lids fluttered closed more and more often as sleep beckoned him, lulled perhaps by the warm water. Despite his sleepiness, his dark brows were drawn together in a frown. Without thinking, Shelley smoothed her thumb over his forehead, as though to wipe away the unpleasant memories recently forged there. Those brown eyes opened wide for a moment to study her thoughtfully before closing once more. He sighed.

It hit her suddenly that she felt as though she had known this man forever. It didn't feel uncomfortable as she had feared, or unnatural to sit this close and be intimate in this way. She felt safe here with him, and from him. That in itself was strange, for she usually felt ill at ease with anyone she didn't know. She was surprised at herself for touching him so willingly; for actually wanting to. She couldn't even remember the last time she had actually touched another human being. The feeling of warm, smooth skin under her finger tips almost brought tears to her eyes. It was far more comforting than she could have imagined.

Squeezing the warm, wet cloth against his neck, she watched the water drip down his chest and disappear into the waistband of his pants. She couldn't help but notice that he was finely made. She ran the cloth gently over muscled shoulders, down his back, up around strong arms, across a chest lightly dusted with hair and down over the taut ridges of his stomach. His skin, usually a healthy golden honey, was mottled with the biggest, darkest black and blue marks she had ever seen, fresher red welts and nasty looking cuts where the skin had split from the force of the blows. She washed all the open wounds again with the antiseptic, then taped dressings over each. "You're going to look like a mummy when I'm done."

He made a sleepy sound of acknowledgment.

There were other wounds as well, that she couldn't place at first. Puckered and waxy looking, these wounds were small and circular, occurring in no particular pattern across his chest and back, even his arms. She examined them closely, noting the darker specks and smudges surrounding each of them. She wiped around one of them carefully but it came to her only when she noticed some of the dark smudge had rubbed off on the cloth. Ash. These were burns. Cigarette burns. Appalled, she looked up into his face, not knowing what to say. Thankfully, his eyes were closed. Tears pooled in her eyes at the thought of such deliberate cruelty. This man had been beaten and tortured. Never in her life had she expected to be witness to such a thing.

Hoping the bandages would not stick to the ruined skin, she covered all the burns and taped them in place before continuing her inspection.

His nose was straight, miraculously intact in his battered face. His lips had been smashed into his teeth, causing them to split and puff out. She actually ran a finger over his bottom lip, feeling the rough scabs before snatching her hand back. His upper body swayed in his sleep, snagging her wandering attention. She put her hand on the back of his neck to hold him upright and called his name, hating to wake him.

"Michael, wake up for a minute. I'm not done."

A muscle jumped in his cheek.

"Michael." She had to repeat it twice more before his eyes opened.

"Sorry," he mumbled. "I can't seem to stay awake."

"You should get those pants off, so you can finish washing up." Digging through the clean clothes he had dumped onto the table, she picked out a soft pair of blue flannel boxers. "Why don't you put these on? I'll give you a minute," she suggested hopefully. "I still have to do something about those wrists and that - is that a bullet wound on your arm?"

He nodded tiredly, pushing himself to his feet. She turned her back to him and shuffled her aching body to another chair near the window to give him some privacy. She heard his pants hit the floor, the sound of water dripping and splashing into the basin, a sharp intake of breath as he no doubt encountered another one of many painful spots on his body.

"All right," he said finally. "Do your worst."

She turned to find him standing, clean and pale, wearing only his boxers and a white muscle shirt. His dark brown hair, clean and wet, was pushed back from his face, with only the shorter pieces falling back over his forehead. Water dripped from the ends at his neck, making wet blotches on his clean shirt. Sitting him down, she made quick work of flushing his wrists with antiseptic. They looked completely awful; she could actually see bone on the outer edges of each one. She bound them with gauze bandaging and tied the ends to keep them secure.

The bullet hole was crusted over, but the skin around it was red and hot to the touch. She decided to leave it for someone at the hospital to do in the morning. That dead tissue had to be removed and she just couldn't do it, not with him awake and feeling everything, watching everything. Shelley said nothing as she worked and the silence grew. His gaze was uncomfortably direct. He opened his mouth several times as though to say something before snapping it shut. Finally, when she was ready to explode with frustration, he got it out.

"Are you all right inside ...from the.." He cleared his throat. "From the rape? You're still bleeding." He gestured lamely toward the towel he had placed under her earlier, now spotted with blood. He took a deep breath and let it out as though he had just survived a fate worse than death.

Shelley felt humiliated. What was she supposed to tell a stranger, a strange *man* how her most private body parts felt? She started to say something simple to ease his mind without embarrassing herself, something flip, but a finger on her lips stopped her mid sentence. The falsely cheerful note died away.

"Don't joke," he said gruffly. "I want to know."

She sighed. "It hurts," she confessed. "But it will heal, like everything else."

Nodding, apparently satisfied with her answer, he settled himself on the sofa bed, pulling her gently down beside him and covered them both with the blanket. Shelley didn't know what to do. Her body was stiff as a board. She concentrated on just breathing, in and out, watching the bulk of her sling rise and fall with each breath. She calmed slowly, knowing he meant no harm, and found herself gradually relaxing, lulled by the warmth of him, the heartbeat under her cheek, the even breathing. She felt safe, and so very sleepy.

The sun had already risen when Shelley awoke and shafts of its light cheerfully beamed through the picture window. The room was a bit chilly, yet she felt comfortably warm and cozy. She never was the type to be instantly alert the moment she opened her eyes, so it took her some time to realize where she was - and who she was with. Her body ached all over, every abused muscle, bruise and bone throbbed with a kind of pain she had never known. She lay half on top of Michael, one leg drawn up over his with her cheek pressed against his shoulder. She noted with growing dismay, the small wet spot on his shirt. Oh, God. Worse and worse. She was *drooling* on his shoulder. Laying on and drooling on a man she had known less than twenty four hours. Shifting carefully, she surreptitiously wiped at her mouth and the wet spot on his shirt, then eased back to peek at his face. His eyes twinkled at her.

"I used to have a cat like that when I was a boy," he said with a grin, ignoring her gasp of outrage. "She would suck on my shirt at night while I was asleep and leave big wet spots just like this."

"I was not sucking on your shirt!" She huffed, pulling away. "My lip is swollen and I couldn't help it." Although she could feel her cheeks colouring, flushing with embarrassment, she couldn't help the mental image from forming. The picture of her sucking on his shirt was so ludicrous it made her smile. Smiling hurt. "If I wasn't so sore I would hit you for embarrassing me," she added. "I'm sure it would have been more polite to pretend you didn't notice." Her look challenged him to disagree. He was still grinning, a painfully lopsided, discolored yet infectious grin.

She impulsively touched one of the scabs on his swollen lip. "Stop it," she laughed. "That looks grotesque. No more smiling until your scabs fall off." Her own smile faded as she studied his face in the bright sunlight. "It's a wonder you're smiling at all," she said softly. "You look terrible."

"Cheerful by nature," he responded. "But you have got to look worse than I do. How do you feel?"

"Rotten," she admitted. "I can barely move."

"Me too," he said, glancing at his watch. "But we have to get up to meet the plane. We have half an hour." He probed cautiously at her temple. "With a lump like that on your head, I shouldn't have let you fall asleep."

They both shuffled to the kitchen, groaning. Her entire body throbbed. "Coffee," she said. Her mouth felt dry as cotton. "Coffee is what I need right now. And some morphine. Two lumps." It wasn't until she sat on the stool at the kitchen counter that she realized she didn't know where she was, or how they got away from the blond man and his friend.

"Coffee I can do," Michael said lightly as he filled the metal pot with water and fragrant coffee grounds before setting it on the flames of the propane range. He reached for two mugs from the cupboard. She noticed it took him two tries to get his arm that high, and he had to hold his side to do so.

"Pretty sore?" She ventured.

"A little," he allowed. "I think they're cracked. Hurts to breathe a bit."

They both watched the coffee pot, thinking and remembering.

"Can you tell me what happened, Michael?" The water started to boil, percolating up through the coffee grounds into the small glass knob on the lid.

"I finally got loose, ripped the tape with my teeth, you know." He watched the coffee perk.

"Then ..." She prompted.

"Then I shot them," he stated simply.

"Come on, Michael. This is like pulling teeth. Both of them? How?"

He nodded. "Both of them. Then I wrapped you up in a blanket and brought you here, to my cabin. We're neighbours, I guess. I thought that place belonged to Mickey McGraw?"

"It did," she agreed. "He passed away this spring. I'm his granddaughter."

"Oh, I'm sorry," he said so sincerely that she almost started to cry again. "Mickey was a great old guy."

"Yes, he was." She had to give herself a mental shake before she lost herself in memories. "Why were you there, with them?" She thought to ask. Truly, it was a question she would have been smart to ask earlier.

Judging the coffee to be done by the wonderful aroma, he turned the burner off and filled both mugs. It looked black and steamy and heavenly. Her mouth fairly watered for it. "Cream and sugar?" He asked, smiling ironically as he added, "Two lumps?"

Lifting one corner of her mouth in a half smile of her own, she shook her head, already reaching for the mug. "No. If you don't have morphine then I'll take it black. Thank you," she said, taking a sip. "Mmmm, coffee." With a sigh she opened her eyes to find him watching her, intently, but with no little amusement.

"Are you one of those people not truly alive until your second cup of coffee?"

"Guilty," she responded without any hesitation.

"I heard about them on the radio," he explained, getting back to her question. "Two men had just robbed the 'Food n' Fuel' convenience store in town. They killed the owner after he handed over the money, apparently." He took a sip of his own coffee then set the mug down so heavily it spilled onto the counter. "I went over to your place to warn old Mickey, if he was around, not to let anyone in. I thought they might come up this way to hide for a while."

"That's it, then?" She looked at him doubtfully.

His features hardened and tensed perceptibly. "Mm hmm. That's it." It was said so tonelessly, she became instantly suspicious and it must have shown on her face, for he relented enough to say, "I didn't want to shoot them."

Her jaw dropped in surprise. "You didn't?"

"No. I wanted them to die slow and ugly like they deserved. I wanted to beat them until they could never move again." He pushed away from the counter. "We only have a few minutes. The bathroom is down the hall if you need it."

It was a dismissal, a bright neon sign saying 'let it die', but there was one more question she needed answered. "What day was it when you went to Grandpa's cabin?"

She could see he didn't want to answer. His teeth worried at his already mangled lower lip, breaking the scab open. A single drop of blood trickled down his chin. Wiping at it impatiently, he levered himself to his feet and left the room, but not before she heard him answer. "It was Monday."

Shelley glanced at the calendar on the fridge and realized with a sinking feeling, that today was Friday.

CHAPTER 3

Shelley adjusted the angle of her pillow. Then the lay of her sheets. God, she was tired of this hospital bed. Tired of the nurses coming in and waking her and poking her and taking her temperature. It had only been three days but it felt like three weeks. Her body ached absolutely everywhere. It felt even worse than yesterday and as hard as she was trying, the tides of self pity were rising quickly. Visiting hours had come and gone several times. No one was lining up beside her bed to hold her hand and tell her that she would be all right or that they loved her.

It seemed to her that being all alone in the world was punishment enough. So why did they have to be in her cabin? Do this awful thing to her? Her stomach growled noisily but she tried to will it away, for she had refused all her meals. Now, alternating between intense, ravenous hunger and nausea, she was too confused and stubborn to even try to eat. Food felt like an award she was miles away from achieving. She couldn't explain it to herself or even make sense of it, but anything she tried to eat just stuck in her throat, refusing to go down.

Maybe it was better this way anyway, she thought crazily. Just to die. To starve myself into a coma and then death. Her thoughts wandered back to the man that had saved her. Michael. The night and following morning in his cabin seemed surreal now. When she thought of him, the coil of misery, of tension and shame in her stomach would just unravel, so she thought of him often. She would remember his voice and how safe and peaceful it made her feel. It was unusual and very compelling, almost like the voices of two men blended together. One average, smooth with the barest hint of a French accent and a lower, gravely growl which would catch only parts of each word. She gave up trying to describe it to herself, knowing only that it made her feel better.

She had asked about him and received a long list of his injuries; fractures in his skull, three ribs and a jawbone, an assorted collection of stitches, staples and tapes, very severe bruising and body trauma. He had some slight internal bleeding which they had repaired in surgery. They said he was going to be all right and she was fiercely glad for him and the many people that must love him. Pushing him from her mind, she drifted off to sleep, losing herself in an emptiness that had been there since childhood. Now it was a deep, dark, yawning abyss - desolate and lonely. She didn't care anymore if she ever got out.

"Ma'am?"

Shelley fought to keep her eyes closed and ignore the insistent though pleasant voice. She didn't want to see even one more person with a needle, thermometer or blood pressure cuff, or she would scream. She was just so tired.

"Miss McGraw?"

Her eyelids popped open, finally resigned to the fact that he wasn't going to go away.

"Sorry to disturb you, Ma'am. I'm Constable Matthews. I need to get a statement from you, if you feel up to it."

She nodded briefly and licked her lips. Police officers made her nervous. She imagined that they were all unfeeling, shifty-eyed individuals, always watching and waiting for you to slip up and make a mistake. Then they pounced.

He dragged a chair over to the bed and gingerly perched on its edge. His shadow loomed over her, stirring up her feelings of unease and causing her hand to convulsively grip the edge of her blanket; to open and close over it, open and close.

He put his own hand over it and gently pushed it into a flat, relaxed position on the sheet. "It's okay, Miss McGraw. Just a couple questions so we can close the file."

Shelley made herself look at him, really look at this big man in his crisp, black uniform. He had kind, sympathetic eyes. Despite his size, he didn't look like the type of man who could hurt anyone. "Is Michael in trouble?"

He smiled. "No, Ma'am, I don't think any charges will be brought against him. There's no reason."

"Good," she said on a sigh. "I was worried."

"But we need the statement just the same," he said pointedly.

She nodded again. "I understand."

"Why don't you start from the beginning and tell me what happened."

Shelley cast one longing glance at the call button. If she pressed it, the nurse would come and probably send him away. It was so awfully tempting. She didn't want to remember. She didn't want to think about it or describe it. "Well," she started, licking her lips again. "I inherited the cabin from my grandfather. I wanted to spend some time in it - you know, to say good-bye. When I went inside, they were already there and those two men were beating Michael. Actually, the tall one was beating him, but they both had blood on them.

They must have taken turns. He was tied up, against the kitchen wall. They saw me. The tall one sent the other one outside, to stand guard, then he started beating me."

Although her voice was as flat and unemotional as she could make it, she couldn't keep the tone of disbelief from threading through it. The whole thing still seemed so incomprehensible. "He broke my arm and then I passed out. That's all I can tell you."

The Constable's eyes fell to the bandage above her collarbone then skipped back up to bore into her own wary green ones. Her mouth felt sticky. She swallowed dryly and wiped at the corner with her finger.

"Did they rape you, Miss McGraw? In front of Mike?"

"No," she whispered quickly. "Nothing like that." Oh, Lord. He knows, she thought with a rush of embarrassment. Somehow, he knows. She didn't want anyone to know. She hadn't even told the nurses and doctors. Look away! She screamed at him in her mind. Look away! But he didn't. He just kept looking at her and tapping his pencil on the coil of his notebook. "Look," she said, steering the conversation back to Michael. "Michael saved my life. He did what he had to do, to get away alive. They would have killed us, you know."

"I know," he agreed softly, closing his little notebook. He stood up and lifted the chair effortlessly with his thumb and forefinger, to place it back against the wall. "Miss McGraw?"

"Yes?"

"We have a peaceful little town here. I hope you don't judge it too harshly. Everyone would ...well, everyone would like the chance to welcome you." With a final, pointless adjustment of his hat, Constable Matthews strode from her room. She couldn't even hear his footsteps echoing down the hall and wondered briefly if he was walking on his tippy-toes. The thought almost made her laugh out loud. Almost.

It was much later when she stirred again, reluctantly opening her eyes. The half moon sent a weak scattering of beams through the window, along with a welcome cool breeze. She didn't realize she had a visitor until a hand reached up to switch the overhead light on. She turned her head to find a pair of concerned brown eyes only inches from her own. She would have known those eyes anywhere, even without the telltale bruised, puffy pockets surrounding them. Michael sat in his hospital pajamas and bandages on a chair pulled up close to the edge of the bed.

He put his finger to his lips. "Shh. If the nurses catch me out of bed they're going to skin me alive. I won." He added abruptly, with a spark of wry humour evident on his battered face.

She pushed her body up to lean against the pillows behind her, feeling slow and groggy from the pain medication. "What?"

"I won," he repeated. "I got more stitches than you."

"I noticed. You look like Frankenstein," she rejoined weakly.

He snorted. "Have you seen yourself recently?"

She tried to smile, splitting the newly formed scabs on her lip. "No," she admitted, dabbing at the blood with a tissue. "The nurses thought it would make me suicidal."

He sobered instantly, placing his hand over hers, covering it completely. She stared at the hospital bracelet around his bandaged wrist. Daillant. His last name was Daillant.

"They tell me you won't eat, Shelley."

She looked at him, startled that he had brought it up. Why should he care? "I wasn't hungry, that's all," she lied.

"For three days?" He questioned skeptically.

"I'll eat. I will," she lied again.

He just stared at her, into her eyes, reading answers to questions he hadn't even asked. She used up every ounce of her willpower to hold his gaze but her traitorous eyes darted away.

"That's not the answer, Shelley."

She didn't try to deny it again, or hedge. He was too good at this. "No one would care."

"I would," he said sincerely.

"No, you wouldn't," she denied. "Not really. You don't even know me."

"I want to know you."

Typically, that left her tongue tied. She didn't know what to say. "Oh," was all she could manage.

"Do you know what will happen if you don't eat?"

"Of course. I'll starve to death."

He shook his head. "They'll hook you up to an IV or a feeding tube."

"I'll rip it out," she challenged stubbornly.

"Then they will send you to Thunder Bay and strap you down in the mental ward. Maybe even keep you drugged. Do you want that to happen?"

"No," she whispered.

"All right then," he said with satisfaction, pulling the rejected food tray a little closer. "Eat with me."

When she didn't move right away, he filled a spoon with plain, cold rice and shoved it quite expertly into her unwilling mouth. He then spooned a shivering green blob of gelatin into his own mouth. "I can't chew," he explained, tapping his jaw. "I'm afraid I have to confiscate your Jello."

She swallowed the tasteless rice. Her empty stomach clenched painfully around it and a wave of nausea threatened to send it back up. "I can't. I don't want to eat. I don't want it," she protested, swallowing yet another mouthful.

"Nobody *wants* it, Shelley," he said, pretending to misunderstand. "It has absolutely no flavour. No one would want to leave if the food was tasty."

His look of innocence was so overdone she could feel the laughter bubbling up her throat and tried desperately to squelch it. Oh, he was charming, but the last thing she needed was this man's pity. The hospital staff probably asked him to visit her. "I don't need you to feel sorry for me," she bit out suddenly.

He blinked at the suddenness of the attack. "To tell you the truth," he confessed, "it's more for me than you. When I'm alone in there, the depression grabs me, you know? I wanted some company and I want to get to know you."

"But why?" She asked, utterly confused by the possibility.

"I don't know. I keep thinking of you. It's important to me."

The visit set a pattern for the days to follow. They visited as often and for as long as they were allowed by the nursing staff. They talked of controversial issues and everyday mundane things. Sometimes they would play cards or chess. Thinking of the last game they played together, she had to laugh. She beat him unmercifully. She had said, feeling mischievous, "Well, I guess that puts you in your man's place. Far behind a woman's intellect."

He had laughed, full of good humour. "That's one theory. How about a gentleman never beats a lady?"

In the ensuing silence he realized, stricken, what he had actually said. "I'm sorry," he apologized over and over. "That was so insensitive."

Amazingly, she had found it amusing, which she thought was a very good sign. "I guess we both know a couple of guys who weren't gentlemen, then don't we?"

Bringing herself back to the present, Shelley flung back the covers. After two long weeks she was finally being discharged. She had to make plans and say her good-byes. She put on her robe and forced herself to walk down the hallway to Michael's room. The door was wide open.

She watched him for a while from the doorway. He was reading a thick, dog-eared Tom Clancy novel from the hospital's collection. He was chewing at his bottom lip again. It's funny, she thought, how important someone can become to you in such a short time. She would really, really miss him.

"I can tell you a story," she called, stepping into the room.

He looked up in pleased surprise, then patted the bed and moved over so she could sit beside him.

"Do I have to pay for it?" He asked, pretending to ponder the situation.

"Of course. One handful of your M&M's. I like the blue ones."

First measuring with exaggeration in one large hand, he carefully dumped the colourful sweets into her lap. "So, about your story - is it as good as this one?" He waved his book in front of her nose.

Shelley grabbed at it, holding it still long enough to read the title. "Clear and Present Danger" she read aloud, already popping little chocolate candies into her mouth. "Oh, you can't compare them."

He raised his eyebrows.

"That's a guy book," she explained. "Mine is a girl's story. It's very short and very ironic."

He stole one of the little chocolates back.

She slapped his hand and launched into her story. "Once upon a time there was a little girl. She grew up in the city of Toronto, amid millions of other people. Toronto could be a very scary place and there were thefts and assaults and murders every day. But miraculously, this little girl was never affected by it, physically at least."

Stealing a glance at Michael, she wasn't surprised to see he was frowning. He knew where this was heading.

"Circumstances led this little girl, now a woman, to leave the big city for a short time, to explore the wilds of Northern Ontario and mourn her last remaining relative." She popped another M&M into her mouth. "This is where it gets ironic."

She could see that Michael couldn't gauge her mood, but she pushed on. "Now, this woman wasn't in the Canadian Wilderness for a day, not even an hour before misfortune struck. She became a victim of a violent crime. Doesn't that just bite you in the ass? That she had to travel hundreds of miles to get assaulted in the boonies? Anyway, she was beaten. And raped. But of course this is a fairy tale and all fairy tales have a knight in shining armour or a handsome prince, and naturally he saved this woman, for she surely would have died without him." She faltered here, unsure how to go on.

"How does it end?" His voice was gravely, husky, so he cleared his throat. "Do they live happily ever after?"

She shook her head. "No, I think she thanks the prince for being so wonderfully kind and goes back to Toronto, where it's safe."

Michael threw his book on the bedside table. "I don't like your story," he stated emphatically. "Quit playing games with me."

"I have to go home," she said desperately.

"Why?"

She lifted her brows. "Why do you think?"

He was growing angry, she could see it in his eyes and the tension around his mouth. He was starting to raise his voice. "Why?!"

When she moved to get off the bed, he snared her wrist with the fingers of one hand. "I don't think you're leaving because of what happened. I think you're afraid. Afraid of me - of getting close to me. You're running away," he accused.

"That's ridiculous," she scoffed. "You have been so kind to me, but I have things to get back to. I was crazy to come up here anyway. Maybe we could write," she tried, "I would really like that."

"Don't do that!" He growled. "Don't put up that wall because I'll just rip it back down again!"

"Why?" She wailed. "I'm not your responsibility."

"Because we need each other, Shelley. Look at me." He had to push her chin up with one finger. "Look at me!"

Knowing he wouldn't give up, she finally did, meeting his eyes with difficulty.

"I won't let you hide from me," he said. "At least look at me and tell me how I make you feel. That's all I'm asking."

Shelley tossed her head, feeling mutinous. This kind of honesty, of closeness, was foreign to her. It made her uncomfortable. In her family, personal feelings were kept personal, bottled up to be released, if ever, in the privacy of her room. So, having shared so much more of herself with this man than she had with anyone else in her life, she felt reluctant to open up even more.

As a teenager, she remembered bolstering her courage, telling one or two girls things about herself, trying to make friends. She had felt at the time that she had imparted great personal secrets, so private was her life. In truth, she had said very little and yet felt betrayed when they tossed something she said back at her in fun. So she was most often alone; too sensitive, labeled 'cool', 'aloof' and worse, 'snotty'.

"I can't," she refused. Her eyes filled with tears at his look of disappointment. Shaking her head, she said again. "I can't, Michael."

"Would it be easier if I went first?"

At her nod, he took a deep breath. He studied the coverlet on the bed, tracing the pattern with his finger, clearly marshaling his thoughts. "We've only known each other for a short time, but I know at this moment that I want you in my life. I want to be all things to you," he clarified. "I want to be your big brother and your friend and someday," his voice dropped, "your lover, and learn everything, everything about you. If you leave, I'll never get that chance." He sat back in the bed.

"Wow," she breathed. "I don't know what to say."

"You do," he insisted. "Look at me and tell me how you

feel."

Shelley swallowed, working past the lump in her throat. "I ...," she began, "I feel ..."

Michael hung his head so she couldn't see his face. She felt awful, hurting him this way just because she was a coward.

"Shelley, if you don't feel ...attracted to me, if you don't think about me or miss me, or if you don't like to be around me, then you should say so."

"No! No, I do! I think you're the sweetest man I know. I think about you *all* the time and I do miss you when you're not with me. You make me feel good inside - special. And comfortable. I have felt ill at ease with everyone my whole life, except my grandfather."

He looked up then, but not with the wounded expression she had expected to see. His eyes sparkled with mischief. He grinned at her. "Was that so hard?" He asked gently.

She sniffled and wiped at her nose with the sleeve of her hospital robe. "You tricked me! And yes, it was!"

He snorted and handed her a Kleenex.

She squinted at him over the tissue as she blew her nose. "It just scares me. What if this isn't real? What if it is some kind of dependence, a psychological reaction to what happened?" She paused and blew her nose again. "So, what now?"

He kissed her forehead. "Now we go back to the lake. We do some healing and thinking and let life play out the way it's meant to. Sound good?"

It did sound good. For once she would let life play out and see where it took her.

CHAPTER FOUR

Shelley had to face facts. She was afraid to fly. Beads of sweat popped out on her forehead. Fingernails dug into the material of her jeans. Her heartbeat seemed to accelerate right along with the tiny aircraft. It was so small that she could touch both walls at the same time and she couldn't stand up without having her head graze the ceiling.

Reminding herself that she had survived this once already did absolutely no good. Her stomach started to churn anyway. His Cessna, Michael had told her with his most serious look, was perfectly safe. Nothing to worry about, he said. Safer than a car, he said. Ha! That cannot be true, she thought. Scrunching her eyes shut in a feeble act of self preservation, her denial instead became a desperate, silent litany. Please be true. Please be true. The entire structure began to vibrate and rattle ominously as it bounced over the chop on the lake.

Abruptly, the turbulent ride smoothed out as the aircraft lifted itself into the air. Thousands and thousands of hectares of trees stretched out beneath the wings. It was jack pine and spruce mostly, but dotting the landscape here and there were clumps of aspen, birch, poplar, larch and willow. The leafy bursts in different shades of green contrasted beautifully with the dark, muted colour of the evergreens.

The land had dips and swells scraped out by glaciers centuries ago to form natural basins; some little more than ponds, others many miles wide, but all filled with the most incredibly blue water she had ever seen. The network of lakes stretched as far as the eye could see, some joined by winding rivers, others completely isolated.

Michael tapped her on the shoulder, startling her. He pointed out her window to a long, dark strip below. The trees, charred and black, were stripped of their foliage, though many still remained upright. It seemed a battlefield of sorts, littered with the sad remains of living things; trees, plants, small animals, creatures that had held no hope of survival against their raging foe. "Lightning fires," he shouted. "Lots of forest fires around here."

She could barely hear him over the roar of the single engine.

"Don't worry though," he yelled with a reassuring wink. "None burning around here right now."

Shelley nodded dumbly, thinking wryly that her list of fears was growing at a rapid rate. On the bright side, though, at least this new fear of forest fires lessened her immediate terror of flying in this itty bitty plane. Looking far off the wing, she could see great, bare patches of earth, strewn with boulders and stumps and felled trees. She stabbed at the window with her finger. "What's going on there?" She yelled.

"Logging," he shouted back. "They clear cut a whole area and then replant. That's what my family does back home."

Shelley found that the process saddened her a bit. She could see rough roads carved into the earth, leading away from the stripped areas. From such a distance the trucks laden with logs heading south looked tiny, like Tinker Toys. Even when the trees grow back, she thought, it will never be as rich, or diverse. Never be the same. The land looked raped.

Violated.

Realizing with a start that she had come back to that, she jerked her eyes away to stare at the hands in her lap. Does it always come back to that, she wondered? How long before my every thought stops revolving around and around it? She wondered what kept her from hiding from Michael in complete and utter embarrassment. He had seen her at her very worst. He had witnessed her rape, seen her naked, seen her beg and cry. Under normal circumstances she would have fled from him as well. Maybe this was different because he had been brutalized too, and in his own way, was just as much of a victim as she was herself. It forced her to acknowledge that what happened to her wasn't about how men treated women. It was about power. It was about people who felt little and worthless, people who had to step on the backs of as many others as it took to make them feel taller and more important in the world. She refused to allow herself the comfort of blaming all men for the sins of two. Those men beat Michael, and tortured him because it made them feel powerful. The one man beat her for the same reason. Raping her was just a bonus.

Anyway, there was a certain freedom in knowing that she could be herself - no pretending, no artifice, no trying to impress. She didn't have to come up with explanations or excuses for her behaviour because he already knew. And for whatever reason, be it guilt, pity or attraction, wanted to spend time with her anyway. She thought about the things he said in the hospital and blushed. He wanted to be her lover. The thought made her nervous and uncomfortable, and saddened because it was probably too late now.

She watched him, peeking through her lashes. Certainly, theoretically at least, men appealed to her. Romantic books and movies and other happy couples made her yearn for a relationship but never had she met a man that really attracted her. None had tempted her beyond casual conversation. She had wondered often as she was growing up, what was wrong with her. She loved romance, loved the whole idea, but never participated in 'boy talk' with the other girls or experienced the teenage crushes they gushed about. Well, now she finally felt something for a man, but who really knew what it was? Maybe she was just confused and grabbing at him like some sort of life raft. He had saved her life and been very kind. Maybe she was just using him to feel safe and secure.

And worse? Would his touch only bring to mind that of another - more brutal and repulsive to her? She didn't know if intimacy would ever be possible without the image of the blond man crowding her. She could picture him so clearly, the mental image so realistic a chill coursed up her spine. The mad look in his eyes. They were blue. A light blue so icy they were almost white. His features would have been normal, good looking even, had they not been twisted with insane rage.

She could still smell him, loathsome and unwashed, breathing fumes of stale beer in her face. Her stomach roiled at the vivid memory. Gorge rose in her throat which she swallowed with difficulty. Just the thought that such an animal had been inside her made her skin crawl. It made her want to worm her way right out of it, to trade in that defiled shell for another. It was a feeling that no amount of scrubbing could erase.

And Dear God, she thought for the millionth time. What if there are more serious repercussions than a sore body and a state of pure emotional hell? What if he was diseased? Had AIDS? All these questions, uncertainties and confusing feelings had her so lost in thought that she barely noticed they had landed and now taxied toward the small dock in front of Michael's cabin.

☙

Michael pushed the door to the last room open, then grabbed her hand to lead her inside. "This will be your room," he said. "I hope you like it."

A double bed sat in the middle, with the beautifully carved headboard against the far wall. A hope chest, carved on the top with the same design as the headboard, sat at the foot of the bed. The coverlet was warm and cheerful in green buffalo checks and the four huge, fluffy pillows in green and white practically guaranteed a comfortable sleep.

There was a night table beside the bed, with a wind-up clock and a lamp. Although electric, the lamp looked hand crafted with wood and a mason jar, and cleverly painted to resemble an old gas lamp. On the far side of the table was a large papazan chair, with a cushion covered in the same material as the bed spread. She was studying the chair, delighted at the thought of curling up in it with a good book, when she noticed its current occupant. The grey and white cat she had mistaken for a pillow sat up and arched its back in a great stretch before reclining once more on its side. The head twisted back with one paw covering its eyes in a tragic pose, as if unbearably appalled at the intrusion.

"That's Amber and apparently that's her chair. Feel free to kick her out."

"No, no. I like cats," she assured him. At least I think I do, she thought to herself hopefully as she continued to survey the room. The other wall had a bay window which overlooked the water. The seat was covered with the same kind of fluffy pillows that graced the bed. The only other piece of furniture was a large armoire beside the window. The floor was polished pine, just like the rest of the house, but placed at the door and the bedside were two colorful, cozy rag rugs.

She loved the room immediately, loved everything about it. "It's perfect," she finally thought to say. "Like it's right out of a 'Country Living' magazine." Her eyes wandered to the wall, to the only picture in the room. It was a large charcoal sketch of Michael.

He looked slightly embarrassed. "My sister Drew is an artist. She did it. I'm hiding it in here," he confessed.

"But it's so wonderful!" She protested.

"She is good - really good," he allowed. "I just feel weird displaying pictures of myself all over the house. She would kill me though, if it wasn't up somewhere."

"I love it," she said simply. "This whole house is beautiful. Comfortable, like you can really live in it. My father was very ...clean. Obsessive really, so our house was never very relaxing. I'm going to like it here. I'm glad you asked."

He smiled. "Me too."

They both realized at the same time that he still held her hand. To cover the slightly awkward moment, he dropped it and looked at his watch. "I'm going to put supper on. You come down whenever you're ready, okay?"

She nodded. "Okay."

After he left, she put away the few items she had picked up at the hospital, holding out one small package.

Sitting on the bed she held it a long time, afraid to open it, afraid not to. Finally, with a big sigh, she pulled the pregnancy test out of the bag and put it in the drawer of the beside table. It was cowardly, putting it off, but she simply couldn't do it. She told herself it didn't matter - there really was no rush, because God would not, could not be so cruel as to curse her with that man's child. On the way out, she stopped to look once more at the sketch on the wall. Michael was younger there, probably just out of high school. He was sprawled carelessly in a hammock, clad only in swimming trunks and a sleepy smile. With a smile of her own and a shake of her head, she surmised he must have been quite devastating to the population of teenage girls.

Shelley followed the aroma of barbecued meat down the stairwell and into the kitchen. At least, she reflected, emotional upheaval didn't affect her appetite. She was always hungry. Hungry when she was worried or nervous or when she had the flu; always. The thought of her trying to starve herself to death was ludicrous.

The chef himself, the man behind the tempting aroma, was standing on the porch in his socks, whistling a tune behind the lid of the smoking barbecue. He poked his head through the open screen door. "Hey, perfect timing. The steaks are almost done. Can you fry up a can of mushrooms?"

"Oh, sure." She rummaged through two cupboards for the can, four drawers for the can opener, and one last cupboard for the frying pan, thinking he'd be done long before she ever got started. She began to open the can, getting no more than two or three turns into it when a keening howl suddenly split the air, followed by a sharp and unexpected poke to her backside. It scared her so much that she dropped the can with a shriek and turned around fully prepared to do battle.

A huge wolf stood there before her, mouth slightly open and eyes shining. The creature almost reached her waist, with a thick, thick coat in varying shades of black, white and grey. Michael, just coming in with a platter of steaks and potatoes, caught the expression on her face.

He started to laugh. "It's the can opener," he explained. "She thinks it means supper time."

Shelley backed warily toward the sink. She tried to keep her voice as even and quiet as possible. "Tell me that isn't a wolf."

"She's not a wolf. She's an Alaskan malamute and my very good friend."

"*This* is one of your dogs? I had no idea they were so huge."

"Yep, this is Darby. Murphy just dropped them off. He was looking after them for me. Watch this," he said, still grinning. With a combination of bizarre movements and goofy noises, he led her into a full fledged, beautiful howl. Over and over she sang, punctuating each verse with a snap of her teeth and a toss of her head. She pranced around him, performing for him in the hope that he might deposit the contents of one tin can into her bowl.

Shelley was enchanted. She had never had a dog, never been allowed, and to be honest hadn't even thought about getting one for years. But then, she hadn't known they could have such personality. Obviously drawn by his mate's enthusiasm, another malamute, even larger than the first, bounded into the kitchen. Dawson greeted her like an old friend, making conversation with a groaning, grumbling sort of noise deep in his throat as she scratched around the ruff of his neck. He ran excitedly back to Michael, turning in four or five happy circles, before standing up carefully on his hind feet. Bracing the sides of his front paws on Michael's hips, his head tipped back, looking around and behind him with an expression of pure joy as Michael returned his hug with a hearty squeeze.

She laughed delightedly, feeling completely charmed. He had spoken about them with such affection while they were in the hospital. She had humored him a little, for deep down, she hadn't really understood how someone could get that attached to an animal. She hadn't expected that they would win her over so completely, so quickly. The love and pride he felt for them was easy to read on his face. They were close friends, she realized, feeling a little pang of regret that she had missed out on that experience while growing up.

After his dogs were fed and with a quick hand signal, told to lay down, she and Michael worked together, setting the table and pouring the iced teas - not saying much, but comfortable with it. Feeling completely incapable of hiding the fact that she was starving for real, non-hospital food, Shelley cut into the steak with enthusiasm and took a bite. She closed her eyes, chewing the tender meat slowly to savor it.

"Mmm, that's sooo good. I don't go to the effort of cooking much. You surprise me, though. I would have pegged you for a vegetarian," she said, pointing her fork at him.

He blinked. "Why's that? You're not going to tell me I look gay, too, are you?"

She laughed. "God, no. No, it's just that you seem like a 'save the Earth and all the creatures too' kind of guy."

"I am," he agreed, cutting his meat into tiny pieces for his still healing jaw. "Well, I try to be, but I still believe in the food chain. Some species have evolved to eat vegetation, others meat. Humans need both. I figure if we were supposed to live on grass like cattle, we'd have four stomachs like cattle."

She nodded vigorously, agreeing as she sank her teeth into a cherry tomato. It simply exploded, sending a stream of seeds and tomato juice to land with a smack in the center of Michael's forehead. The look on his face made her laugh so hard, so suddenly, that it came out a long wheezing sound before erupting into peals of uncontrollable laughter. The tomato pulp slid down his forehead to land neatly on his baked potato where it sat atop the dollop of sour cream like a garnish.

This set them both off again, each's laughter feeding off the other until they were weak with it. Shelley slumped over the table, holding the cramp in her side. Finally, she clapped a hand over her mouth, biting the inside of her cheek in desperation. "I'm sorry."

He licked the tip of his finger and drew an invisible line in the air. "That's one point for Shelley. " He grinned at her. "Great aim."

The meal passed swiftly and amiably. They chatted about the dogs, a little of her life in Toronto and about her grandfather. They shared funny stories and anecdotes about him right through dinner and the clean up afterwards.

Each with a sweater and a mug of tea, they moved to sit outside on the front porch to watch Darby and Dawson play in the clumps of tall, wild grass, snuffling and snorting with abandon. The evening was cool for July and the breeze coming off the lake was almost brisk. Lost in thought most of the time, they sat on the step in companionable silence, enjoying the easy quiet of twilight. Nature itself enriched the hush as the sun rested its ponderous weight in the bed of trees, adding the only accompaniments necessary in a symphony this grand. The water washing up on shore, the raucous call of a merganser, the mournful melody of a loon, the pipping chorus of frogs; each sound was as soothing and hypnotic to Shelley as the near forgotten feeling of a mother's loving hand on her hair. The entire evening seemed like that to her, like a gentle, healing caress.

Michael broke the peaceful silence first. "We should go over there tomorrow."

"I know. I'll be all right."

After another long pause, he yawned; a big, bone cracking yawn that had him grimacing in pain. "Well, I think-" He straightened, suddenly alert. "Don't move, Shelley," he whispered urgently. Putting one finger to his lips and warning her to silence, he quietly ushered the dogs inside the house. Easing himself back onto the step, he pointed over her shoulder down the length of the beach. "Do you see him?"

"See who?" She whispered back in alarm, searching the dusk for threatening shapes.

"A caribou. Down by the water. See him?"

He was a large bull, with a proud, commanding presence. He seemed brown in the dim light of evening, or perhaps grey, with a creamy white neck, mane and underbelly. The epitome of effortless beauty and dignity, he stepped daintily into the shallows, dipping his impressive, many-pronged rack of antlers gracefully toward the water as he drank. "I do," she breathed, her excitement mounting. For a born and raised city dweller like herself, this was such a magical, special thing to witness. "I see him! I thought they traveled in huge herds?"

Michael shook his head, keeping his voice low. "No. These ones stay in small herds and they don't migrate very far, not like the northern caribou. The survival of this particular species of woodland caribou is threatened, though. They may even be gone in my lifetime," he added sadly.

"Why?"

"Habitat destruction mostly, and poaching. We're cutting down their forests."

"But you told me they replant them."

"Oh, they do, but caribou need mature forests. They eat reindeer moss or lichen mostly, and it takes over a hundred years to grow enough to support a herd."

Shelley digested the information reflectively. It was sobering, making her think seriously about the impact the human race had on the creatures that came before them. It was something she had never really dwelled on before and it made her feel ashamed. They watched the bull move stately down the beach, watching even after he disappeared; thinking about him, about the greed and cruelty of people, about what they had to face in the morning. They sat together in thoughtful silence until the sun disappeared completely, leaving the stars overhead and the sliver of waning moon as the only light in the darkening sky.

"Well," Michael said finally. "I'm off to bed with a book, I guess. Do you want one?"

"Sure. I might get a couple pages in before I fall asleep."

They both rose, still stiff and sore, and shambled inside. The screen door slammed behind them as they made their way into the living room. Michael fumbled around in the dark and finally succeeded in lighting both of the propane wall lamps. There was no fire in the grate, but despite the slight chill, the decor was warm and inviting. The room was large and open with skylights in the high ceiling to let natural light in. Large potted plants graced the corners of the room and hung from the balcony of the upper floor. The walls and matching log furniture were golden brown, the colour of aged honey. There were pillows and spreads and area rugs, all with different fabrics in different shades of green. It was a nice room. He had simple but impressive taste.

The bookshelf covered at least half of one wall. The books were crammed in, tightly wedged into every available space. There were large and small novels, hard covers, soft covers, manuals and magazines. Here and there amongst the books were photos in small wooden frames, of him and his family. His huge family; five brothers and two sisters.

"Holidays must have been so much fun at your house," she mused, unaware actually that she had said it aloud. She picked up another picture and glanced at it. "This is you?" She asked incredulously, "In a choir? You sing!" She exclaimed, excited.

He gave her a 'don't get any ideas' look. "No."

"Oh! You do! Sing a song for me."

He shook his head.

"Oh, come on, Michael. I'll make you dessert," she bribed. "I know you really like cheesecake."

He gave in with a sigh. "Okay." He squared his shoulders and cleared his throat.

"*Black fly.*

The little black fly.

Always the black fly, no matter where you go.
I'll die with the black fly pickin' my bones
In north Ontario-io
In north Ontario."

She whacked him lightly on the shoulder with her cast. "No! Sing me a real one. Pleeeeease." She put on her best pleading face, opening her green eyes wide and batting her lashes. It had always worked on her grandfather.

"Okay, Okay!" He cocked his head, plainly searching his mind for a song. His face suddenly lit up with inspiration. She leaned forward eagerly as he took a deep breath.

"Shelley, Shelley, bo belly,
Banana fanna, fo felly - "

"Michael!" She interrupted with another smack and a laugh. "Forget it. But you're not getting cake until I hear you sing."

He just laughed. It took them each about ten minutes to decide on a book to read. They climbed the stairs together, each looking forward to the end of a long day, however enjoyable. Before turning to her own room, Shelley spontaneously reached out and gave him a light hug, mindful of his ribs.

"I feel so much better. Thank you."

He hugged her back, squeezing slightly before releasing her. "Don't thank me. I need it just as much as you do." He surprised her with a light kiss at the corner of her mouth. "Goodnight, Shelley."

CHAPTER FIVE

The path to her grandpa's cabin was narrow and partly grown over with the thick, leafy ground cover so prevalent on the forest floor. The glossy leaves brushed against her ankles, transferring chilly drops of morning dew to her bare skin. The air was damp and dark, making this trek seem more frightening and depressing than it had to be. Shelly looked up at the clouds worriedly. They were gathering low overhead, darkening to an ominous purply blue that raised the goose flesh on her arms. She didn't like storms. Nothing good ever happened in a storm. Thunder rumbled and rolled in the bruised, swollen sky, getting louder by the minute. It looked ready to split open and let go with a mighty force of its own.

Michael led the way, pushing branches away from the path and holding them there so they wouldn't slap back against her face. The dogs trotted behind, often veering off the path to explore some elusive scent before joining the line once more. She hoped the storm could wait until they got back home.

Michael had assured her it was only a fifteen minute walk, yet a half hour had already passed and still they trudged along. She couldn't help but think back. It was for that reason, dreading the memories she would be forced to relive, that she dragged her feet, knowing even so that she merely delayed the inevitable. Not all the events of that day were clear in her mind, so she couldn't really describe what happened in a linear fashion. It was more a serious of images that came unbidden, flashing occasionally behind the closed lids of her eyes. Each one evoked feelings so strong she felt almost choked by them.

Perhaps the most vivid image was one of the first - Michael, strung up by his hands against the kitchen wall. Strangely, the mental picture was a hauntingly detailed one, despite her fear and the fleetingness of the moment. His shirt was hanging loose out of his pants. The blue-green plaid was covered with dark, rusty stains. Dried blood. His hands were clenched into fists above the thick bands of heavy tape. She remembered how he kept trying to twist his body or raise his knees, to protect his midsection from the blows raining down on him, but he was weak and the effort had proven futile.

Of course she had, as nearly everyone in their lifetime has, seen other people in pain, whether it be a car accident, a fall off a bike or even childbirth. It was unsettling if you were at all sensitive, but seeing someone systematically and savagely beaten almost to death was something else entirely. Even though she witnessed only moments of it, she would never, ever forget the sound of solid wood hitting flesh or the look on his face. His features had been ravaged and bloodied and etched with suffering and despair. Later she had seen the hatred and anger blazing from his eyes and heard it in his voice, but still, the memory of him in that one unguarded moment of defeat stayed with her. It probably always would.

Tripping over yet another tree root stretched across the path, she marveled that he managed to get her home in his condition; with wounds of his own, weak from days of thirst and hunger and loss of blood. She shook her head with amazement. It must have been pure adrenaline that kept him going.

The path opened up abruptly, finally, to the clearing in

the rear of the cabin. They circled around to the front. It saddened her, looking at the homey little cabin, because she couldn't feel it anymore; the peace, the sense of homecoming she felt the first day she saw it. It didn't feel like a good place anymore. It was like losing the very last part of her grandfather. She let her hand fall against Michael's, wanting to grab onto it and hold tight, but the fear of his rejection held her back.

"Sorry," she murmured.

Visibly mustering the effort to tear his eyes away from the cabin, he looked down at her, somehow understanding her need. His hand found and folded around hers, swallowing it completely in a small cocoon of safety and reassurance that made her feel a little braver.

"Let's go down to the dock first. I left stuff down there."

Michael held her back. "No. They packed it up. It's all in the cabin."

"Who's they?"

"Daniel. Constable Matthews and his family came up again after they took the bodies. They cleaned the cabin, too."

"Oh, that was so thoughtful. He was very nice …at the hospital."

They stood at the bottom of the steps.

She took a deep breath. "Well, let's go in. It's just a place, right?"

White teeth worried at Michael's bottom lip before his mouth settled into a grim line. His brown eyes hardened. He set his jaw and squared his shoulders. "Right." His steps were brisk and resolute as he led the way up the stairs and through the front door.

The main room, the sitting room, was polished to a shine and had about it the sharp, clean smell of Pine Sol. Nothing looked out of place but still, it had a sinister air about it now. Swinging the empty back pack from her shoulders, Shelley crossed over to the large fireplace and carefully filled the bottom with pictures from the mantel. There was nothing else in this room she wanted, for there was very little in the way of personal touches. Grandpa only surrounded himself with things he needed; junk annoyed him.

Michael was glaring balefully around the empty room; at the faint stains on the floor, even at the sparse furniture. He had never given her any details of his attack and surely now was not the time to ask, but she guessed by his reaction to it that most of it took place in this room. Grabbing his hand again, she pulled him out of there and into the kitchen.

It barely even resembled the room she remembered from just two short weeks ago. The garbage had been cleared away and the floor cleaned, although there were two more large blood stains on the polished boards, one of them spread evenly around a shallow hole in the wood where a bullet had come to rest. The table was pushed neatly against the wall with all the chairs placed upside down on its surface. She noticed with a little lurch of her stomach, that one was missing a leg. Those were the only signs of the whole event.

She felt cheated somehow, that there wasn't more damage to the room. She couldn't even point to anything and say, 'See! There you have it - proof of my struggle, evidence, so that you might understand the magnitude of the terror and pain I felt in this very room.' But there was no such evidence, save the marks of the men's deaths upon the floor.

As bizarre as the notion might be, the scabs and bruises and cast on her arm were more than just unpleasant reminders, they were a kind of validation. Once her body healed she wouldn't have any more physical excuses for the state her mind was in, and that scared her. She had faced this demon at least. It was a start.

"Would you come upstairs with me?" She asked Michael. "I'd like to look through Grandpa's things before we go."

"Of course."

The stairs were creaky and the light was dim, but if felt safer than downstairs, sort of a haven. They hadn't lingered upstairs, she could feel it. The bedroom was almost bare. There were two old shirts hanging in the closet so she grabbed one and brought it to her face, inhaling deeply. It was faintly musty and it didn't have his smell anymore. Most of his things had an individual 'grandpa' smell; a mixture of Old Spice after shave, tiger balm for his arthritis and potent black licorice candies. She missed him. Putting the shirt on and drawing it around her, she continued to look around.

His slippers sat neatly on the rug by the bed, as though they waited patiently for his gnarled old feet to slip inside. She picked them up to run her finger along the faded brown corduroy.

"What's with the slippers?" Michael asked, indicating with a flick of his finger the area that had been sliced off. The entire front and top of the toe was gone, leaving only the sole poking out the bottom.

"His big toe pointed up a bit on both feet and the end would rub on the top of the slipper, so he always just cut it off."

"That's funny," he said with a smile. "And it sounds like something he would do."

The only other personal items in the room were in a small, carved wooden box atop the dresser. It had a pocket knife, old but well cared for, with the image of a bear engraved on its ivory handle. There was a small collection of stones he had found himself over the years; a fairly large one with webs of gold embedded in its surface, another grey stone jutting out at one end in a rough purple amethyst and a chunk of lead. There was also a hammered gold fishing lure, two silver dollar coins and a baby picture of her with her parents. She put everything back in the box and put it in her bag.

"I'm ready," she said softly, turning away to wipe at her eyes.

"Hey," Michael reproved gently, hugging her lightly from behind. "You don't have to hide it from me. I know you must miss him. It's okay to cry."

She shook her head. "I'm tired of crying. I don't know where all the tears even come from. I do miss him though."

He rested his cheek against hers. "I know."

They took one last look around downstairs before gathering up the two duffel bags set neatly at the door. None of the boxed groceries were perishable, so they just left them. They were both relieved that it was over, not so lost in trepidation, so conversation came more naturally during the walk back. They discussed what should become of the cabin.

Michael was very adamant at first that she sell it. "Well, you can't live there," he stated matter-of-factly when she expressed her reluctance.

"Well, I can," she stressed stubbornly. "Just not right away. I need to have a place. I let go of Grandpa's apartment and I'm done school, so I can't live in residence."

He looked at her sharply. "You can't live there." His voice was firm. "Ever."

She stopped walking, needing to rest anyway since her body still ached in places, and sat on her bag. "Oh?" She said impudently, a little rankled at having him tell her what to do.

He sat down on the other bag. "Why are you fighting me on this?" He asked.

"It's not your decision to make."

He regarded her steadily for a long moment, his eyes lit up with frustration.

"Are you just going to sit there and fry me with your eyes, or tell me what this is about?"

He leaned forward until his face was so close she could feel his breath on her cheek, and when he finally spoke, his voice was soft and intensely compelling. "It's just not a place you should be living - not anymore. Sell it."

She shook her head, trying to resist the spell he was weaving so effortlessly around her. "Then I won't have a place to live if ...I need it."

He ran the side of his thumb lightly across her cheek. "You won't need it. I promise. Just ...stay with me. If you don't want to sell it, rent it out."

Shelley forced herself to think beyond what his words and eyes were making her feel. How much did she really know about Michael Daillant? She liked him very, very much and trusted him instinctively, but that meant very little in the real world. Maybe he was simply upset at the thought of her living in a place that witnessed his torture and her rape. But what if he was trying to undermine her independence, foster her need to lean on him, to take all that he offered until she had no way out and nowhere to go? What kind of fool was she, to move in with a virtual stranger, in the woods where she had no way out and no one to run to for help?

Looking at his intent, handsome face, she suddenly felt ashamed of her grim and terrible suspicions. He'd been nothing but kind. He was a good man. "You're right," she said abruptly. "I'll see if I can rent it out. I don't want to live there anyway."

"Good," he said with an audible sign of relief. "Let's go home. Before we get soaked."

CHAPTER SIX

Michael pushed himself out of the chair and crossed once more to the large picture window. Summer storms never failed to exhilarate him, but tonight the weather couldn't be blamed for his mood., or the seething, nameless feeling of discontent.

"What?" He asked faintly, still staring out into the blackness.

Shelley pushed the cat off her lap and came to stand beside him. "Well, you've gone to that window about ten times in as many minutes. What are you looking for?"

Studying the crazy maze of rivulets running down the pane, he tried to follow one with his finger, then another before finally shaking himself out of his trance. He smiled at her ruefully. "I'm sorry. I'm feeling restless, I think. I'm not used to spending so much time inside." It was more than that, he guessed with a sudden flash of insight. "It's withdrawal!" He almost shouted, making her jump. "Withdrawal," he said again happily in the face of her obvious confusion. "I'm so glad I finally put a name to it. The feeling was driving me crazy." His fingers fairly itched to hold his camera. He had never gone more than a day or two without taking pictures or developing film or checking his equipment. Finding the subject, balancing the composition, feeling for the right mood, waiting for just the right lighting - the challenge of bringing all these elements together for the perfect picture never dimmed for him, the excitement never waned. Photography was more than a hobby, more than a profession. It had always been an obsession, at least until the attack almost four weeks ago. At that point he hadn't cared if he ever looked through another lens again, ever, but now he realized with a spark of excitement that he couldn't wait another day. Lightning flashed outside, briefly illuminating the wildly swaying trees and the white-capped fury of the lake. It fired his blood, filling him with restless energy.

Shelley was searching his face with a worried frown. "Withdrawal?" She echoed hesitantly.

He nodded, achieving a sober expression with difficulty. "Yes, I'm sure that's it. Chills, sweats, tremors ..."

She just stared, mouth hanging open, blinking up at him with eyes gone big. It was the disappointment in them though, that made him realize she had taken him completely seriously. "Hey," he said softly, tweaking the end of her nose. "I was kidding about the chills and tremors. I meant withdrawal from work."

Shelley let out a long, heavy sigh. "That's a relief. You had me stunned for a moment there ...I'm pretty good at spotting the junkies and you just, well it just didn't fit." Turning her back on him she went back to her chair.

Michael followed her. "That wasn't funny, was it?"

She flopped down onto the overstuffed cushion and began to flip through a magazine she found on the end table. "No, it really wasn't."

"I'm sorry." He perched on the arm of her chair, not knowing what else to say.

Nodding her acceptance of his apology, she closed the magazine and threw it back on the end table. "That's okay. I'm a bit touchy about it, I guess."

"You don't look like someone that has traveled in those kinds of circles." The comment was tentative but hopeful for he thought maybe, just maybe, she would feel like sharing part of her past with him.

"Oh, well," she shrugged, avoiding his gaze, "I knew someone. I put in my time, so to speak."

"Who was it?" He probed cautiously, knowing his chances of getting more information out of her were slim. She was always closed up so tight that getting her to talk about her childhood was tricky indeed.

She just shook her head, apologetic but clearly determined not to continue the conversation.

Michael let it go, reminding himself not to take it personally. She would come around if he didn't push her too hard, too fast. Unfortunately, patience with people had never been his strongest virtue.

"I've been here all this time," Shelley ventured, obviously trying to ease the tension she had created, "and I've never seen your work."

He smiled at her, feeling his excitement build back up and bubble over, as it always did when he thought about how he made his living. Reaching onto the bookshelf, he pulled two thick photo albums down and handed them to her. "This is what I do."

She took them to the couch and eagerly flipped the cover of the first album open. Unexpectedly, Michael felt a sudden powerful urge to slam the cover back down. What if she didn't like his work? What if she wasn't impressed by it? Other people's opinions had never meant much to him, not until this moment. He watched her face, hungry for some sign of approval.

There were over two hundred photographs in the albums, compiled over the years, and he considered them his best work. He liked to try to capture a force of nature on film, be it beautiful, ugly, frightening or tragic. Just the thought that he could freeze a moment or feeling in time was magical to him.

Turning the pages slowly, she looked at every one, studying them closely. Some she lingered over for minutes at a time, touching the plastic covering, running her fingers over them. A mother black bear shot by hunters and left for dead stared sightlessly forward, sadly incapable of taking in the lush, green beauty surrounding it or the two tiny, frightened cubs that nuzzled at her stiffened carcass. It was a powerful shot, and poignant.

Two wolves with hackles raised and teeth bared, circled each other, exhausted and wary but ready to fight. Scarlet droplets hung suspended in midair and more spattered the snow around them. It was dramatic and he could still feel their desperation every time he looked at it. Now more than ever he knew perhaps, how they must have felt at that moment.

A chubby toddler peered intently into the shell of a startled turtle; a lightning storm that crackled with potent energy; the flames and rolling, billowing clouds of a forest fire. For over an hour she pored over the photographs, completely absorbed. She didn't ask questions and that pleased him, for his pictures were supposed to tell the story on their own.

After the last page had been turned, she looked at him with admiration. "Those are wonderful! They're beautiful and sensitive and ...perfect."

"I sell some to magazines, but my sister Drew sells most of them in her studio in Quebec." He studied her face, captivated by the animation he saw there and the wonder shining from her eyes. Her bruises were completely gone and the swelling was down, leaving her skin fresh looking and naturally beautiful. It gave him an idea. He wasn't normally interested in portraits, but it suddenly seemed very important to do one of her. "Can I take your picture?"

She laughed. "Are you kidding?" When she saw that he was serious, she covered her face with her hands, as though he already had his camera aimed at her. "No!" She said, plainly horrified.

Touching her knees in supplication, he got on his own knees in front of her. "Please," he wheedled with his very best, most persuasive smile. He could see her resistance weakening, wavering the face of his deliberate charm, so he went in for the kill. "Pleeeeease, Shelley. It's just for fun, to help me get back into the swing of things. Please."

He could see the moment that she gave in; a softening of her features, a sudden flash of resignation, a small sigh. The thought that he had the power to predict her actions, to sway her thoughts and ultimately affect her decisions filled him with a rush of triumphant exultation. It was an odd feeling, really, and unexpected. He had never been in a relationship like this one before and it left him floundering sometimes. He was normally a 'go with the flow' kind of guy, rarely making the effort to take control in personal relationships with his buddies, his family, or even with old girlfriends. But Shelley was none of those things and for the first time ever, he felt that he was in a relationship where he could put his wants and needs right out in the open and be irresistible in the process. He was beginning to realize that she could not resist him when he used a certain look or a certain voice and it made him feel good, and to a degree, powerful. That sounded selfish and arrogant, he knew, but the scales would be more than even if she ever discovered how tightly he was wrapped around her little finger.

"All right," she said grudgingly as she stood up, innocently unaware of the deep and complicated turn his thoughts had taken. "I'm sure it's going to be a waste of your film, though. I really am not very photogenic."

"Oh, I doubt that," he said, looking her over with an expert and professional eye, already imagining what kind of shots he wanted. "I want you to go upstairs and put your favourite clothes on. And bring something down with you, something important. A treasure," he added with a grin.

"My favourite?" She asked uncertainly, "or the nicest?"

"Your favourite," he clarified.

Fifteen minutes later he paced impatiently at the bottom of the stairs, too excited to sit down, his equipment long since set up and ready to go. Dawson sat on the couch, looking up the stairs expectantly, as though just as eager to get to work as Michael was. He looked at Michael from time to time, ears up and head cocked to the side, as if asking him what the hold up was. So naturally he began to explain to Dawson, as he paced back and forth, about the nature of woman, and how man had never really figured out what women did behind closed doors when they were getting ready for things. He was just reaching the peak of his explanation when he heard her bedroom door open and the slow footsteps to the upper landing, but she hovered there, reluctant to come down. He raced up the stairs, taking them two at a time, to grab her hand and bring her down before she retreated back to her room and changed her mind. He wasn't at all surprised by her choices, in fact it was exactly the look he had in mind for her; fresh and down to earth in a baggy grey U of T sweatshirt and blue and green plaid shorts. Her hair was still up in a fluffy pony tail and she held a ratty, hairy stuffed dog in front of her like a shield.

"It's a google dog," she explained hesitantly, catching his amused glance. "I've had it since I was twelve. It's the last thing my mother ever gave me. You know what? This is a bad idea. I feel ridiculous and I ...goodnight."

"Oh, no you don't!" He said, catching her arm. "This won't hurt a bit." He let his voice drop again to a soothing, persuasive pitch, roughening the edges into huskiness. "Do it for me."

She gave in, as he knew she would. Using the full bookshelves as a back drop, he positioned her on an artfully messy pile of blankets. She bolted up again, ready with another excuse. "I have no make up on."

"No make up," he said firmly, pushing her back down. "Just you."

At first she wouldn't take her eyes off the floor to look at the camera, as she huddled on the blankets with her arms locked around her knees. Her cheeks were so rosy with embarrassment that it made him wonder what she was thinking about. She looked terribly shy and just so sweet that he knew it would be a wonderful picture.

"Pretend I'm not even here." he instructed as he snapped another picture. He got her to change positions two or three times; sitting cross-legged with her stuffed dog in her lap, to lay on her stomach reading a book with her legs crossed at the ankles and bare feet in the air, to lean against Darby and Dawson. He was having a lot of fun and it felt good to be working again.

Shelley sat up with a yawn after almost half an hour, absently petting the stuffed dog that rested on her knee.

"Tell me about your google dog," he prompted softly. He wanted her to talk about herself and share stories of her childhood. She was so relaxed and unguarded and this seemed a natural place to start.

She smiled a bit self-consciously. "My mother gave him to me when I was twelve. Not long before she died."

"You never told me how your parents died. Was it a car accident?" He took more pictures, casually, as they talked, never making it obvious but always catching the change of emotion; the shadow of sorrow in her dark eyes, the small smile from an almost forgotten, joyful memory.

"No. My mother was ...lost. She could just never find herself, you know?" She looked at him, her eyes willing him to understand what she meant.

He nodded, though he really didn't understand at all.

"She died of a heroin overdose. My dad couldn't go on without her. He killed himself that same year." Her fingers fussed with the hair on the stuffed dog, twisting it into little ropes, but she held his gaze. "I don't like to tell people about that. People judge you."

"Oh, Shelley. I'm so sorry." Filled with genuine sympathy at the surprising revelation, he left his camera to kneel beside her, folding her in his arms for a hug. "I'm sorry you've had such a sad life."

"It was a long time ago, Michael. My life hasn't been all that bad." Her voice was muffled against his shoulder, but she hugged him back hard and didn't let go until Darby squeezed her cold, wet nose between them, nudging and snuffling until she became part of the hug. Michael squeezed out of the embrace, leaving Shelley at the mercy of the overly affectionate dog, laughing as he watched Darby push her down to wash her neck and face.

"Hey!" She screamed, giggling helplessly between licks. "Help me."

"I think I'll let you two bond some more - I'll be back with some iced teas and maybe some popcorn."

"No!" She howled, still laughing uncontrollably. "Don't leave me." Inspired by the sound, Darby raised her head and let loose a throaty howl of her own.

Before Michael even reached the kitchen, Dawson had joined in. He could only shake his head with amusement at the racket the three of them were making. All had fallen quiet by the time he returned. Shelley lay sleeping on her side, curled around a pillow with one dog nestled behind her knees and the other against her stomach. She looked very young and peaceful and strangely untouched by the world. It saddened him to think that two strangers could come along and change a person, just damage their body and spirit in the space of an hour or two. She looked vulnerable and fragile but she had a strength, a quiet strength of character that had kept her going. He felt drawn to it. He took more pictures of her, enjoying the artistic freedom and the unguarded expressions that chased themselves across her face, even in sleep.

For over an hour he watched her sleep, studying her features so closely he could see them when he closed his eyes. He had to acknowledge to himself that no matter how attractive he might find her now, or how very much he liked her and wanted her to stay, he never would have noticed her in his normal, everyday life. She was too quiet, too shy. She wouldn't stand out in a crowd of people, unless you knew her. Like he did. He stood abruptly, deciding that he was finished with the little girl - now he wanted to capture the woman.

Gently waking her up, he positioned her so that she was partially reclining against the pillow. He pulled the elastic from her hair and watched it spill down around her shoulders, like dark, shiny skeins of silk. He combed it with his fingers, arranging it the way he wanted. Her eyes gazed sleepily at him, blinking slowly in unconscious invitation and looking for all the world like she was deep in the throes of passion. He felt a rush of heat as his own body unexpectedly responded in kind.

He tried to ignore it, taking deep breaths and thinking about the picture. Only the picture. But he found himself reaching out toward her anyway, to run his finger over her soft lips, making them look even fuller. He had to force himself to step back and take the picture. He took several, simply letting his imagination run with tantalizing, wicked images, with wonderful fantasies of her stripping off her sweatshirt and throwing him to the floor in a frenzy of lust and passion. He got so involved in his thoughts that it took him some time to notice that she had fallen asleep once more, with her head lolling uncomfortably to one side. It made him laugh out loud - the fact that while he was getting carried away with such thoughts, she was innocently napping.

Realizing that he desperately needed to change the mood, he woke her once more, but this time started telling her jokes and funny stories about him and his brothers growing up. Before long he had her laughing uncontrollably, and he caught it, snapping pictures until he ran out of film.

Hours later, after the iced teas were gone and she had fallen asleep for the third time, he quietly packed up his equipment and carried her up to her bedroom. She didn't stir when he placed her on the bed and covered her up, not even when he kissed her - just the softest touch really, of his lips to hers. He was already thinking about the pictures as he eased the door shut behind him, already looking forward to developing those rolls of film, because he had discovered tonight that Shelley McGraw was one force of nature he desperately wanted captured in his album.

☙

Giving up the third attempt in the last fifteen minutes to french braid her hair, Shelley damned the cast on her arm and settled for two simple braids that hung forward over her shoulders. She scowled into the mirror. It made her look about five years old. Spontaneously, she pulled a simple shorts and T-shirt set from the closet. White cotton with tiny coloured flowers, it was one of her favourite outfits, but she hadn't worn it once this summer. Today felt like a good day for it. She dressed quickly and studied her reflection with none of the apathy that plagued her even a week ago.

Her glance shifted to the chart taped to the wall. She had started keeping track of how many times in a day her mind went over the assault, like a tongue worrying at a sore tooth. Far from making her fixate on it, keeping track made her feel a certain freedom from it. It gave her something on paper - proof perhaps, that the pain would go away and the memories would fade.

After the trip back to Grandpa's cabin, the number was

over fifty per day. Simply everything reminded her of it, but mostly of course, the lingering pain in her body and the cast on her arm. Sometimes at night, she would see his face and hear the sharp echo of snapping bone. Even feel the agony.

Two weeks had passed since then. The number was under ten now and those mostly came at night. She found that every morning she was a little happier, a little more eager to face the day. Of course, it had a lot to do with the fact that she wasn't alone. She spent every day, all day, with Michael. He made her laugh constantly and despite what she had been through, she was sure she hadn't felt such a lightness of spirit since she was a child. Every day with him was like a break from reality. They didn't do much at first; talking, card games, short walks with the dogs.

But today they were going camping, scouting for pictures and she couldn't wait to watch him work. His photographs were so much more than flat, two dimensional pictures. They were different, almost alive. She wondered what the shots of her would look like. Imagine! Getting her to pose for pictures. Ridiculous, she thought, but couldn't stop her lips from curving in a smile.

With one last look in the mirror, she grabbed a small pack filled with 'bush essentials'; bug spray, sunscreen, a flashlight, sunglasses, a compass she didn't know how to use and a book of matches. Michael already helped her pack her clothes and toiletries, since she had a tendency to want to bring too much. She trotted down the stairs in her new hiking boots and was almost at the bottom when a shrill wolf-whistle pierced the air and nearly made her jump out of her skin.

Michael strolled out of the kitchen, drying his hands and eyeing her outfit with keen appreciation. "Wow," he said, then with a grin, belted out part of his modified version of a country song.

"*Green eyes, she's got 'em.*

Legs on the bottom.

She tippy-toed right out of a dream."

Shelley laughed so hard she had to sit down on the bottom step. "Where do you come up with these things?"

He shrugged, still grinning.

"When are you going to sing me a real song?" She asked.

"When I'm ready."

"I'd fall completely in love with you, you know that, eh?"

"Really?" He raised his eyebrows with interest. "Why's that? Aren't my good looks enough for you?"

"Oh, there's nothing more seductive than a man's voice. Very powerful, you know."

He cocked his head to the side, trying to look thoughtful. "Is that so?" He asked in a deep, husky, movie star voice.

"You're such a goof," she laughed, though privately those three little words set off a flutter in her stomach. "Ready to go?" She asked, refusing to get flustered by it.

"Yeah, just let me get the gear."

Michael shouldered his pack, loaded with the tent and his camera equipment, and helped her with hers. Then they were on their way with the dogs in tow, heading down a well used trail that sprouted right from the back yard of the cabin.

The trail led them often near water - a riverbank or lake shore, where they would sit for a short time to watch and wait, to have a drink and a handful of nuts and dried fruit. She didn't want to admit it to him, but the rests felt good. Her pack was lighter than his, but still, the weight of the food and sleeping bags was nice to unload.

Sometime after lunch they spotted a fox sprinting through the trees with a rabbit in its jaws. Leaving the dogs with a firm command of 'stay', they followed it silently, with Michael tracking it when it got too far ahead. The wind was in their favour when they came upon her again, blowing their scent away from the vixen's den. The kits were out waiting for her. Michael was very patient. He waited silently for the right moment, camera poised and ready, until finally the playful kits rolled and tumbled into a patch of sunlight, where the golden rays gilded their fuzzy baby hairs. He started snapping pictures then, catching them chasing each other, chewing on legs and tails and finally settling in next to their mother for comfort and a bath.

Shelley spent as much or more time watching him as she did the fox and her family. He was intent and absorbed. He looked like a man who loved his job. His lips moved as he silently told the kits to roll over again, or playfully pounce, or chase a bug. He either had a gift for anticipating their movements or had simply studied the wildlife so long he knew what to expect, for they almost always did as he silently bid them.

She thought about her years at school pursuing her major in microbiology. She found it interesting of course, but could never imagine working herself into some king of euphoric state of joy at the prospect of going to the lab to check on her petri dishes. It made her think and rethink about what she wanted to do with the next forty or fifty years of her life. She wanted joy. Everything that happened this summer made her see that. She didn't want to have to take a mundane job with a fancy title just because she had put in the time at school. She didn't want to live in the busy, crowded city just because she always had, and she didn't want to live alone and be lonely, just because she always had been. The rape had made her realize that a person's grip on life was tenuous and it was rare to get another grab at it. Spending time with Michael made her see that she could make it better, make it worth something this time.

A light touch on her shoulder brought her out of her reverie. "Such deep thoughts," he teased in a whisper as they moved away, back toward their trail. They picked up the dogs, who waited obediently on the path, and walked for two or three more hours before stopping for the night.

Darkness settled in quickly in the woods, so Michael deftly pitched the tent while she started cooking supper. He was so very organized. She pulled out the zip lock bag marked with the appropriate date and dumped out the contents - two packages of chicken flavoured instant noodles, one can of flaked turkey and one package of dehydrated vegetables. It all went in the one pot to be heated over the tiny, portable camping stove. Completely exhausted, she sat on a smooth, weathered log which had long ago been stripped of its bark, and stirred the thick soup.

Michael hung a small battery powdered lantern on a tree nearby, then sat down beside her with a sigh. First noting the increasing number of itchy red bumps popping out on her skin, she looked over at him. "How come they don't go after you?" She asked irritably, slapping yet another mosquito on her arm.

"They bug me. They just don't bite me. I guess your

blood is sweeter than mine." He peered into the steaming pot of soup. "I'm starving," he said, waving his cup around in a blatant hint.

"Are ye now?" She asked, in a perfect imitation of her grandfather's Irish brogue. "So where's *your* supper, then?"

"I'm only going to tell you this once, Shelley," he said gravely, looking into his empty cup. "I could get anything I wanted from my two sisters when we were growing up and probably still could. Do you know how?"

She shook her head, not sure if he was annoyed or amused, yet intrigued by his question.

"I tickle them. I am the champion of ticklers. I made them pee their pants at least once a week and I can guarantee," he added softly, "that I can make you do the same." He flexed his fingers experimentally and she jumped with a nervous laugh. His smile was big and triumphant and completely irresistible. "Do you want to reconsider?" He asked in a low voice, holding out his cup again.

Looking over at him, it was hard not to laugh. He looked like one of those guys in the 4x4 truck ads, like he could whip a fishing rod out of one pocket and a wrench out of the other, like he should be drinking a cold beer and smoking cigarettes down at the local bar. If she hadn't met him before now, she would never have guessed that he was artistic and sensitive, with a charming sense of humour. Life really was an amazing collection of coincidental events and winding turns that led a person to the here and now.

He shook his cup again to catch her wandering attention, so she gave in with good humour and filled his cup. She couldn't help pointing out to the obvious to him, though. "I hate to burst your victory bubble, but I can tell you that will never, ever happen. I'm not that ticklish."

He arched his eyebrows slightly in disbelief, shrugging one broad shoulder. "Time will tell, eh?"

"Whatever you say, Mr Wilderness Guide. I wouldn't want to get left out here in the forest."

It started to sprinkle then, so they cleaned up and piled into the tent with the dogs. Surprisingly, she fell asleep right away, surrounded by the sounds of even breathing and a strangely comforting doggy smell.

The sound of agitated ravens on the peak of their tent woke them early. They both groaned, stretching bodies gone stiff from the previous day's sudden activity. After a coffee, a quick breakfast of instant apple oatmeal and a brief, chilly wash in the river, they packed up and started on their way. For two more days they hiked through the maze of trails, catching brief but valuable glimpses of wildlife.

Michael got pictures of a beaver studiously chopping at trees on the bank, comically moving from one half-chewed trunk to another. They saw two moose, a cow and her calf, grazing in the weedy shallows. They were so much larger than Shelley had imagined, and fascinating, for although she hadn't detected their presence, the cow kept her baby well protected, flanking it at all times. They also saw a slinky little marten raiding the nest of an agitated squirrel, an otter playing in the ebb and flow of river water under the rapids, and a beautiful bald eagle that gazed down at them from his perch with such majesty and presence that she was held in complete awe.

He used up an entire roll of film on a large, shiny black bear picking at a rotten log, delicately and persistently shredding it to get at the collection of bugs and worms inside. He used yet another roll on a lynx, which had its back arched defensively as it crouched on a rock wall above their tent.

Although disappointed that he didn't get any wolf shots, they decided on the morning of the fourth day to head back home. The trip back was much quicker but just as much fun, since Michael ended up chasing her for half of their last day, brandishing his damn camera like a weapon. He followed her, taking pictures from behind, or sprinted ahead only to jump out and surprise her with another picture.

By the time they got home, getting her picture taken didn't bother her a bit. All she wanted was a long, hot bath, food that required chewing, and a soft, comfortable bed.

CHAPTER SEVEN

Dawson groaned deep in his throat, rolling happily onto his back in the grass. Shelley chuckled, convinced he was smiling in contentment. She ran the sturdy comb through his white belly fur, pulling out dead hair and the occasional burr. The motion was repetitive but unexpectedly soothing, and mindless in a way that inevitably leads to introspection.

The day was beautiful; sunny and bright with a cool breeze that ran through the clearing with enough regularity to keep the temperature at a perfect twenty five degrees. Michael was going to be gone for most of the day shooting pictures, and although it felt strange to be apart, it was quiet and peaceful and the perfect time to reflect on the myriad changes in her life.

It was isolated here, that was for certain. Although they had been to town a couple of times for groceries and doctors appointments and follow up X-rays, Coyote Falls wasn't exactly a hub of social activity. The town was small and though the people were basically friendly, there were some things she did miss about living in the city. She missed going to the movies and nice restaurants. She missed computers, cappuccinos, shopping malls, stores with irresistible sales, fast food, even sometimes just the hustle and bustle of *people*. Thankfully, such feelings of homesickness were rare. Recent events aside, she really did love it here. She had survived, and at the time she thought thrived, in the fast paced life of a busy student for four years, but coming here had opened her eyes.

Here she was beginning to discover what life was really about; cherishing the small moments, learning, living healthy, living right and loving what you have. Stuff like that. The kind of hectic pace she was used to didn't belong here. There was no fighting traffic or watching the clock or standing in line here. Everything just seemed to flow naturally, at its own speed. She loved it all; the bird song in the morning, the wildlife, the rhythmic sounds of the waves against the shore, everything. She knew that when the time came for her to leave this place, she would be very sad indeed.

Of course, some things had taken a little getting used to, chiefly the lack of electricity. Turning on the lights, for instance, was not the simple matter it used to be. They were all propane fueled and had to be lit with a match. She still didn't like doing it; that big 'poof!' as the gas finally ignited scared her every time. The upstairs heaters, fridge and stove, hot water tank, barbecue and clothes dryer were also propane fueled. Michael hauled the propane in during the winter by snow machine and sled, bringing enough one hundred pound bottles to last the entire year.

Making toast was another task she found particularly challenging. The bread had to be toasted in a compartment of the oven, under the flames. She simply didn't have the patience to watch it and as the oven didn't obligingly shoot the bread out when it was perfectly browned like an electric toaster, she burned it time and time again. The kitchen really was the only area where she missed electricity and the wonderful plug-in ease of appliances. It was surprising for a bachelor, but Mike had them all - processor, blender, mixer, even slow cooker, but they were all tucked away in the cupboards, collecting dust. There was a small, gas powered generator behind the cabin which they used occasionally to watch a movie or play music, but it was inconvenient so they didn't use it often.

They did at least have indoor plumbing, thank goodness. The water was pumped to a large, elevated tank from the lake, or rather from under the lake as Mike had explained. They used a sand point, drawing the water from about ten meters below the natural filter of sand and rock. The water was simply fed by gravity from the tank to the cabin. They had a septic system for the waste water but it tended to fill rather quickly, especially in wet weather, so there were no sinfully long showers or excessive toilet flushing. She learned through trial and error to use only the water she needed.

Darby barked and yipped at the water's edge, suddenly interrupting Shelley's thoughts. Dawson reared his head at the sound and pushed at her hand to dislodge the comb. He scrambled to his feet, shook himself thoroughly, stretched first his front legs then back and trotted off without a backward glance. She let him go, admiring the healthy shine of his coat. Both of the dogs had enjoyed the grooming, and she wanted to end it on a happy note. That meant leaving the nail trimming to Michael since they could bleed profusely if cut incorrectly or too far up.

Her stomach growled noisily, rumbling and echoing its awareness of the time. She pulled her tuna fish sandwich from her bag, unwrapped it eagerly and took a big bite, though her enjoyment was hampered somewhat by the racket the dogs were making. They were both barking now and running back and forth along the rocky beach in frustration. She shook her head affectionately. "Darby, Dawson, come! Leave the silly ducks alone!" They came to her reluctantly, though they stopped every few seconds to look back down at the water with obvious longing. She patted and praised them both but they didn't stay to visit, apparently disgusted by her party-pooping attitude. They took off behind the cabin instead, with their characteristic howls and judging by the resultant, teasing chatter of the local squirrel, she had a pretty good idea what they were after. They would most likely stare up that tree, circle it threateningly from time to time, and bark for hours. They were good dogs and loads of fun, but she didn't think they would even place in the 'smart dog' category.

Undaunted by the noise, the ducks swam closer. Michael had pointed out some of the different kinds to her, explaining the differences between the puddle ducks and the diving ducks, giving her some basic knowledge of what they ate, what kind of noises they made and when they molted. The speculum, or colored patch on the wing of these particular birds was a beautiful, iridescent violet, marking them as Mallards. He told her that the males, or drakes, were in full eclipse this time of year, meaning their bright plumage was lost after mating. For a few weeks at least they resembled the drabber hens, making it difficult for an amateur bird-watcher like herself to tell them apart. There was no confusion today though, for this group clearly consisted of a mother and her nine curious ducklings.

With powerful thrusts, one by one they surged straight up from the water to land on the dock in a ruffle of brown feathers. They waddled toward her in a line with single minded purpose, focusing on the soft brown bread of her sandwich. Mike had told her stories about these ducks, even going so far as to say they marched up the hill to pick their own blueberries. She hadn't believed him, but judging by this bold and amusing behaviour, she was beginning to reconsider.

They crowded around her, 'kwek, kweking' comically and she laughed, delighted by the precocious birds. Their funny orange feet flapped against the wooden boards as they jostled for a better position. Ripping a small piece from the bread, she held it out tentatively, a little bit afraid they might snap at her fingers, but their bills only clacked harmlessly over them as she offered small pieces to each in turn. It went well until one particularly bold one craned his long neck to grab the entire piece from her hand and ran with it back down the dock. It did its best to swallow the prize whole but two of the other ducklings raced to join him, to rip their share of the booty from his mouth.

It was just too funny. Between chuckles she picked at the sticky globs of tuna salad on her plastic wrap and put them in her mouth, unwilling to sacrifice her entire lunch. When it became clear there was no more food for the taking, the ducks lost interest and waddled to the end of the dock. She was sad to see them go as they each jumped back into the water, but they didn't go far. They paddled around in hopeless circles, preening, straightening feathers and bickering as siblings do until one by one they tucked their bills under their wings and went to sleep.

They seemed a happy little family, she thought, stifling the unexpected feeling of loneliness that crept through her. What will become of me? Of Michael? How long could they continue to live in this idyllic place, as friends and roommates? Would they become a couple and have a happy little family of their own? It seemed terribly unlikely to her. Pushing herself to her feet, she dusted the grass and dirt from her pants and meandered to the shore, over the sand of their small beach and the outcrop of boulders that separated it from the forest. She didn't want to think about the future.

The snakes were out again. Some of her excitement and joy in the day returned as she counted them, challenging her memory as well as she tried to recall their names. They were all named after lawyers Michael had met at one point or another and the thought never failed to make her laugh. She could tell most of them apart by their side markings; bright red, orange or yellow in varying shades and lusters, depending on when they last shed their skin. All eleven of them were curled up on and around the rocks today, sunning their sleek black bodies amongst the wildflowers and tall grasses. She ran up the hill to the shed where the minnow tank was kept. It had been converted from a small freezer and set up with a filter and pump to keep the water oxygenated. She skimmed the dead ones from the top, two dozen or so, and dumped them in a pot to carry back down with her. The snakes loved these. Michael had apparently been feeding these ones for years and at this point they were fat and healthy and larger than most garder snakes in the area. They simply appeared every summer, unfazed by the dogs and the people, to feed and sunbathe and companionably share their surroundings.

As soon as they saw the pot, the older, larger snakes reached and slithered closer, tongues darting out in anticipation to taste the air. They actually ate right from her hand, slowly working entire minnow bodies into their mouths and swallowing them whole. Their appetites were insatiable when they were hungry and could easily consume two or three dozen minnows *each*, stopping only when they had a noticeable and truly uncomfortable looking lump in the otherwise uniform length of their bodies. They were fascinating creatures and the feeling of wonder that she felt every time they allowed her into their world like this never faded.

Like the ducks, they too curled up in the lazy heat of afternoon for a nap. Yawning hugely, she decided they all had the right idea. She packed up the grooming tools and the remains of her lunch and stuffed them in her bag. After all, a summer holiday wasn't really a holiday unless you could nap when you wanted to.

CHAPTER EIGHT

Michael handed her a slippery minnow. "Hook it like I showed you. In the mouth, out the gill, back through the side."

Shelley held the wiggling minnow up so she could see its face. It had little blue dots on its nose, below eyes that stared at her in direct accusation. It opened and closed its mouth in a desperate search for oxygen, but to her it seemed a cry for help.

Turning her seat slightly toward the bow, she leaned over the side and pretended to rinse her hands, releasing the minnow at the same time. As soon as it disappeared, she dropped her line with its unbaited spinner into the water, then looked back at Michael.

She smiled at him.

His eyes narrowed suspiciously. He cut the engine and began to reel his line in. "Give me your rod," he said.

"No! I'm fine."

"Hand it over," he repeated, getting out of his seat.

"No! Use your own. Michael!" she squealed, as he lunged for it.

They wrestled for it briefly, each laughing but determined to win. He let go with one hand, using it to tickle around her ribs and under her arms. Unable to fend him off, she started to giggle uncontrollably and the rod slipped unnoticed from her hands. He grabbed it, then dropped a kiss on her forehead.

"Thank you," he quipped. "Told you I was good at that." He brought the line up quickly, then dangled the offending bare hook in front of her. "Aha!" He shouted. "I knew it! What the hell are you doing with your minnows?"

"I had a nibble," she lied. "A fishie stole it."

"Oh, right. Goddamn it - you're letting them go, aren't you?"

"Yes," she confessed, laughing helplessly. "How did you know?"

"You gave me that 'I"m hiding something' smile. You show way more teeth than usual." He glared at her in mock anger until she flashed him a real smile, presumably with the correct number of teeth, for he smiled back slowly and so beautifully that her heart slammed into her ribs.

"Oh, you're gorgeous when you smile." She was sure she only thought the words, but ducked her head in mortification when his eyes widened in surprise.

The smile in question grew into a grin. "Isn't that supposed to be my line?" he joked.

Her face burned. Swiveling her boat seat away, she seriously considered biting her tongue off so she could never again be plagued by her own verbal faux pas. She could hear him chuckling and dared a glance back. He caught it and gave her such a phony, deliberate smile that she threw her empty pop can at him.

"I take it back," she said as loftily as possible.

"Oh, it's too late for that," he pointed out. "It's already gone to my head."

Mercifully, he dropped the subject, peering dubiously at the stringer of fish over the side. "I guess we have enough for a shore lunch. Let's go in." He hauled the stringer into the boat, where the three Walleyes flopped weakly in a small puddle. Noting her pitying look, Michael pointed at her. "Don't even think about it! This is lunch."

Being chiefly for trolling, the motor was small and fairly slow as they wound their way through a maze of islands, around rocky points and over large, open expanses. Yet, it was just fast enough to work strands of hair out of her braid and cool her flushed cheeks.

Michael slowed the boat even more as they passed a reef. The rocks reared out of the water in places, forming jagged little peaks and smooth, sloping slabs. Every square inch of it was covered with gulls; the white and grey feathered birds crowded together, squawking and flapping their wings at the intrusion. Clearly familiar with boats and their hopefully fishy contents, a few gulls left the rock one by one until a small flock followed them, flying over and around the boat.

They stopped at an island just beyond the reef, pulling the boat up onto the coarse, red-gold sand of the beach. Michael set to work immediately, expertly filleting and deboning the fish. He threw the heads and entrails far down the stretch of shoreline where the gulls fought noisily for the scraps. Next, he lit a fire inside a ring of rocks, and laying a grate over the flames, proceeded to load it with a fry pan for the fish, one for the sliced potatoes and onions and a pot for the baked beans. She reached into the cooler to help, but he gave her a friendly slap on the wrist.

"Don't touch," he said. "It's my job. I'm the guide, remember?"

He dipped each wet fillet in corn flake crumbs before frying it in the hot oil. He cooked the fish, stirred the beans and fried the potatoes, handling all three jobs with ease.

Within a half hour, he presented her with a paper plate loaded with food. It smelled heavenly. He even had fresh, buttered bread, cherry cobbler and cold bottles of ginger ale from home.

After the incredibly tasty and filling lunch, which she praised him lavishly for, they washed the pans with sand, packed up the cooler and then relaxed for the rest of the afternoon. They spread a blanket out on the beach and snoozed, side by side in the sun until the heat became unbearable. She was hot and excited about swimming in a real lake, so it took little effort on Michael's part to convince her to go swimming with him.

As she stripped down to her bathing suit, Shelley turned away self consciously, wondering how many scars were showing through the open back of her green, one piece suit. His eyes had dropped to the bite mark on her left shoulder; she saw him look. Although healed, it still showed individual tooth marks in a roughly circular, pink scar. He had numerous scars too still, some she was sure would be permanent, like the one over his eye and the bullet hole. He didn't seem to worry about his battle scars, though, so after making an initial, conscious effort, she forgot about hers and had a good time.

They splashed each other, raced and dunked each other, crawling back once in a while to lay down on the blanket and rest or have a cold drink. They swapped childhood stories, told jokes and laughed. They tried to catch quick, silver minnows with their hands, they dug holes in the wet sand and built sand castles. Exploring the beach, they found a natural spring with icy cold, clear water bubbling down to the lake. She also found and collected empty clam shells, pieces of smooth driftwood, pretty rocks, a tiny crayfish skeleton, which she thought was just the cutest little thing, and an eagle feather.

Michael just shook his head and led her a ways into the shaded forest, where he showed her lady slipper orchids and picked her wild roses. They found saskatoons, blueberries, pincherries and wild raspberries and ate them for supper, staining their hands and lips a deep, purply red.

Finally at dusk, as exhausted as two little kids after a day of serious play, they were forced to leave their island and head home before the darkness made it impossible to do so. By the time the screen door slammed behind them at home, it was dark. Darby and Dawson came running, almost knocking them down in exuberant joy. Michael wrestled with them in the living room while she went to the kitchen to put the leftovers away and clean out the cooler. She heard a playful howl and then recognized with amusement, the heavy thud of someone hitting the floor.

Feeling a sudden shiver wrack her body, Shelley put water in the kettle to boil for tea. The air was still very warm and she didn't understand why she wasn't hot. Her head ached, her brain felt slow, her thoughts a little fuzzy.

Michael raced into the kitchen with the excited dogs at his heels. He skidded on the slippery surface, catching her around the waist and slamming her into the fridge. She could barely respond, could only clutch the front of his shirt as her head started to spin. His face started to swim before her eyes.

"Is it chilly in here, Mike?" She asked weakly. "Why am I cold? I don't feel very good."

She sagged back against the fridge with her eyes closed. A hand came up to feel her forehead and her cheeks, peeled up one of her eyelids to peer inside then abruptly grabbed her own hand.

"C'mon then."

She pulled back. "I think I'm just tired. I should go to sleep."

"Nope," he said cheerfully, but with a edge of steely determination she couldn't ignore. "I think you've got sun stroke." He led her down to the small expanse of beach beside the dock. Without asking, he proceeded to grab the bottom of her shirt and whisk it over her head. He reached for her shorts.

"Excuse me!" She said, perking up a little. "What are you doing?"

"Helping," he said with an innocent blink of his brown eyes. "You have your swimsuit on under there and we're going in the lake."

She pulled her own shorts off then they both waded out into the water and just stood there, letting the cold wash over them and lower the temperature of her overheated body. The moon was full and glorious, suspended over the lake, dripping rippled beams along its surface. A loon called mournfully in the distance and she thought the beautiful cry sounded unbearably sad and lonely. The blackness of the night got deeper and darker, but still they stayed in the water, floating around on their backs, pointing out fire flies, constellations and falling stars. She had never seen a night sky so black back home, or seen so many stars in it.

It must have been midnight when Shelley finally felt normal again, if a little wrinkled, and she was going to suggest they go in when, without warning a greenish white glow appeared high overhead. It began to feint and flicker across the northern sky before spreading out in a half ring. The light danced and rippled for a long time, sparking with flares of purple and red before disappearing completely and suddenly, as though it had never been.

"That's the most beautiful thing I have ever seen ...and kind of eerie ...," she said in an awed voice.

Michael swam around to stand close in front of her. "Aurora Borealis. Northern Lights. Wawatay. It has many names."

"Very pretty," she stated, reflexively backing away from him slightly. She started to ask what caused them but decided the scientific explanation would take the magic right out of it. "I feel fine now," she said instead. "Let's go in."

He just came closer again, making her feel nervous. He put his hands behind her shoulders, pulling her slightly off balance so she was forced to lean against him. She had never felt so much skin against her; it was scary yet comforting, calming yet exciting. His body felt warm, even in the cold water. The moonlight caught the droplets of water on his skin, etching him in silver.

"Shell?" He asked in a low voice. She could feel it rumbling in his chest. "How many men have you dated?"

"I couldn't say," she answered stiffly, feeling insulted and a bit defensive. She pulled away and turned toward shore.

"All right. Narrow it down. How many men have you kissed?"

She spun back around and gaped at him in disbelief, looking for some sign that he was joking. He wasn't. She just stared at him.

"Tell me," he prompted softly.

"No. That's a rude question. I don't keep track." She didn't intend to mislead him but she didn't want to admit to none, either.

His expression grew even more intent, his voice even quieter. "How many men have you made love with?"

"Michael!"

"I can't tell," he went on, as though she hadn't spoken, "from your behaviour. You're a mystery - a contradiction. You're shy, yet you promise me exciting things with your eyes. You're - "

"Let's talk about something else," she pleaded, "because I'm not going to tell you."

"How many?" He pressed, pulling her back to him. She could feel his fingers lightly stroking the back of her neck.

Shelley felt the answer slipping out. Why not? He knew everything else. In a brief moment of recklessness, she gave in. "None," she offered weakly, "to all three questions."

He went very still, seemed to suspend his breathing even, for an endless moment. "Are you saying that day in the cabin was your first time?"

She nodded. "I wasn't too impressed," she tried to joke, in the hope that it would ease this terrible tension.

"Oh, Shell, you know that it's not always - "

"Yes, yes." She waved it away. "I know that."

"Why?"

She gave him a blank look.

"Why not before?"

She shrugged, trying to make it look casual, to make him think the years of loneliness didn't matter. "No one ever asked. At least, no one I liked."

Surprisingly, his teeth flashed white in the darkness. "I get your first kiss, then." It was a statement, not a question.

"Says who?"

"Me," he answered succinctly, searching her eyes.

"And you." He leaned forward.

"Now?" She squeaked.

"Unh-huh," he said, already staring at her lips. "I've been wanting to do this all day." He lowered his head very slowly. She watched his mouth as he came closer and felt a flutter of excitement. His lips hovered over hers, touching softly here and there. "Close your eyes," he whispered.

She closed them, wanting very much to please him. She felt his lips curve in a smile before he pulled away slightly.

"You're so sweet," he said softly. His mouth came down over hers again, this time with more pressure, yet he kept it gentle and undemanding. Something flickered again at her insides and she recognized dimly that it must be desire. She felt his tongue sweep over her bottom lip before he pulled back again.

"I feel like a teenager," she said with a shaky laugh.

"No making out in the car? No hiding hickeys from your grandfather with scarves and turtlenecks?" His breath was warm where it fanned her skin. She shivered and goose bumps rose up along her arms.

"No," she said, struggling to think clearly. "No hickeys."

"It's time you had one, don't you think?" He asked with a thread of laughter in his voice.

"No, that's all right." But it was too late. His mouth fastened on her neck just below her ear and began to draw on it. It branded her, incredibly hot on skin gone cold and clammy from lake water. Her knees almost buckled. Her hands ran through his wet hair, then over the sides of his face, where the muscles in his neck and jaw worked in a slow, steady rhythm beneath her fingertips. The flicker inside her became a steady, seductive pull.

"There!" he said, touching the little bruise with a satisfied and slightly sheepish quirk of his lips. "Now I feel like a teenager." He tugged at her hand and she followed him out of the water and up the path to the cabin, trusting his sense of direction, for she couldn't even see the rocky trail.

After they toweled themselves off, he ushered her right into the kitchen, where he reboiled the water in the kettle and made a pot of tea.

"Well, we were too late for the burn, I'm afraid," he said, pushing her under the light to examine her reddening shoulders and back.

"I don't feel burnt."

"Oh, you will in the morning." He grabbed a tube from the first aid kit and handed it to her. "Anywhere that saw the sun today."

She started on her arms and shoulders, rubbing the cool gel into her skin. He sat down at the table and watched her, following the movement of her hands intently. Disgusted with herself for being so jumpy, she planted her elbow firmly on the table, on the forgotten tube actually, accidentally squeezing a large amount of gel onto the beautiful oak. "Maybe I'll go do this in the bathroom," she suggested, feeling like some sort of inept exhibitionist.

"Why? Because I'm watching you?" There was a new quality to his voice; a new timbre that she found exciting.

"Because of the *way* you're watching me," she stressed, deciding to be honest. "It makes me nervous."

He smiled slowly, nodding his understanding but his gaze continued to follow her hands anyway. She rubbed the lotion briskly onto her legs, feeling shy and self-conscious, and darted a glance at him only when she reached her thighs. His look was direct and intense. Too intense. Taking the cowardly, or as she preferred to think of it, the prudent way out, she turned her chair in the other direction. Silently applauding her own cleverness, she quickly squeezed a generous amount in her palm, discarded the tube once more onto the table and proceeded to rub it into her thighs.

"Nice try," teased a voice in her ear, just before a warm hand started to massage more gel into her back.

"I can do that!" She protested, but she didn't twist away. It felt too nice.

"Oh, I'm sure you can," Michael said agreeably, "but I want to help." His hands lingered long after the lotion was gone, but eventually they fell away. He rotated her chair back to face him then returned to his own.

They drank their tea in silence. It stretched out before her, the silence, like a long country road, in a way that it never had before. This kind of mood, of tension in the air was new to their relationship, so she had no idea what she should do or say next. "Michael," she began, "I've had a wonderful day, actually I can't think of a day when I've had more fun, but I'm very sleepy, so I think I'll turn in." She got up to leave the room.

His voice stopped her at the door. "Shelley, did you think of him today?"

She didn't have to ask who he meant. "Just the once," she admitted honestly, "when you asked me ..."

"So, it's getting better?"

She nodded. "You?"

He nodded. "Good!" They said in unison, then laughed.

She left him then, exhausted by the fresh air and the

sunshine and went up to bed. Her last waking thoughts were on the wonder and magic offered by a summer night in the wilderness, but her dreams were about a man; a tall, dark haired son of a French logger, with a voice that made her weak in the knees.

ൟ

As usual, the sunshine and bird song coming in the open window had Michael up early. After a quick shower and a shave, he walked quietly to Shelley's room, thinking to check on her sunburn. He slowly turned the knob on her door and pushed it open. She had kicked her covers off sometime in the night, and was laying on her stomach in a large Toronto Blue Jays night shirt, with one knee drawn up. Her position brought the curve of her backside into prominent focus, and he worked hard at tearing his eyes away. Her arms were tucked beneath her pillow and a heavy cloud of dark hair hid her features.

Carefully easing his weight onto the bed, he leaned over her slightly. "Morning," he called softly, pushing the hair out of her eyes.

Her eyes opened, blinking sleepily at him in some confusion until without warning, they came sharply into focus and she bolted upright in the bed. "What's wrong? What's going on?"

"Nothing is wrong. I just came in to check on your burn. How does it feel this morning?"

She shrugged her shoulders experimentally and winced. She stuck her legs out in front of her and he winced. The front of each was an angry red and in places the skin had bubbled, leaving a slightly yellowed, crackled crust. It looked like second degree burns at least. The tops of her feet were burnt as well, and swollen to twice their size.

"It looks like someone blew air into your feet," he cracked, unable to help himself. "You know, like a rubber glove."

"Ha, ha," she said, poking carefully at the red skin.

He leaned over her to pluck the back of her shirt away from her body and peer down it. Her back and shoulders and even the tops of her ears were covered with dime-sized water blisters. He gave a low whistle. "That's nasty."

"What should I do?" She asked in a worried voice.

"Well, I don't know," he had to admit, feeling at a loss, "I've never even had a sunburn."

They both looked at his arms and torso, where the skin was deeply and evenly tanned.

"Yeah," he acknowledged. "I get pretty dark in the summer. My Mom used to call me her little Indian. She'd tease Dad about it and tell him she had an affair with a First Nation's Chief."

"Did he think that was funny?"

"Oh, sure. He knows she would never cheat on him. Commitment is very important to my family." He gave her a very meaningful look, deciding he would let her read into it however she chose to.

She obviously chose to ignore it, deciding instead to finger-comb her tangled hair, to wind her clock, to fidget with the blanket. "Are you in here for a particular reason, Mike?" She asked finally. "I should get dressed now."

"Yes, you *should* take that off," he said, pointing at her nightshirt, "before it sticks to your blisters. Don't let me stop you."

She gave him a dirty look then got out of bed and

hobbled awkwardly to the door on her puffy feet. Looking at him pointedly, she waited.

Just for fun, he waited too. "Let me find you something to wear," he suggested spontaneously, walking to the closet. He knew he was being obnoxious but it gave him an excuse to stay in her room. He rifled through the clothes, watching her in the mirror at the same time. She yawned, then sat down on the edge of her chair to watch him with amused indulgence.

"Nothing in here is right - do you have a bikini?"

She snorted. "Get real."

He chuckled and went through the clothes again, finally picking a light tank top. He pulled it off the hanger and dropped it in her lap. "I'll leave you alone now," he said generously, leaning into her to kiss her cheek. He resisted the urge to slide down to her lips. "Do you want 'I-feel-sorry-for-you-because-you-have-a-sunburn' pancakes or a 'you-look-like-you're-in-pain' cheese omelet?"

She smiled in pleased surprise. "Umm, the pancakes with sympathy please."

"You got it!" He trotted down the stairs, wishing wistfully for a morning where he could wake up beside her.

☙

It took three or four days for the pain of her sunburn to pass. It was altogether a miserable experience; the blisters popped, leaking sticky fluid all over her pillow and bed sheets, and the burnt skin began to peel off in great ugly swaths. She had vowed at least ten times each day that she would never again leave the house without sunscreen on.

Michael had spoiled her shamelessly in the last days; cooking for her, making her treats, rubbing lotion on her back.

Deciding that she owed him an afternoon of his choosing for being so understanding, she went out the back door to look for him, spotting him eventually in the hammock, down in the shade of a clump of poplar trees. From a distance, wearing a muscle shirt and cut off jeans, he looked healthy and fit and completely relaxed. One bare leg swung absently over the side as he stared up into the leaves. It was only when she reached him that she noticed his somber, thoughtful expression.

She hesitated, not wanting to intrude, but he must have heard her approach, for he twisted his head back to look at her.

"Do you want to be alone, Mike?"

"Hey," he said softly, with a shake of his head. "Join me?"

She looked around the yard in confusion.

"No, join me here." He took her hand. "There's lots of room."

"No," she laughed. "I don't think so. The last time I was in a hammock I tried to read and it made me sick for two days. I'd probably flip us both to the ground. Contrary to the impression I have already made, I am not looking for my next injury."

He held tightly to her hand when she tried to pull back, and looked in her eyes very solemnly. "I would very much like you to join me," he insisted quietly. "Please."

She bit her lip in indecision. He hadn't said or done anything ...suggestive since he'd kissed her in the water that night. A tiny part of her was disappointed, but mostly she was relieved. She would feel a lot less uncertain about things if they kept it the way it was. When he flirted with her she felt pressured by her own fears, desperately wanting to find out what it would be like with someone she cared for and was attracted to, but also desperately sure she would do something horrible and shame them both. She couldn't see even a hint of his usual, teasing sparkle and decided she was worrying for nothing. He was in no mood to flirt with her today.

With surprisingly little difficulty, she eased first her bottom onto the hammock, right near his hip, then lay back onto his outstretched arm. She had no choice but to rest her head on his shoulder. Her bare leg pressed along the entire length of his and though she tried to hold it away, the netting rolled them right back together.

"Relax," he suggested gently. "I won't hurt you."

"No, I know you won't." She breathed in and out with care so he wouldn't notice how nervous she felt here next to him.

"Do you think," he asked suddenly, "that everything happens for a reason? That it's all part of some big plan?"

"Honestly?"

He nodded.

"No, I don't. I don't believe in God, or any supreme being that created earth and animal. Life is evolution - a mere collection of random events, and the survivors win. Period."

He kissed the top of her head very softly. "You're such a scientist. Are you never swayed by thoughts of having some benevolent being watching over you and guiding you through life?"

"No, never. The God in the bible is not benevolent. Not at all. Look at all the sadness in the world, Michael. People suffer from so many awful things every day; disease, hunger, abuse, loneliness. They die from natural disasters, violence on the streets and freak accidents that make no sense in somebody's master plan. And all they can say is, 'have faith, it's God's will'? I don't think so! You tell me why, if this God is so great and powerful, that He cannot even offer one shred of concrete proof of his existence. I mean, why the secrecy? It's ridiculous. There is no way you could get me to accept as fact, fairy tales written by men from a couple thousand years ago -"

Michael playfully cupped his hand over her mouth. "Okay, I get it. Thank you." He lifted his hand away, only to clap it back in place when she opened her mouth to continue. "How do I shut it off?" He teased.

"I'm sorry," she said through his fingers. "I get carried away sometimes. What's your theory then?"

"Well, it does sound rather far-fetched to me, but officially I am the son of a religious woman so I'm not allowed to argue. My mother would kill me. I do like to think though, that this happened to us for a reason." He was silent for a long while. She could feel his hand in her hair, wrapping a thick lock of it round and round one finger. "In fact, I'm going to give it a reason anyway. I don't like senseless."

"Okay, so what's your reason?"

"You."

"No!" She burst out. "Don't do that. I don't want to be the reason for something like that. We would have met eventually anyway. We were neighbours after all."

He shook his head. "No, it wouldn't have been the same. We never would have been anything more than neighbours and you know it." He paused, as though deciding how best to word his feelings without hurting hers. "We've been here what, six weeks? Plus two in the hospital? Together everyday, all day, and still you won't open up to me. You have a wall, Shell. You can talk with me for hours and laugh and have a good time, but the very moment it gets personal you retreat and go to work, fixing your wall, building it a little higher. I think you try to forget I was even there! I was there when that precious wall of yours crumbled to dust. I got inside and saw you bared right to your soul and I'm not leaving just because you're scared. I may have to fight for it but I'm going to know your every thought, every need and fear. Every dream."

Shelley was shaking her head back and forth, trying to push out of the swinging hammock, but the hand wrapped in her hair made it impossible. She felt a shiver of fear course up her spine. He sounded so intense, so fierce.

"Already I can read every one of your expressions, even though you try so hard to hide what you're feeling. You're scared," he continued bluntly, his voice hardening, becoming painfully accusing. "On the verge of panic actually. You think about leaving every time it gets a bit uncomfortable, don't you, Shelley? You run from people, as far away as possible and you don't care who it hurts as long as you're safely tucked into your little shell."

"Michael, stop it!" She cried, helpless to deny what he was saying because there was some truth to it. A lot of truth. "I've never hurt anybody," she did deny finally. "I've never had anyone to run from."

"You're hurting me. Don't you ever think about how it makes me feel when you shut me out over and over again? You won't cry in front of me or show your pain or tell me how you're feeling beyond anything physical. You won't share yourself with me and I feel alone."

"But, we barely know each other, Mike. You have no

right to my personal feelings."

"I do! I saved your life and you saved mine. No one has more right! And no one knows you better than I already do. Why do you keep fighting me? Every time I get a little closer, you push me away and Shelley - I need to be close to you right now. I need to. And it's what you need too, even if you won't admit it." He pulled her gently back down so that she lay half on top of him this time. He rubbed her back lightly and she felt herself slowly and reluctantly relaxing against him.

"You're pushy," she said sullenly.

"I know. Tell me what you're afraid of."

"Nothing," she denied. "I don't do it on purpose. It's just the way I am."

"Just let go, Shell. Let it happen."

"Let *what* happen?"

"Whatever. Let our friendship grow and go somewhere. Summer is over. We'll have to make plans soon."

"Yes. Soon," she agreed, "but not yet."

Again he sighed underneath her in frustration.

"I promise, Mike. We'll have a real talk and I won't run away from it. Soon, I promise."

Using both hands, he cupped her face to lift it up to his and kissed her softly on the mouth. "I will hold you to that promise."

She honestly had every intention of keeping her promise, but her unspoken, nagging worry made her continue to put him off. They filled their days with canoeing and kayaking, swimming, fishing and other fun summer activities, but every evening as they roasted marshmallows on the beach or played cards, he would watch her with heart breaking expectation, waiting for her to open up and talk to him. And every evening she would look into his brown eyes and smile and put it off for just one more day.

CHAPTER NINE

Positive.

Shelley flipped the lid of the toilet seat down and collapsed onto it, clad only in her lacy white bra and panties. The wand of the pregnancy test fell to the floor as her fingers went limp with shock.

Oh God, Oh, God.

Her heart dropped into the pit of her stomach, making her feel sick. She could feel the pressure at the back of her throat and the unease in her stomach build until, without warning, her dinner came up. She barely flipped the toilet lid up in time.

She heaved and heaved, long after there was nothing left to come up but bile. Tears of misery and self pity started to fall as she retched over the porcelain bowl, hair hanging around her face in limp, sweaty strings.

Pregnant. *His* baby. That monster's seed growing inside of her like some vile insect. It gave her an awful, creepy crawly feeling, bringing with it the terrible memories she had almost succeeded in putting behind her. His hands touching her, hurting her. The pain and panic. The shame. She slid to the floor where the cold tiles numbed her bare skin.

Mindlessly, she began to scream and claw at her belly, knowing only that she wanted it out. Why me? Wasn't it ever enough? Why me? Her thoughts were disjointed and desperate but she nabbed one thought with the focus and determination of a pit bull. Get it out. Don't let it grow inside me, not something like that.

She didn't hear the rattle of the door knob or the pounding on the door. The concerned voice coming through the solid wood panel couldn't penetrate the hysteria that consumed her. With a crash, the door flew open, splintering as it ripped small pieces of wood away from the frame. She stopped shrieking and scooted backwards, freezing at the sight of him like a wild animal trapped by the beams of an oncoming car. She had just enough presence of mind to note the expression on his face. It was drained of colour. He looked scared to death.

His eyes dropped to her stomach and the blood on her hands. "What are you doing?" He yelled, so loudly that it echoed, bouncing from wall to wall in the small bathroom.

Sobs began to wrack her body, so deeply that she started to retch again, throwing up foamy bile onto the white floor tiles. "I don't want it!" She moaned, wiping her mouth with the back of her hand.

He fell to his knees in front of her and grabbed her wrists. "I don't understand," he said, his voice now smooth and even, soothing, like he was talking to a frightened child.

"Help me, Michael," she begged desperately, trying to free her hands. "Please, don't make me. Please help me. You have to help me."

He pulled her closer to the door, to a clean spot on the floor, and locked her in front of him with his arms and legs. Her own arms he held crossed in front of her, away from her bleeding belly. She struggled only briefly, too tired to fight him.

Reality slowly seeped into her consciousness. She was

covered with blood, smeared with vomit. Why must this man be witness to all of her most horrible moments? She sniffed loudly. "I'm fine. You can let go."

He didn't move, obviously reluctant to free her. She hung her head so that her hair fell forward, veiling her face. The humiliation was setting in again, as she mentally gathered together the shreds of her composure. She could feel some of the stiffness leave the muscles of his arms and thighs. "Really," she pressed. "I'm okay now."

He released her wrists, then quickly levered himself up to kneel in front of her. "Don't move."

She opened her mouth to protest.

"Don't move!" He barked. "I'm sorry," he relented immediately. "You just scared the hell out of me. Don't move - please."

She nodded.

He sighed with relief then moved across the floor to clean up the mess. He quickly wiped and scrubbed, throwing the soiled tissues into the toilet and flushing them down. He found the pregnancy test on the floor and threw it in the trash can.

Her eyes followed dully as he washed his hands, then wet a washcloth. He wouldn't give it to her when he returned but rather washed her face for her, like he would a toddler, rubbing the cloth over her whole face at once, then her hands, one finger at a time. He rinsed the cloth then returned. "Lay back." His words were terse but his expression was concerned and confused.

She did so, feeling that this surely must be the very lowest point of her life. Slow tears streaked back over her temples to disappear into her hair.

He dabbed at the bloody furrows streaking her lower abdomen. "Why would you do such a thing?" He asked gently.

She shook her head, dislodging more of the tears that glazed her eyes. "I didn't realize," she explained weakly. She felt spent, utterly exhausted.

He got up once more to rummage noisily in the medicine cabinet, muttering to himself. He came back with a wrinkled tube of antibiotic cream, a small one with the end rolled half way up its length. He smeared the ointment over each scratch with a cotton swab, then taped a single, large square of gauze over them.

"Get up," he instructed, firmly hauling her up by the hand. He led her to the sink where he poured a splash of clear blue mouthwash into a small cup. "Rinse," he said.

She obeyed woodenly, automatically, not caring.

"Spit."

She spat into the sink, watching dispassionately as he rinsed it out and turned the wall lamp off. Saying nothing, he led her into her room, where he tucked her into bed.

"I don't want him inside me, Michael," she whispered again, trying to make him understand.

"I know, baby. We'll talk about it in the morning, okay? We'll figure everything out."

She was asleep before he even left the room.

Michael went back downstairs, heading straight to the cupboard for the bottle of vodka. He downed a shot in one gulp. It didn't calm his nerves as he had hoped. Instead, he could feel the now familiar anger rattle at the cage of his self control. He could hear it roaring in his ears.

Before June sixth, he was an easy going man, slow to anger. Lately though, it was an emotion he battled daily.

Mostly it just simmered beneath the surface, waiting patiently and silently for the seal to crack. The further he tried to bury it and the more he tried to pretend it wasn't there, the more relentless it became. It was getting worse instead of better and increasingly more difficult to hide from Shelley. More and more often now, he would find himself making excuses to leave the room and disappear until the rage passed.

Every night he woke up drenched with sweat, desperate and frustrated that he couldn't alter those events, especially of that last day. Their taunts would ring in his ears and the memory of pain, normally forgotten in daylight, would sear him ruthlessly. The hatred and humiliation would ignite anew and burn hot. The flashbacks were vivid and always triggered the release of his frustrated rage.

He silently counted to ten, then twenty, making a conscious effort to slow his breathing and calm the hammering in his brain. When he had opened that bathroom door his heart had nearly stopped beating. All he had taken in at first was the blood on her hands and the look of terror in her eyes. He had thought ...God, he thought she had slashed her wrists. He had thought she had given up and that split second had nearly brought his world to a grinding halt.

He counted to ten again and took a series of deep, calming breaths. So Shelley was carrying a child. A child conceived in a moment of agony and fear. Her screams still echoed in his mind sometimes. Even the memory of the sound made the hairs on the back of his neck stand up.

He shook his head, even thumped his forehead repeatedly with one closed fist, but the image of her wouldn't leave him, that one moment before he had closed his eyes in defeat. The very moment that piece of trash climbed on top of her and raped her. And impregnated her. Her face had been beaten and bloody and utterly, hauntingly empty, like a broken doll.

The helpless anger began to build inside him all over again, along with a hate so powerful, it left him shaking. He wanted to scream and shout his pain out to the world, to vent his violence on the ones who deserved it, but they were dead and so he was left floundering in a pool of his own bitter feelings. Suddenly overcome, he flung his empty glass at the wall then hurled the bottle, still half full, right after it. They shattered into a million glittering pieces.

He stared at the mess, feeling ashamed and confused but perhaps a little less overwhelmed. With a deep sigh, he sopped up the pool of vodka with a rag before it could soak into the wood, and carefully swept up the shards of glass. He then sank heavily into a chair at the kitchen table and sat there for a long time, thinking. More than anything in his life he wanted Shelley to be his. From that first night in his cabin he felt it and the more he learned about her, the stronger the feeling became. He wasn't interested in where the feelings came from or why they were so all consuming. All he knew, all he cared about, was that the feelings were real ...the need was real. With unconscious arrogance he decided he would do whatever he had to, to keep her in his life. But what about the baby? The thought that she carried within her another man's child filled him with unreasonable, uncontrollable jealousy. It made a part of him, just a small part, want to rip it out of her too. He could almost hear that man laughing, laughing at this grim reminder of his presence, like he was reaching a hand from the grave just to muddy the waters of their healing spirits.

There were so many things to consider besides how they both felt about that man. What kind of person would it be? Would it be twisted and heartless, committing with ease the same kinds of crimes and atrocities as its father? Even if it was a normal child, how could they as parents resist any feelings of resentment toward it? How could they not associate it with the most horrible ordeal of their lives? It was impossible to know or predict. He had always been vehemently opposed to abortion. Always. But he was knee deep in it now. What did he think of his narrow, uneducated opinion now?

He had a large family and had always been around babies. He loved them and believed strongly that anyone irresponsible enough to get pregnant ought to grow up and take responsibility for their actions. Everything has a consequence. Learn it and live it. His dad still used that expression all the time. It was his favourite, all purpose lecture phrase.

But Shelley wasn't irresponsible or promiscuous. She was young and innocent and terrified of this baby inside her. She didn't deserve these consequences. There was no easy answer, so he found himself wavering back and forth throughout the night, agonizing over a decision that wasn't even his to make.

He would picture a little blond boy, crazed and unbalanced, mean spirited and out of control and think abortion was the best option for everyone. Yet, over and over he forced the image from his mind only to have another take its place; a pretty baby girl with her mother's big green eyes, shy smile and sweet nature. It would be so wrong to kill this baby, as innocent of any crime as it is possible to be. He turned the problem over and over in his mind until finally there were only two options acceptable to him - raise it as their own or give it up for adoption.

Could he accept another man's - no *that* man's child as his own and love it unconditionally? He was sure it wouldn't take more than one chubby fist clutching his finger to lose his heart to it. Yes. He wanted it. It would be the only positive thing in this whole crazy situation, maybe he thought, even their salvation. Their saving grace.

At last finding some peace in his mind, Michael crawled onto the couch and succumbed to sleep near dawn.

☙

Shelley tiptoed barefoot down the stairs, clutching at the sleeves of her flannel robe. She felt much calmer, more in control than last night. Last night, she recalled with a grimace as she let the dogs outside and filled the kettle with water. How horrible. She had never lost control like that in her life.

She couldn't have thought of so many ways to turn a man off if she tried. Start off with an average woman; a little plain, a little dull. Throw in the recent sexual trauma and confusion and some low self-esteem. Add a little self mutilation, insanity, physical scarring and another man's child. Oh, and vomit. Perfect, she thought sarcastically. Just what he's been looking for. He must be so disgusted. She should just go back home to Toronto, but the thought of running home held no appeal. There was nothing and no one to run home to.

The lid on the kettle began to rattle, bouncing up with each agitated puff of escaping steam. She poured the water into two cups, dipping a Mountain Berry tea bag into hers and an Earl Grey in the other. She added a squeeze of honey to each, grabbed a bag of Fudgeo cookies and carried everything into the living room.

Michael was sprawled on the couch on his back, with one arm and one leg hanging over the side. His mouth was open slightly, lips parted and relaxed. Long lashes rested against his cheeks, making him look like a little boy despite the strong cut of his jaw and the shadow of dark stubble.

A wave of affection for him rushed through her, seizing her chest and squeezing so ruthlessly, it almost stole her breath away. How could she not love someone so completely irresistible? There were so many things she was confused about, but her feelings for him were not one of them. It didn't really matter, though. What they had here, this escape from reality, was over. She couldn't fool herself into thinking that when he opened his eyes she wouldn't see the disgust there. He would be as revolted as she was by this news, even more so. It would break her heart but at least it wouldn't be a shock. That was something, wasn't it?

She sat in the rocker beside the couch, carefully setting the mugs of tea on the coffee table between them. She felt much more able to think on her future this morning, without panicking. She would have to go to town as soon as possible and have it taken care of. Then it would all be over and she could just get past it …just get it done.

She had been sitting there for only a few minutes when Michael's arm moved. He tried to rest it on his chest, where it promptly fell back down, causing him to rap his knuckles painfully on the coffee table. He woke immediately and sat up, grinding his palms into eyes gone bleary from lack of sleep.

"Morning," she said around a mouthful of cookie

crumbs.

He smiled a greeting, rubbing a hand over his face then through hair that stuck out comically at the back in a messy pinwheel. He noticed the cup of tea on the table. "Is this for me?" He asked hopefully.

"Oh, yes. Though it's not so hot anymore."

"That's all right." He took a big sip, then leaned back with a sigh of satisfaction. "Thank you. You look better this morning."

She could hear the question, the unspoken concern. "I'm sorry," she blurted out. "About last night, I mean."

He just looked at her, sipping his tea. "Can we talk about it?" He asked gently after a moment.

"There is no need, Michael. I'll be going to town as soon as possible ...to ...um ...get rid of it."

"I wish you wouldn't do that." His voice was quiet but it rang in the air and replayed in her mind several times before she could grasp what he had actually said.

Her mouth fell open. "What?! What are you saying?"

"Just that you have choices."

"What do you want from me?" She cried, slamming her cup onto the table.

"I want you to think about what you are doing."

"Don't be retarded, Michael! As if I haven't thought about it!" She snapped. "I haven't thought of anything else."

"No," he argued calmly, "I don't think you have. Not beyond the easiest way out. I know it's painful for you, and scary -"

She flew out of her seat. "You don't know!" She screamed into his face. "You don't know anything about it." He looked hurt by that, but she was too angry to care. She couldn't believe she was hearing this from him, the one person who was supposed to understand.

"I'm not trying to tell you what to do -"

"Yes, you are!" She interrupted hotly. "That's what I don't understand. You know what he did - you saw! He ..." She broke off, unable to say it. She enunciated each word slowly, with exaggeration. "I - DON'T -WANT - IT."

"It?" He asked incredulously. "It's not a parasite for God's sake, Shelley. It's a baby. Just a victim in this like you and me - "

"It is! A parasite, that's exactly what it is! Part of him has taken hold inside and it's ...it's ...feeding off of me, growing and ...changing me!" She wiped angrily at the tears on her cheeks.

"I just don't want you to look back at this day and regret it. You can't decide something like this overnight!"

Shelley started to pace. Her blood was raging through her veins, pounding in her head. She had never argued and screamed like this at anyone, ever. It made her feel strange and out of control. She turned on her heel to stomp from the room.

"Shelley!" Michael roared. "Don't you walk out on me!"

She turned back, ready to scream some more, but he whirled away to brace his hands on the back of the couch. He hung his head. "Talk to me," he pleaded hoarsely. "Talk with me."

She closed her eyes. He was right. She hadn't thought beyond abortion. Everything in her had been screaming for a quick solution, to just end this painful turmoil. Her anger drained away as quickly as it had come, so she recrossed the room to sit on the couch. "It's so much harder to think about it," she confessed. "I just want it to be over."

He sank onto the cushion beside her. "I know."

They sat together for a time, each afraid to say the wrong thing. The clock ticked loudly.

"It's part of you."

"It's part of *him*," she countered.

"Yes," he agreed. "But what part?" He touched her belly lightly. "That might be the one who cures cancer right there."

"Or bombs the World Trade Centre."

He tried again. "It might compose the most beautiful music you've ever heard, or become an artist."

"Or a robber, murderer and rapist," she said flatly.

"Come on, Shell. Open your mind up. Quit seeing it as some byproduct of a violent crime. You're blaming this little baby for the sins of its father. It's innocent. Is it really for us - you," he amended quickly, "to decide if it even has a right to enter this world and try like the rest of us to be a good person?"

"What if it can't, Michael? Or doesn't want to, like ...him?"

"For all we know, he could have been the sweetest kid in the world. Maybe he was abused, molested. Maybe he got into drugs and couldn't get out."

"Maybe," she agreed. "Although it's easier to think of him as purely evil."

He nodded. "Yes, it is."

"How could I not see him or think of him when I look at this baby? How could I ever love it?"

He smiled. "I think your heart will melt the moment you see it," he said simply. "But if it doesn't, there is always adoption."

She didn't believe it, not for a second, but he was so sincere. He really thought that it was possible to love it.

"Just promise me," he said earnestly, taking her hand. "That you won't decide until after we spend a day in town, after the weekend."

"For what?" She asked, suspicious.

"Education. Informed decision. That's all I ask, okay?"

She squeezed his hand. "Okay."

CHAPTER TEN

She had pestered Michael in the boat ride down river and in the car all the way to town but he still wouldn't tell her where he was taking her this weekend, or what they would be doing. She didn't get her first clue until they arrived at the Social and Family Services building around midmorning. Reminding her screaming nerves that she promised Michael she would be open minded, she ran up the last couple of steps to open the door for him. With a smile.

He smiled back encouragingly, but clearly wasn't buying her act for a second. The building was huge for such a small town. Following at least three different signs that pointed the way to the Children's Aid wing, they arrived at last to a large waiting room with four or five closed doors shooting off of it. There was no secretary at the desk, so Michael simply rapped on the nearest door, the one marked 'Susan Givens', then opened it.

The woman behind the desk was stunning. Her blond hair hung smoothly and perfectly around her tanned face in a smart looking bob. The red of her blazer matched her lipstick exactly. Sniffing the air as unobtrusively as possible, Shelley had to admit that even her perfume was elegant. The woman looked up from her papers, clearly annoyed at the unannounced interruption - until she saw Michael. She fairly flew out of her seat then, red, red lips curving over perfect teeth in a big smile. "Michael, how *are* you?"

"I'm good," he barely got out before her arms went around him and she pressed her slim body to his. Her beautifully manicured hands traveled up and down his muscled back.

Shocked at the tasteless display, Shelley could only stare, certain that those hands would have continued their downward exploration had Michael not pulled away. He walked back toward her and grasped her hand, pulling her forward into the room. "Susan, this is Shelley. She's staying with me at the cabin."

"Oh?" Susan questioned almost frostily, looking her up and down. "Oh! I had heard there was a woman involved as well. It's sooo good of you to take her in like that. I was simply sick when I heard what happened to you, Michael. Sorry I didn't get up to the hospital to see you ..." Her eyes darted once more toward Shelley, cooling perceptibly before looking away again.

Feeling snubbed and distinctly uncomfortable, Shelley tried hard to slip her hand from Michael's, but he wouldn't let it go. Instead, he pulled her toward the matching chairs and dragged her down beside him.

Susan too, returned to her seat. "What can I do for you both?"

"I'm sorry, Susan. I know we don't have an appointment. We just ...well, we've been told, Shelley and I," he paused dramatically, deliberately stroking her hand, "that our baby options are ...limited. Could you possibly outline the adoption procedure for us?"

Shelley started in surprise. He had intentionally made it sound like they were a real couple that wanted to adopt a baby instead of give one up.

Susan's mouth fell open. "Oh! So soon?! I didn't realize ...I mean, that's ...of course I can do that for you." But still she stared at them in obvious bewilderment, as though she just couldn't grasp the idea of Michael committing to someone like her.

Shelley's eyes fell to her lap, where her hand was still entwined with Michael's. One simple look from this sophisticated woman had stripped her of every iota of self esteem she had managed to build up in her time at the cabin. Why was he? Why was he bothering with her at all? With women like this all over him, why should he? She suddenly felt so small and unworthy of the man beside her and so judged by Susan's cold, stabbing eyes, that she just wanted to run, run anywhere and hide. She pulled yet again to free her hand, panicking inside with the need to get away, but still he only grasped it tighter and tucked their folded hands between his knees. Forced to remain, she fixed her gaze on a random spot on the wall just above the other woman's head and concentrated on her breathing, in and out, consciously slowing it down to calm herself.

She listened with half an ear as Susan outlined adoption procedures, availability of babies, waiting times and what kind of parental backgrounds were supplied. Michael came prepared, asking questions whenever Susan fell silent. "So there could be a long wait then, for a baby?"

"There could be, yes. There is a high demand for newborns, especially, I'm sorry to say, healthy non-minority children. In a public adoption like this, the wait could be as long as eight years and neither the adoptive parents nor the birth mother really get much latitude in the decision making process. The decisions are almost exclusively based on the welfare of the child."

"Does the birth mother get to see the baby?" he wanted to know.

"Yes, of course."

"How long does she have to change her mind?"

"Before the papers are signed - as long as she needs."

"What about after? Do they often change their minds about giving it up?"

She picked up the papers on her desk before answering and squared them neatly, each movement exaggerated with self importance. "Well, no, they don't often change their minds once they have gone that far, but the adoption isn't final for a minimum of sixty days after the baby goes to a new home, kind of a probationary period before the court will grant an adoption order." She looked at Shelley once more, sending undercurrents of animosity her way, then pointedly looked at her watch. "I think private adoption may be the best choice for you."

"Thank you, Susan," Michael said politely, taking the obvious hint, "for your time."

"Anytime, Michael." She inclined her head slightly in Shelley's direction. "Kelley."

Shelley felt a spark of anger at what she felt was a deliberate insult. "Nice to meet you, Suzie," she gushed sweetly, with her teeth clenched in a smile. "Thank you."

She saw the woman's eyebrows shoot up to her hairline just as she was shutting the door. Michael looked at her sideways. "She really hates it when people call her Suzie."

"Really? I never would have guessed that," she said with a straight face. "C'mon, I'm hungry."

☙

The chime dinged as the door swung closed behind them and a gust of artificially cooled air swirled around their bare legs. Two or three people called out to Michael with the casual concern that usually made his trips to town so enjoyable. He greeted everyone that looked his way, chatting briefly with them as he and Shelley worked their way to the back of the busy restaurant.

With her eyes downcast, Shelley headed directly for a table in the corner. Her body language was defensive and practiced and designed to make her as invisible as possible. Head down and shoulders rounded, she settled herself in the booth, taking the bench against the wall. He watched her closely, entranced by this shy side of her and wondered what elements in her past had convinced her she was unworthy of attention. Although he was fascinated by her shyness, he had a feeling that he would have been unable to get past it. Would she have let him in if her defenses hadn't already been smashed to bits? He doubted it. He found that it pleased him though, the shyness. It pleased him that he was the only one to know the real woman behind the shy exterior.

Only moments after taking their seats, a waitress, perhaps in her late forties, walked stiffly toward them, menus in hand. She was tall, rail thin and frail looking with a jerky walk, rather like her joints had been fused together. Her expression was sour, probably from years of pursing her lips in disapproval. Everyone called her Ms. Roland - he didn't think she even had a first name. All he knew was she was a spinster whose life revolved around the church and her self-appointed role as moral judge. He was still thinking about the old waitress, wondering how a person could come to be so constantly unpleasant, when Shelley's voice caught his attention.

"She really likes you."

"Her?" He looked at the retreating figure of Ms. Roland with an appalled expression. "I don't think she likes anybody." Then he grinned, amused at the very thought, if it were true. "Think she'll go out with me?"

"If you play your cards right," she joked. "Leave a big tip."

Shelley looked upset despite her teasing remark, like she was about to say something else. It hit him suddenly and he leaned toward her. "You meant Susan, didn't you?"

Her mouth formed the word no, but she nodded before any sound came out. "It's none of my business," she corrected quickly.

"Don't you want it to be your business?" He asked quietly, knowing it would fluster her.

"I ...I take the Fifth. I get in trouble no matter what my answer is."

He laughed, delighted by her answer. "Very smart, but there's nothing going on. They say she's after every man under fifty, single or married."

"Oh," was all she said.

"Jealous?" He teased, knowing she would deny it vehemently. But she threw him completely when she looked him in the eye.

"Yes. I was."

Privately, he thrilled at the confession. "Ahh," he said. "Tell me more."

"She was fawning all over you!" She huffed, playing

with her napkin, folding and unfolding it. "I'm sorry. I couldn't help it."

"Don't be sorry. I'm flattered."

"I think she was going to pinch your butt," she whispered primly, with a blush staining her cheeks.

He laughed loudly, wishing he could have seen her face. "I think she was, too. Why do you think I pulled you over to sit beside me? I needed protection."

She gave him a wan smile. "Seeing her today though, made me realize ..." She stopped, looking suddenly stricken. "It made me see that you belong with someone like her. I am not ...for you."

His humor vanished in an instant. "No," he denied vehemently, shaking his head. "I want you to stay. I have lived here for five years, Shell. If I wanted to be with Susan or anyone else in town I would have by now." He could see her fighting the truth of that in her mind, unsure how to just accept it.

"How do I know you're not just doing this out of pity?"

He knew just how important this answer was for her, so he thought carefully before answering, feeling the pressure of the moment. Looking in her eyes as earnestly as he could, he tried to show her his sincerity. "I like to think I'm a good person. I try to be, but I'm not a martyr. If I just felt sorry for you or felt only obligation, I would maybe buy you a plane ticket home, or help you settle into Mickey's cabin. I would be your friend if you needed me. Nothing more. But with you, I want more. I want it all. There isn't anything I can do or say to convince you of that, is there? The problem is with you - your insecurities. You have to figure out how to convince yourself that you deserve a relationship. Will you try, for me?"

Shelley nodded mutely, seemingly relieved enough to let the matter drop. Ms. Roland marched up to the table then, looking distinctly displeased as she took their order then grilled them for particulars. Gravy or not? White, brown or rye? Cup of soup or bowl? He answered each patiently, smiling at her each time.

"You're positively blooming Ms. Roland. You must be having a good summer."

"Hmmph." She pushed her glasses back up her nose with a knobby finger, looking at him shrewdly.

"You know," he tried again, "I missed you last month. The service isn't half so good when you're not here." Then he winked at her.

She gasped, drawing back with the menus clasped against her bosom. "Watch yourself, young man," she hissed, as with a smart click of her heels, she turned abruptly and stalked toward the kitchen.

He peeked at Shelley. She had one hand clapped over her mouth, but her eyes danced with suppressed mirth. "Your blasted charm didn't get you very far there," she quipped.

He shook his head ruefully. "It never does. She thinks I'm after her body."

"Do you want all the women sighing after you?"

"Not all," he said, suddenly completely serious. "Just one."

Another pink blush crept into her cheeks. "I'll sigh louder next time." She spoke lightly and he wasn't sure how much meaning to read into it.

"You do that."

The chime dinged and Michael turned to see who it was out of simple curiosity. "Hey, it's Daniel."

She gave him a blank look.

"Constable Matthews. He took your statement at the hospital and cleaned up the cabin."

"Oh."

"There's no tables left - do you mind?"

"Not at all."

"Dan!" He called out, raising his hand. "Daniel! Come join us."

The man scanned the tables, looking for the source of the voice and smiled when his eyes lit on them. He weaved through the aisles, working his way to their corner. "Hey, you two. What brings you to town?" He slid next to Shelley, causing the buttons of his uniform to catch on the edge of the table.

"Just taking a day or two in the big city," Michael replied vaguely.

Dan straightened his buttons absently. "Mike, you look a hell of a lot better than the last time I saw you. Almost as good as new, though I confess, I was looking forward to being better looking for once."

"You don't need to be better looking, Dan," he reminded him. "You've got that lady-killer uniform."

"Right," Dan nodded, grinning, then turned to Shelley. "How are you holding up, Shelley?"

"I'm doing fine, thank you." She smiled shyly at him, then actually reached out and touched his hand.

Michael could feel himself bristling, regretting his impulsive invitation. Though he recognized the foolishness of it, he wanted to grab her hand and pull her fingers from Dan's arm.

"I never got a chance to thank you," she continued,

"for what you did at the cabin. That was very thoughtful."

"Don't mention it. I'm just glad you're doing better."

They shared a friendly smile and a friendly look. Neither of them did anything even remotely inappropriate or suggestive, yet Michael felt his heart starting to pound. Beads of sweat popped out on his forehead and upper lip. His fingers clenched into tight fists and it was only with immense effort that he forced them open, to lay them flat on the table. What the hell? This man was his friend but he had to fight the need to get up and slam his head into the table.

His throat was gripped so tightly by some violent, seething emotion that he couldn't even participate in the conversation. Fortunately though, before he could make a complete fool of himself, Dan's beeper went off.

Dan cursed good-naturedly, then slid back down the bench and got to his feet. "I guess lunch is out today," he said, slapping a friendly hand on his shoulder. "But you take care, Mike. Shelley."

"You too," Michael said, knowing that it came out as more of a growl than anything else, but helpless to correct it. He tried to smile at him but it was lame and unconvincing, even he could tell.

Dan left, looking back over his shoulder once with a worried, perplexed frown.

Even Shelley looked at him strangely. "Are you okay, Mike?" She asked softly.

He nodded briskly, battling for self control. For one scary moment he felt it slipping from him, so he excused himself to beat a hasty retreat to the washroom. Once inside, he splashed cool water on his heated face and studied his dripping reflection in the mirror. His pulse gradually slowed to normal and that mindless, clawing, almost uncontrollable anger dissipated, leaving him shaken. That was not normal, for God's sake. It wasn't normal, but he knew what it was. It was jealousy.

Confused by his own out of proportion reaction to an innocent encounter, he swore at the face in the mirror. "Get a grip on yourself." The day was going to be hard enough for Shelley without those kinds of childish displays.

As soon as he opened the rest room door, he could see that she had her neck craned around, checking to see what was keeping him. He was ashamed to look at her. "Sorry," he apologized, sliding back into his seat. Their food had arrived while he was gone, so he took a french fry, forcing himself to chew and swallow as though he were still hungry. It stuck in his throat.

"Michael, is something wrong?"

"No, I feel better now. Sorry," he said again, hoping she would never know what exactly he had been feeling. It would scare the hell out of her. He tried to pretend nothing happened but she sensed his mood without understanding it, and it cast a pall over the meal, making their usual easy banter impossible.

"Don't you like him?" She asked quietly after long minutes of tense silence.

"Of course I do. He's a good friend."

"Then what is it?"

"I ...just didn't feel myself for a minute there. Everything is okay now. Don't worry," he assured her, though he couldn't stop the worry from gnawing at his own mind as he pictured, over and over, her small hand on Dan's, touching him.

He managed to shake it from him somehow and by the end of the meal had coaxed her smiles and laughter back as though nothing really had happened.

༷

"Michael," Shelley protested. "What are we doing here?"

"Don't worry," he soothed, "nothing scary." He led her through sets of swinging double doors, down sterile hallways, then through one final door marked 'X-ray and Ultrasound'.

She tried to pull back, alarmed. "No! This isn't fair. I don't want to do this."

"Shelley," he said firmly, "you promised you would look at the whole picture. This is part of it."

She felt panicky again, distraught. Her voice dropped to a desperate whisper. "I can't. Please don't make me do this."

He pulled her into the room anyway. Only moments later an older woman wearing a bright purple scrubset appeared from around the corner. She was short and heavy, with graying blond hair pulled back into a messy bun. The myriad laugh lines around her eyes, the red apple cheeks and the happy, booming voice were all familiar to Shelley. Margie bustled forward cheerfully. "Michael and Shelley! You both look great. I haven't seen you since I took your last X-rays." She peered happily into their faces. "You healed up nicely I see. I thought I told you young people to drop in and see me!"

Michael gave her a warm hug. "Hi, Margie. Now, don't get excited. This is our first trip to town in quite a while. How have you been? Nicole and Kerry doing all right?"

"I've been great, as always. The kids are up to no good, as always." She shook her head, as though they were the worst kids this side of reform school, but she beamed at the mere mention of their names. "Nicole won herself a scholarship and she's just started her first year of University, and Kerry is still obsessed with her horses. She came in second at the riding competition and ...oh my goodness! Enough about me! You have an appointment!"

"Yes, we do," Michael said, nudging Shelley forward. "I'm amazed you managed to get us in here with such short notice. We don't even have a requisition slip ...but we really appreciate this."

Margie whipped a folded piece of paper out of her pocket with a sly wink. "Got one right here, obstetrical sonogram, signed by the doctor this morning. Called in a favour. Dr. Hastings says hello by the way." She beamed at them some more, clearly pleased with herself. "Come on back."

Shelley followed her into the dimly lit room reluctantly, with Michael trailing behind. She didn't know how to refuse without making a scene. If there was anything she hated it was making a scene, so she did as instructed by the large, kindly woman and lay back on the table.

"Oh, you're barely showing, dear. How far along are you?" Margie asked with enthusiasm.

Shelley struggled to keep her voice even. "Seventy three days."

"Wonderful. Just wonderful." With a tube of gel poised in mid air, she raised Shelley's sweatshirt, only to freeze, shocked into silence. She stared at the collection of scratches covering her stomach. There were at least twenty of them, all capped by a crusty red scab.

Shelley held her breath, waiting for the questions she was sure would come next. But they didn't. The technician instead carried through with the gel like a true professional, squeezed a warm blob onto her skin and proceeded with the ultrasound. Despite herself, Shelley watched the screen. She couldn't read it, not really, but it hit her hard, unavoidably, that there was a baby in her womb. A flesh and blood, heart and soul, real baby.

"There!" Said Margie. "There's a little hand ...that's the head ..."

Shelley could feel the hot tears pooling in her eyes. She tried not to blink, to keep them from falling, but they came anyway. She turned away from the image on the monitor, biting her bottom lip to keep it from trembling. Little hands. Seeing those tiny hands ...

"Such wonderful timing," Margie announced. "Just what a sweet, young couple like yourselves needs right now, to help you get over that terrible incident this summer. That was simply awful," she clucked.

Michael gave her a sickly smile.

She picked up on his discomfort, quick and accurate as radar. Her eyes narrowed, almost disappearing in the folds of her chubby cheeks. "Isn't this your baby, Michael?" She asked bluntly.

Shelley gasped, stricken by the question. What should she say? What would Michael say?

He looked stunned. His mouth worked soundlessly for a moment before he cleared his throat. "Of course. Of course it is."

Margie looked from him to Shelley and then back again

with a frown creasing her forehead. Shelley was at once relieved and horrified. She didn't want to explain, but she didn't want to lie either.

"Shelley, honey," said the technician gently, reading something in her eyes. "Those men raped you, didn't they dear? You wouldn't be so sad if that was our Michael's baby."

Shelley nodded miserably. "One of them did."

"Oh, sweetie," Margie crooned, drawing her into a hug, almost smothering her against the abounding, comforting softness of her bosom. "You should have told us. We'd have been there for you."

Shelley felt overwhelmed with emotion. She felt validated and understood, safe and loved and so very comforted in this woman's motherly embrace. It gave her an inkling of what she had missed with her own mother - her mother had always been too immersed in her own problems and needs. Her own addictions.

"What you need - what you both need, is some counseling, someone to help you sort through things. What do you think?"

Shelley pulled away and wiped at her eyes. "I don't think I want to tell a stranger those kinds of things." She looked over at Michael. He looked troubled. She couldn't understand his moods lately; what caused them or what they meant. He was becoming increasingly silent and withdrawn.

"We'll think about it, Margie," he promised quietly. "Thank you."

The older woman nodded, wisely deciding not to push the issue. She patted Shelley's hand. "Are you going to carry it to term, honey?"

"I don't know."

The technician efficiently wiped the gel off of her stomach and pulled her sweatshirt down. "I guess I don't have to tell you, you don't have much time to decide. The risks are much higher after twelve weeks. In either case, you should see the doctor for a prenatal exam as soon as you can."

"No, I know. What would you do, Margie?" She asked impulsively.

"Oh, honey, I couldn't say. My kids are my biggest joy. My life would be empty without them, but I know they were conceived with love. It's just not the same."

Everyone was silent for a minute, digesting the truth of her statement.

Michael broke the silence first. "Margie, do you have a pamphlet or a video or something that we can see on abortion? We're ...looking at all the angles today."

"Of course. It's good that you're learning about your options. Follow me, dears." First grabbing a stack of pamphlets wrapped with an elastic band and a VHS tape from the shelf, she led them around the corner and down the hall into a small room with a ratty old couch, a coffee table and a large TV. She quickly set it up and popped the video in then crouched down in front of Shelley. "If you have any questions, honey, or just need someone to be there for you, you let me know. Whatever you decide, I'll be there, okay?" She wiped at Shelley's cheeks. "Don't cry, dear."

"I'm sorry. Just when I think I'm out of tears, they start all over again."

"I know, sweetie." She handed her the remote for the VCR. "Just press play."

It was quiet again when she left the room. Michael sat down beside her and took her hand. "Ready?"

The butterflies in her stomach were almost making her nauseous, but she nodded then pressed the button. The video was good, she had to admit, for it was neither anti-abortion nor pro-choice. It first addressed the legal point of view, stressing that in the eyes of the law, despite the stew of moral, religious and ethical issues surrounding it, every woman in Canada had a right to an abortion.

For the next ten minutes, a group of young women sat in a semicircle in some kind of seminar, discussing alternatives to abortion. There weren't many, and there weren't any Shelley hadn't thought about already. The final part of the video showed a supposedly real abortion, though she suspected they were actors.

A woman sat on an examination table, with her fingers plucking nervously at the flimsy gown provided for her. After a moment of stilted conversation the doctor instructed her to lay back and relax, with her legs up and apart. Shelley wondered briefly if the doctor, a man in his mid thirties, had any idea how impossible it is for a woman to relax in such a position. For modesty's sake, a sheet was draped over her raised knees. Like an impartial bystander, the camera was a fair distance from the table, placed for a clear side view of the doctor, the woman and the tent over her knees.

He explained things to her as he went along, in a voice most likely meant to be kindly, but sounded instead brusque and clinical. He prepared her with a local injection, saying as he did so, "This is injected in and around the cervix, so you don't feel any discomfort." From a nearby tray, the doctor then selected a scary looking device. "I use the speculum to stretch the vagina to see the cervix and its opening into the uterus," he stated, reaching under the tent to do so. Then, with gentle scraping and sucking, a small plastic vacuum tube cleared the fetus from the young woman's uterus.

He unbent her legs and rested them flat on the table in a final 'all-done' gesture. "Some pelvic cramping and spotting is normal for a few days," he said, "but come and see me if you have excessive bleeding or pain, dizziness, chills or fever."

He snapped off his gloves, reminded her not to have intercourse until after her two week follow up appointment, then left the room.

Though that particular doctor hadn't seemed concerned for the woman beyond her physical welfare, Shelley was impressed by the clean sterility of the doctor's room and his obvious expertise. It was a real medical procedure, not some shameful secret in a back alley hovel with a man and a dirty knife. Was it wrong or right? She just didn't know what to do. The dull, nagging pain in her head that had been plaguing her all morning blossomed with the stress of her confusion, throbbing with each pulse of blood her heart sent in that direction.

She flipped through a pamphlet to avoid any discussion of the video. She wasn't ready for that yet. "Listen to this, Mike." She leaned back into the cushions and began to read. "In primitive societies, abortion was often attempted by magical incantations and rituals that implored the gods to drive the embryo from the uterus. Later, medicines and potions were devised, such as mixtures of spices, herbs and wines. An ancient Chinese document suggested mercury to cause abortion. An Egyptian papyrus recommended applying a poultice of dates, onions and fruit of acanthus. Middle Eastern women swallowed foam from a camel's mouth and European women drank water from the blacksmith's bucket. Women had their vaginas packed with animal dung or submitted to starvation, special diets, bloodletting, enemas, hot ashes and potions made from roasted insects and mixtures of arsenic and other poisons, all in an effort to end unwanted pregnancies.

Historical documents report many methods, such as diving into the sea from a cliff, jumping up and down strenuously, beating the abdomen with rocks or clubs, placing a board across the abdomen and having several people jump up and down on it and constricting the abdomen tightly with belts. Papyrus, wool, caustic plants, pointed devices made of wood or metal, and other irritants were inserted through the cervix and into the uterus -"

"Good God," Michael interrupted, snatching the pamphlet from her and flipping through it himself. "Kind of makes you glad to live in the twenty first century, eh? Did you know if you have an abortion before twelve weeks, it's twelve times safer than carrying it to term and giving birth?"

"Really?" She asked, completely surprised. "I wouldn't have thought that."

"No, me neither. This was printed in the early 80's though, so the stats are more than a bit out of date."

She rifled through the other pamphlets in the stack Margie had given them. "Hey, there is another one here on chemical abortion. I've heard about this." Skimming through, she read snippets aloud. "Non-surgical abortion for woman five to nine weeks pregnant. Oh, I'm a bit past that already, but anyway, it involves three steps. The first is the physical exam of course to make sure there are no health issues that would cause complications. Then, if I'm understanding this right, you either take a pill, RU 486 or more specifically I guess, mifpristone, or get an injection of methotrexate. This step blocks the action of progesterone, the natural hormone vital to maintaining the rich lining of the uterus. Deprived of the food, oxygen and fluids he or she needs to survive ..." She faltered, struck by ruthless reality of the procedure, "the baby dies. The second step involves a visit to the clinician thirty six to forty eight hours later, where she is given a dose of misoprostol or some other artificial prostaglandin, which initiates uterine contractions and usually causes the embryonic baby to be expelled from her uterus. This can happen within hours or days of the injection. The third visit, two weeks later, is just a follow up, I guess. It says 'because these drugs cause serious birth defects, a surgical abortion *must* be carried out if abortion has not occurred.'" She flipped the page over. "Several serious, well documented side effects of chemical abortion have been documented, such as prolonged, severe bleeding, nausea, vomiting, abdominal pain and cramping, diarrhea, bone marrow depression, severe anemia, liver damage, methotrexate induced lung disease and even death ..."

She dropped the pamphlet and watched it flutter to the floor, then suddenly pushed them all off of the table with one violent sweep of her arm. Moving over, she curled up on the couch and sank against Michael. She needed his strength. "Oh, Mike, tell me what to do. I'm so confused. What I should do, what I want to do, what I'm afraid not to do - they're all different and I don't know how to decide."

"Me neither," he said again, stroking her hair, "but even if I knew, it's your decision."

She sighed into his neck, feeling sorry for herself.

"But I'm here for you, no matter what, okay?"

She nodded, thinking how different it could have been. Let's see, how would it go in a romance novel? She would arrive in the boat and step to the dock, disheveled but breathtakingly beautiful, of course. Then there would be Michael, the gorgeous stranger, tanned and shirtless, pruning Grandpa's roses in a sweet, neighbourly gesture. They would see each other and the sands of time would simply stop running through the proverbial hourglass. Overcome by passion, he would ignore her maidenly protests and sweep her into his arms, where he would cart her off to his cabin and make mad, passionate love to her.

Then, after struggling through arguments and misunderstandings for about two hundred pages, they would declare undying love for each other and live happily every after. And this would be his baby. They would feel nothing but joy at the promise of this new life inside of her.

A voice on the intercom, paging Dr. Wilson, brought her out of her fantasy. She didn't live between the covers of a getaway romance. She didn't have a writer planning out her life, carefully weighing her tragedies and victories. And she didn't know the ending. She sighed again. There was just no escaping this twist in the plot.

03

The little girl stared up at Michael with silent, shy adoration throughout dinner. He would speak to her occasionally; ask about her puppy or how many times she had gone swimming this summer. Although she didn't always answer, she positively beamed whenever he even looked her way.

Michael had told her a little about his friends just this afternoon, when he informed her they would be visiting for the evening. Norman and Marylin Keeper were both First Nations people, specifically of the Ojibwe Nation, though they called themselves *Anishinabe* or 'original people'. They lived with a pleasant combination of Indian and White traditions and beliefs.

Norm was a miner, working his shifts underground without complaint and without fail. He was quiet, with black eyes that twinkled with amusement and mischief all the time, as though he knew a joke that he refused to share. Very much a family man, he spent his evenings at home.

Marylin was much more outgoing, with a friendly, boisterous personality. She worked as a teller in the local bank, well known and very well liked. She was involved in the community, heading the library and homeless shelter boards, she was involved in the town council and the hospital board and she was a leading member of the fundraising committees for both cancer and children born with fetal alcohol spectrum disorder. She was a very busy woman, but clearly adored her family and made them a priority.

Together Norm and Marylin endeavored to show their only child, Rosie, the best of both worlds; teaching her both Oji-cree, the language of her ancestors, and English; reading her Dr. Seuss and relating old Indian lore; making her moccasins and buying ballet slippers. At almost four years of age, she was a delightful child.

Shelley looked around the room, admiring the cozy feel of it. Tastefully placed here and there were traces of their Native ancestry; traditional paintings, intricate beadwork and carvings. The rest of the decor was contemporary, with light carpeting and dark furniture. It was an interesting combination but very inviting.

She shifted uncomfortably in her chair. The evening

with Michael's friends seemed very long to her. She wasn't good with strangers, never knowing what to say, hating the strain and pressure of trying to come up with something bright and witty. She tried but typically, her words never failed to come out tangled or simply inane. She would end up talking too fast, or too quiet or lose the thread of her conversation. It was an old and familiar feeling of inadequacy, one that kept her in her room for her last three and a half years of University. She watched Michael with affection and some envy as he laughed and chatted. He draws people to him, she thought, like bees to a blossom.

"Rosie," he called suddenly, putting his cup of coffee down. "Little Flower, you promised you would dance with me the next time I came to visit, remember?"

The little girl nodded, setting her two glossy black pigtails into motion, then held her arms up with a sweetly trusting smile.

Marylin looked at Shelley. "He walks on water as far as Rosie is concerned," she said fondly, then got up to put her baby's favorite song in the CD player. It was a country song, so Michael swung her up, resting one arm under her little bottom and clasping her hand in his in a classic two-step position. He whirled her around the room; two slow steps, two quick steps, with Rosie's smooth baby cheek pressed against his raspy, manly one.

Shelley watched them play, touched by the looks on the their faces. He was so genuine and would make such a wonderful father, she thought, struck anew by the unfairness of it all. It started up an ache in her heart. She let herself imagine just for a moment, that the baby was his; a part of them both and borne of their love. But, neither of them had mentioned love and the baby was most assuredly not his, as much as she might wish it otherwise.

She studied the child in his arms, noting the large, dark eyes, the tiny hand on his shoulder, the little button nose and infectious giggle as he dipped her playfully. What if Marylin had decided to have an abortion? Had her scraped from her womb like leftovers from her plate? This beautiful little person just wouldn't be. It was so like murder when she thought of it that way. How is it different? Withholding food and nutrients from a six week old embryo or a three year old baby - it was the same thing, wasn't it? She might not be able to love the baby inside her, but it was a living thing, a human being special in its own way, and she could no longer convince herself that she had the right to kill it. It didn't matter how much she feared carrying such a blatant reminder of the worst day of her life around for months, she simply had no right. She couldn't keep it, but some wonderful, childless couple would fight for the right to give it the love it needed. The knowledge of what she had to do simply clicked into place and the heavy weight of agonized indecision lifted off her shoulders.

She looked away from them, surprised to see that both Marylin and Norman were watching her speculatively instead of their daughter. Shelley squirmed inside. What were they thinking about her? What had they heard? She tried to smile at them but it was merely a showing of teeth; more grimace than smile. She wanted Michael to take her home - away from the looks and whispers of the townspeople. They didn't mean to be unkind, she was sure, but she felt as though she had been placed on a block for everyone to talk about and point at, as mere grist for the gossip mill.

Michael must have sensed her growing desperation, for

within minutes after his dance, he thanked their hosts for a lovely dinner and had her out the door. They strolled down the sidewalk as the streetlights went on one by one to keep the darkness at bay. A car whizzed by. A dog barked. The church bells pealed in the distance, marking the hour. She had gotten used to the absence of such night sounds.

"They're nice people," she said, for wont of anything better.

"Yes, they are," he agreed, breathing deeply of the night air. "But you didn't have a good time?"

"Oh, well sure I did. It's just been a strange day."

He reached for her hand and folded it in his much larger, warmer one. "Do you think any of it will help you with your decision?"

"Yes." She realized she was about to commit to something that still terrified her. "After reading those horrible pamphlets and seeing that precious little girl in there ...I've decided to carry it to term. I don't think abortion is a decision I can live with."

He squeezed her hand. "I'm glad. I don't want you to think I was trying to push you into anything -"

"But I can't keep it," she interjected quickly. "That's not an option for me. The baby *will* go up for adoption." She paused, searching for the right words to explain. "All the reasons for having an abortion were all about me. *I* was scared. *I* didn't want to be reminded of him. But I realized today that it shouldn't be about me anymore. I want this baby to live and be loved." She smiled up at him self-consciously. "If it's a girl, I want her to have the chance to dance with a man like you."

He looked at her thoughtfully. "You seem to be a little

was a friend, that he was a nice guy, that he was already married. He had wanted to hurt him.

He might as well get a club and drag her around by her hair, he thought with self disgust, and just beat everyone off. It's how he was behaving. He could recognize the fact that this all stemmed from the attack, that his anger from it kept breaking loose, but he couldn't stop it or channel it. It was taking his feelings for Shelley and twisting them into something ugly. Help. Help. Help. Unable to say it aloud, the thought echoed in his mind. God help me, before it turns on her.

She flipped on her back at that moment with a sigh, flinging her arms out. Her sweatshirt had ridden up, bunching beneath her breasts and leaving her stomach bare. He stared at it. He wanted to touch it, touch her. He wanted to lay beside her and feel the warmth of her body. He wanted her to love him and touch him and soothe his spirit. But she was sleeping. She didn't know what he needed and probably wasn't ready to give it anyway.

Ignoring the other bed only three feet away, he crawled carefully onto Shelley's bed and eased his body next to hers. He let his hand just skim over the smooth skin of her stomach before putting his arm around her. God. He didn't know what was happening to him. He was scared of what he was becoming. Scared that she didn't need him, that she would leave. Despair and confusion washed through him and he buried his face in the fragrant softness of her hair. He tried to ignore the tightness in his chest, to swallow the lump in his throat, but he couldn't stop the tears from squeezing out beneath his lashes, to wet the silky strands of her hair.

༃

The earth continued its slow spin, opening its arms a bit at a time to the fiery red morning sun. The pink light washed gently over the main street and the frost covered brick walkway of the waterfront park. Shelley's breath misted on the hotel window, obscuring her view, so she wiped it away with the sleeve of her sweatshirt. Sunrise wasn't something she ever took the time to notice when she lived in the city, but here, even in town, it was a peaceful, wonderful way to greet the day.

She peeked back over her shoulder at Michael, noting that he was still sleeping, sprawled carelessly on his stomach now with both hands tucked under his pillow. There was just something so endearing about the sight of a sleeping man. This one, anyway. She went to stand by him, debating whether she should wake him up or crawl right back into his arms. It had been nice, waking up with him beside her.

Feeling the devil stir within her, she decided it was time he got up, too. The day was wasting. She tickled the sole of his foot with her nails but he only twitched once or twice then moved it away. She knelt beside the bed and tried blowing in his ear but he just turned his head, burrowing deeper into the pillow. "Hi, handsome," she said finally, giving up on her subtle tortures.

He woke up instantly then, as though highly attuned to flattery and nothing else. He opened his eyes with a smile, flipped onto his back and knuckled the sleep from his eyes before letting his hands flop back on the pillow behind his head. "Do I get a good morning kiss?" He asked with such a mixture of hope and suspicion that she laughed.

"Sure." She leaned over him and placed one quick, innocent kiss on his cheek.

His right arm came around her instantly, first resting on her bare back where her top rode up, then quickly sliding up under it. He held her lightly to him, arching his back and stretching the kinks and knots from his long, lithe body. She was unresisting, taken by complete surprise, especially when he started rubbing his raspy cheek against her jaw, back and forth like a great, friendly cat. He took a deep, deep breath and released it in a warm, ticklish rush against her neck, kissed her cheek and then pushed them both up into a sitting position.

"Promise me you'll wake me up every morning," he said with a little smile, but his voice was heart wrenchingly solemn.

Part of her wanted to say what he wanted to hear, but the other part of her wanted to scoot off the bed and put as much distance between them as possible. She felt flustered by the undercurrents that kept surfacing between them. "I don't make empty promises," she blurted out.

Michael's smile fell and he backed away to the end of the bed as though she had slapped him. He got off the bed without a word and walked to the bathroom, closing the door behind him with a quiet click.

She had seen that wounded look in his eyes before, when he got lost in memories, but she had never, ever imagined that she would be the one to put it there. She felt a dull, constricting pain in her chest and a suffocating, panicky sense of loss. What had she done?

He wouldn't look at her when he came out of the bathroom, instead moving about the room, gathering up little items they had left strewn about.

"Mike?"

His shoulders tensed slightly, but that was the only outward sign that he had even heard her.

"Oh, please, please don't be mad," she begged him, grabbing his hand as he walked by. She pulled him down to sit beside her so she could look into his eyes. "I didn't mean it that way, really." She felt the tears start in her own eyes at the closed, unforgiving set of his jaw. "Michael?" She pleaded, "It's just we've never talked about the future. I know that's my fault. I know that. Especially now, with the baby …it's all so confusing for me. I just don't believe in promises. They're not fair and people break them all the time."

He finally looked at her. "What about marriage vows? Don't you believe in them, either?"

"Yes, of course I believe in marriage vows."

"They're just promises," he pointed out.

"I know they are, but those promises are between two people who know where they stand. Normal people with honesty between them -"

"Honesty?" He exploded angrily. "I have never misled you! I have been very honest about how I feel and what I want from you."

"I know," she admitted softly. "It's me. I can't give you what you want."

"I haven't asked for anything!" He said, throwing his hands up in exasperation. "Except that you open up a little and talk to me."

"No, but you will."

He looked frustrated and genuinely perplexed.

"You should understand," she said helplessly.

His expression softened a bit. "Well, I don't."

"Sex!" She practically spat the word out.

"Sex?" He echoed it perfectly, even giving it the same desperate intonation.

"Yes. I don't think I can do it again, ever. Not even with you. So it would be wrong for me to make you promises. Do you see?"

His brow smoothed out suddenly as his frown disappeared and he relaxed visibly. "Yes, I see," he said gently. "You've never had sex, Shelley."

"Oh? What? I swallowed a baby seed?"

"I don't think rape is something I have to explain to you," he said deliberately. "And rape is not what I want from you. Sex is altogether different though, Shell. Sex is a basic, elemental urge. It's powerful."

She opened her mouth to interrupt, but he held up a finger. "Sex is not what I want from you, either."

"Then what -"

He put his hand over her mouth. "I want us to make love. I want to show you how I feel, to pour my heart out to you without saying a word; using only my hands, my mouth and my body. I want you to do the same for me. Do *you* see? Think about it and try to understand the difference."

With that said, he got up and crossed over to his overnight bag, where he grabbed a set of clean clothes. "I'm going to have my shower now."

He left her to herself, with her own confusing feelings. She closed her eyes, remembering the feel of his body next to hers, his breath on her neck and his lips on hers that night at the beach, and knew that she already understood the difference.

It was still fairly early when they left the hotel. The awkwardness from their frank conversation lingered in the air, following them stealthily along the sidewalk on their way up to the grocery store. She wasn't even sure who said it, but one simple word broke the tension. He took her hand. She walked a little closer. By the time they got to the plaza, their conversation was as animated and comfortable as it ever was, and his hurt feelings seemed completely forgotten.

The plaza was in the centre of town and the closest thing it had to a mall. Besides a grocery store, there were law offices, an employment centre, a post office, a bank, a fast food outlet, a liquor store and a large clothing store. Shelley noticed several groups of people, with four or five men and women in each, milling around the plaza. Some stood in little circles, some sat along the concrete parking divide, and still others were actually laying down in small patches of grass. Some were dressed poorly, others with brand name clothes, but all appeared dirty and unkempt.

"They're all Indians," she whispered. "What are they doing?"

"Probably waiting for the liquor store to open," Michael answered with evident disgust.

She looked at him sharply, wondering what prompted such a racist remark.

"I'm completely serious," he said, catching her look. "I'm not going by stereotype here. Let me show you." He led her up and around to the back of the clothing store, where the long grass was sectioned off by several well beaten paths. There was garbage everywhere; take-out food wrappers, discarded pieces of clothing, pop cans and even what appeared to be used toilet paper. But mostly empty bottles littered the ground - liquor bottles, after shave bottles, mouthwash bottles, anything that might have once contained alcohol.

A man and woman were passed out in the grass, oblivious to them and the chill of the morning. Oblivious to everything. Dirty, lank locks of black hair fell forward over the woman's face, which was somewhat skewed, as though she had been seriously beaten at one time. Under her opened, black bomber jacket, her colourful checkered dress was soiled and rode high up on thin legs. She wore black leggings underneath with dirty white socks pulled up to at least mid calf. Her high top Nike running shoes looked new but they had no laces.

The man beside her was laying on his side, facing away from them so Shelley couldn't see his face and she realized with a shudder that she didn't want to. His jeans were filthy and faded almost white on the seat.

They were a pathetic pair and Shelley felt a twinge of pity as well as an uncomfortable, guilt ridden surge of distaste. It made her feel ashamed so she tried to hide it, but Michael was watching her, looking for a reaction.

"You think I'm a racist?" He asked. He stared thoughtfully at her for a moment and then nodded, answering his own question. "I am a bit. The way they're coddled by the government makes me angry. It's unbalanced and it doesn't seem to do them a damn bit of good. There is a lot of bitterness and tension on both sides, Shell. The unemployment rate for aboriginals in this community is five times higher than for us. They think whites keep them downtrodden with prejudice and the whites think they spend too much time drinking and collecting welfare cheques. It's a mess. I think there are good people and bad people, hardworking people and lazy people and it doesn't seem to matter what colour they are.

This bunch," he indicated those around the plaza with a sweep of his hand, "give all the First Nations a bad name. Most of them are on Welfare. They live off of tax money that they never have to pay into. They get vouchers from the government for free, brand new winter jackets. Expensive jackets." He nudged the man's boot with his toe. "All this guy has to do is get a meal and a good night's sleep at the Shelter and clean himself up. The Friendship Centre could get him some clean, second hand clothes and point the way to the Employment Office. As long as they have a treaty card, they don't pay sales tax, income tax, eye care or dental care. There are government subsidized apartments that seem to be just for them. When they are on the reserve, many of them don't pay for housing or even hunting and fishing supplies, and God only knows what else. When they do get money they buy anything that will give them a high - hard liquor, beer, wine, mouth wash, Lysol spray, hairspray. They will sniff gas or paint or whatever they can get their hands on until they end up just like this. Over half of the ambulance calls are picking up drunks that have ingested something that was never meant to be ingested." He paused again, taking a deep, frustrated breath. "He could take Adult Education classes here to improve his English and writing skills, or to learn a trade. They are free for him. He could go off to College or University. The government not only pays their tuition, they also give them living expenses. Did you know that?"

She shook her head and he gave a short, bitter laugh. "My parents worked all their lives to help send us to school. We worked summer holidays and after school jobs and passed down our clothes and we're still paying off student loans. Yet here they lay. In a haze of alcohol so thick they can't even see their own opportunities." He shook his head. "I just don't get it."

Shelley tore her eyes from the pair on the ground to study his profile. It was chiseled and proud and uncompromising. He wasn't the type of man to respect anyone, of any race, that squandered life that way. He expected people to do something, become someone and make their way in life, somehow. "Maybe they are happy this way," she offered lamely, for lack of anything better to say.

He started leading her back down the path. "Even when their toes and fingers freeze off in the middle of winter, when the Shelter kicks them out for sneaking booze inside? Or when they're so sick from drinking hairspray that they just want to die? I couldn't stand that kind of happiness."

"Me neither," she agreed. "They are missing a gene, you know. I think I read that in one of my textbooks, somewhere."

Michael smiled at her over his shoulder. "Oh, yeah? What kind of gene?"

"Without this gene, people can't effectively metabolize alcohol."

"Are you making that up?"

She laughed. "I don't think so. Don't quote me on it, though."

"Okay, professor," he teased, "enough deep and depressing subjects for today. Let's get our last ice cream cone of the summer. Then we have a lot of groceries to buy if we want to eat this month."

CHAPTER ELEVEN

The days turned into weeks, passing swiftly and formlessly until suddenly, without any warning at all really, it was fall. The leaves began to turn, mellowing into shades of yellow and brown, though Mother Nature dabbled here and there with her brush, painting select clumps of trees and shrubs vivid reds and oranges. Shelley collected some of the fallen maple leaves, rare in this area, to add to the collection of flowers she had dried over the summer. She now had a very colourful assortment of pink wild roses, purple fireweed, delicate violet blossoms of hairy vetch, sweet yellow clover, bluebead lily stalks with berries and small white moonshine blossoms. All the different kinds of trees and flowers and birds were still as fascinating to her as when she first arrived. And the moss! In some places, it was thicker and more luxurious than any carpet, even in the cooler weather. She had carefully collected some to see if she could grow it in pots, to transplant to the garden in the spring. She was sure it would be a beautiful ground cover for the more shaded areas.

Such was the stillness of the place; the absolute isolation, that for the first time in her life, Shelley could actually hear the leaves fall, the dry clacking sound as each leaf crashed through the branches below it on its final, graceful journey to the earth. The weather was pleasantly cool, hovering around ten degrees during the day and dropping to near zero at night. It was often overcast and drizzly, but still, she thought it was perfect. Never before a morning person, she found that here, at this time of year, it was her favourite part of the day. Just after sunrise, while the ground still shivered under its blanket of frost and the mist rolled in silently from the bay. The birds greeted the morning cheerfully, although many of the smaller songbirds were already gone.

The seagulls disappeared. Flocks of noisy Canada Geese flew overhead on their yearly quest for warmer climes. The black bears wandered closer, sometimes even onto the porch, lured by the smells of food and the increasing need to store fat for the long months of winter sleep ahead. The wolves and coyotes too, seemed much closer, and the almost otherworldly yips and howls in the dark distance often gave her goose bumps.

Perhaps hovering in a state of denial, neither she nor Michael mentioned the future, or the baby, or brought up the past. They simply lived day by day, in the moment. They hovered, too, in a strange state of suspended physicality. Haunted by memories and worries, Shelley at least was content to hold hands, sit close and share sweet but chaste kisses goodnight. She got the feeling sometimes, from a lingering look or a special tone of voice, that he wanted more from her. He never pushed though, and she was grateful.

A comfortable pattern developed to fill their days and evenings as they learned and adjusted to the quirks and habits of the other. As before, they took long walks, played outside with the dogs, learned new card games and read quietly by the fire, but mostly they talked. Despite the fact that before that fateful day in June their lives had been so different, they found much in common and never seemed to run out of things to talk about.

Michael worked a few hours a day when the need took him and she sometimes helped in the darkroom, though she felt a need for something more demanding to keep herself busy and challenged; something for herself. So she began to pore over cookbooks, discovering an interest she hadn't been aware of. Often then, she would spend hours in the kitchen, stirring sauces over the propane range or rolling dough for a new pie.

Cooking for one had always been a chore to her and so she had rarely bothered, opting instead for cereal or canned soup and sandwiches. But she found, to her surprise and his delight, that she loved to cook for Michael. She couldn't have found a more appreciative roommate, for he made it clear as he pilfered cookies and tarts from the cooling racks, that he considered her newfound interest in cooking a gift to him from God. He sighed in ecstasy every time he even entered the kitchen.

She made blueberry jam, pincherry and kinnick kinnick jelly from the bags of summer berries in the freezer. She pickled fresh fish from the lake. She learned how to make delicious soups and chowders and flaky pastries, loving it more and more everyday.

But time continued to fly by relentlessly, and the realities of past and future that she had tried so hard to deny began to push in on her. Her pregnancy began to show. Michael started to withdraw from her, with mood swings triggered by something she had said, or a memory that he wouldn't share. He would disappear outside without a word more and more often, sometimes for only minutes, sometimes for hours, and return cheerful, as though nothing had gotten him down. But he would never, ever speak of it.

She would turn quickly sometimes and catch him unguarded, revealing a look that was hungry and lonely and desperate. The intensity of it scared her and she knew that soon, very soon, decisions would have to be made. Let him get closer or push him away. Stay or go. Go back to school or get a job.

Life wouldn't wait for her to be ready. If she didn't stand up soon and make up her mind, time would do it for her and she would have nothing. Sometimes she could almost hear it in her mind; the ticking, ticking of a clock. It would go off soon, like her kitchen timer, and then what would become of her?

CHAPTER 12

After tossing and turning for over an hour, Shelley gave up. Unaffected by her restlessness, Dawson slept peacefully beside her. He took up most of the bed and he had long ago claimed the other pillow for his own. She ran a hand through his fur, marveling at the texture and thickness of it. His forepaws twitched into running motion and she watched for a while, amused, wondering if he was chasing rabbits in his dream. She released a frustrated sigh though, as he continued to sleep on and pushed herself out of bed. She stripped her nightshirt and panties off, shrugged into her robe and tiptoed down the hall to the bathroom. A nice hot bubble bath had never failed to make her sleepy.

While she waited for the tub to fill, she piled her hair in a messy knot and secured it with a flannel scrunchie. Choosing a berry scented bath bomb from the basket, she added it to the water; it frothed and fizzed in a foamy explosion, permeating the entire room with fragrant, steamy puffs.

Just as she was about to step into the scented, sudsy water, she caught her profile in the full length mirror behind the door. She studied her reflection briefly, noting the changes in her body. Her breasts were bigger, she was sure of it. Running a shaky hand over the tight swell of her pregnancy, she looked away, unable to bear the sight of it. She kept her face averted until the mirror was veiled in steam. Yes, she had made the decision to carry this child, but the resentment she felt did not just go away. Every time the nausea of morning sickness forced her to crouch by the toilet, every time she felt the slight stirring inside her, memories crowded her thoughts; memories she wanted to forget.

Resolutely, she pushed it from her mind. There was nothing to be done about it now - except wait. She sank into the bubbles with a sigh and tried to clear her mind of the worries that were starting to tie her in knots. She closed her eyes and with deep, slow breaths began to relax her body. Starting with her toes, the arches in her feet, then the clenched muscles in her calves, she worked her way up, consciously relaxing each and every tense part of her body. It left her with a pleasant, heavy limbed kind of languor and the certainty that nothing could disturb her sleep after this.

☙

The cat woke him up around one o'clock, licking his eyelids raw. "Amber!" He pushed at her furry little body but it sprang back like an elastic band. Her raspy tongue didn't stop for a second. "I won't have any eyelids left when you're through," he said, forcibly picking her up and dropping her on the floor. "Plus, I have to go to the bathroom."

He walked down the hall in his shorts, pausing by Shelley's room. The door was open. Most of the room was dimly lit, awash with moonlight, except for the bed. It hid in shadows, so he couldn't see if she was sleeping. Or what she was sleeping in. He could see a pair of skimpy panties discarded hastily on the floor. The blood rushed to his loins. Before he gave in to the urge to step inside and close the door, he turned on his heel and strode resolutely to the bathroom. He was too agitated to notice the signs that usually indicated the room was already occupied; the door was closed and a light shone from the crack under it.

He walked in and pushed at the door, hard enough to swing it back but not actually close it. He even had one hand at the drawstring of his shorts before he realized he shouldn't be in there.

Shelley was in the bath tub. She gaped at him, her soft lips rounded in a surprised O of dismay. Her arms crossed reflexively over breasts not quite hidden by the sudsy water, but not quickly enough. The image was branded on his brain, arousing him even more. Her hair was pulled up in a casual knot, with little tendrils escaping to curl around her face from the moisture.

Her knees were raised, so the water lapped suggestively at her thighs and he stared, completely transfixed. He almost groaned out loud when a stab of desire knifed through him.

"Out!" She squeaked, finally finding her voice.

He didn't want to leave; couldn't make himself, so he walked towards her instead. He hunkered down beside the tub so she wouldn't see what she was doing to his body. "I could wash your back," he said very softly.

"No, I don't think so."

The bubbles were popping, fading rapidly and she was plainly worried that her cover would soon be gone. He prayed for it, stalling his departure.

"Get out, Michael," she pressed, but her voice was breathless and uneven and it only made his heart pump faster.

"I'll go," he promised, reaching his hand out to touch her shoulder. She tried to shrink back but there was nowhere for her to go. Her skin was slick and wet and almost more than he could bear. Sliding his fingers around to the back of her neck, he cupped it and urged her forward slightly toward him. Then, closing the distance himself, his lips touched hers as they had many times before. But it wasn't enough for him this time. Just thinking about her bottom lip was enough to excite him. He kissed it, ran his tongue over it, nibbled on it.

"I dream about you," he confessed in a low voice against her mouth.

Her arms, crossed so rigidly in front of her before, slipped a notch and her lips parted on a soft sigh. He took instant advantage, slipping inside her mouth to touch her tongue with the tip of his own. She let him for a moment, just for a moment, but pulled away when he tried to deepen the kiss.

"Michael, this is-"

"Shh, baby. Don't be afraid. Just a kiss, I promise." He began to speak softly to her in the same low voice, caressing her with it and punctuating each heartfelt utterance with gentle, teasing kisses. Only when her lips finally clung to his and parted on their own did he once again slip inside. Cupping her face in his hands, he took full possession of her mouth, kissing her deeply and hungrily, knowing it would overwhelm her but unable to hold back. The taste of her, the smell of her skin, the silky feel of her in his hands; the force of it all sparked around him, fueling his already heightened senses and testing the limits of his self control. He became so lost in the need to get closer, so lost in the longing that he started to lift her from the tub.

She tore her mouth from his with panic in her eyes. "No! You said just a kiss!"

He let her sink back down into the bubbles, reluctantly

releasing his hold on her. "I'm sorry," he apologized hoarsely. "You're right. Just a kiss." His arousal strained uncomfortably against his shorts and he couldn't stop himself from reaching out again to run the pad of his thumb over her lips. "Goodnight, Shelley. Sweet dreams." Then he pushed himself up and left the bathroom.

By seven o'clock the next morning, he was on his stool at the kitchen counter, frowning into his coffee. He wasn't sure if he was doing the right thing. He had done some hard thinking last night, after his blood cooled down. He knew Shelley cared for him, maybe even loved him, but it was possible to love lots of different people in different ways and not stay with any of them. She was strong enough to be on her own now and he couldn't see that there was anything holding her here. They were healing and rebuilding their lives together - he refused to let that slip away from him. He needed to gain control. If her feelings weren't already as all consuming as his, then he would make them that way. And make her admit it. He decided to begin a relentless campaign to break down her defenses. She had every right to deny him and he had every intention of respecting her wishes, but it was time for some tangible, physical proof of commitment. He was looking for some kind of tie that would bind her to him and he knew that for most women, making love was a very powerful one. He was beyond wondering if his thoughts and fears and plans were rational. He was alert, excited and eager to begin.

Shelley came down later than usual. It was in fact almost eight thirty before he heard her footsteps on the stairs. She peered hesitantly around the corner before stepping into the kitchen, like a deer checking the forest for danger. She was dressed in baggy jeans and an oversize sweatshirt. He guessed that she was trying to compensate for her lack of clothing last night.

"Good morning," he said cheerfully.

She looked everywhere but at him and muttered a good morning as she fumbled in the cupboard for her coffee mug. When she heard him scrape his stool back she jumped, spilling the coffee she was trying to pour.

He moved toward her.

She tried to move away but succeeded only in knocking the whole mug over and sending a steaming river of coffee down the length of the counter.

He reached around, one arm on each side of her, to pull a length of paper towel from the roll, and kept her pinned there while he sopped up the hot liquid. "Shelley," he said gently in her ear, "are you mad at me?"

"No."

"I don't want you to be mad at me," he confessed helplessly.

"I'm not."

"Good." He put his hands on her waist. "Does it scare you when I stand this close?" He asked.

"No," she breathed. "It doesn't scare me."

"Why are you trying to get away from me then?"

Her back stiffened. "This is my personal space," she snapped defensively. "And you're in it."

"I want to be in it."

She sighed and tried to sidle away.

Instead of following her down the counter, he turned her around to face him. He needed to see her face, her expression and the look in her eyes to know what she was thinking and feeling. She didn't look scared, he noted with relief, just uncomfortable and maybe embarrassed. And shy. Her cheeks were pink. It was strange that she would be shy with him now, after all they had been through. He caught her staring at his lips and she flushed an even deeper pink.

Ahh. She did like his kisses.

"Why this sudden change?" She surprised him by asking. "Things were going so well ..."

"Things have been changing for a long time - we can't keep ignoring it. Can't you feel it?"

"I don't know," she hedged.

"I think you do," he insisted, sliding his hands up from her waist to rest beneath the soft weight of her breasts. He let his thumbs brush against them provocatively, back and forth, barely touching. But they tightened anyway, hardening almost immediately into little buds that pushed out against the material of her shirt. She gasped in horrified embarrassment and tried to wrench herself away.

He held her arms firmly to keep her there, with her body flush against him from chest to thigh. "Wait," he whispered. "Just for a minute." Placing his hands back around her waist, he lifted her onto the counter, resting her bottom on the very edge of it. Before she could jump down, he pushed her knees apart and placed his body in between them. He looked in her panicked eyes, then grabbed her hips with a sharp pull, fitting them together.

Her head fell back. Her eyes closed.

"Can you feel it now?" He rasped. "The wanting?"

She wouldn't look at him, but she nodded.

He folded his arms around her and held her, willing her to relax and simply enjoy the contact.

Her arms came around him after a moment to grip

fistfuls of his shirt and hug him tightly. "Please don't run from me, Shelley. Don't let me scare you away."

"I'll try," she promised.

༄

Shelley poured the thick, red raspberry sauce over the cheesecake and spread it evenly before cutting one large piece and putting it on a plate. "Mike?" She called, wandering from room to room in search of him.

She found him finally, sitting at his desk, completely absorbed by the papers laid out before him. She couldn't see them from the door but he studied them intently. "Mike?"

He jumped, so startled that he knocked a jar of pens to the floor. "Good God, woman!" He bellowed, clapping a hand over his heart. "You almost killed me."

"Sorry. I made some cheesecake. You said you were craving something sweet."

He grinned at her. "I meant you."

She rolled her eyes with a nod and held the plate out. "Sure you did, but you'll have to settle for this."

He wheeled his chair eagerly toward her to claim the treat. "I thought you weren't going to make cheesecake until I sang to you."

"I'm reversing tactics. I thought maybe you'd be so grateful that you would spontaneously burst into song."

He ate the rich dessert with gusto while she watched from the doorway; he
even dabbed at the crumbs on the plate with his finger and put them in his mouth. "That was fabulous."

She looked at him expectantly but he only laughed. "Nope, sorry."

"Why?" She wailed, disappointed.

He shrugged with a frustrating half smile before shoving the empty plate onto a bare corner of his desk. "I'm not ready. Anyway, I want to show you something." He led her closer to the desk and pushed her gently down into his chair. He hadn't been looking at papers, but rather pictures - of her.

"Ohhh, I don't want to look at them, Michael. I don't like seeing pictures of myself."

"C'mon now, don't be a coward," he coaxed, pulling the glossy pictures into a pile and rifling through them. There were shots of her just sitting, reading, lots of her sleeping. She was pleased to see that the scars on her face were faint and didn't look that bad.

"This is one of my favorites," he said, pulling one from the pile.

It was one of her laughing, really honestly laughing. Her head was thrown back and her eyes were crinkled at the corners; she looked happy. It was hard for her to look at herself objectively, but she had to admit the picture itself was beautiful; the lighting, the angle, the mood, and it showed a side of herself she had never seen before. She studied it a long time then finally admitted, "I like this one, too."

His voice took on a husky quality. "But this one ..." His hand reached around her shoulder to place another picture on the desk in front of her. "..is my very favorite."

"Oh my God!" She tried to flip it over, but his hand flattened over it.

"Look at it," he whispered in her ear.

She did. She couldn't help it. She was clothed in the picture of course, fully clothed, but with that look on her face and in her eyes she may as well have been naked. She didn't remember posing like that at all, that evening in her shorts and sweatshirt. It had all seemed very innocent at the time. "I don't remember this, Mike ...this ...that's a 'come-and-get-me' look I really *don't* remember that." Her cheeks were burning a fiery red.

Michael laughed at the accusing tone in her voice. "Hey, I didn't do a thing. You were sleepy, that's all. You had snoozing on your mind and that's about it." He laughed again. "I was the one having naughty thoughts that night." He ran one finger over the picture. "I look at this picture often, though."

She almost choked. "Why?"

He moved the curtain of her hair aside to nuzzle at her neck, making her shiver.

"Because it excites me."

She could barely find her voice. "It does?"

"Oh yes." His teeth nipped at her ear. "I end up imagining all kinds of things." He pulled her chair out and to the side, kneeling in front of her with his forearms braced on the arm rests. "I want to kiss you," he said in that special voice that made her heart pound in her chest. "And I want you to kiss me."

Her body automatically swayed toward him, head dipping down to his before she caught herself and paused.

He smiled slowly. "No, that's it," he whispered. "Kiss me."

She lowered her head consciously this time until her lips touched his. She pressed little kisses against his mouth but he remained passive until she pulled back in confusion. Then he followed her with a low laugh, wrapping his hands in her hair and kissing her thoroughly. His lips nibbled their way down her neck and then back up to her mouth, where finally his tongue parted her lips to rub up and down the length of hers, to twine around it and draw it into his own mouth.

He made all her senses spark to life. His kiss tasted of the tart-sweetness of raspberries. She could smell the clean scent of his soap and her skin tingled everywhere their bodies touched. Even the sound of his breathing, heavy and harsh, caused her stomach to flutter with excitement.

"I should stop," he groaned, pressing his body tightly to hers and stealing one more taste of her before sitting up. He trailed his finger tips over her collarbones, letting them rest on the pulse that fluttered there. "Are you afraid?" He asked softly.

She nodded. "A little bit."

He kissed her hand. "I understand. We'll take it slow, but you understand that putting it off will only make it more difficult for you?"

She nodded again.

With a final, gentle kiss on her lips, he stood up. "Well then, I'm going to put those two pictures in my 'greatest hits' album."

She gasped.

"And I'm going to send a copy of *this* one to Drew to put up in her studio."

She gasped again and surged to her feet. "No, you're not!" She lunged for the stack of pictures but he beat her to it, holding them easily out of her reach, laughing delightedly. "We can stencil our address on the bottom and see how many letters you get from lonely men."

She jumped at his outstretched hand. "Oh! I would kill you! Give me those!"

"Shelley."

She continued to dance around him, jumping, trying to grab the pictures.

"Shelley." His voice was sharp and finally succeeded in getting her attention. He put the photographs down on the desk very deliberately. "That picture of you is incredibly sexy, Shell. I can weave all kinds of fantasies around it - but it's my picture and I don't want anyone but you to see it. I don't want another man to see that look in your eyes, ever." He pulled her close for a hug. "I was just teasing you, baby. But that doesn't mean I won't blow it up and hang it above my bed." He sprinted out of the room then, tearing down the hall with her hard on his heels in determined pursuit.

CHAPTER THIRTEEN

Michael pulled a box of movies from the bottom shelf of the handmade wall unit. "These are my brother's," he said, blowing dust off the top edges of each. "He left them here in case he gets bored during his next visit."

"Anything good in there?" Shelley asked. "I don't want to watch a cheesy horror movie."

"Not even on Halloween?"

"Nope, not even on Halloween."

He rummaged through the box, pulling movies out at random, only to toss them on the floor after a glance at the title. "Half of them don't even have covers," he complained. "I can't tell what they're about." He picked another out of the box. "Prince of Tides," he read. "That could be about anything. Dare we gamble?"

"I think I can take a chance," she responded with mock seriousness. "I'll be right back - don't start without me," she warned as she hurried into the kitchen. She loved it when they had movie night; entertainment, snacks and lots of cuddles. There had been many changes between them in the last four weeks. It was like that night in the bathtub had flipped some sort of switch for Michael. Since then his attentions had been constant and passionate and sometimes overwhelming; kissing, making out like teenagers on the couch, touching her through her clothes until they were both hot and breathless. But it reached a point every time where she was simply unable to go on. Her hands would push against his chest, she would struggle for breath and for freedom from his body and his hands, gentle as they may be, and whisper 'no'. Again. She was too afraid. Not of him, or the act of love itself even as Michael thought, but rather what would become of them as a couple when it became obvious that a physical relationship was never going to work. She sighed as she filled two glasses with ice cubes. The problem was, she was getting tired of saying no.

She rushed back into the living room with a large bowl of salt and vinegar chips and the two frosty glasses of Coke. Michael was already sitting on the couch with his head resting on the back of it. "You're planning on sleeping right through this, aren't you?" She accused lightly, plopping his Coke down on the table beside him.

His voice dropped to a conspiratory stage whisper. "Don't be alarmed, but I think this is going to be a 'chick flick'."

"What's it going to take to get you to watch it with me, then?" She asked, sitting down beside him. "A chip? A bowl of chips?"

A wicked little smile played at the corner of his mouth. "I can't think of a thing," he sighed dramatically.

She knew exactly what he was up to and leaned in to kiss him on the cheek.

Ruefully, he shook his head. "I'm afraid that just won't do. Do you have anything else to offer?"

Enjoying his playful mood, Shelley swung her leg over to sit on his knees facing him. "I'll give you a real kiss if you watch the movie with me," she bribed.

"You've got a deal," he said thickly, suddenly serious.

She touched her lips to his, lightly moving over them, teasing him. He brought his hands up to cup her face and opened his mouth slightly, urging her to deepen the kiss. She did so, wrapping her arms around his neck, but she rapidly lost control of the situation. He became the aggressor, taking over and making the kiss hungrier and more intense than she had intended it to be. His hands were sliding over her thighs, grasping her hips. The warmth of his fingers burned through her cotton pants. Reluctantly, she ended the kiss and rested her forehead against his.

"Will that do?" She breathed.

"One more," he groaned.

"Movie," she reminded him, resisting the urge to give in.

"More."

"Movie." She got off his lap and settled beside him. "We had a deal." Shoving a chip into her mouth and another into his, she arranged the quilt over them and pressed 'play'.

The beginning was slow and Michael obviously wasn't getting into it. A young woman attempted suicide and her therapist was trying to get information about her past from her brother. Shelley peeked over at Michael again. Although he was staring at the television, he was obviously only pretending to be engrossed because every time she looked away from him he started to play with her fingers, running the tip of his own along the sensitive inner skin and round and round on her palm. Her put his arm around her next, snuggling even closer. His other hand began the same teasing motions on her neck.

Shelley suppressed a smile. If he was trying to seduce her, it was working. She was so involved in what his hands were doing and where they might go next, that she could barely follow the dialogue in the movie. But when they heard the word 'rape', they both sat forward, snapping to attention. The sister had been raped.

"Let's turn it off," suggested Michael. "It's not like we need a reminder, eh?"

"No. I think it will be good for us. What do they call it - desensitization?"

He leaned back again, clearly disagreeing but saying nothing. They both watched tensely, playing no more games, waiting for the character to describe the incident in detail. The tale unraveled slowly. Three men had broken into the house and raped his sister and his mother, but when the man reluctantly admitted he had also been a victim of rape all those years before, Michael surged to his feet to turn the TV off.

"This is sick," he said. "I'm not watching this. I'm going for a walk."

Dumbfounded, Shelley could only watch as he rammed his arms through the sleeves of his parka. His boots and mitts went on with the same barely suppressed violence. "Michael, tell me what's wrong," she pleaded. She knew it was futile. He just wouldn't talk about it. What about the movie set him off? "It's just a movie, Mike," she began hesitantly. It was the wrong thing to say.

He pinned her with an angry glare. "I know what the fuck it is!" Then he and the dogs were gone in an icy blast of winter air. It would be pointless to follow him. She knew that. She agonized over the need to help him, but he wasn't letting her and she didn't know how to make him.

Shelley dragged herself up the stairs, feeling depressed. She couldn't help thinking that he needed someone who didn't remind him of a nightmare. Someone who could reach him. It certainly didn't seem to be her. She brushed her teeth and washed her face slowly, dawdling, hoping that he would come back so they could talk. She changed into her pajamas, even folded her clothes and tidied the room. But still no Michael. She crawled into bed. The minutes ticked by painfully slowly. She tried to stay awake, to wait, but Amber purred with contentment by her ear, lulling her into unwilling slumber.

She started violently awake sometime later. She flicked the beside lamp on so she could read the hands on her clock. They pointed to 2:00am. The sound that woke her came again. Breaking glass. Someone was crashing around downstairs. The fear was immediate and paralyzing, robbing her of breath. Ignoring her instinct to run and hide, she forced herself to get out of bed, to walk toward the upper landing of the stairwell. With a white knuckled grip on the railing, she crept half way down the stairs. It was Michael. She clapped a hand over her heart and sank to the step with such immense relief she almost wept. The relief was short lived however, as she realized what was happening. He was in a wild rage, breaking everything in his path.

She quietly moved down the remaining stairs, not knowing what to do. The dogs cowered in a corner, terrified of this stranger in the guise of a master they loved. She looked around the room, noting with dismay the empty bottle of vodka. He hardly ever drank. The movie that had started it all now lay on the floor. The plastic covering was smashed into little pieces and meters and meters of shiny black tape were strewn about the room. The shattered remains of a crystal vase glittered in the lamplight and the wildflowers she had picked and dried herself were broken and crumbled. His winter clothes as well as his shirt and socks added to the clutter on the floor.

The last stair creaked mournfully under her foot and she cringed at being discovered as he whirled around to face her. He swayed slightly from the sudden movement but didn't advance as she had feared he might. They stared at each other, she rooted to her spot with growing tendrils of uncertainty and he by his secretive demons. He just looked so lost. Breaking free of the moment, she moved toward him slowly.

"Please, Mike, tell me what's wrong."

"Nothing. I'm fine," he said stonily.

"You're not fine. Look, Michael. Just because you're a man doesn't mean you can't talk about it. It will - "

"I'm not a man," he cut in desperately. "Things like that don't happen to a *man*." He sat down heavily, leaning far forward over his knees and hiding his face in his hands.

She sat beside him, rubbing his bare shoulder. She felt like a soldier picking her way through a mine field in the dark. She didn't know which direction to go, yet one wrong move could set him off. "Men get mugged every day, Mike. Beaten. Taken hostage. It's not uncommon."

He didn't answer.

She took a deep breath and ventured further. "I know we can't understand exactly what the other went through -"

"The hell I can't!" He roared suddenly, moving to the other end of the couch. His breath was ragged and uneven and his jaw was clenched so tight the cords of his neck stood out. He wouldn't say another word, wouldn't budge from his spot on the couch.

She tried to sit beside him to comfort him but he

pushed her away.

"Go to bed," he yelled. "Leave me alone!"

Deeply hurt by his rejection, tears pricked her eyes and her lower lip started to wobble. She brought one hand up to cover her mouth, willing him to look at her, but he didn't. She turned from him with a heavy heart and trudged back up the stairs.

Lying in bed, she thought about him for hours, trying to understand. The same scenes kept flashing in her mind: his pale face just before he switched the TV off; the look of self loathing as he was slamming the door; his final words; the glaze of tears he was too proud to shed. Oh God. It couldn't be. But it explained so much, bringing together all the little pieces of the puzzle she thought were missing. The signs were there all the time but she was just too naive to put them together. They raped him too. Oh Dear God. They had kept him there for four days. It was a question she had been afraid to ask him. Why keep him alive? Why for so long? Now she knew and her heart broke for him.

She could barely grasp it, that something so horrible could happen to a man like him, so she cried for him, cried with complete abandon into her pillow. She had shed so many tears in the last six months; for her grandfather, for herself, and now for the man she loved. The pain was wrenching. The tears ran their course, slowing eventually to an occasional hiccough. She mopped at her eyes and blew her nose then went back down stairs, determined this time. She would not let him push her away.

He looked so wretched, sitting there on the couch. He hadn't moved, hadn't slept. She marveled that he had been able to hide this from her for so long. Perhaps the fates had picked that movie last night so he could unload this burden before it killed him. She knelt at his feet in her pajamas and looked up at him with red, puffy eyes. "I'm sorry," she said softly. "I should have guessed."

He closed his eyes in resignation. "I didn't want you to know."

"Why?" She cried.

"Because it's ...because ..."

"It's shameful?"

"Yes."

"It's embarrassing?"

"Yes."

"You feel violated and repulsed every time you are reminded of it?"

He shuddered visibly. "Yes."

"You don't want people to see you as less than a man?"

"I want *you* to see me as a man! Not ..." He swallowed with difficulty. "Not some ..."

"I understand. I *know* how you feel."

He shook his head and whispered. "It's different."

"Why? How?" She asked earnestly.

"Because I'm a man! It's not supposed to happen to a man!"

"It's not *supposed* to happen to a woman, either!"

"No! I know. That's not what I meant. It's just not something I ever imagined happening to me. I can't ...I can't process it."

"I think the only way to make it go away, Michael, is to let it out. If you don't want to tell me, write it down. Whatever. Just share with me. I didn't have that choice because you were there. In some ways that made it worse, for a while, that you saw me like that, but being able to share it with you is what is helping me get past it. It's going to eat you up inside."

He looked at her finally and shook his head sadly. "I don't know if I can, Shell."

She got up to sit beside him on the arm of the couch, tucking her chilly feet under his knee. Her hand lifted to touch his hair as she studied his face. "Nothing anyone could ever do to you, could make me see you as less of a man."

He closed his eyes at her touch. "All right," he relented with a slight nod when he opened them again. "I'll try." He started slowly, as if unsure how to begin. "Well, you know I went to check on Mickey. When I got there I could hear the radio blasting and I thought that was odd."

"It would be," she interrupted softly. "The radio got on Grandpa's nerves and he never played it loud."

"Exactly," he agreed. "So I just listened for a while from outside. It didn't really occur to me that they were in there until the radio went off and I heard them arguing. Anyway, I was still worried about him so I went around to the side. There's a wood shed that slopes right next to the cabin. I climbed that and then from there I could reach the little balcony off his bedroom. His bags weren't there and none of his stuff was in the bathroom, so I knew he wasn't there. I decided the smartest thing would be to go back to my place and radio the police. I wasn't armed and I knew they had at least one gun.

On my way back down though, the corner of the shed roof gave way. It was rotten. The support post snapped off and I fell to the ground. One of them, the bald one, heard it and came running outside. I started to run. He shot at me, got me here," he indicated, touching the scar on his upper arm. "He said he'd shoot again if I didn't stop. So I stopped. If I'd known what was going to happen I would have taken my chances and run like hell. He said 'get on your knees', so I did. Then he rammed the butt of the gun into my head. Knocked me out.

When I came to, in the living room, it was evening. My hands were taped behind my back. It felt like a freight train was running over my head and I couldn't follow a thought. Couldn't think. They talked for a while, trying to scare me, you know? Telling me things …then the tall one …the blond one …his name was Scott." He spat the name out, like a bitter taste. "He pulled back the hammer of his gun and told me to get up on my knees again. When his other hand pulled his fly down I said, "Fuck you. Go ahead and kill me."

That made him mad. He just went crazy. They both started punching and kicking me. I couldn't defend myself, I couldn't fight back. It went on for a long time but I was still conscious when they pulled my jeans off, then dragged me to the coffee table and retaped my hands in front of me, real tight, through the posts at the end of the table. I couldn't believe it, what they were going to do."

Shelley watched his hands clench and unclench as he relived the events in his mind.

"Desperation gives you strength you know, when you don't think you have any left. I fought them with everything in me but it didn't matter. They did it anyway. Both of them. They left me there like that for three days. I fought them every time, but it didn't make a difference. I was losing a lot of blood, getting weaker and they didn't give me food or water. I dozed a few minutes here and there, but they slept in shifts and made a point of keeping me awake and in pain. When they got tired of ...using me and beating me, they burned me with cigarettes." Michael blinked rapidly, trying not to show what he was feeling. "I asked them to kill me once. They said they would, when they were finished with me.

They were getting ready to leave, on the afternoon of the fourth day. The day you came." He stared fixedly at a callous on his palm, then started to pick at it, stalling. His mouth opened several times to continue, but then snapped shut. Long minutes passed before he could make himself continue. "Scott said, 'we should at least let the bitch die with his pants on'. They thought it was real funny."

Shelley felt such an explosion of fury, she didn't know how to contain it. If only she could have them sitting here in this room, right now, bound and helpless. She would make them pay in ways they couldn't even imagine.

Some of what she was feeling must have shown on her face, for Michael chuckled mirthlessly. "You look like an avenging goddess with that fire in your eyes. Anyway, they let me get dressed. I almost couldn't do it though. I had lost all the feeling in my legs - I couldn't even stand up. They dragged me to the kitchen and taped me up again, but over the pot rack this time. I'm not sure why and at the time, I didn't care. I thought I was ready to die. They were going to beat me to death I guess. They said they didn't want to waste another bullet. You know the rest."

She shook her head. "I know the middle. What about the end? How did you get free?"

"Well, it was the first time in four days that no one was watching me. It took a long time because I wasn't strong enough to hold myself up for long, but I ripped the tape with my teeth. I told you that before."

"That is so awful, Michael. I didn't realize it was so awful for you."

"I should have done something. My brothers wouldn't have let that happen to them. They wouldn't have just watched him rape you either."

Shelley debated what approach to take. She was in way over her head, but she had to try and make him defend himself, not attack. Working on the beginnings of an idea, she said, "If I told you a story right now, say about one of my boyfriends-"

He looked up sharply.

"My boyfriend," she corrected smoothly, "that, while trying to do a good deed, was set upon by two men. They were armed, he was not. He was beaten, tied down, sexually assaulted and held prisoner. Despite his pain and exhaustion, he managed to save the life of another victim by killing both men. If I told you that story, what would you think of him?"

"I don't know." His tone was surly.

"Okay, would you call him a coward or a brave man?"

"Shelley -" he started to protest. "This is dumb. It's not a him - it's me and I can't play this game!"

"Humour me, please?" She pleaded.

He gave an exaggerated sigh, then said. "Coward."

That was the answer she had expected. "Why? He went in the cabin, right? When he knew they were there? He tried to redirect the anger from the other victim to himself, didn't he? When he broke free, he stayed behind to kill them, didn't he?"

Silence.

"Didn't he?" She asked with more force.

"Yes, doctor," he said dryly. "He did."

"Okay, so we agree cowardice was not his problem?"

He weighed that for a while, chewing his lower lip. Finally he nodded. "Agreed."

"Good. What do you think his problem was, then?"

He slammed his body back against the couch, irritated. "He was weak, stupid."

"Why? Start with stupid."

"Well, his plan didn't exactly work, did it? He should have waited for the right moment to leave."

"But he couldn't wait, in case they left, right? And hurt someone else most likely."

"Right."

"And it would have worked if that post hadn't collapsed under him?"

"Yes, I suppose."

"So, going on what he knew, the plan was sound. Just bad luck, wouldn't you say?"

He sighed again. "I guess."

"Okay, weak. How about that one?"

"Weak? You know, not as strong?" He snapped sarcastically.

She ignored the sarcasm, just rotating her hand in a 'let's move it along' gesture. "He had four days, surely he could have gotten free somehow," he said contemptuously.

"How though?"

"How the hell should I know?"

"He was always securely taped to something, right, and guarded at all times by at least one man with a gun?"

"Yes."

"I don't see a way out of that one."

"He could have fought them harder."

"But they would have killed him."

"So?"

She blanched. "They would have killed the second victim too, after a while."

His eyes met hers again, seeming startled by the thought.

"He didn't do her much good," he denied.

"He saved her life! Saved her from days of repeated torture. She wouldn't have lasted four days, Michael."

"No," he murmured thoughtfully. "Maybe not."

Shelley gathered up her nerve for the next question. The big one. The one that was bothering him the most, she suspected. "Would you think of him as a homosexual now, then?"

The air hissed between his teeth. He looked at her, his eyes big and clouded with hurt. "Would you?" He rasped.

"I'm asking you."

"No! He didn't ask for it or want it or consent to it or enjoy it and they didn't get it without a fucking fight!" His voice rose higher and became more agitated with every point.

"I know," she soothed. "*I* know that. So, then you think that this man that I love - he might be a brave, strong, clever, completely heterosexual guy who did as much or more than any other guy in the same situation? *You* wouldn't think any less of *him*, would you?"

After long moments he grudgingly replied, "Probably not."

"Nobody would. Nobody will, Mike."

"I know what you're trying to do, Shell, and thank you. You made me see it a different way, but it's just not that simple."

"I know, Mike. I just wanted to make sure you understood that you're the hero. You should be proud of what you did. It will take some time."

"Time heals all wounds, is that what you're telling me?" He asked with a half smile.

"Yeah, or maybe it's 'time wounds all heels'. Forget I said anything," she joked.

"Oh, funny too, eh? C'mon, let's get some sleep," he said, pulling her off the couch.

She trailed along behind him, glad of this moment of levity after the depressing tension of only moments ago. "Oh, of course. I'm your cook slash therapist slash comedienne slash cuddle bunny."

He raised his eyebrows comically. "Wow, just how much am I paying you an hour?" They laughed going up the stairs but the humour was forgotten as they curled up together on his bed. Michael took her hand and placed it on his bare chest. "When you touch me, Shell, I feel like nothing else matters," he said simply. "I don't know what I would do without it." Then he went to sleep.

Feelings were complicated things, she reflected as she lay there beside him. There's so many of them at the same time it messes a person up. He was the most honest and forthright person she had ever known, yet his own shame had forced him to keep this monumental thing from her. Her own feelings were no less complex. His vulnerability just caused the bonds he held her with to cinch her heart a little tighter. It aroused her protective instincts which was ridiculous, since he was easily twice her size. She was enormously relieved and pleased that he finally trusted her enough to confide in her, yet hurt that he hadn't done so sooner. She was still battling doubts about the authenticity of their feelings for each other; were they real or simply a product of their ordeal? She worried at her own memories of that day, fighting her denial and shame and anger just as he was. Then of course, there was the stew of confusion surrounding the life inside her. She hated it yet felt drawn to the thought of a little being in there, a little bit of her, growing and changing, slowly becoming a person who would have thoughts and feelings and dreams just like she did. It was all just too much. Denial. Guilt. Fear. Love. Hate. Hurt. How was a person supposed to sort them all out?

Her thoughts chased themselves round and round, accomplishing nothing, resolving nothing. More than an hour later, as her heavy eyelids fluttered closed, she could only conclude that yes, feelings were indeed very complicated things.

CHAPTER FOURTEEN

There was a crackling pop, then a hiss as the fire in the hearth eagerly claimed a new log. Shelley watched it, completely mesmerized by the flames, lost in a world of fire and memory and inner conflict. Her novel lay open but forgotten in her lap, though she turned the page now and then. The sounds around her seeped into her subconscious, but she wasn't really aware of them; the clock chiming five times, the music going off in the dark room, the door opening and closing again, Michael's foot steps approaching behind her. They all just floated around her as part of her trance until Michael spoke.

"What are you thinking about?" He asked softly, resting his hip on the arm of her chair.

She felt his hand smooth over her hair in a soothing gesture she loved. "Nothing," she lied, not sure how to put all her feelings and fears into words, so she didn't try.

"Nothing," he echoed flatly, letting his hand drop down to his lap. "We need to talk."

"I know," she agreed quickly. "But I was just about to make supper -"

"No. Now. Right now. We've been through this before and you've been putting it off for weeks. Months. Tell me what's happening here, Shelley. Where is this going?"

"I don't know," she said in a small voice.

Angrily, he grabbed the book from her lap and threw it

to the floor. "Bullshit. Be honest with me for once. Just once, look me in the eyes and tell me what you're feeling! What am I to you?"

"You're my friend."

He let his head fall back for a moment in frustration before nodding wordlessly three or four times, as though unable to think of an appropriate response. "Yes," he agreed finally. "I'm your friend."

"My best friend," she clarified tentatively, knowing even as she said it that it wasn't what he wanted to hear.

"Don't you care for me at all?"

"Yes!" She assured him. "Of course."

"You know what I'm asking! This is a relationship for me. The most serious, meaningful one I've ever been in and I can't even get one word from you about how you feel! Getting closer physically is a battle I can understand. God help me, Shelley, I want to touch you. I want to touch you all the time, but I understand that you're not ready. I *understand*." He stressed. "Emotionally though, you're still a thousand miles away and I don't get that! After all we've been through, why? Is this just a comfortable place for you to heal and hide? Are you just biding your time here?"

"No! It's not like that."

He stood abruptly and bent over her, looming, but his voice was controlled once more, gentle even. "Why can't you talk to me?"

She just shook her head, helplessly unable to explain or even look him in the eye. He refused to accept it this time. Cupping her face in a determined grip, he turned it toward him and kept it there. "Why?" His hands slid up and back to thread through her hair. "Why can't you tell me what you're thinking?

Share something personal with me. Why can't you do that?"

"Michael ...I..." Her shoulders slumped. "I just don't know how." Damning her own limitations, she leaned into him for one brief moment before pulling his hands from her hair. She had one idea, one last desperate idea she hoped would make him understand. He had to understand how badly she wanted to share. He had to understand that she just needed to learn how. Without a word to him, she ran up the stairs to her room, where she rummaged in her bedside table for a book. She clasped it to her chest in a moment of indecision before running back down the stairs.

He still stood in the same spot, with his hands in his jeans pockets, staring at her in bemusement.

"I don't know how to share myself but I swear to you that I will overcome it, if you help me. This is the best I can do for now, because I want you to understand. I don't want you to hurt anymore because of me." She thrust the book into his hands then fled once more up the stairs to her room.

☞

The key dangled from a frayed velvet ribbon in his hand. He ran the tip of one finger over the cover of Shelley's diary, over the collage of printed flowers and wrestled with his conscience. Reading someone's diary made him feel sneaky, like an intruder in someone's private world. It was her choice, he reminded himself again. It's not like he stole it from her room.

With one final look up the staircase, he came to a decision. He settled back onto the couch, unlocked the diary and opened it up to the first page. It was dated August 28, 1999. Her first day of University. 'I look forward to this challenge," he read. 'I look forward to recreating Shelley Rae McGraw. This is my chance ...' He skimmed through entries detailing classes, schedules and roommates and the normal general concerns of a young woman with newly acquired and much awaited independence. She had a wonderful, dry kind of wit that made him laugh out loud and it wasn't hard to imagine himself there with her, reliving his own first weeks in college. She wrote freely about past and future events, hopes and feelings and he got a growing sense of *her*; how she measured people, how she thought and how deeply she felt about all kinds of things.

The change in her writing was gradual but painfully unswerving, picking up speed and snowballing as the weeks went by. Her positive, hopeful outlook slowly plummeted into despair as she uncovered truths about herself she didn't want to or couldn't accept.

'Nov. 8/99: Midterms were finished today. I did well, I think. Everyone went to the bar to celebrate. I wasn't invited ...'

'Nov. 20/99: I went out with Marlene and her friends tonight. I hardly said a word the entire evening and when I did they just looked at me strangely, with blank stares like I was speaking some alien language. No one asked me to dance. The rum made me sick. They left the bar - left me puking in the bathroom. I don't fit in here and I never, ever will. I refuse to try again.'

She seemed to close up after that. For the next three years the entries she had bothered to make were brief and dry, filled with grades and scores and self recriminations. It took the death of Mickey McGraw to force her into some kind of awareness of her feelings. She finally unburdened herself, needing the release and relief that came with it - even if it was only to her diary.

'Apr. 19/03: Grandpa is gone. He passed away last night and now I am completely and utterly alone. I don't even know how to put it into words anymore, how I feel. How can I describe the emptiness? The lonely ache in my heart so terrible it wakes me from a deep sleep? I have found myself wondering for months now, why? Why do I continue going through the motions of my life? I need someone to tell me everything will be all right in the end.'

Though she never wrote the words directly, Michael sensed she couldn't have been more than one step from suicide. The entries after that were so bleak and depressing that he couldn't shake the feeling of impending tragedy. He had to remind himself that this was history. She was past that now, healing and well on her way to being the happy young woman she once was. He marveled that someone so sad and full of despair had survived the kind of attack that often brought the strong to their knees.

Pushing himself up from the couch with a stretch, he wandered thoughtfully into the kitchen to grab a cup of coffee. Just walking into the room brought his stomach to life, reminding him noisily that it was half past six and they hadn't eaten supper. He wondered, with a rush of sympathy, if Shelley was going to hide from him in her room all night. Her gesture wasn't at all lost on him. He knew how hard it must have been for her, such a terribly private person, to hand that diary over to him, exposing all her secrets and feelings, leaving her open for rejection and ridicule.

The coffee was hours old, black as mud and bitter as hell, but he filled his cup anyway and took it back into the living room. Nothing could keep him from reading the rest of her journal and he wanted to finish it all before she changed her mind and came down for it. He took a large, scalding gulp, grimacing in pain and distaste as he opened the book again to the page he had marked. He realized with a start that had the evil black liquid sloshing against the sides of his cup, that the next entry was their first night back from the hospital.

He felt a sudden, overwhelming rush of cowardice shudder through him. He would no doubt be in these entries and it might not be what he was hoping for. It might be devastating. He took another, more careful sip of his coffee and made himself read on.

'Jul 3/03: I resent having to explain it to you. Crazily, for some reason, I feel that you should already know where I am and what has happened to me in the last weeks. Of course you know. It's my thoughts on this paper. You know what I know. It's a good thing, for I *can't* explain it. I *can't* say it and I *can't* write it down. To do so would make it seem so much less horrific than it really was and at the same time, lend HIM an importance he does not deserve.'

Tracing that last line with his finger, Michael thought about it, wondering at the truth of it and shook his head in answer to his own silent question. No. He couldn't have written it down either. Every additional detail committed to paper would make it seem more clinical and unreal and pointless. It would trivialize it, while driving the ragged memories deeper and deeper into himself.

Very few entries after that even alluded to the attack, though now and then she wrote brief updates on her physical progress or small disturbing memories.

'Jul 9/03: Grandpa would have three fits if he knew I moved in with a man I've only known for a few weeks; a complete stranger to me in a place so isolated no one would hear a thing. But unbelievably, it's the law of probability that keeps me from dwelling on the stupidity of my decision. The odds of something else terrible happening to me here so soon are just too low to worry about. I know that's a ridiculous way to make such a big decision, but honestly, when I think back I realize my brain had no part in this decision at all. Michael was just so irresistible. He's so kind to me and funny and spending time with him is the most wonderful thing I've experienced in a long time. So when he asks me to come stay with him, well, how could I not? I admit I wanted to hide from him at the hospital at first. I never wanted to see him again - or to be specific - I never wanted him to see me again. After all, he's seen me at my most humiliating moments. He wouldn't let me hide though and I'm glad. I like him so very much and when I'm with him I feel like a normal person. I know it's a temporary arrangement and that we will be well enough to move on soon, so I try not to let him be the first thought when I open my eyes in the morning, or the last when I close them at night, but I fear I am losing the battle ...'

Such relief bubbled up through him at her cautious confession that he almost went up to get her at that very moment, but he tamped it down and read on. She wrote a little more every day, with a little more detail, about the ins and outs of her day. Things they did together, funny things he'd said or the silly antics of the dogs - just simple things, little ideas and thoughts; things he wished she would share with him more often. The writing became easier as well, more light hearted, though now and then it became thoughtful and weighed down by the uncertainty of her future. He didn't skip a page of it, for he was as strangely enthralled with her carefully written thoughts as he was with her.

She wrote at length about her pregnancy, page after page, giving him some idea of the depth of her many fears. She was afraid she would never get over giving up her baby. She was afraid that the child would remind her of its father and she would never get over keeping it, and surprisingly, she was afraid of his own reaction either way.

'Sept 20/03: Sometimes I feel it, that longing to hold this little body tight to me and love it and protect it from the world, but these feelings are mixed up with such *hate*. Raising his baby, even letting it live, is like forgiving him. I'm learning that forgiveness is the hardest thing ...'

Most of the remaining entries were about him. He felt nervous now that the moment had finally come. With a deep breath, he read on.

'Oct 10/03: I've hurt Michael's feelings again. He thinks I don't want to confide in him. He thinks I don't want him to be close, to touch me. Sometimes I catch him watching me, scrutinizing, and it feels like he's turning me round and round in his hands, trying to figure me out like one of those Chinese puzzle boxes. I'm not trying to be a mystery. I just have all these feelings inside me and I don't know how to sort them out, never mind let them out. I want to share them with him, but I don't even know how to begin. Sometimes when you try to describe how you feel, the words are so inadequate and inaccurate that it just seems pointless. It diminishes my feelings if I can't get it right and then he won't understand.'

'Oct 18/03: I told him I'm afraid, but he misunderstands. I'm not afraid of sex or that he'll hurt me. I'm afraid I'll hurt him.'

Incredulous, Michael had to go back and read that part again to make sure he had gotten it right. He had. Hurt him?

'What if horrible memories flood back over me and I freeze up or freak out? What if I never get over it, what's he supposed to do with me then? If he didn't mean so much to me it wouldn't matter - it would be an experiment more or less. But no matter how I tried to explain it, I know if I rejected him or reacted badly, he would take it personally. It would hurt him. I don't want to lose him. What do I do? I wish I had someone to talk to ...'

'Oct 24/03: If I could do it, if I was able, I would tell Michael how I feel about him. I would tell him how much I love to look at him, even when he's got whiskers and sleep wrinkles and messy hair.'

He smiled at that and self consciously smoothed a hand over his hair.

'I'd tell him how much I love his voice. Sometimes I get so lost in the sound of it that I forget to listen to the words. I remember the feel of him, of his skin under my hands and the taste of him when he kisses me and I would tell him how much I love that too. And how much I love his sensitivity and sense of humor, his kindness and love of living things. I love the way he can be profound one moment and silly the next. I would tell him that he's my excitement and my comfort. My strength and my solace and everything that is important to me. I would tell him I love him, but we've proven time and time again that I'm a coward.'

That was the last entry. He felt blown away by what he had just read. He couldn't stop himself from playing passages over and over in his head like scenes from a movie - the kind of movie that always left him awed and overcome by the drama or thrill or tragedy of it. His mood was quiet and contemplative as he closed the diary and locked it before climbing the stairs to Shelley's room. He didn't knock, thinking the gesture would be empty and absurd after all that he had learned about her in the last hours. She had no privacy left to her; had relinquished it freely when she had handed him that key.

She was curled up in the chair with the cat, staring absently out the window.

He crossed the room to sit on the bed directly across from her, patiently waiting for her to look at him. He studied her as though for the first time, mentally fitting the parts of her she had kept hidden from him together with the Shelley he already knew.

"Aren't you going to say anything?" She asked finally, still avoiding his eyes.

"No, not until you look at me."

Her gaze dropped to the cat, where her hands rubbed and scratched and petted, probably in an effort to soothe her own unsettled nerves. "I don't think I ever can, now. I guess I'm in for a long, quiet winter," she quipped.

He waited. He waited for her to look at him because he didn't know what to say. Say too much and it would sound trite and insincere. Say too little and it would make her feel like he didn't understand the value of her sacrifice. "In some ways I feel I have a right to you, to have you here with me and that I can't explain." He held the diary out to her. "But I know I don't have a right to this. Letting me read it was a gift and it means more to me than I can say."

She looked at him finally. "It was hard, sitting here,

knowing you were reading my private thoughts. I've always guarded them so well."

"I know you have. It was a big step." He moved closer. "You express
yourself very well on paper, though."

She frowned in thought. "It's different than saying it to someone. My diary can't judge me. There's no risk."

"I'm not a risk, Shelley."

"Oh yeah you are. You're the biggest risk. Now I have something to lose." She wrinkled her nose self consciously at the confession. "Do you know what I mean?"

"I understand the thinking, yes. It's not right though."

She snorted. "I never said it was rational. I wanted to run down there and grab it back. I feel like you have all this power over me now."

"I don't have any more power than you do," he pointed out gently.

She nodded thoughtfully. "Do you think we'll ever get this right, Mike?"

"You know," he said, drawing her to her feet, "I'm sure of it. We just have to keep working at it." His stomach rumbled loudly, changing his focus completely. "Are you as hungry as I am?"

She smiled at him and he thought again with wonder about how it lit up her entire face. "Are you kidding? I was about to eat the cat. Let's go forage."

CHAPTER FIFTEEN

Michael sat on the floor near the fireplace. With his back propped against the wood box, he had one hand resting on his bent knee and the other restlessly twirling a toothpick around in his mouth. Shelley sat no more than a meter from him, cross legged on a large floor cushion. The smell of her light perfume wafted toward him every time she moved and he breathed it in deeply. He closed his eyes and let it filter down through his senses where it settled uncomfortably in his groin.

The neck of her oversize sweater had slipped to the side and he couldn't stop his eyes from roving hungrily over the exposed skin of her neck and shoulder. It looked smooth and flawless in the flickering glow of the firelight. She was concentrating on her crossword puzzle, apparently unaware of him as she ran the end of her pencil rhythmically back and forth across the fullness of her lower lip. His breath came faster as his imagination played out scene after scene in his head. It was becoming an obsession. Everything she said, every look she gave him, every slight movement made him think about making love to her. It dominated his thoughts day and night, interfering with work and sleep, alternating between earthy, carnal fantasies and simple yearnings to sleep beside her at night and feel the closeness and comfort of her body in his arms.

He did have misgivings. They had both been sexually assaulted - there were bound to be repercussions of that. He worried about his reaction. He worried about hers. But his body didn't care; it screamed its denial as well as its demand to touch and taste and claim her in the most basic, personal way a man could claim a woman.

"Hey," she said suddenly without looking up. "What's a four letter word for 'exigency'?"

He waited for her to look up at him for the answer and only when their eyes locked did he give it. "Need," he said hoarsely.

Her gaze fell once more to her puzzle to fill in the word then flew back to his, startled, as she recognized the strain in his voice.

Abruptly coming to a decision, Michael threw his toothpick into the fire and pushed himself away from the wood box. Damned or no, he couldn't wait anymore.

Shelley watched him, wide-eyed, as he approached on his knees. He gently took the puzzle book and pencil from her hands, throwing them aside.

"What are you doing?" She whispered.

He pushed a lock of hair from her face with one large hand, tilting her head back slightly at the same time. He dipped his head, grazing her lips lightly with his own, once, twice. "I won't hurt you, Shell ..." He kissed her again, keeping his lips soft and only slightly parted.

Despite the softness of his kiss, she held her body stiffly, not even breathing. She clearly sensed his intentions were different this time, but she didn't pull away.

Emboldened, he ran his tongue along her lower lip, then nudged at it slightly with his own, trying to coax her mouth to open. He could taste the sweetness of her peppermint candy. "Let me inside, Shelley," he said softly against her mouth.

Her hands went to his shoulders and she parted her lips with only the barest hesitation, welcoming him with a brush of her tongue against his own.

Thrilled at her response, he pulled the clip from her hair and tunneled his fingers through it, loving the feel and smell of it. Grasping a fistful, he tipped her head back even further to give himself better access to her mouth. He devoured it, using every trick and technique he knew to make her lose herself to him. They kissed a long, long time; deep slow kisses that inflamed him and brought him to the most mindless state of wanting he had ever experienced.

Easing the cushion out from under her, Michael gently pushed her down onto the rug, then straddled her body, placing his knees on either side of her hips. In an effort to keep control of his hands, he ran them slowly down her arms to thread his fingers through hers and press her wrists lightly into the floor above her head. While his thumbs moved back and forth over the soft skin of her inner wrists, he explored the contours of her face with his mouth; her cheekbones, the curve of her chin, the shells of her ears, the pulse in her neck.

She squirmed deliciously beneath him. She tried to pull her hands free, to arch her upper body into his chest. She tossed her head, moaning in frustration as she tried in vain to capture his lips with her own.

He sat up to look at her, breathing heavily. Her long hair lay disheveled around her in a silky fan. Her green eyes were heavy lidded, gone dark and smoky with desire. Her cheeks were flushed and her lips were red and swollen from his kisses. He'd had many, many dreams about that mouth. The sight of her like this, warm and wanting, was like the touch of a match to dry grass. His passion ignited, burning so hot for a moment he had to fight for breath. A bead of sweat ran from his temple down the side of his face.

He shook it off. "Do you want me to stop?" he asked roughly.

She hook her head. "No, don't stop."

"Thank God," he said with feeling. "You have no idea how much I want you." He peeled his T-shirt off, then brought her hand up to place it flat against his chest. "Touch me, Shelley." Her hand was hot, exciting, as she ran it over him. Soon her other hand lifted to join in the exploration of his upper body; the stubble of his jaw, his neck, the muscles of his shoulders and chest. Everywhere her hands could reach. He closed his eyes, suppressing a groan of pleasure and frustrated need.

Unable to keep still, his hands began to move with a mind of their own, sliding up under her sweater to touch the silky warmth of her ribcage and the slight swell of her stomach. He moved his body down the length of her to trail hot, moist kisses along the same path his hands had taken. Touching his lips to the skin just above her hipbone, he heard her sharp intake of breath. He tickled her there with his tongue and she moaned, and when he started to suck on that small sensitive patch, she went wild. Her body jerked, hips thrusting upward and her hands clenched in his hair.

Laughing softly against her, he dragged his mouth over her navel to the other side, searching out and finding all the sensitive areas along her ribs. His hands slid under her, then up her back to release the catch on her bra, only then sitting up to gather and pull the sweater over her head. Easing the bra straps from her shoulders, he stretched out full length so half his weight rested on her, and slipped one thigh between hers. He bent to kiss her again but froze when he saw the tears pooling in her eyes. They clung to her spiky lashes a moment before slipping down the sides of her face.

He jerked his hands away. "Oh Christ, Shell. You're crying! I'm sorry. I'm such a bastard! I knew I shouldn't have rushed you!" He started to get off of her but she grabbed at his arm.

"No! No, you don't understand."

Reluctantly, he stayed where he was. "Tell me, then," he said, dropping his forehead to her shoulder. His voice was harsh and gravely but he couldn't help it. He felt like a heel, rife with lust and the guilt because of it.

"I've never felt any …real desire," she admitted, a confession which had him on his forearms, so he could look into her eyes. "I thought there was something wrong with me. And after …it happened, I thought that was it." She turned her face away for a moment but met his eyes again when he touched her face. "But it's so different with you. I was just scared that it never would be, you know? And then it was and it feels so good with you …I can't explain," she wailed softly. "I just wanted you to know, that's all. That it's different. Because I love you."

Her simple words moved him; shot right to his centre. "Thank you," he whispered, gently kissing the tears from her cheeks. He finished undressing her then, slowly and sensually, with tender and lingering hands. Taking his time, he caressed her everywhere, with his hands and mouth, eliciting wonderful sounds from her that brought his own excitement to a fever pitch. On and on he continued, until their bodies were slick with sweat and he could feel her body humming, her blood racing with the same need as his own.

"Tell me what you want," he whispered into her ear.

She was panting, her breath hot and thrilling on his neck. She shook her head, trying instead to pull him over her, between her knees.

"No," he resisted, only half teasing. "Tell me what you want." At the same time he moved the callused tips of his fingers over her lightly, ready to begin again.

"I want you," she gasped.

Something came over him then, a feeling he had never experienced before. Sex for him had always been fun and casual. But this - this was an all-consuming need to possess and claim and dominate in a purely male way. It was raw and primitive and completely out of character for him. "You're mine. Always mine," he said fiercely. "Only mine."

She licked her lips then nodded, keeping her eyes closed. It wasn't enough for him. "Say it," he growled, then immediately gentled his tone. "I want to hear you say it."

She opened her eyes, searching his for something. Then with a half smile, she brought her hands up to cup his face, to bring it closer to hers. "Only mine," she echoed smartly. But her eyes said it, what he craved. They were warm, clouded with passion and need and surrender.

Quickly kicking off his pants and boxers, he finally moved over her. He found the contact of skin against skin heady and exotic. Soft breasts pressed against his chest, smooth thighs brushed against his own as they parted to cradle his hips. Feeling as eager and shaky as a teenager, he entered her slowly, terrified he wouldn't be able to make her forget or bring her pleasure. He withdrew then thrust again, deeply this time, setting a rhythm that she responded to with a moan. He was so relieved at that moment, and excited by her need that he almost lost control completely.

Nothing could be as good as this, he thought. Bracing his weight on his arms, he kissed her neck then her mouth, kissing her deeply until her back arched against him. Her nails dug into his shoulders and she screamed into his mouth. The sound of her, sexy and breathless, pulled him right over the edge to follow.

He rested his full weight on her, for she had her arms tightly wrapped around him and wouldn't let go. Before their breathing even slowed to normal he rolled over, taking her with him in a sweaty tangle of limbs. He tugged at her hair lightly until she looked up at him. "I love you," he said, for the first time in his life.

"Thank you," she said groggily, planting a sweet, chaste kiss on his chest before drifting off to sleep.

When she awoke it was still dark. They no longer lay stretched out before the fire, but upstairs in Michael's bed. His big, warm body was curled around hers. One hand moved between them, up and down her back; massaging the base of her spine with the ball of his thumb, grazing the length of it with his fingertips, skimming her shoulders with his palm. Lost in the sensual languor he was creating with his hands, she had only a muzzy, half formed plan of waiting him out, pretending sleep to see how far he would go. Her plan was foiled when one masculine hand slipped over her hip and up to capture her breast. Her body shivered.

"I thought so," he said, nipping playfully at her neck.

Moving her onto her back, he covered her mouth with his, parting her lips to delve inside with the velvet of his tongue. What started as a gentle exploration, a mere sharing of breath, soon became impassioned and uncontrolled. He moved over her, rubbing against her provocatively, his body a great welcome weight pressing her down into the mattress. It was exciting, yet she wanted more; wanted to give him more. She pushed at his shoulders.

"Michael, stop ...don't."

He stilled immediately, his breath harsh and uneven on her neck. She felt him swallow. "Why?"

She could hear the worry in his voice and feel the vulnerability that tensed his muscles. She put her arms around his neck. "No - don't think that. I just ...I want my turn. Please."

He rolled off of her to lean back against the pillows and looked at her warily, clearly not sure what to expect. She sat up on her knees to get a better look at him. A dim light spilled in from the hallway to rest, lovingly it seemed, on the skin of his chest and shoulders. Gripping a fold of the quilt, she began to pull it down, pausing to look at his face with one delicate brow lifted in silent inquiry. He nodded, smiling slowly. The quilt came down, over his stomach, then slower, over his hips and down his long legs. She held her breath, letting her eyes play over him. "You're beautiful, Mike. You really are."

His eyes smoldered and his hands reached out to her, to draw her down to him. She caught them, placing them one at a time above his head. "My turn, Michael," she reminded him playfully. She began to touch him then, starting with his hair. She ran her fingers through it, lightly raking her nails over his scalp time and time again before moving down. She lingered long over his chest, loving the solid breadth of it, the warm smooth hardness of it. She let herself be swept away, doing whatever came natural; massaging his muscles, letting her hair trail over his skin as she kissed and licked her way down. He tasted of salt and smelled of warm, male skin.

He was breathing hard.

Enjoying his reaction, she worked down to his stomach and stuck her tongue in his navel.

The muscles clenched and he tried to sit up. "Shelley," he groaned. "C'mon, that's enough."

"Please," she implored. "I'm having fun. Are you …not?"

He gave a short laugh and when he spoke his voice was thick and raspy. "Yes, but you're driving me crazy."

"Good."

After he laid back down she moved to the bottom of the bed and, starting at his feet, worked her mouth and hands up to his hips. She teased him there, drawing closer and closer to the bold evidence of his arousal. She breathed on it, skimmed over it with her hands and hair, but never actually closed over it.

His lips began to move, to mutter a rough combination of French and English words from deep in his throat, words she couldn't even begin to understand. His fingers clutched convulsively at the tangled sheet and she heard it tear. Finally crawling up his body, she touched him with hers, sliding her legs along his, breasts against his chest. It was healing and liberating and so exciting that the insistent, throbbing pulse deep inside her became almost unbearable. She moved up even further and rocked against him, so that his manhood just brushed against the juncture of her thighs.

"Sweet Christ," he hissed just before he pushed her off to roll on top of her, ending the game and filling her with a swift, deep thrust. They were both too aroused for it to last long. It was no more than a minute before she exploded. The pulsation reverberated inside her, on and on until his powerful body shuddered against her in release. She held his shoulders as his pleasure took him, finding it glorious to behold, marveling at the love surging inside her, marveling even more that at last, at long last, someone loved her too.

When she awoke again it was well into morning. Michael was still there, leaning on his elbow, supporting his head with his hand and watching her intently. Don't you ever sleep?" She grouched. "You're always staring at me when I wake up. Bit of a waste of good sleep time, don't you think?"

She stretched, realizing after a moment that the quilt was bunched around her waist, leaving her entire upper body bare before him. "Mike!" She reached automatically for the blanket to cover herself but stopped when he shook his head. His gaze moved to her stomach, where his hand rested flat against her skin. "I can feel the baby move," he murmured with a sad smile.

She could feel it too and as always, the mixed emotions left her confused. "What are you thinking?" She wanted to know.

He looked up at her in reluctant wonder. "You have a little person there inside you, fathered by a brutal …" He just shook his head, unable to find the right word. "A man who didn't know you, never really looked into your eyes or even touched his lips to yours. He didn't know how easy it is to make you laugh or that you splash in puddles when you think no one is looking, or that you're scared of spiders but won't kill them. He didn't know these things, but I do. I know you. He never felt the love I feel for you, yet it's part of him in there, not me. It's just not …fair that someone like that could create a life in one violent act." He sighed heavily and his hand started to move in little circles while he searched for the right words to express his feelings. "Nature shouldn't allow such a thing. Not without love, the kind that was here in this room last night. It would have been right, to conceive here last night, with me. It would have been right." Suddenly shaking off his mood, he bent to drop a tender kiss on her stomach. "This is your baby, though. Part of you and I can find joy in that."

Shelley was touched by his sensitivity and also by the fact that he echoed the very feeling that surfaced every time she thought of the baby. She wished it was his too. She could find no joy in the baby otherwise, she was convinced of that.

He moved up then to kiss her mouth but she held one hand up in front of her to ward him off and clapped the other over her mouth. "Whoa there," she said, muffled. "This isn't the movies, you know. Morning breath is a common occurrence here in my world. I have to go brush my teeth." Feeling too self conscious to walk naked to the bathroom, she cast her eyes around the room, deciding eventually on the sheet. She tugged at it but it was trapped beneath his big body.

"It's a bit harder to make the bed while we're in it, no?"

She coloured slightly at his amused, quizzical tone. "I need it. Get off."

"What on earth for?"

She glared at him, eyes narrowed until she caught the telltale twitch of his lip. "You know what for. Get off you big oaf."

Instead of doing as she asked, he rolled onto his

stomach and braced his chin in his hands, anchoring the sheet even more in the process. "Shelley, you can't possibly be worried about letting me see your body after last night."

"It's broad daylight," she protested feebly. "You'll see all the faults you missed in the dark."

"Nonsense," he scoffed. "But I'm a patient man. I can wait here all morning."

"Oh, you're mean. Don't you have anything better to do than ogle a naked woman?"

"No," he said, sounding surprised, as though he wasn't aware better pastimes even existed. After only a minute of her stubborn refusal, he got off the bed, naked himself and perfectly at ease, and stretched his hand out to her.

She sighed. Giving up, she put her hand in his and let him pull her off the bed to stand before him. Without letting go of it, he twirled her slowly in a complete circle, his eyes traveling the length of her before he drew her to him for a hug.

"You're completely gorgeous. I love everything about you." His hands went to her hair, where it fell loose almost to her waist. "But especially this." Grabbing a handful, he brought it to his face and inhaled the fragrance of it. "C'mon," he urged with a grin, pulling on her hand. "I'll even escort you to the bathroom. A naked woman should never walk alone."

CHAPTER SIXTEEN

"No," Michael said flatly, not even deigning to look up at her.

"What do you mean, no?" Shelley's voice was sharp. "Why not? I have a prenatal appointment today. You knew that."

She had just about given up on an answer when he finally looked up and squarely into her eyes without even a flicker of contrition. He squared up the negatives on his desk into a neat pile and put them in his desk drawer. "I mean no. I'll cancel it for you while I'm there."

She shook her head, incredulous that he was talking to her this way. "You can't just tell me no." She was trying her best to keep calm, but her temper was outpacing her self control. "You're not my dad. I want to go to town with you."

"I *can* tell you no. I just did and you heard it perfectly - so drop it."

She gasped, as shocked as if he had slapped her. His callous words, his tone, his cool lack of respect for her wishes - these things just weren't him. Or at least they didn't used to be. The hair rose up on her arms as a tiny prickle of buried fear wriggled to the surface. What was happening here? A disturbing thought struck her and she voiced it without thinking. "Mike are you ashamed to take me to town, to be seen with me?"

"No!" He exploded. "Christ, no."

A little voice in her mind, long ignored, whispered a warning but she ignored it and stood up to face him. "I need a reason then." She challenged him with her stance and the look in her eyes.

"You want a reason?" He snarled, turning on her. "I can give you a whole handful. One, you're pregnant and you shouldn't be driving around in the bush. Two, I won't have room on the four wheeler for you and all the groceries. Three, someone should stay to look after the dogs. Four, it's going to be a long trip in and out and you're just going to get in my way-"

"Okay! Okay!" She yelled, backing off, hurt and disappointed by his attitude. Shelley flopped herself down on the couch after he left. This was their first real fight and though it was upsetting, it was more confusing than anything. None of it made any sense. She thought they had already tackled the tough stuff and won. They had taken so many steps in the right direction; confiding in and supporting each other like true partners, and physically, they were closer than ever. She had moved into Michael's room where their nights were loving and passionate and so very natural, but lately, when the sun crept through the windows in the morning, the tension inevitably crept in with it. It was getting more and more difficult to dispel that tension. She wondered sometimes if it was because they had crossed over the line that marked them as friends only. She just didn't know. Why would his moods get worse over time instead of better? What reason could he have to keep her here instead of enjoying a trip to town? The reasons he had given her were ridiculous and clearly manufactured. Had she ignored that little voice in her head one too many times and put herself in peril?

❧

It had been a lazy walk, Shelley reflected many hours into the day, but enjoyable. The sun filtered through the trees on each side of the path, made easier now by winter's arrival. The bright green leaves were but a memory of summer, as were the needles of the tamarack tree, leaving the forest in the shadow of its former glory. It was still pretty though, with snow and frost clinging to the boughs of the evergreens. The wind moved through the tall pines, stirring the tops of them, and they creaked and moaned in gentle protest. Despite the beauty up above, she kept her eyes mostly on the ground. Tracks crisscrossed the trail here and there, of all different shapes and sizes. She enjoyed the challenge of trying to identify them. She'd decided that the tracks with two long indents were made by bunnies, the small ones with sharp little claw marks must be squirrels and the roundish hoof shaped ones were most likely moose or caribou. There were small dog-like ones as well, smaller than Dawson's and Darby's, so she figured they might be fox tracks, or even a small coyote. It was all guesswork, but always the best part of her winter walks. They had almost reached the cabin when the dogs started to yip, bounding ahead of her into the clearing. That could only mean Michael was back from his trip to town. Despite his atrocious behaviour this morning and their argument, she was anxious to see him. It was distressing, parting with bad feelings, even just for the day. She had almost convinced herself she had imagined the worst of it and was eager to make amends. Plus, it was always fun to see what kind of goodies he brought home.

"Hey," she called out happily as she hung up her coat,

slipped off her boots and hurried into the kitchen. She was greeted only by the silence of the room; the same silence she had endured all day, so her first thought was that she had been wrong, that he hadn't arrived. But he had. The empty grocery boxes were piled neatly by the door and he was there, sitting at the kitchen table. He sat sideways on his chair with his back slumped against the wall.

She recognized the change in him immediately, in the set of his jaw and shoulders, but especially when he raised his head. His eyes blazed furiously at her.

"You're still angry," she realized in confusion. "Why? What happened?"

He jabbed at an envelope with his finger and pushed it along the table toward her. It was addressed to her. "Were you going to tell me?" His voice was deadly quiet.

She reached for it. "I haven't even look-"

"Were you?!" He yelled, suddenly trapping her hand with his own, pinning it to the table before she could pick up the envelope. "Or would I just wake up and find you gone?" He jumped out of his seat suddenly to tower over her. "Well?! Nothing to say?"

She was completely bewildered. "Let me see it!" She wrenched her hand from beneath his and pulled the letter from the torn envelope with shaky fingers. "It's just my ...my notice of acceptance into the graduate program, for the winter semester."

"I know what it is!" He roared, knocking the chair over with a sweep of his hand. He snatched the paper from her, crumpling it in one large fist before letting it drop to the floor. He looked so terribly furious.

Her eyes fastened on the frantic pulse beat at his

temple and she felt a spark of fear. Without thinking she fled from him, through the kitchen and back out the door, grabbing her coat and boots on the way out. Although he yelled her name, he didn't try to follow as she ran down the very same trail she had taken earlier. She had no destination in mind, she just needed to get away from him, from his anger. She had first hand knowledge of what a man's rage could do, even had the scars to prove it, and it terrified her completely.

She ran until her leg muscles burned, until her breath was so labored she felt lightheaded. Spotting a fallen, rotting log just off the path, she made her way over with rubbery legs, brushed the snow off and sat down. It took ages to slow her breathing to normal and the time took the edge off her fear, allowing her to finally think rationally. She'd overreacted. No doubt about that. But her fear was real, and she still believed the danger was as well. She had seen it coming for weeks; his moods, his terse words, his increasing irritation at everything around him. It was all getting worse. This anger, this rage, was going to be the end of them both if they didn't do something about it.

Shelley sat on the log for hours, wrestling the problem, searching for a solution as the cold seeped into her bones. In the end, all she came up with was a temporary one. She needed more time to think this through and her Grandfather's cabin, her cabin, was perhaps the place to do it. Unhappy with the decision but at a loss, she finally headed home at dusk. Getting lost in the dark would only add to her problems.

She stole back into the cabin, closing the door as quietly as she was able. Tiptoeing into the living room, she noted with relief that Michael dozed fitfully on the couch. She moved silently up the stairs, grabbed an overnight bag and packed it hurriedly, just enough for a day or two. Then, finding a pad of paper and a pen in his office, she wrote a hasty note, folded it up and stealthily placed it on the coffee table by the couch.

☙

Shelley had barely taken her coat off in her grandfather's cabin when she heard the banging on the front door. Michael had come already and he was getting louder and angrier by the moment.

"Shelley! Open this goddamn door and let me in!"

Unable to bear it, she ran up the stairs and into the bedroom, where she slammed and locked that door too. Flinging herself onto the bed, she covered her ears, desperate now to block out his voice, because even laced with fury and the threat of retribution, it had a power over her she could not fight.

It stopped abruptly. She cautiously removed her hands from her ears at the sudden quiet, listening intently, but the silence was swiftly broken by the tinkle of shattering glass. She listened with a sinking feeling of inevitability to the sound of his approach; the heavy tread of his boots, the creak of the stairs, the opening and closing of the first two doors in the hall, then the ominous rattle of her own doorknob.

"Open it!" The command filtered through the door, low pitched but still vibrating with emotion.

"No," she yelled. "No! Go home!"

"You know I can break it in."

She sat up in alarm. "Don't you dare! You can't just -"

The door latch, old and barely attached to the wall, gave on the very first blow and the door flew open.

"You can't just go around breaking things," she finished faintly.

Still hanging onto the knob, he just stood there, staring at her, breathing hard. He held up the note clutched in his hand; it looked as though it had been crumpled into a tight ball and then smoothed flat again. "What's this?" He asked finally, sending it sailing across the distance between them with a flick of his wrist.

It fluttered back and forth in slow indecision, finally landing propped against her right knee. She could see only one or two sentences from that angle, but her clear round writing was unmistakable. 'The best thing for both of us is some time apart', it said. It said a lot more than that; some she regretted, for it was written in anger and hurt, but mostly it was full of truths that had to be voiced. "I might be naive about a lot of things, Mike, but I'm not stupid. We both know what's happening. Surely you don't need me to spell it out for you?"

"Yeah," he answered quietly. "Spell it out for me."

She took a deep breath. "You want to hurt me -"

He flung the door away from him, slamming it loudly, though the broken latch caused it to pop back open slightly. "I have never hurt you!"

She closed her eyes, trying to find the words that would best explain the turmoil she sensed in him. "You have a need to lash out, Michael. I can feel it. You want to ...retaliate, to cause pain because you feel pain. You're bitter and angry and frustrated because there is no one left to take it out on. I'm afraid ...one of these days your going to take it out on me. You already do in some ways."

He paced agitatedly in front of her, back and forth. "I

try so hard not to."

"Maybe so," she allowed, "but you do anyway. You get short with me. You make sarcastic remarks, say hurtful things. You won't take me to town anymore ... And today, you got so angry. I can feel it all unraveling, Mike. I'm afraid."

"Are you leaving me, Shelley?"

She studied him, taking in each of his features. His dark hair was getting too long; it was starting to curl out at the collar. He wasn't handsome in the modern day model sense. Their look was often gaunt, with prominent cheek bones and lean, long lines. In contrast, Michael was taller, with a bigger, sturdier frame. His face was fuller, a little rounder, giving him a look that was at once boyish and manly. His mouth was inviting, lips full, except where he had drawn part of the bottom in to bite at with his teeth. And his brown eyes, even bleak and stark with despair, pulled her in. The overall effect of him was irresistible, and the force of it slammed into her all over again.

"I don't want to," she answered truthfully. "I applied for the graduate program before I even left Toronto, in case I couldn't find a job in the fall. A lot of things have changed since then. I never gave it another thought."

Some of the angry tension seemed to drain from him and he sat on the bed. "I'm afraid too," he admitted so quietly she could barely hear him.

"Of what?" She prodded softly

"Lots of things. I'm afraid of these feelings. I have been for a long time. I am afraid I'll hurt you. I'm afraid if I take you to town anymore, you'll meet more people who want to get to know you. Maybe ...a man. Someone like Dan, someone that hasn't been ...wasn't ...you know." He looked at her searchingly. "And you won't want to stay."

She moved closer and his arms came around her waist to draw her close, to stand between his knees. He rested his head against her stomach. "I'm sorry."

"Oh, Mike. That's so wrong. Things were going so well between us. I'm not looking for anyone else. You must be able to see that."

He smiled sadly. "My heart knows it. I'm just having a little trouble with my head."

She smoothed a hand over his hair. "What are we going to do?" She asked hopelessly.

He sighed, tickling the skin under her shirt with his warm breath. "I don't know, Shelley. I'm trying."

"I know you are." She hoped trying would be enough to keep the anger in him from spiraling down into madness. For both of their sakes.

CHAPTER SEVENTEEN

Just as she plunged her hands into the new batch of stiff cookie dough, there was a knock on the front door. "Mike?" She called. "Someone's at the door."

There was no answer. It dawned on her that he was still in his dark room developing film. He played his music so loud in there, he would never hear her. With a sigh, she shoved a stubborn lock of hair behind her ear and grabbed a towel for her hands. Who could it be anyway, way out here in the bush? Hurrying through the living room, she jerked the innermost door open. There, blurred by the frosted screen door, were two young men standing on the porch. She froze, her friendly greeting dying on her lips.

Dressed in brand new, expensive winter parkas and boots, they were clean cut and handsome. About her age too, she guessed. Two men. She grabbed the screen door handle convulsively, holding it closed. The fear was irrational, she knew. It wouldn't happen twice. After a deep, fortifying breath, she opened the screen door and made eye contact. "Yes?"

They smiled at her. Open, friendly smiles. "Is this Michael Daillant's place?"

"Daillant," she corrected nervously, wondering what to do. "It's French. The L's are silent."

The two men exchanged looks. "Is he home?" One of them asked patiently.

"Why are you here?" The question was blunt and

unfriendly, but she couldn't help it.

"Oh sorry. I'm Derek and this is James. We're here to move into the cabin down the lake. We talked to Mike on the radio last week. He said to come here for the key."

"Oh," she said, flushing. "I'm really sorry. You must think ...please, come in, it's cold out there. Would you like some coffee or something while I get Michael? He should be almost finished."

The bigger one, the one named Derek, stepped closer. His hand reached toward her face and she flinched back, suddenly wildly certain he was going to hit her. His blue, blue eyes looked down at her with concern as he plucked a glob of cookie dough from her hair and dropped it into her hand. "Don't interrupt him then," he suggested gently. "We'll just warm up with that coffee and wait for him, if that's okay?"

"Of course." She led the way to the kitchen with the uncomfortable certainty that she was under intense scrutiny. She was terribly embarrassed by her own peculiar behaviour and knew they must be thinking she was a 'couple sandwiches short of a picnic', as her Grandpa had been fond of saying. "Have a seat if you like." Pouring them all a coffee, she joined them at the table to wait.

"So, are you Mrs. Daillant?" Derek asked with a cheeky grin. He had pronounced it correctly this time.

"No, I'm not." Smiling back, she handed them each a cookie still warm from the oven. "I do live here though."

There was a moment of thick silence as the men nibbled on their cookies, made a thousand times worse by Derek's steady stare. He studied her curiously and openly and by the time he had eaten his second cookie she felt ready to poke his eyes out. "We scared you," he finally said perceptively. "We didn't mean to."

"No," she scoffed with a wave of her hand, wanting to hide her moment of irrational fear from them. "You didn't scare me." Derek looked at her so skeptically though, she felt compelled to say something more. "The last two men to come through here weren't so friendly," she explained faintly.

"No?" His eyes skipped to the smaller fading scars on her face.

"No." She said it with finality and he let the matter drop.

They all made small talk, fortunately stumbling onto common ground in only minutes. They had both just graduated from her University. In fact, they must have been in half her classes, since they all now had the same degree.

"Hey," she said spontaneously as a funny thought struck her. "You must have had professor Larson?"

"Yes," they said in unison with a dramatic groan. "Organic chem."

"That orange turtleneck just killed me!"

"I know! He wore it everyday."

Their conversation dissolved into laughter at the memory. She closed her eyes, picturing the middle aged man perfectly in her mind; black Lycra leggings and that awful shirt stretched so tightly over the giant mound of his stomach that one could see the indent of his belly button. "I was so fixated on that outfit I could never follow his lectures."

"Too much fun ogling his body?"

"Oh yeah." She laughed again, tickled by thought of her swooning over that eccentric man. Still smiling, she got up to refill their coffee cups, only then noticing the figure just outside the kitchen. Michael stood there, leaning against the door frame with his arms crossed over the wide expanse of his chest. His brows were drawn together in a frown. "Michael," she said happily, ignoring her twinge of unease at his expression. "This is Jim and Derek. They're here for the key to Grandpa's cabin. You didn't tell me you rented it for December."

Derek took another cookie. "We were trying to convince Shelley here to move in with us and bake cookies."

"Really?" Michael said, moving into the room. He sounded friendly enough but she could see the muscle ticking in his cheek. He was grinding his teeth! If he didn't like these men, why did he rent them the cabin?

Fervently hoping that he wasn't going to have some kind of outburst and embarrass them all, she pulled another cup down for Michael, poured the coffees and returned to her seat. Ignoring the proffered cup, he came around to stand behind her chair, then leaned down to drop a kiss on her forehead.

Still confused by his obvious displeasure, she angled her head back to look at him. Something wasn't right. It wasn't the little kiss; he did that all the time, but his hands gripped her shoulders a little tighter than usual and though his words were perfectly civil, his voice had an edge to it that left her wondering.

"I think she's busy enough baking cookies over here." He held Derek's gaze. Shelley could actually feel the undercurrents passing between them until the younger man nodded subtly.

"Well, if we could just get that key then, Mike?"

Michael fished around in a small, cluttered drawer for the key. It was filled with receipts, spare change and all the miscellaneous odds and ends that didn't belong anywhere else. Every additional second he spent searching added more tension to the room, stretching it like a wire until it was screamingly, unbearably tight. When he did finally find the key, Derek pulled a check from his pocket and they switched, rather like two people caught up in a ransom exchange. Despite her confusion, Shelley found the situation amusing and her lip twitched with suppressed laughter. They were being so ridiculously solemn.

"The damage deposit you get back in full before you leave," Michael was explaining flatly, with absolutely none of his usual charm. "If you have any questions or need any help with anything, I'll be here until the twenty third. We'll be gone for Christmas through to New Years."

Derek juggled the key in his hand absently, turning to Shelley once more with a thoughtful look. "All right, thank you. We'll be on our way, then."

Seized by an impulse, Shelley quickly filled a plastic container with cookies and ran after them, just catching them at the door. "Here. In case we don't see you. Merry Christmas a little early."

Jim accepted the cookies with a smile, but Derek snatched the container from him with a wink at Shelley and stuffed it into his coat. "Thank you, Shelley. That's sweet of you, but we'll ...ah ...drop around for coffee before you leave."

"Yes, do that," she encouraged warmly.

Michael turned on her, accusing, as soon as the door closed. "You were flirting with them!"

She gasped. "I was not!"

"You were!"

"I was not," she insisted.

"They couldn't take their eyes off you!"

She laughed merrily at the absurdity of it. "That's ridiculous."

His eyes narrowed dangerously and she suddenly realized how very real his anger was. She sobered instantly. "I don't understand you." She started backing toward the kitchen.

He followed, advancing slowly. "I don't want them here!"

"But why? They seemed really nice."

"Nice, eh?" He grabbed her wrist in a punishing grip. "Do you know what Derek wants from you?"

"My cookies?"

"He doesn't want your frigging cookies! He wants you! Can't you see that?"

"No," she denied, shaking her head. "You're wrong. I don't know where you're getting this from, but you're wrong."

"I'm not wrong!" He yelled fiercely. "Do you think I'm blind?! I will not have him here - and I don't want you going over there, either!"

"What are you saying? Do you think I'm going to run over there and hop into bed with him?"

"Are you?" He challenged rudely.

Shocked, she could only stare at him wordlessly. She had no intention of ever doing such a thing, but her own anger at his behaviour prodded her to say, "Maybe. I'll go if I want to. You don't own me."

She didn't even see it coming. One moment they were glaring at each other in anger and the next she was sprawled on the floor, clutching at her mouth. Disbelief paralyzed her. It couldn't be real, she thought blankly, this wouldn't happen.

But the pain was real. The taste of blood in her mouth was real. She raised her eyes to Michael and her denial gave way to a sense of betrayal so great she wanted to die.

"Shelley? Oh God, Shell. Please..." He hunkered down beside her, reaching out a shaky hand to touch her. "I'm so sorry. I don't know where that came from. Shell?"

She slapped at his hand with mounting fury. "Don't touch me!" Scrabbling backwards out of his reach, she pushed herself up to stand. "Don't ever touch me!"

He moved to follow her. "Shelley, please," he implored. "You don't know how sorry I am."

"Don't!" She screamed at him. "Don't come near me." She wanted to run at him and strike out for hurting her in this way. He was supposed to be her refuge; her solace. He was supposed to love her and protect her from the world. She glared at him, too angry yet to cry.

He stood completely still, pale faced and stunned, but his eyes beseeched her to understand. "I didn't mean to," he said in a raw whisper. "I swear to God, I didn't mean to."

Unable to look at him, Shelley turned her back and mounted the stairs slowly, determined to keep her dignity if nothing else this time.

"Shelley, you know me," he entreated, "you know I wouldn't do this on purpose ..."

"I don't know you," she refuted coldly without even turning around. "It seems I don't know you at all."

She slammed the door of her old bedroom and locked it behind her before sinking onto the mattress in a bleak fog of despair. She just sat there, willing the numbness to overtake her; she simply couldn't face this all at once. She rocked herself back and forth on the bed, despondent and so overwhelmed by a vast sense of loss she was convinced that everything in her life had just hit rock bottom.

It wasn't long before she heard his quiet footfall outside her door, then a soft knock. He rattled the knob. "Baby, please let me in. We need to talk about this ...what can I say?"

She heard his voice break with emotion but she hardened her heart against it, nursing her anger instead. Only the stupid women fall for this, she reminded herself when his retreating foot steps echoed dully in the hall. Only the stupid ones get sucked into the cycle. She refused to be one of those women - they suffer abuse and open their hungry hearts in forgiveness for the tender words that come after, then suffer all over again, becoming smaller and weaker and more pathetic with each spin of the wheel. She refused, because she knew that the wheel keeps on spinning, doling out the pain and humiliation and sick dependence until finally, at the end of the game, they don't know how to live without it.

Spurred by her horrible thoughts, she yanked her suitcase from under the bed, sending a fury of dust bunnies swirling around her feet. She threw it on the trunk and unzipped it with frantic movements, afraid to be still in case she weakened like the other nameless women the statistics claimed. Grateful she had never bothered to move her clothes to Michael's room, she threw armfuls of them in the case, grabbing pants and sweaters and underwear at random, but froze when she heard the whine of the snow machine outside. Michael was leaving! Dropping her load of clothes, Shelley ran to the window in time to see him disappear through the trees, on the winter trail that led straight to town. Now that the swamps and small lakes were frozen over, it was a perfectly serviceable short cut. In the summer, anyone unable to come up the river to reach their lake would have to muck through that trail; six or seven miles of mosquito infested marshland. It was obviously that route that the two criminals had taken this past summer.

What am I doing, she thought with sudden clarity. I have no way to leave here. Worse, I have no where to go. She sat woodenly on the window seat. I have no money of my own left. I have nothing. I'm a pregnant, unemployed nobody with no one to turn to.

The numbness she had earlier prayed for settled in like mist. She had perfected this as a child, and at one point was able to draw the dark, comforting mantle over her with ease. She blinked slowly out the window and allowed herself the escape this blank drowsiness offered. Pulling the folded blanket from the seat beside her, she spread it over her and let herself go, helplessly adrift in her own darkness.

ೞ

Michael pounded on the door with his fist. Though muffled by his leather mitt, he pounded desperately hard and didn't stop until it was jerked open.

Daniel looked beyond annoyed, but the angry words died on his lips when Michael pulled his helmet off. He smiled a surprised greeting but that too faltered when he saw his face. "Mike," he queried in concern, pulling him inside and closing the door. "What's wrong, man? You look terrible."

"Dan," he said hopelessly. "Dan, I need help." Looking past him, he was taken aback by his own wild-eyed reflection in the foyer mirror. His breath had frosted his lashes and his hair, aging him considerably. He had forgotten his scarf and balaclava in his panic and his helmet had been no match for the ferocious wind. It had scoured his cheeks and chin to a bright red, but the rest of his face was dangerously white. His eyes were bleak and deeply shadowed and they looked a fathomless black against the paleness of his face. He did look terrible.

The house smelled deliciously of cabbage rolls and perogies with bacon and onions and he could hear the happy chatter of children coming from the kitchen. He realized with dismay that he had interrupted their family dinner. "I'm sorry, Dan," he apologized. "I didn't even stop and think about the time. Please, go and finish your dinner. I'll just wait here."

"It's no trouble, Mike." He patted his stomach. "I ate too much already anyway. Come through to the kitchen for a coffee, buddy, to warm you up. Then you can tell me what's going on."

"No!" Michael burst out, then finished more calmly. "No, I need to talk to you alone."

Dan nodded gravely. "Okay. Give me two seconds." He disappeared into the kitchen and the chatter rose in a crescendo of questions before stopping altogether. Michael paced the room uneasily, wondering if he had made a mistake in coming here. He couldn't make it right and neither could Dan. He thought about leaving; he even took a step towards the door, but a moment too late, for the lively prattle resumed in the other room and Dan returned with two mugs of coffee.

He set them on the coffee table, waved Michael over to the couch and took a seat across from him. He waited expectantly.

Michael wrapped his hands around the warm cup and took a sip. It was strong and black and so hot that it burned the entire length of his tongue. He decided he deserved that and more, so he took another punishing mouthful. He wanted nothing more than to sit here and weep. He was so deeply sorry and ashamed of what he had done; he didn't want to admit to this man what a horrible person he had become. But he had to. For Shelley. "I hit her, Dan," he confessed quietly. "I hit Shelley and I don't know what to do."

The softer more jovial edges to the man hardened perceptibly as he shifted from good friend to professional police officer in the blink of an eye. He regarded him steadily without a trace of sympathy. Michael knew he was debating whether he should write up a formal report. He'd expected that, wanted it even, and so was surprised when Dan put his coffee back down and leaned forward.

"First of all, is Shelley all right?"

"Yes." Michael met his eyes with difficulty. "She's locked herself into her room, though, and won't talk to me."

"Good. Tell me what happened."

Michael told him everything; what really happened in June, his building anger, the two young men that had fueled his jealousy and the argument afterwards. "It just happened so fast," he finished. "I didn't even get a chance to think about it."

Dan rested his elbows on his knees, rubbing his hands together slowly, thoughtfully.

Michael steeled himself for the scorn and condemnation, but it didn't come.

"Mike, I know you. I know this isn't like you and any fool can see where this is coming from. I'm going to do what I can, because you're a good friend, but let me make one thing clear. If you lay one more violent hand on that woman, Mike,

I'll have you in a cell before you can blink. Clear?"

Michael nodded with relief. "Clear."

"Okay. Let's go."

ଓ

Shelley floated in her warm cocoon of numbness, content in her apathy. Though she fought against awareness, the sounds and voices finally cleared the fog from her mind much as a gust of wind drives it from sea.

She heard a faraway voice; a worried voice which grew steadily louder and sharper. "Shelley. We've been calling you. Are you okay?"

She shook her head to clear it, finally focusing on the broad shouldered man crouching in front of her. "Daniel?" She asked in confusion. "What are you doing here?"

"I came to help. Is that all right?" His voice was gentle and soothing, and his eyes held hers with genuine concern. Instantly, she felt the intense pain of betrayal, the fear and sense of loss return, rising within her, building and frothing and eddying dangerously. It was like white water rushing the dam, beating at its foundation with a force she could barely contain.

But it wasn't until Michael entered the room to sit tentatively on the edge of the bed, that she began to cry. Daniel held her as she cried great convulsive sobs, and patted her back consolingly. Over his burly shoulder, she reached up to wipe at her eyes and found herself looking right at Michael.

He watched them, looking as scared and forlorn as a lost puppy. The tears ran in silent trails down his cheeks, but he didn't wipe them away. He met her eyes briefly, showing her the shadowed depth of his regret until his gaze fell to her split, swollen lip. His eyes scrunched tightly in instant response and he turned his head away from her.

Pulling away from Daniel, she straightened and wiped at her face with the blanket, smiling at him sheepishly. She didn't know what to say, or what was supposed to happen next.

"What happens next is up to you, Shelley," Daniel said gently, as if reading her mind. "Mike told me what happened. He told me everything," he confirmed at her questioning look. "The first question is, do you want to proceed with a police statement?"

She was already shaking her head. "No."

"I'm supposed to report this-"

"No, please, Dan. Don't do that."

He sat back to look at her. "All right. Tell you what - I'll write the report but I won't file it unless it happens again. This should be documented, Shelley."

She darted a glance at Michael but he looked away quickly. She waved a hand at the discarded, half packed suitcase. "There won't be a next time. I can't stay."

His eyes flew back to hers, alarmed, and she was the one to look away this time. "You're not supposed to stay when they hit you," she whispered.

Daniel sighed. "No, you're not," he agreed. "That is your decision of course, but will you listen to what Mike and I have come up with?"

At her reluctant nod, he pushed on.

"First let me tell you I've known Mike a long time. I know him well and I can tell you, it's not him doing this."

She opened her mouth to point out the obvious, but he held up a hand. "I'm not defending what he did, at all, but it's not him, Shelley. What happened in June has affected you both. Mike loves you very much and he's come to me for help. For both of you, if you want it.

I'm not a therapist - I can't help him that way, but I can find him an outlet that will keep you safe and I can give you a way out, if you need one."

"Go on," she urged, feeling at last a kernel of hope swell in her chest.

"Mike said this comes on fast, but he thinks he can key in to the warning signs. We've brought him a heavy bag, so he can go pummel that until he's exhausted. So, most important, let him go do it. Talking will be more effective later, anyway."

"That sounds good, Dan, but what if he doesn't make it to the heavy bag?"

Michael pushed a duffel bag closer with his foot and his friend unzipped it to rummage around inside.

"This is pepper spray," he explained, pulling it from the bag. "It's horrible stuff and it *will* subdue Mike long enough for you to get away, if you have to, so keep it handy."

Shelley couldn't imagine ever being able to do that to Mike, but she reached out to take it anyway. "What then?"

"All right, suppose he's lost control. You spray him then get your ass out of here and come to me. Have this bag packed, Shelley. Always. Keep it in the closet maybe, near the door. Have a change or two of clothes, basic toiletries and your wallet in there." He reached into the duffel again and pulled out a wad of money. "Mike took out one thousand dollars - keep it in the bag. You'll need it if you have to get away in a hurry."

She looked from him to Mike, astounded. It touched her that they really were trying to cover all the bases to keep her safe.

"Lastly, I believe, you need these." He dangled two keys from his fingers. "One is for the snow machine, the other for the boat when the ice goes out. Mike will make sure you know how to use them both. Keep those in there too, where you can get at them."

She rubbed at the keys, absently polishing them with the sleeve of her sweater as she thought about what she wanted to say. "I was scared," she admitted finally. "It's so isolated here and I felt trapped. This would all help so much - I would have a place to run to, a way to get there and enough money to start again."

"That's right. We've also agreed that I will come every Monday to check things out. Mike will talk to me about how he feels he's managing his anger and that kind of thing, at least until he's found himself a therapist. You two have to talk about going to counseling together."

Shelley opened her mouth to protest but again he held up a silencing hand. "You know what happens if you break a bone and it heals wrong?" He didn't wait for her but answered himself. "It never works properly again and sometimes," he glanced meaningfully at both of them in turn, "it doesn't work at all. You two talk about this. I'll be downstairs."

Before he turned to leave, he pulled one last item from the bag, and before she could even register what it was, Dan had snapped her picture with a Polaroid camera. He smiled slyly. "Evidence for my report. Watch your step, Michael my friend."

Things felt even more awkward after Daniel left the room. With their buffer gone, Shelley didn't know what to say. She looked at the floor, at the duffel, at the keys in her hand, anywhere but at the man in front of her. She was still hurt. She was still angry. But she still loved him fiercely. He had done a lot to make amends and that alone had convinced her how serious and committed he was to keep this from happening again. It was enough this one time; this one and only time. She could forgive him and put it behind her.

Michael shifted on the bed and cleared his throat. "I don't know what to say first, so I'll just say it all. I'm so sorry, more than I even know how to put into words. We've been through so much together, seen so much violence …and in a split second I did the unthinkable - I did the same thing to you. *I* did it and that's a terrible thing to live with. I love you, Shelley and I swear, I *swear* that I will not let my anger take control of me like that again. I swear on my life. All I can do now is ask for your forgiveness and hope that you can give me another chance."

Her heart fluttered in a weird kind of nervous happiness and the cloying feeling of doom slipped from her shoulders, crashing down the mountain of her fears to land as harmless rubble at the bottom. She moved from her window seat to hug him tightly. "I can and I will. One chance. I can't be here for you, with you, if it happens again, though. Do you understand that?"

His hug was crushing in its relief. "Baby, I will personally escort you to town if it happens again."

His arms were a comforting balm to her wounded spirit and when his lips whispered over her injured lip she reveled in the tenderness, basking in it like a cat in the sun. The tentative kiss - an apology, tenderly rendered and graciously, helplessly accepted. She sighed deeply. It's strange, she thought, how everything in life is so up and down, and stranger still, how it can all change in an instant.

CHAPTER EIGHTEEN

Before she even opened it, Shelley knew who would be at the door, and sure enough, Derek stood there, smiling at her through the screen. With such mixed feelings, she didn't know what to do. Derek was nice, fun to talk to and it was always a pleasure to make a new friend, but was it worth making Michael angry? Well, she decided, she couldn't be rude.

"Hi, Derek. Nice to see you. Where's Jim?"

"Jimmy is sleeping off a hangover this morning. I got impatient and bored. So here I am. Is the coffee on?"

"Coffee is always on," she assured him, stepping aside to let him in.

They sat again at the kitchen table, briefly discussing the weather and the upcoming holidays until he put his coffee cup down with deliberation. "Shelley, where's Mike?"

"He took his dogs for a snow machine ride."

At his raised eyebrows, she laughed. "They run behind. They love it. He's usually gone a while though. Can I give him a message for you?"

"No. I came here to see you."

"Oh ...umm ..."

He leaned closer to her with eyes so very direct and intense that she felt a flutter of unease in her stomach. "I'm worried about you."

"Why?"

He rubbed his chin with the knuckles of one hand, back and forth, and sidestepped the question with one of his own. "Does he beat you?"

The question caught her in mid swallow, causing her to suck coffee into her lungs with her gasp of air. "No," she wheezed when her coughing fit had passed. "Whatever gave you that idea?"

"You've been beaten by somebody. Don't bother denying it - I can tell."

All that remained of the cut on her lip from Michael was a small scab and she quickly folded it under her upper lip. Her hand too, lifted up unconsciously to trace one of the many faint silvery marks on her face; reminders of that fateful day.

"No, it's not just the scars. It was the fear on your face and the way you flinch back when I get too close. It's the way he looks at you, like you're something he owns. It's the way you keep looking at the door, afraid he'll see me here, alone with you." He leaned forward earnestly, touching her hand, smoothing his thumb over the faint circlet of bruises on her wrist. "I can help you get away from him, Shelley. Don't wait until it's too late."

"It's not like that Derek, really."

"No?" He queried in disbelief. "What happened to your lip, then? Let me guess ...the door hit you? Did you give yourself these bruises?"

The heavy sarcasm made her feel stupid and she could only shrug helplessly. "I admit, he got very angry last time you were here and we argued, but ...it's not what you think."

"Why protect him? Why lie for him, Shelley? It can't be worth it."

"I'm not lying -" She gave up, realizing suddenly how

it must appear to him. There was no way to make him understand. "Thank you for your concern, Derek, but I'm fine."

He sat back in his chair, clearly bewildered, and regarded her steadily. "I'm sorry, Shelley, but I'm going to report him if you don't. My sister was almost killed by her husband and I can't stand by and let the same thing -"

"No," she interrupted firmly. "Michael only hit me once, accidentally. I swear to God." She gestured lamely at the scars again. "This wasn't Michael. It wasn't!"

"Who then?"

"I told you, two men ...This is how Mike and I met," she explained hesitantly, not knowing how much to say to make him understand, at least enough to stay out of it. "I came up for a summer holiday, in June, to stay in the cabin you're renting. Only, there were two men there already, hiding out from the police. When I walked in they were killing Michael - beating him to death. You'll have noticed his scars, too?"

Derek nodded, shocked.

"Well, I got banged up a little before Michael got free and killed them." It's amazing, she thought, how one could fit such a terrifying ordeal into one neat little sentence.

Derek released a relieved sigh. "Honestly then, he treats you all right? What about your lip, and the bruises?"

Her eyes softened. "Honestly, he treats me wonderful. It's just ...he's still really angry inside, you know? And sometimes its more than he can control. He hit me the one time, the last time you were here and you have no idea how devastated he was by it."

"What if he hurts you again. If he can do it once he can do it again."

She shook her head, completely certain. "We've taken

very careful and serious steps to make sure it doesn't happen again. We have a good friend from the police department helping us out and we're trying to line up some counseling. Seeing what happened to me this summer and living with what he did ...it well, it haunts him. Nothing could make him hurt me that way again. I'm sure of it."

"They must have hurt you badly," he observed.

"Mike's injuries were a bit more serious than mine. Oh, I had lumps and bumps, some shallow stab wounds, bruises, stitches and a broken arm. Just enough to make me heartily sick of the whole hospital scene. I plan never to set foot in one again, except of course in the spring when the bab-" She caught herself, cutting the word off, but not before understanding dawned in his eyes.

"You hide it well. It mustn't be easy, carrying your attacker's baby."

Her first instinct was to flee. Her chair scraped back across the floor and she planted her palms flat onto the table, bracing herself to stand, but the memory of Michael's oft repeated accusation kept her seated. She would not run away from this, no matter how uncomfortable she felt. "Kind of jumping to conclusions, aren't you?" She forced out coolly.

"Why else would you hide it? Look," he said sympathetically. "I didn't come here to dig into old wounds. I just wanted to make sure you were okay. I know I'm a nosy, interfering neighbour, but I meant well. I also know I'm no counselor, but I think it would be good for you to own up to it."

"Maybe," she whispered, then after a lengthy hesitation added, "you're right. One of them did rape me." It took more courage than she had imagined to say those words out loud. It gave her an inkling of just how difficult it must have been for Michael to confess that, even to her. She felt a surge of respect and love for him so great it almost brought tears to her eyes.

Derek cursed softly, apparently at a loss for words to have her actually confirm it. "I'm sorry again for prying. It just seemed all the signs of an abusive relationship were there."

"No need to apologize," she said, reclaiming her composure. "You were on the right track. Just the wrong train. Actually, I'm touched that you cared enough to bring it up."

He took one final gulp of his cooled coffee and got to his feet. "Shelley, we're only here 'til the new year, but I'm going to give you my number back home. If Mike loses control, you can count on me for help. As a friend, okay? Anger is a disease - don't underestimate it."

"I won't," she promised. "And thank you. That means a lot."

She walked him to the door and handed him his coat and mitts. "Thank you again," she said sincerely. "You're a nice guy."

He zipped up his coat. "Nice?" He echoed in mock horror. "What about cute? Or exciting?" With a smile and a wave of his hand, he went out the door and skipped down the steps. His voice trailed off, still tossing out preferred adjectives. "Sexy. Handsome ..."

"Bye," she called, shutting the door with a laugh. Well, now one outsider knew her tale and she hadn't been struck down with shame. Progress was slow, but it really did feel amazing.

CHAPTER NINETEEN

By the time Michael came in from his ride, Shelley was a bundle of raw nerves. Tell him. Don't tell him. Would this set him off, or would he keep control of it? Was he even able to? Would Daniel's intervention be a pointless endeavor? It was all so uncertain. The next few minutes could be another turning point in their lives and they hinged entirely on his reaction to her visitor.

He was happy but cold, and so perched himself on the seat closest to the fire. He grinned at her, wiggling his bare toes near the flames. "I think I froze my feet."

Unable to put this off and banter with him she looked at him steadily, hiding the fear mounting in her heart. "Derek was here this morning to visit."

Michael's smile faded. "Just Derek?"

She nodded, watching him closely. His expression was closed and unreadable as he swirled the tea around and around in his cup. "How is he?"

The question was flat and patently insincere, but Shelley was ecstatic. The bubble of tension in her chest popped and the need to jump up and down and clap her hands like a child at a party was almost overwhelming. She couldn't keep the grin back though, and beamed at him with pride. "He's fine. They're both fine and having a good time."

He nodded wordlessly, then sipped at his tea until she couldn't stand it another minute.

"What are you thinking?" She blurted out.

He put his empty cup down then stretched his hand out toward her. She took it gratefully, sinking to the floor at his feet. "Why, I'm thinking 'Shelley loves me so all is well'.

Laughing, she started to rub his feet, chafing the warmth back into them. They felt like blocks of ice. "You're really not angry?"

"A little. I'm counting before I speak, I'm breathing slow, thinking happy thoughts. It's helping, and it's a hell of a lot better than last time."

Her sigh of relief was huge. Only one more hurdle to go. She put his foot down and started working on the other. "Do you want to know the real reason Derek came over?"

A look of worry crept into his eyes, but he nodded.

Shelley rubbed his foot a little faster, nervous about telling him this part. "He thought you were beating me."

"What?" He exploded, yanking his foot from between her hands.

"Settle down," she said calmly. "I explained. You can't blame him though, for thinking that. He said I was jumpy around him. Between that and the scars and my lip and the bruises on my wrist ...plus he said your possessive attitude gave him the willies." At his horrified expression she added quickly, "Not in those exact words."

Not at all mollified, he stuck his icy foot back in her lap. "What did you tell him?"

"I told him it wasn't like that. I told him we were both assaulted, that I was raped and that we were working on things together. He said if things go badly, if I need help, I can call him anytime, as a friend."

He raised his brows. "As a friend, huh?"

"Yes," she insisted, begging him with a look to believe her. "Just as a friend."

"Whether that is truly how he meant it, I believe that is how you see it and want it, and that's enough for me, Shell."

She had forgotten about his feet until they both worked their way under her sweater. She squealed then started to giggle as his cold toes trailed an icy path across her ribs.

He tortured her for a couple of long minutes before pulling her up to sit on his lap. "Where's my reward, Shelley-belley?"

"What reward? And don't call me Shelley-belly."

"I passed your test, didn't I?" He asked against her lips, pressing teasing little kisses at the corners.

"How do you know it was a test?"

"Wasn't it?" He whispered before threading his hands through the hair at her temples and kissing her properly.

"How about a hot bath," she suggested.

"With you?"

"Could it be a hot bath without me?" She shot back pertly.

He shook his head slowly, clearly remembering the night he walked in on her in the tub. "No bubbles this time. I couldn't see a damn thing."

CHAPTER TWENTY

The plane rolled to a smooth stop and the 'please fasten seat belt' light went off with a ping. Shelley didn't want to get off the plane, she was so nervous. Meeting his family terrified her completely; his parents, five brothers, two sisters and a large handful of spouses and nieces and nephews. They were going to hate her. They wouldn't think she was good enough for Michael; not pretty enough, not witty enough, just not enough. Her stomach churned, threatening upheaval. If she threw up, she would just die of embarrassment.

"You okay, Shell?" Michael's voice intruded on her thoughts. "You're so pale." He reached over to unbuckle her belt, since she hadn't moved to do so herself.

"I'm so scared." It came out as little more than a whisper.

"We're already on the ground, Shell," he pointed out. "I'd say the worst part is over."

"What if they hate me?"

"Hate you?" He just laughed at first, but after taking a closer look at her pasty complexion, he realized how truly terrified she was. "Shelley, they're going to adore you. Just be yourself and don't worry about a thing."

"All right," she said gloomily, taking a big, shaky breath. "I'll try."

Before they left the cabin, she had made Michael draw her his family tree. Of his five brothers, he was the youngest.

Taylor was the oldest at forty, then the twins Keith and Kevin, his sister Drew, then Mark, Jared, Michael at twenty five and lastly, the baby Janet at twenty three.

Of all his siblings, he was the closest to Jared. His expression had been one of bittersweet nostalgia as he shared the memories of his youth with her; describing many of the crazy antics and mischievous plots that had earned them their reputation as pranksters. Despite the differences in their personalities, they could hardly be separated, always choosing each other over other friends. They competed for grades and girls and summer jobs and sometimes fought like demons, all the while giving each other the drive to become better men. They were, he said, as close as two brothers could be - they were the very best of friends. Moving away had been one of the hardest things he had ever done, but as the youngest of so many popular, fun loving and in their own way successful brothers, it had been important for him to strike off on his own and find his own identity and independence.

Jared was supposed to meet them at the gate then drive them to the family home. It was almost a two hour drive - plenty of time for her nerves to settle, she hoped. She spotted him immediately, for the resemblance was impossible to miss. He was a little taller, a little leaner, but the hair, the eyes, the shape of the face was all Michael. Her heart reached out for him instantly, wrapping around him and tucking him into one of the empty chasms gouged out by years and years of lonely yearnings for a family. She couldn't help it, he just looked so much like the man she loved.

Michael spotted him too and excitedly tugged her over to him. The two men locked each other in a bone cracking bear hug, with enough happy shouting and back slapping to make

for a boisterous reunion. She could only ima
going to be like with all of them. Loud
wonderful.

They stepped back, grinning ider
Jared had a small chip in one tooth. She t!
special kind of reckless charm. He looked Michae
thoroughly and Shelley held her breath, waiting for the
reaction, wondering what form it would take. His smile faded
as his eyes skipped over Michael's features, taking in the big
scar crossing over his eye and at his lip. The others were faint
but still discernible to one who knew his face well. He took in
the damaged wrists and the general overall change in his little
brother. He frowned, then shifted his gaze over to her, eyes
widening as he noticed her scars, too.

"What's going on, Mike?" He asked in complete
bewilderment, picking up one of Michael's hands to study the
scars on his wrist. "What the hell happened to you both?"

"Later, Jared. I'll tell everyone later, okay? Right now I
want to introduce you to Shelley McGraw. She's been living at
the cabin with me since this summer."

Jared's mouth fell open. "Why didn't you tell me, man?
I didn't know you were *living together* -" Catching his own
lapse of manners, Jared smiled crookedly at her and took her
hand. "Wonderful to meet you, Shelley."

This was Michael's favourite person in the whole world.
How could she make a good impression when she was a
bundle of raw nerves? She felt her heart slam into her ribs.
"Nice to meet *you*, Jared." She meant to sound breezy and
carefree; casual, but it came out altogether ...pathetic.

Jared looked down at her. "Awww," he said, in the
same tone people use when they see a small animal doing

ing cute. He brought her hand up to show Michael; her ... ty, clammy palm. "She's nervous, Mike. What did you tell ... r about us?" He smiled at her again. "We're not going to eat you up."

She blushed furiously as the two men laughed over her head.

"She's not nervous, Jared. She's scared to death. Let's get out of here."

The windshield of Jared's Explorer was already frosted over on the inside, so they waited with the heat blasting. "We're all anxious to hear what's kept you so quiet for almost six months, Mike. You used to call every week." It was a gentle rebuke, but she could see that for Michael, because of his feelings of guilt, it was a barb that sunk deep into his already tortured conscience.

"I'm sorry, Jared. I will explain, but it's a long story and I don't think I can do it more than once."

Shelley felt herself relaxing again once they were on the highway. The two brothers kept her laughing constantly, giving her a painful stitch in her side and making the hour and a half fly by. Their humor was sharp and witty and they complemented each other perfectly, but it was their laughter mostly that got her going. It was completely infectious. Wouldn't it have been wonderful to have a sister or a brother like Jared - a friend to grow up with and do things with? He was so likable and charming and concerned about his brother that she very much wanted to be cherished by him too, as a sister.

Before she knew it, they turned up a long narrow driveway, lined with large, snow covered white pines. The snow was at least a meter deep, higher even in places where the wind had blown the white powder into drifts. The golden glow from the lamp posts lining the drive caught the icy flakes on the top crust, causing them to sparkle like thousands of tiny diamonds. There were already at least six vehicles parked in the yard, and Shelley experienced another powerful, unsettling surge of panic.

She climbed out of the vehicle on Jared's side, while Mike went around to the back to grab their bags. She stood there in the cold, playing with the zipper on her jacket, pulling it up and down as she fretted about the sudden silence. Jared turned toward her, hands in his pockets, and stared at her boldly. His look was neither lewd nor calculating, but ...assessing. The zipper moved faster. He was probably trying to decide if she was good enough for his brother, or maybe blaming her for Mike's sudden lack of communication. Jared watched her fidget for a moment before surprising her with a hug.

She caught Michael's eye over Jared's shoulder and flashed him a big, happy smile, wanting to share her warm glow of acceptance. He smiled back with a nod of understanding.

"Don't worry so much," Jared said reassuringly before pulling away.

The door to the house opened suddenly, spilling more light onto the driveway and their three chilly figures as they hurried toward the beckoning warmth. A whole crowd waited there at the door, maybe fifteen or twenty people, all shouting happily. They pulled them all inside and Michael was instantly engulfed by the welcoming sea that was his family. She felt overwhelmed and touched by all the joy and love in the room. In all her life she had only had one person happy to see her and he had been too conservative to show it.

The room gradually quieted somewhat as the children were herded back to the play room and the others began to notice what Jared had noticed earlier. The questions flew.

Michael held up a hand. "Settle down, everybody. I promised Jared already that I would explain everything - later. For now, I'd like you all to meet someone very special. This is Shelley."

The welcome was friendly but reserved. Open yet cautious. She couldn't blame them really - Michael hadn't even told them about her, mentioning only that he would be bringing a friend. She felt a little spark of anger at that, although she knew why. He hadn't known how to answer normal questions about their relationship without lying or blurting out the whole ugly truth. 'How did you two meet?' wasn't such a simple question anymore. He didn't want to tell them over the phone.

Although his mother's coloring was lighter, all Michael's brothers and sisters had dark, dark hair like his and the same melting brown eyes. In fact, they all bore such a marked resemblance to each other that it was kind of eerie.

His father came forward first. He was an older version of his boys, with pronounced laugh lines around his eyes and bracketing his mouth. His dark hair had lightened with age and silvered at the temples but he was still a handsome man. He took her hand much as Jared had, except he kissed it.

"I'm enchanted," he said with a smile in a charming French accent, "Welcome to our house, Shelley."

"Thank you. I've been looking forward to meeting you all." She could see out of the corner of her eye, Michael's mother, Faith, watching her avidly, not exactly with suspicion but with a watchfulness that made her feel like she was under a microscope back at the lab. One by one, the family members stepped forward to greet her and welcome her.

The twin boys Keith and Kevin were gorgeous, could have been models even, with a more polished, pretty boy look than the other brothers. Although already very masculine, it was obvious they tried hard to look as rough as their brothers, both sporting two or three day's growth of whiskers. Their sleeves were rolled up over their bulging biceps. They both gave her a brief but friendly hug.

Everyone was introduced to her by name, even the kids, and it wasn't long before her head was spinning in an effort to keep them all straight. She would never remember them all. The kids were getting cranky from hunger and the lateness of the hour, so it was decided that the men should go watch the hockey game while the women and little ones prepared a late supper. Michael looked at her with a worried expression, obviously torn.

Determined not to show her misgivings about being left alone with so many strangers, she gave him a gentle shove. "Go! I'll be fine."

He smiled at her gratefully before being swept into the family room to watch the game and drink beer. A man's heaven could sure be different from a woman's, she thought, smiling after him.

The kitchen was soon chaos, with kids running here and there, yelling with excitement and arguing over who had to do what. Pieces of pepperoni and sausage fell to the floor at regular intervals for the dogs to clean up. The dogs were Jared's - two brindle, muscular Boxers. They were a breeding pair and absolutely gorgeous. Their tags said Thor and Freya, names she thought suited them admirably. They sat near her feet to look with longing at the cheese she was shredding. Their brows wrinkled in apparent concern and Thor, the male, had lengthening, glistening ropes of drool that dangled from his wrinkled flews.

Keith's little boy, Cameron, hauled himself onto the stool next to hers. He held a little block of cheese and a grater in his hand. He grinned at her, looking like a true Daillant with his inky hair and big brown eyes. He studied her closely for a long while, with frank curiosity, grating small bits of mozzarella and eating them. "Are you Uncle Mike's friend?" He asked around a mouthful of white cheese strings.

"Yes, I am."

He ran the little block of cheese over the grater one or two more times before giving up and taking a bite out of the block. "What happened to your face? Were you in a car accident? My friend Brian was in one and he got lines like that on his arm. *He* had to get ten stitches! Did you need stitches?"

His mother, Melina, was just passing by with a pan of partially cooked dough when she heard his innocent but tactless questions. "Cam!" She scolded, automatically taking the rapidly disappearing square of cheese from his little hand. "Don't ask questions like that. It's rude." She looked at Shelley apologetically. "I'm sorry."

"That's okay."

Melina picked up her pan and continued across the kitchen where Mark's wife, Rosalie, slathered pizza sauce on it. As soon as he felt his mother was out of earshot, Cam leaned toward her. "Well, did you? Need stitches?"

Shelley laughed. What a precocious little fellow. "Yes. I got one hundred and twenty stitches."

His eyes got even bigger and Shelley wanted to grab him and hug him he was so cute. "Cool," he said, hopping down to go in search of another snack. "Bye."

At that point, Faith efficiently assumed the role of Kitchen General - issuing calm orders to each of the kids. "Ryan, you can put the cheese on the bottom. Cameron can do the meat, Regan the mushrooms and onions. No, no, Cameron, wait until the cheese is on first. Carey and Colleen can put a bit more cheese on top. Ladies - let's clean up this mess."

When the pizzas were finally popped into the oven, the women sent the kids downstairs to play on their Playstation and settled for a few minutes of much needed peace. Janet sat next to her with a big sigh. "Kids are messy, eh?"

Shelley nodded with a shy smile. She felt a little bit in awe of the young woman. She was beautiful; her glossy hair in a neat but casual twist, her make-up neatly applied and her nails done with an elegant French manicure. Michael had told her she was almost done with school; just one more year of journalism. "Mike says you're a wonderful writer," she ventured in an attempt to make conversation.

Janet dimpled. "Well, my family thinks so, but they're a wee bit biased. Hey," she said, suddenly changing the subject, "has anyone bothered to show you your room yet?"

"Actually, no."

"Come with me and I'll give you the grand tour."

Grabbing their bags, she followed Janet upstairs and settled everything in Michael's old bedroom. After pointing out where the bathroom was and the location of the laundry room, she gave Shelley some fresh towels and an extra thermal blanket from the linen closet. She gave her a quick tour around the beautiful log home, making it back to the kitchen just in time to help dish up the steaming slices of pizza and distribute them to the hungry masses. Every seat and every inch of floor space in the family room was soon occupied.

Michael called her over to him and ignoring her embarrassed protests, pulled her onto his lap and proceeded to eat. "You okay?" He asked gently.

She nodded, chewing thoughtfully. "I bet you were just like Cameron when you were little," she guessed.

"That's what my mother says."

"He's adorable."

"Does that mean I'm adorable?"

She nodded again, with a slow smile.

He rubbed a hand absently over her knee, looking into her eyes. "I want to get it over with tonight, after the kids go to bed. Are you up to it?"

"I think so," she said, touching his hand. She turned her head to find, once again, Faith watching her shrewdly; taking her measure and probably finding her wanting. She pushed Michael's hand off her knee and sat up straight. She pretended to watch the game for the next hour, soothed somewhat by the warm hand on her back, but too soon it was ten o'clock and the last little one was tucked into bed for the night.

The television was clicked off; coffee was poured. The air was thick with quiet expectation. They were expecting an explanation and they were expecting it now.

"Are you sure?" She whispered to Michael.

"I don't want to lie to them. Are you having second thoughts? We talked about this—"

"No," she denied quickly, feeling tears start in her

eyes. "No, I'm just nervous. I wanted them to like me."

"They do. They will," he said with conviction. He gave her a very soft, lingering kiss then turned to face his family. They were all watching with interest, waiting for him to begin. He cleared his throat. "This is very hard for us to talk about, but I - we felt it was important for you to know, and to understand. Before you all fire the same question at me, I didn't call or tell you because I was embarrassed. I didn't want anyone to know."

They all exchanged looks, making sure that everyone was equally uninformed.

"On June sixth, I heard an announcement on the radio," he began in a strong voice. "Two men had robbed a local store and killed a man. They were in the area somewhere. I never knew when Mickey, my neighbour, was up using his cabin, and he would have invited a gang of convicted felons in for coffee." He spared a smile of fond remembrance before continuing with the story. "So, I went to warn him, just in case, maybe have a drink with him and hear the latest about his lovely granddaughter." He looked at Shelley then and she heard a few hushed voices as they made the connection. She blushed, unaware that Michael had even known she existed before that day.

"Anyway, Mickey wasn't there. But the two wanted men were."

"Oh, my God, Michael!" Gasped his mother, before clapping a hand over her mouth. "Oh, what happened?" She asked through her fingers.

"Well, I didn't get to put up much of a fight, I'm afraid. One of them shot me, here," he indicated his upper arm with his finger, "then knocked me out. I was unconscious for the first day."

Voices erupted into chaos. Shelley could catch bits and pieces, but the outrage that someone could harm their Michael was clear. He let the uproar calm down on its own.

"When I came to, they took turns beating on me and r ...and ...beating me." He faltered, clearly unable to force the word out. She knew how hard it was for him to bare himself that way, yet it was so important to him to try.

He looked at his mother, who had tears running silently down her face; of anguish at what he went through, and fear of what he was about to say next. But her look also conveyed love and support. Shelley squeezed his hand, silently urging him to go on.

"For the next four days, they took turns beating me and raping me." He said it really fast, making it sound like one long word.

Shelley watched his family closely, studying everyone and judging their reactions. Not one of them recoiled or avoided his gaze. Their expressions ranged from pained sympathy to protective rage. The women cried for him, the men got angry on his behalf and she could see that no one thought any less of him.

"On the fourth day I begged them to kill me. I couldn't get away - one of them was always watching, and I ...well, I wanted to die. But then on that afternoon, Shelley marched right into the kitchen, mad as a hornet that someone was in her cabin. She looked like an angel." His voice trailed off a bit, as if lost in the memory.

A loud sniffle from one of his sisters brought him back to the present.

"She was smart about it, making them think she had

friends outside, so one of them went out to look. The other one, though, he turned on her. He attacked her with his fists, his feet, his teeth ..." He unconsciously traced the bite mark on her shoulder, circling it through the material of her red sweater. "Then, when she couldn't get up anymore, he broke her arm. He raped her. Right in front of me and I couldn't do a damn thing, not until it was too late, anyway."

When it became apparent that Michael wasn't going to say any more, his father cleared his throat gruffly and asked in a voice thick with emotion, "What happened to them?"

"I killed them. I had to kill them," he added quickly, as if afraid his father would disapprove, but the older man just nodded and his troubled eyes flashed with a glimmer of satisfaction.

Michael held up his hand again. "Wait. There's more."

Everyone quieted once more, looking horrified at the prospect of 'more'.

He laid a hand on Shelley's belly, flattening the protective cover of her roomy sweater. "This is his baby."

Following a moment of stunned silence, there arose complete pandemonium.

"Hold it! Quiet, will you?!" It took several minutes to bring the room to order.

Shelley tried to block the voices out. She was sure that having his family know and support him in this would be healing to his spirit, but the pitying glances they were now sending her way made her feel ashamed, as though they could all picture her pinned naked to the floor by that animal.

It was too much all at once; more than she could handle. All these people, these strangers she had so desperately wanted to think well of her, knew her disgrace.

This would be the foundation for them to build on, to base their perceptions of her on. They were all staring. Her breath started to come faster, yet she couldn't get enough air. She slapped at Michael's hands, struggling to get off his lap, out of his grip, suddenly frantic to get away. She was wrong to come here. She tore from the room and up the stairs, where she flung herself on Michael's old bed in the dark.

The door closed softly behind him sometime later, but she heard it anyway. There was the rustling, sliding sound of his clothes hitting the floor, then the bed dipped down as he sat on the edge and pulled her to him.

She buried her face in his shoulder. "I'm sorry, Mike. I panicked."

He helped her undress, then slipped her under the covers before crawling in beside her.

"Shh, that's okay. I shouldn't have done that to you on your first night here. I didn't think. Meeting family is stressful enough in an ordinary situation. It will be better tomorrow, I promise."

He started to move his hands over her, sweeping them down her arms, her stomach, her legs. She gave herself up to it and to the voice whispering in her ear, forgetting for the moment the judgment she had imagined in the eyes of his loved ones downstairs.

ଓଃ

It was still fairly dark when Shelley opened her eyes, but it was morning. Reaching across the bed for Michael, she was surprised and disappointed to find that he wasn't there. She showered and dressed quickly before tiptoeing down the stairs to the kitchen.

All the women were already up, sitting around the dining table with a cup of coffee. They fell silent when she entered, making her feel like she had been the topic of conversation. She hovered uncertainly at the door, unable to meet their eyes. She was about to do the cowardly thing and turn back when Janet jumped to her feet to pour another cup of coffee. She beckoned Shelley into the room with a friendly smile and wave of her hand.

"Mike said you don't function until you've had your caffeine," she said, handing her the coffee. "He made me promise to say 'Good Morning' and give you this cup and to tell you he would be back before brunch. They've gone to get the Christmas tree," she explained cheerfully. "Tradition. The men chop it down, since they're the loggers." Her eyes twinkled at that. "Then we decorate."

Shelley held up the cup to look at the picture. It was a silly cartoon with a timid grey mouse pushing a big mug of steaming black coffee toward a cat that just happened to be sharpening its nails. The caption at the bottom read, "You're just a pussy cat after you've had your coffee." She snorted and took a sip. They made room for her at the table and conversation started up again in a rally of fond complaints about husbands and kids. She could hear the distant gurgle of running water and even the buzz of morning cartoons. Shelley sipped her coffee silently, content to just listen and absorb the sounds of family. It was nice.

The conversation turned inevitably to last minute Christmas preparations, giving her the opportunity she needed. "Is there a mall close by? I couldn't do any shopping back home - "

Janet perked up. "I have to go into town for some last

minute gifts too - I'll take you. Hey! We can make a day of it, go shopping, maybe some skating. I can show you Drew's studio. That sounds like fun. I have to go get dressed." Excited, she flew from the room without even waiting for confirmation.

Faith shook her head. "That girl does get herself worked up."

One by one, drawn by the sound of stirring children, everyone got up from the table and left the room except Faith and herself. Shelley stared at the tablecloth for a moment, determined to stay and have a nice, normal conversation with this woman. About what though? Her grandchildren? Michael? The weather?

Her thoughts were interrupted by a light touch on her arm. Startled, she looked up into the older woman's face.

"Shelley, I wanted to thank you for being there for Michael, for helping him through such an awful thing. Since he chose not to …confide in his family, it means a lot to all of us that someone was there for him to turn to."

"Oh, it's not that he didn't want to-"

"No, I understand," Faith interrupted kindly. "I really do. He told us when he was ready and that's enough. Thank you," she repeated. "For being there for him."

"I love him," she answered simply.

"I can see that." Faith seemed to be searching for the right words. "I felt in my heart that something was wrong but …I didn't want to push. I feel so very guilty that I didn't go to him." She shook her head sadly. "Anyway, despite the circumstances, believe me when I say nothing would make me happier than to welcome you to our family."

Shelley felt her lower lip start to wobble and her eyes

fill up with tears. Though she damned her self a thousand times over, she started to sob right there at the table. "I'm sorry," she wailed. "That just means so much to me. I didn't want to come between you if you didn't like me, because Mike loves you all so much." She mopped ineffectively at her face with her sleeve, but couldn't stem the tears leaking from her eyes any more than she could the words spilling from her mouth. "I listen to his stories, and I look at his pictures of you all sometimes, and I wish with everything that is in me that it was my family..." She trailed off finally, embarrassed at her own behaviour. "I have to go get ready."

Faith stood up with her, but held her back, drawing her into a loving embrace. "We are your family now, honey. Now go find little Janet and buy my son a Christmas present."

ങ

Much to Shelley's relief, conversation between them was easy and relaxed as they drove to town, for Janet was a veritable chatterbox. Shelley was enthralled by tales of her college mishaps and disastrous dates. She had an ability to take an everyday, almost boring event and spice it up so much in the telling that it became an adventure.

Drew's studio, 'Picture This' was closed for the holidays, so they were able to stroll through without interruption. There was one whole wall of Michael's work - a lot of which she had already seen in his albums. Janet led her to a panel of three or four large, beautifully framed photographs. "These are his newest ones." She pointed to one with a dramatic sigh. "This is my favourite." Captured in those few fleeting moments after sunset, against the background of calm water and smooth beach sand were the silhouettes of a man and woman kissing.

Shelley looked at it for a long time, remembering the night they spent in the water at their beach. "He has a real talent, doesn't he?" She said at last.

"Oh, yes," Janet agreed with enthusiasm. "Wait till you see Drew's stuff."

They spent a full hour looking at her work; mostly charcoal sketches and oil paintings. They were truly brilliant and quite expensive. She was impressed not only at the quality, the talent of each piece, but the incredible variety. Drew painted flowers, landscapes, stylized fruit and portraits of human models. She sketched the forms of animals, studies of leaves and moths and even fairies. They were incredible.

One corner of the studio was devoted to figurines. They were carved or sculpted out of a light, porous material that she had never seen before, but they were charming and very life like. There were bears, raccoons, different breeds of dogs, cats, even dragons.

"Mark did these," Janet pointed out.

Surprised, Shelley picked one up for a closer look, admiring the detail. It looked like Dawson and she felt a little pang in her chest as she thought about how much she missed the dogs. "I'd love to buy this for Michael," she said wistfully.

Janet looked up from the sample album she was flipping through. "Oh, you can't! Mark made him some for Christmas." She smiled. "Sorry, that would be too easy."

Shelley laughed. "Yeah, I guess it would. So, which one of your parents passed down all this artistic talent?"

"Well, neither. That's the weirdest thing. If either of them had it, they didn't pursue it," Janet said with a shake of her head as she locked the door behind them. They walked briskly down the main street, which was busy with last minute shoppers like themselves. "So, do all of you have these amazing talents?" Shelley asked interestedly.

"Well, all the boys sing beautifully and have a natural understanding of music. Drew and I learned an instrument but we're not very good and we can't sing a note - not in tune anyway. Let's see …Taylor's the most talented musically. He can play all our instruments and he only has to hear something once to play it. He teaches music at the high school. Mark carves those figurines in his spare time. Keith and Kevin decided they would rather play hockey than do anything artsy. And I'm the only writer. What have I left out? Oh, yes, of course you know Drew is an artist, but Jared is too, sort of. He's a really good cartoonist. They used to run his comic strip in the local paper every week, but as you can imagine, he's not too good with deadlines. Plus he has the best singing voice of all the boys."

They moved down the row of small stores as they talked, stopping inside each one to browse and wait for inspiration to strike. Thankfully, Shelley didn't have to buy a gift for everyone. Michael told her the family was so large, they decided years ago to draw two names for regular gifts and then two more for small stocking presents. They hit every store in town in under two hours and by the time they reached Janet's car their arms were laden with brightly colored bags.

Enjoying the easy companionship, Shelley readily agreed to Janet's suggestion that they go for coffee with some of her friends. She even agreed, with some trepidation, to go skating with her at the river.

ꙮ

Blasted skates! Shelley pulled herself up from the ice yet again, wind milling her arms for balance. Her ankles flopped back and forth uselessly in a desperate and ungainly attempt to remain upright.

Janet though, skated graceful circles around her, doing an occasional spin or jump. She was smiling, laughing even at her expense, but the face was so like Michael's that Shelley couldn't find it in her to be offended. "This isn't working," she found herself saying, "I'm just too awkward."

Janet stopped suddenly in front of her, kicking up a spray of ice. She put one mittened hand over her mouth. "Oh, my God! I didn't think! You shouldn't even *be* skating. Falling down like that - I forgot, completely forgot that you were preg-" She gasped again then winced at her perceived thoughtlessness. "-nant. I'm sorry."

"It's not your fault, Janet. Frankly, I just didn't realize how much time I was going to spend on my butt." She carefully maneuvered herself over to a brightly colored bench; one of many conveniently placed on the bank of the frozen river. Collapsing gratefully onto it, she smiled at the young woman reassuringly. "Don't worry about it."

Janet followed her to the bench and sat beside her. She rubbed at her legs to warm them for a minute or two, looking over at Shelley from time to time. "Shelley," she began tentatively, "would it be horrible and insensitive of me to ask you about it? The baby I mean?"

Shelley was startled by the question, though she knew she shouldn't have been. Janet was a journalist, after all. "No," she answered slowly, realizing she had come a long way in her acceptance of this pregnancy. She was not afraid. Janet was not here to pass judgment. "What is it you want to know?"

Janet shifted on the bench, turning toward her. "Are you going to keep it, you and Michael?"

She shook her head. "No, I don't think so. I don't think I could. Mike wants to though," she added absently, thinking of their first explosive argument about it.

Janet's eyes opened wide. "Really?" She questioned incredulously. "But why?"

Shelley nodded. "Hm, hmm. He thinks it will be our saving grace. Our salvation. The only positive in a big mess of negatives. How ever you want to word it."

The younger woman frowned, silent for a time. "How is he doing really, after ...you know, how is he handling it all?"

Shelley chipped idly at the ice with the toe pick on her skate, wondering how to answer such a complicated question. She was tempted to give her the sugar coated version, but as his sister, obviously caring and concerned, she decided to tell her the truth. She needed to confide in someone. She needed advice, and who better than his sister? "Better. Better all the time, but still so angry. He was pretty good at hiding it at first, but either I'm getting better at reading the signs or he's getting worse at controlling it." She thought of the signs that prefaced one of his rages; the dilated pupils, twitching hands. His wonderful, soothing voice hardening, clipping his words and sharpening them into deadly little weapons.

"No," Janet said emphatically. "Michael doesn't have a temper. I've never seen him angry. Never."

Shelley nodded miserably. "He does now. Full blown rages. He screams at me and throws things, breaks them ..."

Wiping at the moisture stubbornly welling from her eyes, Janet shrugged self consciously. "I'm sorry. It's just so sad. He used to be so confident and happy, cocky, you know?

But in a charming way. Always cheerful and funny." She dug a tissue from her pocket and blew her nose noisily. "I just hope that part of him isn't gone forever."

Shelley touched her hand, trying to comfort her. "I don't think it is. I didn't know him before, but as hard as this is for him to deal with, he hasn't forgotten how to laugh or play. He hasn't lost his passion for his work or his love for his family. He'll get through this - once he learns how to quit hating himself."

"Why would he hate himself? He was assaulted for God's sake."

"I don't know how to explain," Shelley said. She took a deep breath of cold winter air and let it out again, watching it condense into a moist puff around her face. "Rape makes you feel ...small, maybe? And unworthy. Ashamed. Dirty. Violated. But it's different for him even, don't you see? Just by its very unnaturalness. I don't think he can even put into words how low this has made him feel. He feels robbed of his very masculinity. He recoils from himself and the shame sometimes takes him to a dark place." She fell silent for a moment, as she watched two little girls skate by, hand in hand. She envied them their innocence.

"When he's hurting I just want to take him in my arms and hold him tight and make all the pain go away, but I can't. He's got to work it through himself, just like I do."

Janet was looking at her with those lovely brown eyes, her Michael-eyes. She couldn't read what was there in her expression; it was concern, maybe empathy, but it was a soft look. No woman had ever looked at her that way before. It made her feel close and understood in a way only Michael had been able to.

"You really, really love my brother, don't you?"

She smiled. "Do you know what he said to me at the hospital? He said he wanted to be all things to me, and that's what he is. He's the father I lost, the brother I never had, the friend I always wanted and the lover I only dreamed about - " She stopped suddenly at the look on Janet's face and blushed. "T.M.I?"

"Yeah, way too much information," Janet agreed with a laugh.

"Sorry," she said, embarrassed. "I forgot myself and got carried away."

"So, what's so great about him?" Janet asked with a mischievous smile that lightened the mood considerably.

Shelley didn't even have to stop and think. The answers just started spilling out. "I love the way he sings when he's cooking, the way he loves his dogs, the way he can see so much through his camera lens and capture it, the way he cares about his family and me. I love his eyes when they go all deep and dark like melted chocolate. And I love the way his two front teeth are just a little bit bigger than the rest. It makes his smile really special, don't you think?"

Janet snorted.

Undaunted, Shelley continued with her list. "I love his height and his shoulders and the way his hair starts to curl around his collar when it gets too long. And I love the way he always smells like pine trees -"

"Oh God, stop it! You're making me sick. You made your point."

They joked back and forth as they changed back into their boots and sipped the hot chocolate Janet had purchased from a busy vendor in the park. Though she hated to ruin the happy mood, Shelley felt she needed to ask about Michael's past now, while they were alone. She might not get another chance.

"Janet," she said gravely. "I need to ask you something."

"What?" She asked, sitting up straight in alarm.

Shelley leaned in a little closer and lowered her voice, embarrassed that she had to ask these questions and not sure where to start. "Mike had girlfriends in high school, right?"

"Yeah, a few. Why?"

"Was he ...possessive or jealous? Controlling?"

"No," Janet scoffed. "Hardly. Why?" She asked again. "Why are you asking?"

Shelley found herself telling her about Michael's reaction to the letter from her university, to Constable Matthews in the restaurant and again to Derek's visit. "He was very, very angry. He admitted to me even, that he doesn't want anyone else in my life, at all. He returned most of my mail, he wouldn't take me to town ...The thing is though, that it's getting worse instead of better."

Janet looked troubled. "Has he hit you?"

Shelley nodded reluctantly. "Just once."

Janet looked devastated. "No, Shelley. Michael was anything but possessive. He had no interest in serious relationships. I just don't know what to say. Maybe ...maybe Mom and Dad will know what to do-"

"No, no, Janet. I don't want to tell them about that. We'll work through it. I just needed to know if that's how he was before. I didn't think so." She stood up and threw her empty paper cup in the garbage bin. "I guess we should go, eh? It's getting late."

Janet, Shelley was soon to discover, was like a Cheerio - unsinkable. She bounced back from their serious, depressing conversation quickly, declaring that moping wouldn't solve a thing. As a result, they were once again chatting happily as they bustled their shopping bags through the door. They shrugged out of their winter clothes and stomped the sticky clumps of snow from their feet.

"Where have you been?!" Intruded an angry voice, so loud that it dropped between them like a bomb. They sprang back with a cry and their bags fell to the floor in a jumbled pile.

Janet just stared at Michael, her eyes rounded in disbelief. His expression was thunderous and so foreign to the Michael she knew, she clearly didn't know how to react.

"What the hell were you two doing? Why did you keep her out so long, Janet? Didn't it occur to either of you that I might be worried when you didn't show up for brunch?" His voice rose with each question he fired at them.

Finally finding her voice, Janet tried to defend them both. "We were just shopping, Mike, and skating. I introduced her to some of my friends and we had fun."

"Fun?!" He roared as he stepped closer, crowding them with his height. "With who? Where'd you go?"

"None of your busin-" she began rebelliously, in typical sister fashion, only to be interrupted by Shelley, who stepped forward to grab Michael's hands.

"Mike, stop. Take a deep breath and think about what you're doing."

He tried to shake his hands free but she held on tightly. "What *I'm* doing?!" He yelled.

"Please."

He looked into her eyes for a long moment before pulling his hands free. He smoothed his palm over his jaw, visibly agitated and breathing hard as though he had run miles to get there. His hand shook.

They all stood there, silent, watching each other, waiting for the awful tension of the moment to pass.

He took a deep, calming breath and then another. His was the voice that broke the silence, and when it did it was even and low pitched. "I was worried."

"I know."

"I'm sorry."

"Me too. We should have called."

He lifted his shoulders in a helpless gesture that was far more eloquent in its simplicity than any string of words could have been. Just as clear to her as his outward anger was his remorse, his frustration and despair at his own lack of control. "I can't protect you if I don't know where you are."

She reached up to give him a hug and a kiss. "It's not your job to protect me. Now, I'm going to put my gifts under the tree." She kissed him once more, a peck on the chin, then bent to sort the bags on the floor.

Janet stepped close to him then, sticking her face into his shoulder and breathing deeply.

"Jan?" He questioned in confusion. "What are you doing?"

"Shelley thinks you smell good, like pine trees. Frankly, I'm not getting it."

Shelley laughed merrily without looking up from the assortment of bags. "You weren't supposed to tell him, Janet," she scolded.

"Sorry, but he doesn't."

"He does too. He smells good."

Michael gingerly lifted the collar of his shirt and sniffed at it.

"You guys were discussing how I smell?" He asked, sounding affronted. "What else did you talk about, dare I ask?"

"Oh, your many quirks and attributes," Janet answered vaguely. She slapped him on the back. "I almost gagged, Mike. I didn't want to hear another word about you - that's why we finally came home." With a secret smile at Shelley, Janet selected her bags from the pile and left the foyer with a cheerful whistle.

Michael hunkered down then, to help her with her parcels. "What else did you talk about? You didn't tell her anything embarrassing, did you?"

"Nothing," she said, waving a hand in dismissal, then grinned at him. "Nothing I'm going to tell you, anyway."

"Oh, come on. Tell me."

"No way. It was just girl talk."

"Just one thing," he wheedled.

Shelley balanced on her heels, sitting back to look at him. He looked like he was going to just explode with curiosity. "I told her I loved your teeth."

His face fell. He looked more than a little disappointed. "My teeth?" He echoed in apparent disbelief.

"Yes, I love your teeth."

He moved in a little closer. "So you love my teeth and the way I smell?" She could hear the thread of laughter in his voice. "What else do you love about me?"

"Your family. I love your family."

"What else?" He whispered now, against her lips, before his mouth opened over hers, hot and demanding in the kind of kiss she loved to share with him.

"If you two were looking for the mistletoe, you're way off," interrupted his mother in a dry voice. "We're about to decorate the tree, Shelley, if you're interested."

Shelley sprang back so quickly she hit the wall behind her and she could feel the familiar colour of mortification flooding her cheeks. Of course they would be caught kissing like teenagers on the floor of the foyer. Of course it would be his mother. Naturally.

"Yes," she said as coolly as she was able. "I'd love to help." She scrambled to pick up the gifts again. "I need to put these under the tree anyway."

She got to her feet, dropping half the boxes that had spilled earlier from their bags. Bending carefully at the knee to retrieve them, she lost another for every two she picked up. She was annoyed with herself for being so inept, but more with Michael for putting her in such an awkward situation. He was laughing at her. Both of them were.

"Go ahead, Mom." Michael said, "I'll help her with these."

"That was your fault," she hissed as soon as they were alone again.

He shrugged one shoulder in casual dismissal. "I'm sure it was obvious you weren't interested in kissing me back," he said outrageously, with more than a touch of sarcasm.

"Ohhh-" she steamed.

"Shhh," he whispered with a boyish grin, placing a finger over her lips. "I have a surprise for you tonight. We've been working on it all day."

She forgot her irritation and embarrassment instantly. "You do? A surprise?"

He nodded excitedly. "So be good," he teased, before grabbing the parcels and leading her into the living room.

Decorating the tree with so many people was a novel experience for Shelley, and a wonderful one. It was confusing with so many hands, and to be honest, the spruce looked downright ugly when they were done; the lights were clumped in spots, the angel listed precariously at the top, the garland was twisted around half the ornaments, hiding them, and the kids put way too much tinsel on, but she had never had so much fun.

The whole family just sat around for over an hour, drinking holiday cider or eggnog, reminiscing about past Christmases and telling funny stories. It was a time Shelley would remember always, a precious moment that if she could, she would capture forever. Bottle it maybe so when she felt the need she could simply uncork it to experience it all again. To smell the real smells of Christmas; roasting turkey and the sharp scent of evergreen. Or to hear the happy sounds of children laughing and a crackling fire. Or see so many lovable people gathered together in a room made festive and homey with pine boughs, candles and homemade decorations. To taste the cider and sample once again from the trays of sinful baking. To feel Michael next to her and experience the kind of joy she had never, ever known at Christmas.

It so moved her that she found herself lifting her glass in a toast. She meant it to be silent and private, but Michael caught her eye. She shook her head, as if to tell him it was nothing, but he persisted, refusing to look away. So she lifted her glass again and spoke quietly, so only he would hear. "To Scott and Mark, for bringing us together and making me a better, stronger person."

She thought for a moment that she had made him angry, but after a lengthy pause, he lifted his own glass and touched its rim lightly to hers. "To Scott and Mark."

☙

After dinner, everyone shoved their chairs back from the table, some even unsnapping their pants.

"Why?" Groaned Janet. "Why do I eat until I'm in utter agony? Where's the logic?"

"It's tradition," explained her mother. "And it's insulting to the cook if you don't eat until you're in pain."

They all nodded gravely, grasping the excuse. No one moved, no one spoke; minds dulled and bodies weighed down by too much food. Except Michael. He shifted continuously in his seat, fiddled with his cutlery, flashed her big smiles. He practically emanated waves of excitement. He shared secret looks with his brothers that left her wondering just what kind of surprise he had in store for her.

Suddenly, he shot to his feet and began to stack dishes and clear the table. Everyone watched in amazement as he systematically and single handedly loaded the dishwasher, packaged leftovers for everyone to take home, and wiped the table. He even swept the floor and brewed coffee and tea.

Shelley looked around the table. They all just watched him, held transfixed by this, what must be a rare performance indeed, if she was to judge by the expressions on their faces. He gave the shiny counters a final wipe, folded the dish cloth just so and circled behind his mother. Bending to her, he kissed her cheek. "Thank you for a lovely dinner, Mom. You outdid yourself again."

Out of the corner of her eye, Shelley caught Keith mouthing the word 'lovely?' with a look of incredulous surprise on his handsome face. Kevin, his twin, started to laugh then, setting off a reaction as everyone else joined in.

"Let's give him a break," suggested his oldest brother Taylor between chuckles, "and move into the other room."

All the brothers, six total, appeared in the living room after everyone else, each with an instrument in hand. Michael hushed the room. "I'd like to sing Shelley a song now," he announced with the most irresistible little boy smile she had ever seen on a grown man. It was self satisfied, mischievous and a little bit vulnerable. "It's a Bryan Adams song, called 'I'm Ready'."

Shelley burst out laughing, causing the entire family to look at her strangely. Of course, they couldn't know that every time she asked him to sing, he would say 'I'm not ready.' She covered her mouth with her hand, to hide both her laughter and her excitement. Michael understood her laughter and he winked at her.

At his signal, the room was filled with magic. It began softly, with the beautiful strains of Taylor's cello and Keith's guitar. Michael looked straight at her and began to sing. His voice was rich and husky and it made her heart do flip-flops in her chest.

> "*I'd like to see you*
> *Thought I would let you know*
> *I want to be with you, every day,*
> *Cause I got a feeling*
> *That's beginning to grow*
> *There's only one thing I can say"*

The music built up slowly behind him, adding the violins and the piano as he reached the chorus.

"I'm ready - to love you
I'm ready - to hold you
Baby, I'm ready, to love you
As ready as I'm going to be"

Between verses Michael played a wind instrument, a Celtic one called a low whistle. It sort of looked like a flute, only played vertically. The ethereal sound gave her goosebumps. It was haunting and so very beautiful that it brought a lump to her throat. Although the song was a perfect choice, the sweeping music and sexy voice had such a powerful effect on her that it wouldn't have mattered what he was singing.

When the music died away all eyes turned to her expectantly. Michael came to her and handed her a box, roughly the size of a toaster. "We only pick one present out of the bag on Christmas Eve. This is it. Open it."

She took it from him and unwrapped it with care, slowly removing the paper without ripping it to make the moment last. Peeling back the cardboard flaps, she peered inside. It was full to the top with green Styrofoam packing. With an eager smile, she plunged her hand into it and fished around, spilling little green pieces onto the floor. Her fingers bumped into a small object on the bottom. It was velvety. It was ...on a stick? She felt around, frowning in concentration and finally pulled it out. It was shaped like a red rose; a velvet bud on a leafy green stem.

"May I?" Michael asked, reaching for it. He grasped the red bud and snapped the top half back to reveal a ring nestled in the satiny bed.

It was fashioned from interconnecting gold hoops to

show two hands clasped together over a central heart. She had never seen one, but she knew it was called a love ring, because although the hoops could be separated, they could never be torn apart.

He took her hand. "Shelley Rae McGraw, will you marry me?"

She was stunned. Completely floored. They had never even discussed it. She couldn't think beyond the pounding of her heart, so she did as it bid her and opened her arms wide. "Yes. Yes, of course I'll marry you. I told you, didn't I?" She asked, hugging him tightly, "That if you sang to me I would fall hopelessly and irrevocably in love with you?"

"I was counting on it," he said, then kissed her soundly in front of his whole family. They all cheered and the next half hour passed in a flurry of hugs and kisses and heart felt congratulations.

The next couple of hours were spent singing Christmas carols with the kids. For once Shelley didn't care that she couldn't sing; she joined in loudly, even, after much prodding, singing a verse of 'Silent Night' all by herself. She clapped enthusiastically for the children after each of their solos and heckled the adults for more.

When it came to Jared's turn for a solo, Michael lunged at him playfully to try to cover his mouth, but Jared darted around the piano. "Don't sing it this year," Michael ordered.

"I want to." Jared sounded hurt by such an insensitive suggestion. He opened his mouth to begin, but every time he did, Michael would hum part of the song, but in the wrong key.

"Michael!" Scolded his mother. "What are you doing? Let him sing. It's tradition."

He sat back sullenly. Shelley leaned toward him to whisper, "What's wrong with you? You're being a baby. Janet told me he can sing better than any of you."

"I know he can sing better than me," he hissed back quietly. "I don't want *you* to hear him sing!"

"Why not, for God's sake?"

He just glared at her until she figured it out. "What, you think I'll want to marry him instead because he has a better voice?" She just threaded her fingers through his and shook her head at him, waiting for Jared to begin.

He did sing beautifully, like an angel really. It was the most powerful, unforgettable version of 'O Holy Night' that she had ever heard, but his voice didn't wrap around her heart like Michael's did. She squeezed his hand reassuringly and brought it up to her heart.

He smiled sheepishly at her and the matter was promptly forgotten as they all stood up to get ready to go to church for the midnight mass. By the time they crawled into bed that night, Shelley was exhausted but happier than she could ever remember being.

03

A combination of things woke her in the morning; the happy squeal of a young child, the sound of water running in the bathroom down the hall and the feel of warm lips moving on her neck. Rubbing the sleep from her eyes with one hand, she ran the other through Michael's hair, playing with it. "Can't we have Christmas in bed?" She groaned with a little stretch.

"We can," Michael allowed in a muffled voice, since his face was still buried in her neck. "I don't know if everyone will fit in here with us though."

"We could start a new tradition," she suggested.

"Let's do that," he agreed softly.

The door swung open, and little Cameron's face peered around it. He wore a pair of Spiderman pajamas and clutched a ratty teddy bear under one arm. "It's Christmas," he announced as though ignorance of the date was the only possible explanation for them to still be in bed. "Aren't you coming down to see what Santa brought you?"

"Absolutely, Cam," Michael said. "I was just trying to convince your lazy auntie to get out of bed."

"Liar!" Shelley accused, whipping out her pillow to bean him over the head. Before he could retaliate, she scrambled off the bed, grabbed Cam's hand and her robe and raced out the door, pausing in the hall just long enough to shove her arms through the sleeves of the fuzzy garment and loosely knot the belt.

"He'll get you later," Cameron predicted wisely.

"Probably, but don't worry. I'm tough."

With ill suppressed excitement, he shifted the stuffed bear to a more comfortable position. "C'mon, Shelley, hurry. We can't open our presents 'til everyone comes down."

"Well, lead the way little guy, before your Uncle Mike gets me."

By the time he clumped down the stairs after them in his boxers and a T-shirt, she and Cam were seated safely in the crowd around the Christmas tree. He met her eyes as he sat across from her and gave a cheerful wink that somehow promised retribution.

One of Taylor's kids was elected as 'Santa's helper' to hand out presents from the giant stocking. It had to be at least six feet high and stuffed full with little presents. She handed them out one at a time and waited for each person to open it before moving on to the next. The kids got books, movies and CD's, small toys and gadgets, and the adults got little personal items like a new sable paint brush for Drew or a box of Turtles for Michael's sweet tooth.

Shelley got two items from the stocking. One was a framed cartoon drawing of her as a 'mad scientist' in her microbiology lab. On the counter in the drawing was piled a stack of empty petri plates and she held aloft a sandwich dripping with agar and globs of colorful bacterial growth. It was hilarious and she loved it. Of course it was from Jared. From Janet she received a set of paperback books she couldn't wait to read and a bookmark with a written promise to give Shelley the first copy of her book, if it was published.

They let the kids open their presents under the tree next and they all rapidly disappeared, gone like a puff of smoke with their new clothes, Playstation games, in-line skates and Barbies. The atmosphere was more relaxed after that. The grownups drank coffee and opened their gifts at a leisurely pace that would, quite simply, have killed the kids.

Shelley had drawn Michael's father, Sylvain, from the pot of names, and after much thought had decided on a sheep skin hunting vest. He seemed to really like it, declaring, "Just what I needed, since Kevin stole my other one."

The other name she had picked was Mark's wife, Rosalie. It was difficult buying a gift for someone you didn't know at all. She had asked Mike for suggestions but he had only shrugged, saying she liked to read, cook and run. With so little information to go on, she had decided to put together a baking gift basket, filling it with cookie cutters, two recipe books, a cookie and cake decorator kit, pretty oven mitts, jars of spices and cinnamon sticks wrapped in ribbon.

Although it too, was well received, she noticed that there were very few gifts that weren't creatively homemade and she felt self conscious. The presents she picked out seemed more and more inadequate as 'Santa's helper' continued to pass the gaily wrapped boxes around.

After much prompting she opened one of hers next, the one from Faith. It was a photo album full of pictures of Michael growing up, with little stories and expressions, special notations like when he took his first step and what his first word was. She loved it. The little card attached said, 'The single most difficult thing a mother can do is let her child go, because she knows that people will try to knock him down. She knows that sometime, he will fall. In passing this to you, I can let go now with a light heart, knowing that you have already caught him.' Shelley was moved by the blessing and smiled a tearful thanks.

As much as she loved the gift, it was the one from Michael that took her breath away. It was a large, framed photograph of her, the one of her laughing, but somehow superimposed over two other pictures. It appeared that she was sitting in a field of colorful flowers, leaning back into the tall grass, and hovering in the air all around her, lighting on her hair, her knee, everywhere, were hundreds of monarch butterflies. It was like a fairy tale, magical yet so realistic even she almost believed she must have been there. She told him how much she loved it and that it was the best present she had ever received. She meant every word and it must have shown on her face, for he positively beamed with pride and excitement.

"I have a whole year," she said with feeling as she

touched the presents laid out before her, "to make you all something as wonderful as these."

Her gift to Michael was the last to be opened. He held the pendant between thumb and forefinger, letting the thin silver chain dangle across the backs of his fingers. He looked at it for a long time, an impossibly long time, with a frustrating lack of expression.

"The phoenix," she explained. "A mythical bird that dies by fire every one hundred years, then rises again from the ashes, completely renewed." She hoped he understood that he could do the same, that he could bring himself up and out of the ashes of his ordeal. He could start again and be a better man because of it.

Finally, he flipped it over, and though he rubbed his thumb back and forth over the inscription, 'all is well, love Shelley', he didn't read it aloud. Her heart sank as she realized he didn't seem to like it, but she ruthlessly stomped on the growing need in her to babble excuses and explanations, reasons why she had bought such a gift. She saw his brothers send uneasy glances to each other, obviously as confused by his reaction as she was.

"It's a moonstone," she offered despite herself, to the absolute silence of the room. "It captures the sheen of the moon to bring good fortune."

Michael still stared at the charm, seemingly fixated. Janet shifted uncomfortably in her seat and Shelley had the further realization that now they probably all thought she was some kind of new age nut; into tarot cards, incantations and crystals. She wasn't, but she had liked the symbolism of both the phoenix and the stone. Unable to control herself, she babbled some more. "The stone is symbolic of the moon, of tenderness and ..." She swallowed hard and it sounded loud in the stillness, "of lovers."

Pushing aside her embarrassment at being on display like they were, she crawled over to him and her hand moved to his knee to touch it softly. "Michael?"

He looked up at her finally. His gaze was troubled, his eyes bright and glassy and very close to betraying him.

"I can get you something else," she whispered, trying to ease the pendant from his grip, but he pulled it away from her with a jerk.

"No!" Then more softly. "No, I like it. I love it," he corrected, placing it deliberately in her palm. "Put it on for me."

Michael didn't know how to explain his unexpected reaction to the simple chain and pendant beyond a peculiar sense of identifying with it. It just clicked inside him in a rare moment of clarity, triggering an embarrassing array of emotions.

Mighty, yet gentle and delicately fashioned, the bird seemed to surge from its nest of hellish flame, not with fear or desperation but with purpose, determination and even joy. Finally nudged toward understanding by Shelley in this sweet and insightful way, he was beginning to see what she had known for a long time. He had been wallowing in his hell, running around blindly in denial and shame, only working his way deeper in. He had to stop. He had to take it all in, use it and rise above it.

She fastened the clasp around his neck then sat back to look at him. Suddenly oblivious to the presence of others, she reached up to him, to run her fingers along his cheekbones then down along the line of his jaw. He didn't know how to tell her what the gift meant to him, didn't have the words inside him to explain. *I feel it. I understand. I can do this now. I love you.* He wanted to shout these things to make her understand, but the words seemed small and inadequate. She held his gaze for a long moment, then nodded almost imperceptibly. He let his lips touch briefly to hers before whispering in her ear. "All *is* well. Merry Christmas."

The remainder of the day was wiled away in a lazy fashion. Taylor, Keith, Mark and Kevin left with their families, promising to come back New Year's Eve, leaving the house strangely quiet and empty. Jared and Michael decided out of boredom to teach her how to play poker. No one had enough change on them so they played for jelly beans and lemon drops. Unfortunately, the game was declared an equal loss for all parties when the steadily shrinking pot finally and mysteriously disappeared.

Sleepy from the inactivity, Michael fell asleep beside her on the couch around three o'clock, and she used the time to get to know his favorite brother a little better. While they were chatting, Jared pulled out a small bag, one which was obviously familiar to his dogs, for they scrambled to their feet so fast, one almost did the splits on the slippery surface of the hardwood floor. He dug in the bag and tossed Thor a giant rawhide bone, before he had a chance to get the drool started. The other one sat at his feet, pleading with her eyes.

"Can I give her one?" Shelley asked.

"Sure." He tossed her a thin, brown treat in a triangular shape.

"What is this thing?" Freya was starting to whine softly, making the cords in her muscular neck stand out. Her eyes were big and they darted eagerly from her to the treat and back again.

"It's a pig ear."

"Yeah, but what is it?"

"No, it *is* a pig ear," he repeated with more emphasis.

Just then she noticed the fine network of blood vessels still visible in the dried ear. "Yuck!" She squealed, barely resisting the urge to toss it back. Freya, obviously tired of waiting for instruction, flopped down to her belly and then rolled right over. "Oh, here baby, good girl."

Despite her eagerness, the boxer took the treat gently, briefly caressing her fingers with the little hairs on her velvety lips.

"She's sweet, Jared."

"Thank you," he beamed, proud as any father of his baby.

They talked about dogs for a long time, then his drawing. She learned who did what in the sawmill the brothers took over from Sylvain. It was the largest, most successful one in the area. The conversation however, was cleverly steered back to her time and time again, despite her attempts to avoid it. She found that subtlety wasn't one of Jared's virtues.

"Have you decided what you're going to do about the baby?"

No one besides Janet had mentioned her pregnancy, or even acknowledged it in any way since the announcement that first night, so the question again caught her off guard.

He smiled at her reaction. "I don't like pretending things don't exist," he explained. "I'd rather face them head on, right away."

"I think ...I've decided to give it up. I want babies, I do, but I can't help but wonder how I will feel about this child as it grows. I don't want it to feel unloved or unwanted and I won't be able to help how I feel. Do you think that's wrong?"

He shrugged sympathetically. "No, but it doesn't matter what I think. I don't envy you your decision." He stood up with a stretch. "Mike's making me sleepy just looking at him, I'm going to give that a try." He was at the door when he turned around to say, "If you keep it, I've had a little practice at being an uncle. I'll love it the same as all my nieces and nephews."

She smiled at him gratefully, then he left her to her thoughts. She circled round and round the problem in her mind as she often did, until she fell asleep beside Michael on the couch.

○₃

Later that evening, after a filling dinner of turkey leftovers, Shelley was stretched out on the rug in front of the television, watching 'City of Angels' with Janet. Michael sauntered in and before she even realized what was happening, he had rolled her onto her back and straddled her hips.

"Remember this morning?" He asked. "The pillow?"

She nodded.

"Time for my revenge." He smiled his bad boy smile and began to tickle her, expertly and ruthlessly. "This could get ugly, Janet," he called over his shoulder, "you may want to leave the room."

But Janet didn't move, other than angle her body for a better view.

"Stop," Shelley begged weakly. "Oh stop, Mike, I can't breathe." But he went on tickling, on and on, his long fingers unerringly finding her every sensitive spot, and she went on laughing. Before long, her laughter changed, becoming silent; the kind where time stands still and the lungs fail to draw in enough air to sustain it. Her muscles went so lax that she was incapable of even the attempt to bat his hands away.

Finally, after a desperate eternity, it stopped and silence reigned once more. She dragged in one wonderful lung full of air before smacking him on the side of the head.

"Oh," Janet said in sympathy from across the room, "Oh, he's done it, hasn't he? Made you pee your pants?"

Michael loomed over her with fingers poised, anxiously awaiting her answer.

"Yes!" She bit out furiously.

Michael's arms shot up into the air in the age-old sign of victory. "Yes!" He shouted, as though he had just caught the fly-ball that ended the inning. "Haven't lost my touch," he boasted, getting off of her and hitching his pants in a perfect Don Knots impression. Then he darted from the room.

"Now he's going to brag to all the guys," Janet informed her.

Shelley sat up abruptly. "He wouldn't!" But even as she said it, she heard a burst of male laughter float in from the other room. "He's done this to you?"

"Oh yeah. Drew too."

"How could you have let him live? I'm going to kill him."

"Every time we tried to get back at him he'd just do it again. You'll get tired of losing too. Trust me. Just let him get away with it."

Shelley got to her feet, pulled her cardigan off and tied it around her waist.

"No way. I *will* get him back." She climbed the stairs with as much dignity as the situation would allow.

"Trust me, Shelley," she heard Janet call after her. "I know what I'm talking about."

Just before midnight, all three guys joined them in the living room. Michael handed her a cup of tea and a smile and sat down on the rug next to her.

"Come near me and I'll rip your lips off," she warned.

"At least you would have a better view of my teeth. You do love my teeth," he said, unperturbed.

She gleaned only a moment's satisfaction from her imagined vengeance before the mental picture of a lipless Michael got the best of her. She laughed. "You just be on your guard, Mr. Man. I'll figure out a way to get you back."

ଓଃ

Boxing day promised to be just as lazy and relaxing as the day before. Company came and went all day, so everyone just visited and snacked and drank too much coffee. It was late afternoon before the house became quiet once more.

Shelley pushed herself from the couch and stretched. Some of the grand kids had come and gone, leaving toys scattered across the carpet. She moved around the room, absently picking them up and placing them in the charming wooden toy box in the corner. "What do you want to do, Mike? We could go for a sleigh ride," she suggested hopefully.

"We're doing that on New Year's Day," he reminded her.

She dropped another toy in the box. "We could go skiing. You said there were extra pairs of skis downstairs."

He grinned at her. "That sounds like too much work

right now." He closed his eyes and leaned back into the cushions of the couch.

She picked up a toy gun from off of the floor, still loaded with three plastic, brightly colored balls. "You're being difficult, Mike," she warned before pulling the trigger and she watched with glee as all three balls thwacked him harmlessly in the side of the head. It so startled him that he surged to his feet, promptly tangling in them and falling to the floor. His flailing arm sent the full glass of ice water on the end table falling after him, where it landed on his forehead, spilling over his face and chest.

Of course she laughed. Laughed and laughed.

He pushed himself to his knees. "That wasn't funny," he complained, rubbing his head.

"Oh, it was!" She howled, collapsing onto the rug. She wiped the tears from her cheeks and dissolved into fresh peals of laughter, picturing over and over the surprised look on his face.

He pulled at the snaps of his shirt and ripped it open, to shrug off and toss onto the table in a soggy wad. Then, he rolled her over onto her back and leaned over her. "You have no compassion," he sighed dramatically. His new pendant hung down, just touching the skin where her shirt lay open. It was still warm from the heat of his body.

"I love you," she said spontaneously, reaching up to pull his face to hers.

He kissed her hard once and bent his head for another when she started laughing all over again against his lips. He moved away in disgust, rolling her shaking form back over. "Never mind. A man doesn't like to be laughed at when he's kissing his woman."

When she finally had the strength, she pushed herself up. "Sorry," she said, without a trace of genuine repentance. "It's a weakness. I always laugh when somebody gets hit in the head." At his mock glare, she held one palm up in a half shrug. "I can't help it. Call it a character flaw."

"I'll kiss it better for you, Mike," teased a voice from the open doorway.

"Jared!" Michael fairly snarled. "How long have you been standing there?"

"Long enough to see you make a fool of yourself," he chuckled. "I thought I was going to have to break up something embarrassing for a minute there."

Shelley made a hasty exit, mumbling something about going to help with supper, but they could hear her laughing still, all the way down the hall. Michael stared fondly after her for a moment then pushed himself easily to his feet and plopped down on the couch again.

Jared switched the T.V on and flipped through the channels, eventually settling on the sports channel. They watched the last period of the hockey game, nibbling at leftover holiday baking and arguing about the players and penalties during commercials.

Michael grabbed the remote when the game was over and surfed through the channels.

"Mike?"

"Yeah?" He answered absently, shoving a butter tart into his mouth.

"Why don't you tell me about it?"

Michael swallowed the half chewed tart and turned the T.V off. "I told you enough." His voice was suddenly gruff. "More than enough."

"I didn't mean about that. I meant, what's going on in your head?"

"You wouldn't understand."

"Since when, Mike?"

It was said quietly, but it hit home. He ached to share this with someone and if anyone could help him sort it out, it would be Jared. He rubbed the back of his neck, wondering how to start; what to say. "Since I don't understand it myself." He smiled wryly. "Shell's got it all figured out though."

"Oh yeah?"

"Yep." Resting his head against the back of the couch again, he took a deep breath and closed his eyes, as though preparing to quote from a text book. "Apparently my self-esteem took a beating along with the rest of me, and my insecurities, bitterness, residual rage and feelings of helplessness have mingled together to make me behave in a jealous, possessive and overprotective manner."

Jared laughed, despite himself. "And?"

"And she's probably right. It just doesn't feel that simple. It gets out of hand sometimes."

"What do you mean?"

Michael chewed at his lip, wondering how to explain it.

"Do you remember Pete?"

"Pete?" Jared squinted, trying to remember. "Pelletier? The big guy that beat Mark up for looking at his girlfriend?"

Michael nodded, letting his brother come to his own conclusions. It took only seconds.

"You?! You're kidding, right? It's just not in you, Mike. You never cared less before."

"Well, it's in me now," he said with a depressed sigh. He was ashamed to admit the rest, but felt compelled to do so anyway. "She doesn't have anyone else, Jared. No close friends, no family. She's alone and I've worked very hard to keep it that way. I even convinced her to rent her cabin out, so she couldn't live there. She has next to no money, with a baby on the way and no one to turn to but me." He dared a sideways glance at his brother, not surprised at the shock he saw on his face. "She eats with me, works with me, sleeps with me ...but Jared, it's just never *enough*."

His brother gave a low whistle. "Jesus, Mike. That doesn't sound healthy. Are you sure getting married is a good idea?"

Michael's head snapped up and he looked at Jared sharply. "Why don't you like her?"

"I do like her," Jared protested. "I like her a lot. She's sweet and smart and obviously worships the ground you walk on. It's just ...listen to yourself. You've been through a rough time and you barely know her, really. I mean, why rush into it like this? It sounds like obsession, not love."

Michael started to pick at the hole in the knee of his jeans, pulling at the loose threads, fraying them. "It is obsession," he agreed finally. "But if there's one thing I've managed to sort out of all of this, it's that I love her. I can't let her leave me, Jared. I need her."

Jared let the air out his lungs with a grunt of surprise. "You think she'd cheat on you?"

"I said leave, not cheat," he bit out. "She wouldn't cheat."

Jared snorted. "How can you be so sure?"

"She's just not the type, that's all."

"How do you know, though," Jared pressed. "You can't really know someone in six months, I'm telling you!"

"I just know, okay?! She had never even been with a man before ...that day."

Jared sagged back against the couch. "Oh Christ, really? How old is she?"

"Twenty three."

His brother quirked an eyebrow, eloquently if silently making his suspicion clear.

Michael shook his head. "There's nothing wrong with her, believe me. She just had a lonely childhood, a troubled one, you know? She just chose to keep to herself."

"So, what then? Why would she leave? You don't - you're not saying you hit her?"

He could feel his face coloring with shame.

"Mike ..." Jared read the answer in his face. "Mike, what are you thinking? She can't have deserved that."

"No! God, no. She didn't deserve it at all." He covered his face with his hands, overcome with the memory of that night. "I just feel so angry all the time. I don't know how to control it."

"You just do," his brother said firmly. "Just make that choice, Mike. You have to or it will only get worse. You can feel it coming on, can't you?"

He thought a moment, feeling miserable and hopeless. "Yeah, usually. A friend from back home brought me a heavy bag. I can punch the hell out of that. It's just - how do I stop it from happening in the first place?"

His brother stared at him thoughtfully and Michael felt a small ray of hope rise through his despair, just at having another person on his side, working the problem with him.

Jared made a face. "I don't know. I'm not a shrink."

Michael just waited. He knew his brother wouldn't leave it at that; he was a born problem solver, unable to resist the process of working it out. He almost smiled at the expression of intense concentration on his face.

"Okay, what triggers these things?"

"I've thought about that, but you know, it seems random. It can be something so small, something that before would have been mildly annoying. Mostly, it's just always there, under the surface."

"They're dead, Mike," he said wisely. "You can't take it out on the people who caused it because they're dead, right? That's why it won't go away?"

Michael nodded. "I guess so."

"But, you shot them," he reminded him.

"So?" He spat out. "They died almost instantly. They tortured me for four days!   How is that revenge?"

"Mike, you have to make peace with it."

"Make peace with it? I can't," he growled. "They ruined my life! I'll never be normal again - no one will look at me the same again."

Jared shook his head vehemently, opening his mouth to argue, but Michael interrupted, pointing to the healed scars on his bare chest. "It's not these, they could be from anything." He traced his finger over the faint lines and ridges of scar tissue. "It's not this," he added, moving to the long scar on his stomach. "I was bleeding slowly inside - they repaired it in surgery." Moving his finger again, this time he traced one of many puckered, circular scars. "It's not even these cigarette burns, as ugly as they are." He stuck his hands out toward Jared, fists closed and held together, as though bound. "It's these. Look at them. There's no denying what caused these; what they represent. It's in my mind every time I look at them, and probably in Shelley's and yours and everybody else's. It's sick. It's just so sick that she'll eventually feel ashamed of me, you all will. And it's their fault." He jabbed a finger in the air. "It's their fault and there isn't a fucking thing I can do about it!" His voice broke. "Don't look at me like that, Jared!" He swiped angrily at his eyes.

Jared was looking at him with such sadness and understanding and his eyes too were bright with moisture.

"Shit," Jared exclaimed, pushing his thumb and forefinger against his closed eyelids, trying not to cry. "Shit! It kills me to see you like this. Can't you see that we're all proud of you?"

"Proud?" Michael almost shouted. "Proud that I was raped repeatedly by two men?"

"Yes! Proud you survived. Proud you saved her life. Proud you risked yours in the first place. We all love you, Mike. Give us some credit. You're a fighter - you gave it all you could," he said gently, clapping a comforting hand on his back. "You just lost. There's no shame in that. Make peace with it."

☙

The remainder of their days with Michael's family flew by at an alarming rate, but they managed to fit in hours and hours of visiting and board games, eggnog, food, more food and even more food. They went for sleigh rides on New Year's Day, as promised. She went skiing with Janet, Jared and Michael for a couple of hours and then with the help of all the kids, built a crowd of snowmen in the front yard. Shelley felt that she got to know most of them quite well in that time and enjoyed them all immensely. They were a sensitive, thoughtful, fun family and her memories of the holiday were ones that she would treasure always. Meeting them all made her feel rewarded somehow, and enriched.

Saying good bye had been difficult for Michael, and he was as a result, morose and depressed on the flight home. But it didn't last. Seeing his family and basking in their love and understanding had finally begun the healing he so desperately needed.

CHAPTER TWENTY ONE

"Hey, Shelley-belly! You ready?" Michael's voice floated up to her from the foyer.

"One minute," she called back down the stairs. "I have to go to the bathroom. Again," she muttered to herself irritably. At seven and a half months, she wasn't just noticeably pregnant, she was huge. The pressure on her bladder felt constant now, her back ached all the time and her legs and ankles were unpleasantly swollen. Mike was on the right track when he called her Shelley-belly, she reflected as she flushed the toilet, for her belly was round as a melon and so large that it was beginning to affect her balance.

As annoyed as she was with her ungainly, uncooperative body, the day, the weekend, promised to be an enjoyable one. They planned to spend it with the Keeper family at the winter festival, visiting, playing outside and watching the other events. It was a nice way to break up the long winter and she was so looking forward to it. The weeks since they had returned from Montreal had been quiet and peaceful. Almost too quiet. It had given her far too much time to think and reflect. Michael's behaviour had been exemplary. He was working through his anger issues with great success, combining suggestions from Daniel, his family and the local therapist he was seeing every second Wednesday. His success raised a hope in him that buoyed his entire outlook. He was learning to let go of his rage and self loathing and it was a wonderful thing to see.

Despite that, she found herself slowly sinking into a depression. She felt fat and ugly and furious with this role she had been cursed with. Her emotions were up and down, changing in a flash, raging like a hurricane one moment and calm as a misty morning the next. It wasn't just what was happening to her body, though that was certainly horrible enough. It was the feeling of helplessness and well, bondage.
She felt as though she were being forced to give this being life, to harbor it, nourish it and keep it safe. She was being forced to carry this child as though she *forgave* him, as though he had been her chosen one, as though she had chosen *this*. It made her feel so trapped and mad that she could hardly stand it. She wanted to feel the magical wonderment that expectant mothers are supposed to feel when the baby moves or when they see its ultrasound image on the monitor or think of its future. But she couldn't, because she couldn't bring herself to forgive him for doing this to her, and to Michael. It wasn't fair.

She forced the confusion of her thoughts aside, determined to enjoy herself. The skidoo ride to town always boosted her spirits, so it was as good a place to start as any.

☙

After paying a small fee at the door, Shelley, Michael and the Keeper family shuffled with the crowd into the welcoming warmth of the building. The large hall was alive with the buzz of many noisy, high-spirited people as they mingled and moved from table to table to chat with friends. The decorations were festive and wintery, with giant, glittering snowflakes hanging from the ceiling as well as loops of silver garland interlaced with strings of white lights. A popular local duo strummed their guitars and sang fun folk songs on the stage. Shelley found it all rather enchanting. The Native Trapper's Committee really had outdone themselves. They were always an important part of the Winter Festival, Michael explained to her as they moved into the buffet line. Every year they put this dinner on, providing the wild meat gained from fishing, hunting and trapping. The smell of roasted meat hung heavy in the air and Shelley felt her stomach lurch unpleasantly in response. Baby apparently didn't like this new smell.

There was a great variety of meats to choose from; beaver, rabbit, walleye, pike, moose, grouse, duck, deer and caribou, all prepared in different, appetizing ways, as well as roasted winter vegetables, wild rice, salads and hot buttered bannock. It was an impressive feast. Following the dictates of her near-nauseous tummy, Shelley opted for a small fillet of the fresh fried fish and a helping of each side dish. She found the bannock especially delicious and as a lover of bread, even unleavened as this was, she found it to be pure comfort food.

This loud, merry atmosphere was a nice change. Everyone at their table laughed and talked loudly with such enthusiasm that they interrupted each other constantly. No one minded, in fact, it made them laugh all the more. Shelley found herself wondering briefly, watching Michael's face as he listened intently to another of Marylin's jokes, what had changed to make her feel so much more comfortable. She felt at home in this social setting, possibly for the first time in her life. It was beyond wonderful ...it was, well, she couldn't even begin to express the joy she felt at this unexpected sense of 'fitting in'. She felt the happiness rise within her like fuzzy champagne bubbles. She knew now without a doubt in this sudden moment of clarity, that she was a different person than she had been a scant eight months ago. She had suffered, yes, suffered and cried and wallowed in self pity, but she had also grown. Her confidence and self-esteem had received a brand new foundation. Now, she at least knew which way was up. Even with the curse of this pregnancy, she felt like a new person. A better person.

Her moment of deep self-analysis was swept away by more infectious laughter and forgotten, as they mopped up their plates with the last bites of bannock and drained their cups. They moved on to browse at the sales tables set up across the hall, which were laden with home crafted goods of all sorts. There were soft furs and pelts and squares of supple hide. There were beaded wall hangings, moccasins, mittens, watchbands and even jewelry. Many local artists proudly displayed their native paintings and carvings.

Shelley stopped to admire the dream catchers. Each was a web of sorts, woven around a circular frame, and feathers of different colours dangled from thin leather straps of various lengths. She found them charming and watched with interest as Marylin sorted through the selection, eventually purchasing two of them.

"Hang these by your bed," Marylin said with a sweet smile as she handed one to Michael and the other to Shelley. "They will catch your bad dreams," she added with a searching look at both of them. "You still dream of it sometimes, no?"

She didn't seem to expect an answer, brushing off their thanks and hugging them both in turn before moving along to the next table. Norman shared a smile with them, eyes twinkling, and took his daughter's hand, leading her too away to the next table. Shelley was touched by Marylin's gesture and by her easy concern and vowed to make an effort to get to know this woman better. She could be a very good friend.

They made their way through the cold, blustery weather back to the Keeper's home, where Norman immediately brought the banked fire to life in the sooty hearth. Excited by the company and her fun at the festival, it took rounds and rounds of hugs and kisses and tickles before Rosie was tucked into bed for the night. Marylin made everyone a warming cup of wonderful, spiced tea with sugar, cinnamon, cloves and slices of orange and lemon. It smelled as good as it tasted and Shelley wanted to just envelop herself in the comforting aroma. Though the heat of the fire and the tea relaxed them all, the evening was far from winding down, for they played a hearty game of Pictionary into the wee hours of the morning. It was perhaps the most fun Shelley had ever had. They laughed so hard at Norman's attempts to draw even the simplest ideas that they had to wipe tears from their eyes.

Shelley couldn't even remember laying her head on the pillow that night, but she woke with the pale winter sun at about eight o'clock, wrapped in Michael's arms and the warm blankets of the Keeper's guest bed. She smiled at the memory of last night and hoped this day would bring more of the same kind of enjoyable companionship. It was going to be a busy day. After only a few more treasured moments of snuggle, she prodded Michael awake. He's always the same when he wakes up, she thought affectionately; sleepy-eyed, dopey and irrepressibly good-natured. It made her day all the better and she hugged him tightly.

"Ah, ma petite," he said with a greatly exaggerated French-Canadian accent. "Dis morning, eet is a good one, no?

We play all day in da snow, and on de hice ...eet will be 'uge fun. Geve me a kees to start da day ..."

Giggling into his chest, she reached up to kiss him then emerged from the warm cocoon of blankets. She dressed hurriedly, brushed and braided her long hair then grabbed her toothbrush and toothpaste from the overnight bag. With a mocking little wave at the man still lounging in bed, she headed for the bathroom.

His voice followed her playfully down the hall. "You call dat a kees?"

By the time Michael came to the breakfast table, Shelley was into her second waffle, which was deliciously sweet and sticky with syrup, and playing 'Eye Spy' with Rosie. She smiled up at him with her mouth full. "Morning Monsieur."

"Morning babe," he said with a wink, returning the smile. "Morning everyone." He caught sight of Rosie in her high chair and pretending to be startled, clapped a hand over his heart. "Rosie," he gasped dramatically, "my favorite little flower, do *you* have a kiss for me this morning?"

Her little face shone up at him and she nodded so he leaned in, presenting his cheek down at her level. With lips puckered, she closed her eyes and pecked him blindly on the tip of his nose. He chuckled, tweaking her little nose with his finger tip. "Thank you, sweetie, that just makes my whole day perfect. Hey, Rosie, my girl, are we going to have fun today?"

She nodded again and her dark eyes went round with irrepressible excitement. "Puppies!" She exclaimed with a grin. "Puppy ride!"

"Yes, puppy ride," Marylin echoed affectionately as she put her plate in the dishwasher, "but if you want a puppy ride then we have to go get you dressed. Come on kiddo." She hoisted her out of her chair and onto one hip where Rosie gibbered happily all the way up the stairs.

Shelley's gaze lingered after the little girl for a moment, thinking about the comfortable ritual Marylin and her had. Feeding Rosie breakfast and playing games and getting her ready for the day, though probably just routine to her mother, seemed suddenly a very special thing to her. She felt a sudden surge of longing for it, unconsciously placing a hand on the mound of her belly. It was with the familiar rush of disappointment and claustrophobia that she pushed the longing away. The growing feelings of motherhood were borne of hormones and nothing more. Still determined not to dwell on it this weekend, Shelley turned her attention back to the men, who were presently arguing over which of them was going to be the victor of the snow poker and consequently, the proud recipient of the one thousand dollar prize.

"What's a snow poker?" She interrupted.

"It is a course for the snowmobiles with stops set up," Norman explained in his quiet way. "The riders stop at each and pick up a card, and whoever has the best poker hand wins."

"Ah, I see. And what else are you boys going to be up to today?"

"Well," Michael stated, "we have to enter the races, of course. They're giving away a brand new snowmobile for first place."

"You already have a snowmobile," she pointed out around her last mouthful, but the men only stared at her, agog, as if she had suddenly gone simple.

"Shelley," Michael said, exchanging a pained

look with Norman, "This is a *Thundercat*! They don't make them faster than that."

"Oh, how *silly* of me," she said with a roll of her eyes. "Well, I guess I'll hang with the girls this morning. We can all meet up at lunch, then?"

"Sounds like a plan, Stan,"

"So we're good to go, Joe?"

"Yep. Have a good day, Ray."

"Thanks. Can we take the truck, Chuck?"

"Yep. We'll take the sled, Ned."

"OK," she laughed, giving him an abbreviated bow. "Stop. You are the king of rhyme. You win." She gave Michael a happy hug and Norman a smile. "You guys have fun, and good luck! I'm going to go and attempt to squeeze into my ski pants."

It was almost another hour before Shelley, Marylin and Rosie were bundled up in scarves and mittens and toques and standing in line for their first event. Dog sledding was something she had never tried but since she had met Darby and Dawson, she had thought of it often. She felt almost more excited than Rosie looked, if that were possible. The little girl was hopping up and down in excitement, pointing at one 'pretty puppy' after another. They were very handsome dogs. Their coats were predominantly black, with white masks, legs and bellies. Their tails curled over their backs in true spitz fashion and some of them had eyes of the lightest, clearest, most beautiful blue. They all seemed even tempered and affectionate, though she was sure some of the more independent, feisty ones battled now and then for a better position, or rank, in their 'pack'.

There were four different teams harnessed and

waiting. Marylin was seated with Rosie in the front sled, and Shelley in the one directly behind. The dog owners drove their own teams and though this was intended only as a quick pleasure tour, the one in charge of Shelley's sled, who introduced himself as Barry, saw her interest in the dogs and their traces and explained briefly how they were harnessed and even some of the rudiments of proper mushing. The sleds themselves were handcrafted from ash, he explained, and large enough for a decent load of provisions or as was the case today, an extra person. He explained that his team of six dogs, all Siberian Huskies, were true athletes and could run for hours, easily covering thirty five to forty kilometers in a single day.

The huskies moved restlessly in their traces as Marylin's sled took off ahead of them and they yipped in excitement as Barry moved into position behind her. He held neither whip nor rein, but before the word 'mush' was even out of his mouth the dogs surged forward, eager to race, to feel the joy of running and the freedom of speed. Their tongues flapped happily behind them as their muscles bunched under heavy, healthy coats. Their joy was infectious. Shelley felt it too; the joy in the crisp winter wind, the sparkling snow, the blue sky. In life. She felt all these things as the sled flew over the blanket of fresh snow. There were only the smooth sounds of the runners and the dogs breathing and it seemed to Shelley a magic moment, moving so silently in this wonderland, this beautiful, rugged wilderness.

Barry commanded his team skillfully, but entirely verbally, using familiar words, tone and inflection of voice to control their speed and direction. They were well trained, turning right when he yelled 'gee' and left at a command of 'haw'. He had a rapport with his dogs, a clear bond of love and discipline and there was too, a mutual respect that she was sure had been earned over many kilometers.

The ride ended too soon, she found, for she was disappointed when they completed their loop and slid to a graceful stop behind the group still awaiting a ride. Inexplicably, this had been an emotional experience, one she discovered she would cherish for the rest of her life. She climbed reluctantly from the sled and thanked Barry, stopping to pat each of the dogs in turn.

Rosie was thrilled with her ride as well, and she chattered on like a happy magpie. Shelley watched, amused by the sight of her. Her pink snowsuit was big and bulky and it forced her to walk funny, making her tilt from side to side with arms out as she went, like a little pink penguin. Their next stop was the community hall once again, where the Trapper's committee was putting on a fashion show. They settled themselves at a table with cups of steamy, if a little watery, hot chocolate and divested themselves of one or two layers of clothes. The festival was well planned, Shelley reflected, ensuring that there were activities throughout the day that took place indoors, so the kids could warm up periodically and the parents could relax.

The music cued up right on time and the emcee opened the show with some jokes and the regular thanks to so and so without whom this show would not be possible. The committee had rounded up some locals for this event, and Shelley hooted with laughter when, about fifteen minutes into the show, who but Daniel Matthews came strutting down the catwalk in a buttery hide coat with fur trim. Though he actually looked very handsome, she couldn't help but snicker through her hands at the sight of him. Modeling just so wasn't him. He was such a good sport though, smiling and posing, being his jovial self as the emcee described the coat, named the tailor, the price and where it was currently available. She chuckled through the rest of the show, her laughter continually buoyed by the image of Daniel spinning on the catwalk.

Despite her irrepressible humour, she couldn't help but admire the craftsmanship of the clothes being displayed. They were beautiful and as with the feast of the previous night, all that was being displayed was originally trapped or hunted locally. There were luxurious fur coats, leather gloves, moccasins, slippers and much more. The thought of wearing fur revolted her somewhat though; she much preferred the skins and furs on the animals they belonged to. But still, the show was entertaining and interesting, and the hot chocolate had warmed her up nicely.

It wasn't until the applause signaled the end of the show that Shelley and Marylin realized it was already past noon. They donned their winter clothes in a hurry, this time packing the snow pants into back packs for later in the day, then rushed off across the street to meet up, as arranged, with the men at a local restaurant called 'Kipper's'.

Neither Michael nor Norman was the proud new owner of a brand new snowmobile, or the recipient of the one thousand dollar prize, but they were in good spirits nonetheless. Lunch was a quick affair of grilled cheese sandwiches, noodle soup and animated chatter. They were off again by one o'clock, bundled back into full winter gear. They walked the short distance to the next event quickly, trundling little Rosie along, sometimes passing her from one set of arms to another.

The dog sledding had been exhilarating, the fashion show amusing, but nothing was quite as fun as making the snow sculpture with Michael and his friends. Though they had decided as a team to sculpt a polar bear, most of their time was spent horsing around, throwing and dodging snow balls, and even making snow angels. So it was with no surprise that when the whistle blew an hour later, the bear was little more than half done. Completely undaunted, they moved along to the sliding hill.

Norman procured an inner-tube and crazy carpet from the booth at the base of the hill and with Marylin, took his daughter's hand. They ran all the way up the massive slope. Shelley eagerly started up the hill behind them but Michael squeezed her hand with a pointed look at her belly. She was terribly disappointed as she watched the Keepers race back down on the inner-tube, piled together in a messy jumble of limbs. She had never been sliding and very much wanted to try it. Admittedly, she had forgotten for a moment, but she realized that her advanced pregnancy would make it just too difficult. And unsafe. Her resentment resurfaced with a vengeance and she thought briefly of throwing caution to the winds and doing it anyway. If the baby got hurt somehow, what did it matter? She wasn't planning on keeping it anyway. A wash of guilty shame rushed through her immediately for thinking such a cold thought and her spirits plummeted.

Michael must have followed her thoughts for he sensed the mood change immediately and turned with evident concern to study her expression. "Hey," he said with gentle reproof. "Don't let it ruin your day." He pulled one soggy mitten off and brushed his knuckles along her cheek. "I've never seen you so happy, baby. Your laughter this weekend has been the most wonderful thing." He kissed the tip of her nose. "I've missed it."

Shelley stared into his brown eyes. The warmth of them was always such a comfort to her. As always, something in the depths of them made her realize that the feelings of self pity and resentment that she wanted to hug to herself in a good pout were more self-destructive than satisfying. She felt her mood lift but gazed into them still, watching as one fluffy snowflake settled on his lashes, clinging then melting before being replaced by another.

He looked up at the lazily falling snow. "You've been like a pretty little winter fairy." He smiled his little boy smile. "Sprinkling laughter over us all like magical snowflakes."

A smile finally tugged at her own lips.

Michael pulled his mitten back on. "C'mon, m'lady," he urged playfully. "This will be fun too - I planned *our* next event over there." He pointed to the far side of the field where a group of twenty to thirty people were gathering. "We'll meet up with the Keepers at dinner time."

She found the task fun as promised, but very challenging. Everyone was divided up into teams of six. Michael and Shelley were grouped with two sweet teen aged girls and an older man with a son of about ten years of age. The goal was simple; one by one, wearing snowshoes, the members of each team were to negotiate the bright orange pylons for a distance of about forty meters, then using a simple bow, shoot at least one arrow into the snowman provided some distance away. Any extra arrows fired into the hapless target were considered a bonus and could be the deciding factor in a tie. There was one portly looking snowman for each team, complete with top hat, scarf and even a carrot nose. Someone had gone to a lot of trouble building these cheerful characters, taking extra time to paint a colorful bull's-eye on each round tummy ball. Great pains were also taken to make this event a safe one, including the placement of festival personnel at each archery station and a lot of orange tape. It was stretched across the entire length of the field to prevent anyone from wandering into the target area.

Most of the available snowshoes were the old fashioned kind, made from ash or hickory with rawhide lacing, but there were two more modern looking pairs; both aluminum, one a beautiful electric blue and the other a candy apple red. Michael picked the red pair for their team and having volunteered to go first, strapped himself quickly into the shoes. The first person of each team hovered expectantly over the starting line and when the shrill whistle blew, he took off with the others with a comical but efficient gait, appearing as comfortable on them as a snow shoeing veteran. He shot not one but three arrows into the snowman before heading back, all done so quickly that their team had already gained a substantial lead.

Sarah, one of the teenage girls, was next. Perhaps eighteen or nineteen years old, she was small and slim with locks of beautiful, bright red hair peeking out from beneath her toque. She had the biggest, roundest, most startling blue eyes and her fair cheeks blossomed a lovely pink. She was so perfectly formed and fashioned that Shelley decided she looked like a baby doll. She was such a nice girl too; polite, seemingly mature and full of laughter. Michael buckled her into the shoes and she too was off. She did well on the run, stumbling once or twice but still making excellent time. She was clearly lost however, when she picked up the bow. She fumbled with it, trying to figure out how to hold it, until the attendant stationed there helped her find a comfortable position, guiding her hands and showing her how to draw the string back. Despite his assistance, the arrows landed short, or flew off to one side or the other. The team began to despair as they fell further and further behind, but her sixth arrow finally found the mark, low down near the bottom of the snowman. She almost flew back to the starting line with a rueful smile and repeated apologies.

"Don't you worry about it," Michael said with one of his most charming smiles, as he unbuckled the shoes for her with nimble fingers. "You did great."

She blushed prettily, sharing an 'Oh, my God, we have to talk about this later' look with her friend before fixing her beautiful eyes on her feet. Shelley smiled with understanding, amused by the instantaneous nature of teenage infatuation. Michael was a school girl crush just waiting to happen.

The young boy, Connor, went next, taking off like a bullet and performing admirably at the archery station. He hit not only the snowman, but the target painted on it with his very first attempt. After him went Melissa, Sarah's friend. Her long legs carried her quickly through the course as well, and after only three arrows, hit the target. The team jumped up and down, yelling and cheering their encouragement.

Shelley felt her nerves buck wildly as Melissa rushed back. She just knew she was going to perform poorly, embarrassing both herself and the team. She glanced at Sarah, surprised to find her looking back.

"Don't be nervous. It's all in fun," Sarah reminded her wisely. She smiled, wrinkling her perfect little nose with a self-deprecating shrug. "You can't do any worse than I did."

Shelley had never seen a more angelic smile. Sarah radiated such guileless innocence, such goodness. Shelley felt moved by it, though she had but a brief moment to reflect on it before she realized that Michael was already strapping the snowshoes on her own feet. Between the awkwardness of her pregnancy and the snowshoes, she felt she moved very slow indeed, but the sounds of her teammates cheering her on with such enthusiasm made it more fun than stressful. She finally rounded the last pylon, teetering to a stop and flinging out her arms for balance.

"Help," she squeaked to the attendant as she lifted the bow.

The young man had a build up of frost around his scarf and hat and she guessed he must have been at this for most of the day, but he flashed her a cheerful, toothy grin. "Right handed?"

She nodded.

"Then that will be your drawing arm," he stated, placing the bow in her left hand. "Stand sideways to the mark. Your shoulders should be in line with the flight of your arrow. Feet six to eight inches apart. Good." He helped her as he had done with Sarah, nocking the arrow by placing it's notch correctly on the bowstring, on the right side, positioning her fingers, and finally explaining how to draw the string.

"Okay, draw it back. A little more. Let your back take the weight. Good, now aim."

With a sense of hopeful excitement, Shelley aimed for the bull's eye, sending up a silent prayer for accuracy, then loosed the arrow. It landed squarely in the middle of the target.

The attendant's mouth fell open. "Good job!" He

boomed, patting her on the back.

She smiled gratefully, so thrilled with her success that she actually hugged the young man, jumping up and down at the same time.

He laughed heartily at her excitement. "You still have to get back."

"Oh! Yes. Thank you." Weaving around the pylons, she hustled back to the starting line. They unbuckled her snowshoes in record time and transferred them to Gary, the boy's father.

Michael kissed her soundly on the mouth. "You did great!"

"Holy cow!" Sarah exclaimed. "And you were worried?"

Shelley smiled self consciously. "Archery could be my very well hidden talent, but I'm thinking it was just luck."

Gary was fast, comfortable with both the snowshoes and the bow, and returned to the starting line about fifteen seconds ahead of any of the other teams. They had actually won the relay! Grabbing Shelley and Connor, the girls squealed, hugged and jumped up and down in a boisterous victory dance while the men looked on in amusement.

Shelley very much wanted to stay in touch with the girls, Sarah especially, and so impulsively invited them all to meet at the evening bonfire for a warm cup of celebratory cider. They all agreed without hesitation before heading off in different directions. It dawned on her that she had just done something big, something new in making that simple invitation. She had never initiated anything like that before. It gave her a sense of satisfaction and pride and a feeling of contentment within herself.

Michael peeled the sleeve of his jacket back to look at

his watch. "It's almost three thirty. We have about one hour to kill before we meet Norman and Marylin. You doing okay? You look pretty tired."

"I am exhausted," she admitted, rubbing at her back. "But it's been tons of fun."

"There's an igloo-making demonstration in the ball field. It started at two thirty but they should still be at it. It would give you a chance to sit for a bit. Would you like to see it?"

"Sure, that would be great."

They arrived in time to see two men cutting the last of many snow blocks with a small, toothy saw. Taking a seat in the stands, Shelley and Michael watched with fascination as the men began lining the blocks up on their edges, leaning them slightly toward the center to form a circle around the tramped down snow. After completing one circle they started a second level of blocks, using the saw to bevel the edges before piling them on top. Each new level closed the circular structure in a bit more until finally, one last block at the top completed the igloo. Small chunks of snow were crammed into cracks and crevasses and smoothed with their mittens. Two remaining blocks were placed at one end and covered with a third to form the protective walls around what was going to be the entrance. The smaller man began to dig the snow out from beneath the sheltered entrance, deeper and deeper until he actually dug under the wall of the igloo.

Michael explained the final steps as they made their way to the park. "Now all they have to do is leave a lamp burning in there long enough for a small bit of melting to occur. If you rub the wet snow with your mitt," he said, demonstrating with one hand, "it smoothes it out and refreezes into a tough, leak proof shelter. A well built igloo can reach temperatures of about sixty degrees Fahrenheit in the dead of winter."

"That's pretty cool," she said. "And it ranks way up there in the cheap and affordable housing category."

It was shortly after five o'clock and dark as midnight when they met up with the Keepers at the bonfire. Their teammates from the relay did show up and they all enjoyed the festivities together. The bonfire itself was perhaps six feet across and surrounded by a low wire fence to keep the children from falling into it. For seating, logs and stumps had been situated around its perimeter. They each grabbed a stick, roasting wieners and marshmallows and filling their empty bellies with them, along with cups of hot chocolate and tasty mulled cider. The kids ran in noisy, crazy circles and the adults told jokes and stories, relating funny accounts of the winter's events. Shelley stared into the fire as she listened; she found the flames and sparks hypnotizing and the warmth felt delicious. She felt herself growing drowsy but it was only when Rosie, overcome by her sleepiness, lay her head against her mother's breast and fell into slumber, that they left for home.

CHAPTER TWENTY TWO

Shelley caught Michael glancing at his watch again, only moments after the last time. He crossed over to the window to look out expectantly, once more searching the wintry distance for some sign of them and sighed heavily. "I can't imagine what's keeping them. They should have been here hours ago."

Although Shelley and Michael had made it home before ten o'clock last night, it wasn't supposed to be the end of the activities. The plan was to round out the weekend with a Sunday afternoon of ice fishing and then dinner, but Norm and Marylin were two hours overdue.

She joined him at the window. "It's going to be dark soon, should we go look for them?"

"Yeah," he said. "I think it's more than them just changing their minds. He would have contacted me on the radio. I'm sure of it. Let's go check out the trail. Maybe their sled broke down."

The weather had taken a nasty turn overnight, leveling out at a chilly -32 °C, so they dressed warmly, donning long underwear, snowsuits, extra thick socks, heavy winter boots and insulated helmets. The temperature alone was dangerous enough, but with the wind chill, exposed skin could freeze in less than a minute. Secretly, Shelley hoped that the Keeper's sled had broken down. They would have to give them a ride in and would consequently have no time for ice fishing. The thought of sitting outside in that extreme weather seemed ...well ... it seemed masochistic. She would much rather sip a hot, steamy beverage and sit by the fire. Even so, she enjoyed the ride out. The powerful engine of Michael's Arctic Cat snowmobile purred like its mythical namesake under the brightly painted hood. Sitting behind him on the heated, padded seat, she gripped the pockets at his hips, since the ever-growing mound of her pregnancy made it impossible to reach her arms around him. She tipped her head back and marveled at the beautiful, cool serenity of the day. The sky was a clear, cloudless blue and as lovely as she had ever seen it. There was no sense of foreboding, no feeling of impending doom as she flipped the visor on her helmet back down.

They moved moderately slowly, for they dragged behind them a wooden box sleigh meant for hauling. It had a tendency to tip over when it was empty, but all three of the Keepers would fit in there for the ride back if they had indeed broken down somewhere. Luckily, within half an hour, they spotted figures in the distance; two dark spots against the white of the snow covered ice. With a sudden burst of speed, Michael closed the distance between them, bringing the sled to a stop many meters away and turned off the engine. Shelley didn't at first understand the scene before her, or comprehend the tragedy of the situation. There was no sign of another snowmobile anywhere and there were only two people instead of three, but there was no doubt that one of them, laying prone on the ice, was Norman Keeper. They approached him slowly on foot, calling out to him, yelling his name, but he didn't even look at them. The reason became clear as they drew nearer.

Shelley felt her chest constrict in shocked reaction.

Norman was stretched precariously over the delicate webbing of cracked ice, leaning over the jagged edge. "Marylin!" He screamed over and over, in a voice gone hoarse and raw with emotion. He plunged his arm and shoulder down into the cold blackness of the water, fishing desperately for a lock of hair or a scarf; some trace of his beloved wife that he could grasp to pull her to safety. But he found nothing.

A small rivulet of blood trickled down his forehead and into his eye. It was only when he moved his head to shake it away, breaking his concentration, that he saw them coming. "Mike!" He yelled in desperate relief. The normally quiet, reserved man began to stammer in tearful panic. "W ...ww ...we hit the ice ridge. I didn't realize it had moved so far in ...and it knocked us into the o ...o ...open water. She never came back up, Mike. Oh, help me find her - she went d...down! Shelley, please- watch Rosie and get her warm for me. I couldn't leave her."

Then he inched his body forward, preparing to dive in.

Michael lunged after him, wrapped one large hand around his ankle and forcibly hauled him back from the edge.

Norm began to fight him, kicking out with his heavy boots and flailing his fists aimlessly, but his movements were weak and slow from the cold. "She's drowning, you bastard. Let me go! Help me!"

Michael pinned him easily, face down on the ice, saying as gently as he could. "She's gone, Norman. You can't find her that way. You'll never see her in there. It's black as pitch and the currents are strong here. You know it will have carried her away already. You know you'll die too if you go down there. You have to think of Rosie now."

Before Norman could respond, a loud, ominous crack

split the air as the ice gave way under their combined weight and dumped them into the frigid waters.

Shelley screamed. Her instinct to protect a loved one overrode her common sense and without caution or thought, she started to run toward them. The terrible sinking feeling in her gut eased somewhat when she saw first one and then the other bob to the surface with the slabs of broken ice.

Michael roared from the shock of the cold, cold water. "Stay back!" He yelled savagely when he saw her coming. "So help me God, Shelley, if you take another step I *will* beat you! Stay with Rosie."

Both men grappled desperately for the edge, for something secure to hoist themselves up on, but every seemingly solid piece of ice crumbled, one after the other, taunting them with the promise of safety. It seemed an eternity passed as she stood helplessly, watching them thrash around, wild-eyed with panic in the bitterly cold, black water. They wouldn't be able to keep it up much longer at such a temperature. Her mind raced, searching for something she could do, some tool she could use, but they had come ill equipped in a rush, never expecting such a disaster. She ran back to the snow mobile and ripped open the pack Michael always kept tucked in the back. Dumping the contents in the snow, she pawed through them frantically. There were wooden tip-ups for fishing, with packages of hooks and lures, a flashlight, a GPS or global positioning system, three flares, four thin stakes with fluorescent red flags on them, extra gloves, matches, a chocolate bar and a shiny thermal blanket - the kind that comes in first-aid kits. There was also a small axe and two rope stringers for fishing.

She tore off her mitts and with shaking hands quickly

threaded one of the stringers through the ring on the other. Grabbing the axe, she made her way back to the men. The cold had stiffened their muscles, rendering them sluggish and ineffective and so by this point they were capable only of hanging limply onto the ice edge. Shelley closed her eyes in a brief moment of indecision. This could end up breaking the very ice she was standing on, but what choice did she have? She would never be able to hold the rope on her own. With all her strength and a fiercely muttered prayer, she swung the small axe, embedding it deep into the ice. When she was positive that the ice beneath remained solid, she wrapped the stringer around the neck of the axe and threaded it through the ring to hold it tight. Her fingers were numb from the cold, so numb she couldn't feel the slight rope between them as she gathered the length of it and tossed it into Michael's pale, grasping hand.

Pausing just long enough to see him pull himself out, she raced over to Rosie, who lay still and silent on the ice, bundled in her father's wet parka. Her black pigtails were frozen into stiff, frosted ropes. Her little chest rose and fell, but the breaths were slow and shallow. Her face was deathly pale, with her lips and eyes ringed with blue. She blinked up at Shelley once, with a sleepy, faraway look before the lids slid closed. They didn't open again and Shelley felt her heart begin to race in fear. She pulled the toddler from the folds of the jacket and unzipped her own snowsuit. It was actually Michael's and even though her belly filled out the lower part, there was still enough room to tuck Rosie in there and zip it back up.

She moved awkwardly with the extra burden but hurried back to where the men had crawled along the ice to collapse in exhaustion. Time and cold were her enemies now, she knew. If she couldn't get everyone warm soon, hypothermia would kill them. She roused Michael without too much difficulty and together they half dragged, half carried Norman to the sleigh and placed him inside. She covered him with the blanket from the kit and placed the wet parka over it to keep the wind from whipping it away. Dropping to her knees, she sorted through the gear she had dumped in the snow, looking for the GPS to pinpoint their location. She did her best to commit it to memory then hurriedly repacked everything but the flagged stakes. Those she hammered quickly into the ice, several feet apart and as close to the hole as she dared. The ice ridge was on the other side of the open water and should be marked as well, but she had no time and no way of getting to it right now.

    The ride to the cabin seemed unbearably long; the wind whistled under her helmet, biting into her cheeks and stealing her breath away. Michael was seated behind her this time and she could only imagine how it must be stinging him, already wet and chilled to the bone. She tried her best to shield him from it with her body, but he was so much bigger than her that blocking him entirely was impossible.

    Norman was unconscious when they arrived, so they carried him upstairs to the bathroom. She watched Michael for a moment, while he awkwardly stripped Norman of his wet clothes. His jaw was clenched tightly at the enormous effort the simple task required of him. His hair, frozen in messy clumps, framed a face so pale that the stubble on his jaw seemed unnaturally dark and his eyes were like two bleak, black holes. She moved forward to help but he waved her away.

"I can manage," he assured her quietly, nodding toward the unmoving form still tucked into her snowsuit. "Do what you can for Rosie."

"We have to get you into some warm, dry clothes," she protested.

"After."

"Michael -"

"After," he insisted, just as quietly as before, but with a firm stubbornness she rarely glimpsed in him. "He's my friend. If I hadn't sat around here so long wondering, we might have been able to save Marylin. The least I can do is make sure they survive. Now go."

Muttering to herself about pigheaded, intractable men, she marched to the laundry room and started to fill the small tub with water, stripping off her bulky snow suit while she waited. She fretted over the temperature, testing and readjusting until it was only slightly warm, then peeled Rosie's thawing winter clothes off; the tiny Arctic Cat snowsuit and beaded leather mittens, then the pretty red dress she and Michael had sent her for Christmas. She held the little body close, appalled that a person's flesh could get this cold.

Poor baby. Shelley felt a knot form in her throat as she remembered this little face shining with joy just yesterday and her tears spilled over at the thought that this little angel might not wake up. And if she did, she would never again feel the comfort of her mothers arms around her. She lowered her into the water, supporting her head with one hand to keep it from slipping under. She sang to her, crooning any snippets of lullabies she could remember, adding hot water as it cooled each time and praying all the while to a God she didn't even believe in.

As Rosie's core temperature increased, the blood vessels began to dilate and the skin gradually flushed with colour, losing much of its frightening pallor. After drying her briskly with a towel, Shelley bundled her up in a fuzzy blanket and cuddled her close to her own body. "Please wake up, sweetie," she begged, running her fingers over the smooth baby skin of her brow and cheek. She rocked her back and forth, talking to her, sometimes singing, hoping something would make her open her eyes. But she slept on, the long black lashes never fluttering as they rested undisturbed on her flushed, chubby cheeks. She looked deceptively peaceful.

Suddenly, it just became too much. Her hold tightened on the sleeping child and she began to sob. Her heart ached with such sorrow and worry and though she fought for this little life with everything she had, in the only way she knew, it might not be enough. As if sensing the crumbled defenses, the budding feelings of maternal love she had been suppressing exploded out of her control, blossoming like a summer garden, surrounding Rosie and her own unborn baby with a love so fierce and complete that it seemed a tangible thing. She felt the baby move inside her as if responding to the unfamiliar rush of feeling, pushing at the walls of her womb with insistent little feet. It touched the deeper core of her sorrow, unrelated to the day's tragedy, and only made her sob that much harder.

"Her spirit is strong."

Shelley held her breath, cocking her head to the side in sudden concentration. She'd just heard Marylin's voice, as clearly as if she'd been standing right there. A chill coursed up her spine, causing the goose flesh to rise on her arms before she remembered. Of course. Marylin had said that only yesterday. She'd said, 'Her days will not all be happy ones but her spirit is strong, and she will accomplish much in her lifetime. I have seen this in my dreams.' Shelley had smiled and nodded, thinking it to be a powerful but nonsensical mixture of motherly pride and spiritual native lore. But it echoed now, in her head and today it had so much more meaning. The chill came again and she pushed herself to her feet, knowing now that she had done all she could. It was time to bring Rosie to her father.

She stopped in Michael's office to radio the police, giving them the details of the accident, Marylin's name and description and the coordinates she had memorized from the GPS. She was assured that a search would be launched at first light.

Laboriously, she made her way up the stairs in time to see Michael settle Norman on her old bed, then sink to his knees on the floor in an exhausted slump. She tucked the little girl beside her father and covered them with every quilt, comforter and blanket she could find in the chest at the end of the bed. She remembered seeing a heating pad in the bathroom and quickly went to fetch it. Although their skin felt warm, their bodies weren't yet able to efficiently produce enough heat on their own. All the blankets in the world wouldn't help unless there was heat trapped under them. She filled it with hot water and placed the covered pad under Norman's feet. Now all they could do was hope for the best. And get Michael warm.

She took his hand and started to lead him back through the hall to the bathroom. "Let's get those clothes off you and get you into a hot bath."

"No," he managed, as his fingers fumbled uselessly at the zipper to his cold, wet suit. "There's no hot water left."

Deciding on the best way to get him warm, she helped him step out of the suit and pull off his boots, then led him, quiet and unresisting, down to the fireplace in the living room. She poked at the fire, stirring embers and half burned logs, inciting the flames and coaxing from them a transformation. She teased the lazy red-orange licks of fire to a roaring, ravenous blaze, adding more and more wood, then she pulled a stack of blankets and pillows from the trunk type coffee table and made a makeshift bed right in front of it. She unsnapped his pants and began pulling, tugging and peeling at the sodden garments until he stood, naked and pale, in the middle of the room.

He held out his hand. His look was unfocused, his flesh alarmingly cold, but he sounded lucid when he spoke. "Come warm me up."

Stripping down to her underwear, she took his hand and crawled under the blankets after him. With his back to the warming blaze, he curled around her, skin touching skin. She jumped at the icy contact but only snuggled deeper in and closer to him. The warmth gradually returned and she dozed, as he did, until the shivers started, until his muscles were finally able to generate heat on their own. His big body shook, wracked continuously by chills so severe her worry became a palpable thing. His arms convulsed around her and she grabbed his hand in a white knuckled grip.

"Michael?" She whispered.

"It'll pass," he got out through clenched, chattering teeth. "Just don't leave me."

"No, I won't," she promised.

She didn't know how long the tremors lasted, but even as the fire died to a slow burn, to hardly more than glowing embers, still he shivered. She tried to ease out of his embrace to add more wood but his arms locked around her even tighter than before.

"No," he groaned. "Don't go."

"Just for a second, baby. I have to stoke up the fire. We can't let it go out - it'll get too cold in here." She smoothed the hair back from his brow, now dried in an unruly collection of curls and spikes. "I'll be back."

He let go, immediately rolling into a ball as she slipped out from beneath the blankets. She added more wood, loosely stacking pieces of pine and slower burning birch over the charred remains of the fire. Mercifully, the flames caught the dry wood quickly. She straightened, stretching unconsciously with her hands at the small of her back. It ached even more than usual.

Michael tilted his head back to look at her and she realized that lit up as she was by the growing flames behind her, she knew he had an unrestricted view of her stomach. She had nowhere to hide without making herself look ridiculous. Though she slept in his arms every night, she was vigilant in her attempts to hide her nakedness from him; this steadily increasing girth that had to make him feel ...uncomfortable at the very least. It wasn't shame exactly that made her do it, nor strictly vanity, it was the wrongness of it all. It just felt wrong laying with him, knowing that the baby within her wasn't his. It made her feel guilty and cheap, like she had done something wrong. So, even recognizing the futility of it, she continually tried to hide it from him.

He smiled at her.

She crossed her arms reflexively over her middle. "I'll be right back."

She ran up to their room to shrug into a fleece night gown that came to her knees and hid her belly. She stopped to grab something for him to wear too, though she had to dig way down to the bottom of his sock drawer for the plaid pajamas. Quickly checking on Norman and Rosie on the way back down, Shelley was relieved to find them sleeping with even, regular breathing and good colour. She was sure they would be all right come morning.

Michael was almost sleeping when she bent over him again. "You'll be warmer with these on," she suggested softly, rubbing the red and black flannel across his cheek.

"No thanks," he answered in a drowsy voice, barely even glancing at them.

"They're warm," she coaxed.

He woke up enough to give her a steady look. "No. I hate pajamas," he insisted, setting his mouth in a mulish line. "I can't feel you next to me with those on."

"Yes, you can," she scoffed, but the idea of dressing a full grown, reluctant male held little appeal, so she tossed them on the coffee table. She added one final log to the fire then settled back in beside him, wiggling backward into his arms. She could still feel the occasional shudder run through him, just small ones now, but his body finally felt comfortably warm against her back.

He sighed and his breath ruffled the hair at her nape. She felt a hand slide up her leg underneath her night gown, pulling it up. The garment went up and up, over her hips where it bunched over the swell of the baby. Then, easing one hand under her, he lifted her just enough to pull the gown right over her head and toss it across the room.

"I just put that on!"

"Yeah, I guessed that," he said lightly, mocking her outrage. "I hate your pajamas, too. I was trying to be understanding but I only just realized what you've been up to these last two months. You've had some pretty good excuses, but you're just trying to hide from me." He ran a hand over her stomach. "It's not like I don't know it's there. I still think you're beautiful and I miss your skin against me." His lips lightly touched her shoulder.

Shelley grew pleasantly drowsy in a silence punctuated only by the popping and crackling of the burning wood, and was almost asleep when he spoke again. "I love you," he whispered fiercely. "I don't know what I would do if that was you lost under the ice somewhere."

She kissed his palm and held it tight. As sad as this day had been, from it she had finally learned an important lesson, a key that she had never before been able to grasp. Marylin was a good person; many loved her and a great many would keenly feel her loss. Her death was in no way a reflection of how she lived her life. It was not a punishment for her deeds nor some cosmic force of karma. Since the attack last summer Shelley had asked herself many, many times, what have I done in my life to deserve this? What have I done? She understood now. At long last, she finally understood. The world keeps turning, time keeps marching on. It wasn't about her, or Marylin. The world was just so much bigger than that. Life was full of hardships; drought, hunger, sickness, toil and pain. But it was full of wonder too; it could be joyful and bountiful and full of blessings. If one could just hang on through the storm, the sun would shine all that much brighter when the clouds cleared. Michael was her first blessing and now she had her eyes and arms wide open, ready to embrace any and all that came her way. Even with this new understanding she felt the sorrow weigh heavily as she waited for sleep to claim her once more, and though she wept for Marylin and the loss of the great friendship that could have been, in a strange way, she also wept in relief and in the enlightenment of her own spirit.

CHAPTER TWENTY THREE

Shelley rose early the next morning, long before the day had even thought about pushing the sun up over the horizon. Her sleep had been fitful and uncomfortable, full of disturbing dreams of death and loss. The sadness was a living thing in the cabin this morning, greedily gobbling up all the happiness and joy from the weekend. She didn't want to face Norman. She didn't want to be a witness to his grief or share in Rosie's pain. It would all be so impossibly difficult to do without her heart breaking all over again. Sipping at the one precious cup of coffee she allowed herself every morning, she sat on the window seat in the kitchen, in the dark, and made a mental list of all the things she had to accomplish before everyone else got up. Leaning her head against the pane, she watched the colors of the night shift from deepest black to a lighter shade of midnight blue and then finally to the grey of early dawn.

When she drained the last drop from her cup, she tiptoed up the stairs and dressed quietly, pulling out clean clothes for Michael as well. She fed the dogs and let them out, fed the cat and got the fire going. She collected the wet clothes and winter wear that had been scattered throughout the house and put them in the dryer, gathering the boots up as well to set by the fire. Next, she whipped up a french toast strata with bread cubes, milk, eggs, cream cheese, apple pieces and cinnamon and put it in the oven to bake. She was quite sure that no one was going to want to make a big affair of breakfast, but they had to eat and she thought this simple dish would be ideal.

As was her usual habit, she gathered the clothes from the dryer and collected them in a basket, moving to the living room couch to fold them. Michael still slept soundly before the fire. Every time she looked at him she felt a relief so intense she wanted to weep. In her months of healing and growing, she had built her life up around this man. If he had disappeared under the ice like Marylin, the devastation she would feel would be unthinkable. It worried her sometimes, that she loved him so much, that she depended on him for her own happiness. She could only hope that if something terrible happened to him, she was strong enough to take the happy memories, hold them to her heart and move on. She had learned much about herself in the time she had been here; finding new hobbies, skills and interests. She had grown both emotionally and spiritually and it left her feeling far better prepared for the world than she had been before. Reaching down, she felt his forehead, reassured by the healthy warmth and let her fingers run back through his messy hair.

With a sigh, she selected the items that belonged to Norman and Rosie and climbed the stairs to their room. She was just raising her hand to knock on the bedroom door when she heard Rosie's baby voice through the crack.

"Daddy?"

Although immeasurably relieved that the sweet, black haired child was finally awake, Shelley hovered uncertainly at the door. She didn't want to intrude on what promised to be a private, painful and awkward conversation.

"Daddy?" Said the little voice again. "Where's

Mommy?"

"Rosie ...Mommy is ...gone. She's gone up to heaven."

"Okay." There was a small silence. "But when is she coming back?"

Shelley heard a heavy sigh.

"*Aginibag,* my little Rose Flower. Mommy won't be coming back." His voice caught, ragged with barely suppressed emotion. "She died, Sweetie. Do you know what that means?"

"Kelpie died," the little girl remembered.

He sounded slightly relieved. "Yes. Your goldfish died."

No one spoke for a moment and Shelley could tell by the child's very lack of reaction that she didn't understand. There was a rustle of blankets.

"It's okay, baby girl. We'll get through this. One day you'll understand. You'll remember how wonderful your mother was and how very much she loved you. *Gi zah gin.*"

"I love you too, Daddy."

Shelley leaned against the wall and wiped at her eyes, aching for him. Rosie might be his heart, but Marylin had been his sunshine. He had adored her. Actually, they had adored each other and that's what made them such a special couple.

Cursing her cowardly nature, she firmed her resolve and knocked.

The soft response was immediate. "Come in."

She held the clothes in front of her like a shield as she moved into the room. It was foolish, for the moment she met his dark eyes the grief in them hit her, solid as a wall. She realized sadly that before this moment, she had never seen them without their usual mischievous sparkle, lit up from within so brightly that he was always able to make her smile without saying a word. Now they were dull and flat, those inner lights dimmed by the emptiness of his loss.

Steeling herself against it, she placed the stack of folded clothes on the end of the bed. She didn't know what to say. Everything that came to mind seemed inappropriate; nothing she could say would make it better. Her upbringing had made her poorly equipped for expressing her emotions. She felt such compassion and sympathy for him and his little girl but she just didn't have the words to tell him. "I'm so sorry, Norman," she said finally with a helpless shake of her head. "It's not fair."

"No," he murmured with a sad smile. "It's not." He reached forward to touch her hand. "Thank you, Shelley, for the clothes and well, for everything." His gaze fell to his daughter, still clasped tightly to him in a hug. "I couldn't go on if I'd lost them both."

She stood there for a moment, wringing her hands, unsure how to offer assistance. "I'm not sure what your plans are today, Norman, but I'd be more than happy to look after Rosie for you." She didn't wait for him to answer, rushing to add. "You should probably go to the hospital and have a doctor look at the frostbite on that hand. Whatever you decide, just let me know. They will have started the ...search by now. I gave them the coordinates last night." Unable to stop, she rambled on. "Breakfast is ready whenever you are. I know you probably don't feel like eating, but ...you should. Umm ...Michael will be up any minute now-" She closed her mouth so abruptly to stop her own babbling that her teeth clacked together painfully. "I'm sorry."

"Don't be," Norman said gently. "You don't know what to say. Neither do I. It is enough that you and Michael are here for me. Words are not necessary." He touched her hand again.

"We will be down shortly."

At his simple words, the tension that had been stretching and growing in her neck and chest snapped, retracting to manageable levels like a released rubber band. With a grateful nod, she left them to dress and for Norman at least, to brace himself for the difficult day ahead.

Michael was up and dressed when she got back downstairs, standing in front of the open refrigerator. He was drinking milk out of the carton.

"Oh, you're so refined, Mr. Daillant. That's *so* elegant."

Startled, he tipped the carton too far back, and two white rivers of milk coursed down his chin, dripping onto his clean shirt. He smiled disarmingly. "Oops. Caught in the act."

"Men stay little boys forever, don't they?" She asked, returning his smile.

She moved to the sink to start the dishes and he followed, standing behind her, automatically massaging her lower back as he often did for her these days. "How are they? Are they both awake?"

"They're both awake. Rosie is confused, poor thing. Norman is …well, he's alive. His hand seems to be fairly frostbitten though."

"How are you holding up?" His breath ruffled the hair at her temple, relaxing her one exhale at a time.

She angled her head up and back to look in his eyes. "Me? Oh, I'm doing all right. How about you, though? She was your friend for a long time."

"I'm mostly …stunned right now, I think."

Lost in their own thoughts, they both watched the water rising in the sink, watched the water swirl and eddy under its rich blanket of soap bubbles. Shelley found herself imagining, not for the first time, what it would be like to be swept away by such ambitious water and trapped under the ice somewhere, disoriented by the cold and the darkness, completely panicked as the last vestige of oxygen disappeared from her lungs. She didn't want to die that way; just the thought of it made her shudder against Michael's chest. With one arm on each side of her, he reached around, twisting the taps to off, then began to wash the dishes.

"Mike, why was there open water there? It's been cold enough."

He rested his chin comfortably on the top of her head. "It's near the mouth of the river. The current is too strong there to form a lot of ice."

"But why would the trail run so close to the mouth of the river?"

"Because it's the shortest route. Normally it's not a problem. It usually has at least a thin layer of ice, but anyway, the sleds nowadays are so fast that they can run over open water. People do it all the time. It's only a problem when you have to stop, or in Norman's case, when you hit an ice ridge."

"I assume the normal properties of ice apply? With temperature increases, the ice expands, buckling in weak spots to form ridges and with temperature decreases, the ice contracts, sometimes cracking open?"

He scrubbed hard at the crud caked on the side of one of the dog bowls, splashing dishwater on her prominent belly. "Mm Hm. Sounds right to me."

"I wonder why he didn't come through on the bush trail, like we do?"

"He likes to check his trap line on Caribou Lake. They were probably heading back from there."

"Oh." Turning in his arms, she wrapped hers around his waist and tucked her face in his neck for one greedy moment of pure comfort. It was going to be a long day.

Breakfast was somber and depressing. The men ate quickly, having decided to head out to the accident site to see how the recovery divers were doing, and to help in any way they were permitted. Marylin's body could have moved a long way under that ice and though no one said it out loud, they all knew there was a chance it may never be recovered. Shelley hated to see them go out there again - the ice was too unstable. In her mind it was like tempting Fate, tossing their survival back in its face and giving it a second chance to finish the job. But she didn't plead with them as they dressed in their winter clothes, she didn't grab at Michael's hand and hold him back. She held her tongue for Norman's daughter. She was going to need closure some day when she was old enough to understand, and she wouldn't get it if they never found her mother's body.

Rosie still sat in her makeshift booster seat after they left, unnaturally quiet. Her little face was so grave; lips pursed in concentrated thought and her daintily arched brows drawn together in concern. She might not fully comprehend what happened to her mother, but she had sensed from the tension in the room during breakfast that it was something horrible. "Mommy isn't here?" She asked Shelley tentatively, as though afraid of what the answer might be.

"No, sweetie." Shelley swallowed hard. Things like this shouldn't happen. "She's not here. God called for her when she went under the ice and so she's gone to live in Heaven."

The little girl slipped her thumb in her mouth and stared at her blankly for a moment. Her understanding dawned as if in slow motion. Her large, dark eyes glossed with tears, her face crumpled in a heart wrenching display of misery. "I want my momma."

Fighting tears of her own, Shelley reached out to lift her from her seat. "I know, baby. I know."

Rosie clung to her, wrapping around her with her arms and legs like a frightened baby monkey, sobbing now with complete abandon. "Momma," she wailed pitifully over and over until finally, exhausted and hoarse, the child could only hiccup brokenly against her shoulder.

Shelley rubbed her back and tried to swallow the painful lump in her own throat. Rosie was hardly more than a baby - she was supposed to be all giggles and dimples and cherub-like smiles, safe and happy in the security of her family. Watching her cry for her dead mother was the saddest, most heartbreaking thing she had ever seen.

Now silent and spent, Rosie's round baby eyes were swollen and they stared woefully up at her, beseeching. "Doesn't she want to be my momma anymore?"

Oh, this was so hard. "Of course she does," she assured her. "More than anything."

"Then why did she go?" Two more tears welled at the corners of her eyes before trailing down her flushed cheeks. "Daddy says she won't come back."

"She can't, Rosie. People don't get to choose when they die and they don't get to come back. I can tell you though, that where ever your mother's spirit is, she is even sadder than you are right now."

She could tell her that it would hurt less in time. She could tell her that the memories would fade and eventually, she would forget her mother altogether. To Rosie, Marylin would be little more than a picture in the family photo album. But as she watched her slip her thumb back in her mouth, reclaiming a habit she had left behind months ago, Shelley just knew she couldn't tell a child these things.

The men left early every morning the following week to accompany the divers to a new site, leaving Shelley to care for Rosie. The little girl's moods were all over the place. The tantrums came quickly and without warning; she cried and screamed and dumped her food. She begged for her mother. It became clearer, as time went on, that she still didn't understand the permanence of death, or the inevitability of it. She still talked about her mother as though she might show up in time for dinner, or to tuck her in at night and listen to her bedtime prayers like she used to. It was heartbreaking. Yet, with her sweet nature, she was always open to hugs and kisses and fun distractions. With only a little persuasion, she was all smiles again, happy to work on puzzles, play games and make tasty cookies. They went for walks in the snow to pass the time, playing follow the leader, pointing out birds and following the rat-a-tat-tat of the woodpeckers in the trees. She was bright though, for four years old, understanding some things that Shelley thought would be beyond a child that age.

One particular conversation they had in the woods convinced Shelley that it wouldn't be long before she understood, and accepted, what happened to her mother. They had spotted tracks in the snow that day and followed them a short distance down the path. The tracks were large and crescent shaped, with characteristic dew claw imprints. They seemed to her to be wider, rounder and more widely spread for support than the moose tracks she had studied earlier in the season. "Caribou," she had declared, proud of her improving tracking skills. She remembered admiring the big, proud bull on the beach those many months ago on her first night back from the hospital, remembered his grace and presence and sent out a silent, reverent hope for his safety, where ever he might be.

Rosie had quickly moved to one of the marks and planted her feet squarely over it. She grinned up at Shelley. "You know what my mommy says?"

"No, what does she say?"

She pointed to the print. "If you stand in these, and be good and follow the path, the caribou spirit will look after you. She says I claimed his spirit when I was really little and that he will keep me safe."

"Wow, sweetie. Those are some big words. Do you know what it means?"

"Yeah." She jumped up and down on the hoof print. "It means a little part of him watches over me, like an angel."

"How did you claim his spirit?"

Rosie had frowned in thought for a moment and then shrugged. "I stood in his footprint. It was easy." She tugged at Shelley's arm with her little hands. "You do it." She pulled a little harder. "You stand in it too, Shelley."

"My feet are too big, Rosie."

"No!" She'd insisted, suddenly tearful. "You stand in it! If you don't, he can't keep you safe and you'll go away just like my mom."

To mollify her before it led to a full fledged tantrum, Shelley moved quickly into another hoof print, covering it completely with her winter boots. "There, all done," she pointed out cheerfully. "You know, you're extra specially lucky, Rosie. Now you have two spirits watching over you. The caribou and your mother. You have two angels."

The little brown face had lit up. She was close, really close to understanding this violent upheaval in her short life.

The games and walks kept her grieving heart busy and passed the time, but the men always returned before dark with growing shadows under their eyes and drawn, pale faces. And no news. It was five long, difficult days before Marylin's body was found.

After the funeral, the Keepers moved back to town. Norman went back to work, Rosie was placed in day care and his sister-in-law kindly moved in with them to help carry them through such a difficult time. Michael, in melancholy moments, would reminisce about Marylin and the good times they'd had together as friends, celebrating her spirit with happy memories. Life went on for everyone around her, but Shelley felt that for her, everything had come to a sudden stop. Strangely, out of the entire chaotic tragedy, she felt the loss of Rosie's presence in their house the most keenly. It just felt so empty. Her yearning for the little girl fueled the vicious cycle of bitterness and resentment she had been fighting all winter. Though pregnancy had at first seemed to her a fate worse than death, time, circumstance and no doubt the relentless output of hormones had steadily created in her a longing, a need even, to be a mother. Though it seemed a monumental, challenging task, she considered it one of the most meaningful things she could ever choose to do. Sharing her life with Michael had given her so many sweet, unexpected rewards and she just knew that doing the same with a child would be even more wonderful. What she resented the most, what she could not fix, was that she did not consider the unborn baby to be hers. She never had and she was certain that she never would.

From the moment she decided to carry it to term she thought of herself as a surrogate, no more than a vessel and now, it seemed more unfair than ever.

CHAPTER TWENTY FOUR

The winter sun was surprisingly cheerful, blazing through the living room picture window. Mother Nature dangled the promise of spring before them with an absolutely beautiful first day of March. Shelley settled back into the cushion of the couch, trying to create a more comfortable position to ease the ache in her back. There was a book propped on her upraised knees but as usual, she ignored it, choosing instead to watch the winter birds jockey for a better spot on the feeder outside. So far this morning she had spotted both red and yellow gros beaks, whiskey jacks, woodpeckers, a blue jay, and of course her favorite, the black capped chickadee. They were such delightful little birds and the *chick-a-dee-dee- dee-dee-dee* that they sang to her each morning always made her smile. The ravens too, were fun to watch. Bigger than most cats, the crafty birds would take the bread crusts and scraps left out for them and bury them in holes in the snow or under the roofing tiles, storing them for later like a clever dog. She had even seen one pull the candy bar bag from the hidden storage space of Michael's snowmobile, actually peeling the Velcro flap up to steal it! It was hilarious.

Her peaceful bird-watching was interrupted when Michael purposefully cleared his throat to get her attention. He was standing at the end of the couch, looking at her with a strange, nervous expectation. "Shell? I've written two letters."

She smiled at him from around her book, amused by the matter-of-fact statement, and lifted her brows in question.

"To *their* families. Scott's and Mark's."

Her brows dived instantly from their current elevation to meet in the centre of her brow.

"Don't frown at me," he said patiently. "It's part of my therapy. I can't confront the men I killed. They can't make me understand why they did what they did, so I decided to write their families."

"Are you crazy?!" She slammed her book down onto the coffee table and the birds outside fluttered off in alarm. "What do you think you're going to get out of that? Probably a law suit because you shot their sons!"

"Shelley-"

"You're asking for trouble, Mike! I'm telling you, leave it alone."

"Shelley, I need to do this. It feels unfinished, unresolved, unexplained. You must know how I feel. Don't you want to know why?"

Shelley felt a sudden throbbing in her temple. She wasn't sure why she felt so strongly about it, but she didn't want him to send those letters. He would be opening Pandora's box, surrounding them once more with an atmosphere of danger and bitter, bitter feelings. There would be accusations and finger pointing and it filled her with an unspeakable fear. "There is no why, Mike. Marylin's death helped me figure that out. It wasn't part of some grand design, it just *happened*. I was there, you were there and they were there! That's it. That's why. It's all you're going to get."

He was already shaking his head. "No, baby. You're wrong. They can tell us why. What happened in their lives to make them capable of such a thing. They can help us understand."

"I already understand, Michael," she said more venomously than she meant to. "I understand that they raped us and beat us and were going to kill us. I get it."

He flinched back at the sting of her words, but didn't give up. "I need this to help me forgive them. It's time to forgive them. Both of us."

"I don't want to," she refused stubbornly, crossing her arms over her chest like a willful child. "They don't deserve it. They don't deserve my forgiveness and nothing their families can say will make me change my mind."

Michael's gaze was intense, boring into her own eyes and she felt his disappointment weigh heavily on her shoulders. "What if Scott's family wants the baby?" He asked softly.

"I'm not giving them this baby!" She hissed violently, shocking herself with the force of her own words.

He tilted his head with sudden focus. "Really? Why not? You don't want the baby. You've told me so a hundred times."

"Because they're monsters. Those men couldn't have come from anything less. Anyway," she said, intentionally dismissing the conversation with a flip of her hand, "I don't want any part of your letters. If you feel like you must send them, then send them. I'll come visit you in prison." That was a ridiculous thing to say and she knew it, but the whole thing made her so angry. She was thrilled that Michael's therapy was helping him but this was too much. Way too much. Forgiving them was something she could not do. The frustration mounted; her eyes filled and her chin wobbled as the blend of emotions threatened to get the best of her.

Instead of getting angry at her belligerent words as she had expected, Michael pulled her over to him and gently folded her into his arms. "That's not you, Shelley-belly. I know you, remember? You're sweet and thoughtful and compassionate. You're forgiving." One hand stroked reassuringly over her long hair. "Let it go for your own peace of mind."

"I can't, I can't, I can't." She protested tearfully into his shoulder. "I'm just not there, Michael. I *want* to be angry with them. I want to hate them and part of me is really, really angry that you're ready to just leave it behind."

"I have to. I can't risk letting my anger loose and hurting you, not again. I don't want to let them ruin the rest of my life. I've had a lot of help to get this far but it's the right thing to do."

She couldn't bring herself to write a letter of her own. Sitting in Michael's office after lunch, she got out a piece of paper and a pen and tried, really she did, but she couldn't even get past the opening. 'Dear Mr and Mrs Houseman' was hypocritical. They certainly weren't dear to her and she couldn't pretend they were. After an hour of doodling flowers and curlicues on the page she gave up, crumpling the paper before tossing it in the trash.

She had refused therapy when Michael decided to go in January. '*I* don't have an anger problem' was her excuse and at the time, it had seemed like a good one. But as she noticed the improvements in Michael's attitude, the amazing success he'd had at controlling his temper and even the healthy way he was dealing with Marylin's death, she had to wonder if she'd made a mistake. Was her own bitterness poisoning her mind?

Was she holding herself back? She felt that she'd made a lot of breakthroughs on her own; she'd actually been proud of herself until today. Now she felt ashamed of her own thinking, her own feelings, and she just didn't know what to do. Did hating those men make her a horrible person? Or not wanting to keep the baby? Did that make her a horrible person? Whatever, she thought finally. I can't change who I am - I'm not Michael and there is no point in thinking about it anymore.

But as the days went by, getting closer and closer to her due date, she thought about it a lot, so much in fact that sometimes it made her feel physically, horribly ill. She started getting tension headaches. She couldn't sleep. She found it difficult to eat and vomited violently when she did force something down. She even broke out in hives. Michael tried everything to cheer her up; he pampered her, rubbing her swollen feet, running her bath, reading to her, making her healthy snacks, but nothing seemed to help and he was starting to get frantic with worry. He even went to town to discuss it with her doctor since she felt too sick to go. Not surprisingly, all the symptoms were narrowed down to one underlying cause: stress.

෴

Having awakened reluctantly from her afternoon nap, Shelley forced herself to get out of bed, even though she felt miserable, and shuffled to the bathroom for a drink of water. Catching her own reflection in the mirror, she felt perversely compelled to study it, to note the changes this sickness of body and spirit had wrought in her. Her face was wan and almost gaunt. She didn't have to step on the scale to know that she'd lost weight in the last two weeks. She was thirsty all the time and dehydrated because she still couldn't keep anything down. As a result her hair was getting dry and brittle, her lips were chapped and peeling and her skin was unbearably itchy. She decided, with a tiny spark of her old humour, that she looked like she'd been dragged behind a bus. In the desert.

She took a few careful sips of water then brushed her teeth and washed her face. Sometimes that made her feel better. She slathered lip balm on her parched lips, dusted a tiny bit of blush on her pale cheeks and was just finishing her braid when she heard the dogs bark downstairs. A kernel of excitement quickened her steps as she started down the stairs, thinking perhaps Norman had come with Rosie for a visit. She worried about them still and had thought about them often in the last few weeks, though she had been too ill to run into town with Michael to check on them.

When she stepped down from the last stair she realized the room was absolutely, eerily silent. Rosie and Norman hadn't come to visit. Instead, a woman, a very thin, delicate woman perched on the edge of the plush couch cushion, clutching her purse with both hands. She looked about the room in a birdlike fashion, moving her head in small increments, tilting it this way and that. Her hair was a fashionable ash blond, subtly threaded with grey and stylishly cut. The grey slacks she wore were elegant and clearly expensive, as was the matching blazer. Shelley was burning with curiosity, so much so that she didn't at first notice Michael or Daniel. Flanking the room like the points of a triangle, they all sat as far from each other as possible.

The tension was tangible and almost claustrophobic.

She felt exhausted already from the short flight of stairs and wanted to sit down, however she had to pass in front of the unfamiliar woman to join Michael on the love seat. Pushing aside her instinctual reservations about their guest, she decided to approach her and make her own introductions to speed things along. If she appeared the gracious host while doing so then all the better. "Hello," she said politely, extending her hand. "I'm Shelley. Are you a friend of Michael's?"

"Ah, no," stammered the woman, suddenly looking much less poised. She reached out to shake the proffered hand. "I'm Natalie Houseman. Scott was my son."

Without thinking, Shelley pulled her hand back in alarm. She looked at Michael in direct accusation and felt the full force of her nausea return. She didn't have time to run. She didn't even have time to turn away before her upset stomach hurled the small amount of water she'd sipped on right back out. It splashed over the cozy area rug and the tasteful black dress boots of her rapist's mother.

Shelley was stunned, mortified and enraged but could only stand there, unable to express any of it as her body continued to heave, trying to purge something, anything from her aching, empty stomach. Michael was up in an instant, cupping her elbow for support. "Come with me, baby," he urged gently, ignoring Natalie, her horrified expression and her soiled footwear.

He helped her to the downstairs bathroom where she retched and retched, so violently that she worried the baby was going to come early. Caring hands rubbed her back and strong arms held her as her stomach convulsed. "Try deep, slow breaths," he soothed. "That's it. Breathe slow."

"Did you invite her here?" She asked shakily when it finally passed. "Tell me this wasn't some horrible surprise." She felt too weak to do anything but slump against the sink.

"No, I didn't. Daniel brought her and I'm just as surprised as you. Well," he amended with a little smile. "Maybe not quite as surprised as you. I didn't throw up on her shoes."

"It's not funny," she said resentfully.

He kissed her cheek. "Yes, it really is. Come on, let's go see what she has to say."

Shelley didn't want to hear what she had to say. She didn't want to talk to her at all and she most especially didn't want to look at her, but she couldn't stay in the bathroom forever. Grudgingly, she let Michael help her back to the love seat where he tucked a blanket around her, gave her a glass of juice with a vitamin and even placed a basin near her feet just in case. She was relieved to see that Daniel had already rolled up the soiled rug and taken care of Natalie's boots. Despite her embarrassment, she couldn't bring herself to apologize.

"I'm so sorry," Natalie said first, surprising them all. She looked from Shelley to Michael and then back again. "I shouldn't have come unannounced like this. The last thing I wanted to do was upset you."

"Shelley has been ill, Mrs. Houseman." Michael volunteered when Shelley didn't answer. "It wasn't your fault."

The older woman acknowledged his kindness with a slight nod. "It's Natalie, please." Shelley heard a slight tremor in her voice and realized suddenly that her cool demeanor was nothing but a well practiced, polished front. It bothered her that she wasn't as cold as she appeared.

Michael cleared his voice. "Can I offer you some tea or coffee or anything, Natalie? Daniel?" When they both declined, he finally, thankfully, got to the point everyone was waiting for. "Why exactly have you come, Natalie?"

"I came because of your letter, of course, Mr. Daillant. It was difficult, very difficult and painful to read and I felt ...well I simply felt I had to come. Mostly I wanted you to know, both of you, that I am so deeply sorry for what Scott has done." Her long fingers clutched at the purse she held until her knuckles whitened under the pressure. "And, if you like, if it will help you that is, I can tell you about him. And why he was the way he was."

Shelley worked to keep her expression closed. What did the lady expect? That she and Michael were just going to laugh and say 'goodness, that's okay'?

Looking at her searchingly, he gently squeezed her hand and when he spoke, it was a whisper for her alone. "Are you ready for this, Shelley-belly?"

She knew he wanted this for his own peace of mind and so she nodded, squeezing his hand in return.

"I think that might help," he said to Natalie. "Please, go ahead."

Some of the tension visibly drained from the older woman and she pursed her lips for a moment as she thought about how to begin. "Scott was a difficult child right from the beginning. He was forever beating up on his baby sister or pulling the cat's tail or taunting kids at school. I used to think that good parenting could conquer any behavioral issues in a child but that just isn't so. My husband and I tried everything; more discipline, less discipline, family counseling, grounding, spanking, reasoning. He was diagnosed with an 'antisocial personality disorder' and nothing helped. What worried me the most, what scared me to death, was that no matter what he did or how horrible it was, he never felt sorry afterwards. Never." She fell silent, blinking those pale, icy blue eyes that were so like her son's slowly, as if lost in memories. "When he was ten, we found the charred remains of the family cat in the back yard. I loved her," she added softly. Her mouth tried to curve in a wry smile but it faltered, giving her a tragic, pathetic air. Despite her intention to remain aloof, Shelley found that the woman's sorrow moved her.

"When he was twelve, he beat up a sweet little boy in our neighborhood, very, very badly. Scott wanted his bike and so he took it. The boy lived but he sustained permanent brain damage and will never function independently, never above a five year old level. Scott went to reform school not long after and was in and out of there until he was eighteen. We never saw him much after that. I didn't even know where he was, until I got your letter." She paused, pursing her lips again. "I don't know you, Mr. Daillant, or how you feel about what you had to do, but I want to make sure you understand that killing my son was the only thing you could have done. He had no conscience. I *know* he would have killed you without batting an eye." She leaned forward, her expression grave. The last, lonely light of afternoon glinted off the tears in her eyes, making them shimmer like precious diamonds, but she did not cry. "That's hard for me to say because I brought him into this world and despite everything, I loved him. I changed his diapers and kissed his hurts like any mother, but I couldn't make him a good person."

Natalie looked Michael over carefully before moving on to Shelley. "Were those scars ...did Scott do that?" She asked, swallowing visibly.

Michael nodded. "Yes. Most of it." He fingered the thin

silvery scar above his eye. "It's the scars you don't see that are hard to put behind you, though."

Her narrow shoulders sagged with the burden of this new knowledge. "I understand." She shifted in her seat, this time hugging the purse to her chest. "Please forgive me for asking, Shelley, but were you already pregnant when he …when he assaulted you?"

Shelley stared at her, wishing her feelings of hostility hadn't deserted her so completely. She thought about lying, but she simply didn't have the energy for subterfuge or deceit. She was tired of being confused and ashamed of her own emotions. She suddenly yearned to have a woman to talk to and cry with and she knew with certainty that Natalie would understand her fears. Even as Shelley thought about it she shook her head at the irony of it all. It would be like confiding in the mother of Satan, but strangely, it felt right. "No," she said firmly. "I wasn't."

Natalie straightened her spine and took a deep fortifying breath. "Gentlemen, would you mind giving us a moment alone?"

Michael looked at Shelley in concern. "Uh, is that necessary? I don't think she's up to it-"

Shelley interrupted with a touch on his arm. "It's okay, Mike. I'll be fine. It's okay," she said again when he hesitated. "We won't be long. Maybe you and Dan can make us all some tea."

He frowned. "All right."

After the men left, they looked at each other, woman to woman, with an understanding and respect that instantly forged a bond between them. Shelley felt the words building, climbing in her throat faster than she could get them out. It was a release that she hadn't even known she desperately needed and she gave into it. "I'm so afraid," she whispered. "I'm afraid to give birth, Natalie but more than anything I'm afraid I will hate myself for the rest of my life when I give this baby up."

Natalie sat beside her and took her hand. Tall and blond and cultured as a pearl, she had seemed cool and untouchable to Shelley, but her hand was warm and comforting. "My dear girl. I wish I could tell you it will be all right. I wish I could tell you that birthing was easy and that babies came with guarantees, that this child will not be like my son. I wish I could tell you that you will be happy with whatever decision you make, but I can't. We both know I would be lying. What I can tell you is you are strong, I can see it, and that you can handle what is coming. Use your logic and your heart and you won't go wrong."

They talked naturally and comfortably of so many things in the next quarter of an hour that Shelley felt almost purified, and she imagined that was what confession felt like for a true Catholic. She'd had so many worries building up on her shoulders all winter and although Michael was wonderful; caring and patient and understanding, he wasn't a woman and she didn't always know how to explain her concerns to him. Natalie gave her tips to help her get through the last two, difficult weeks of pregnancy and to battle her recent bouts of nausea. She gave her a better idea what to expect from childbirth itself and how she might feel afterward. They even discussed the assault, how they felt and how it was still affecting them all.

A voice floated out from the kitchen, interrupting them. "Your tea is getting cold."

The older woman smiled with amusement. "He's worried about you. We best go join them."

She braced herself to stand but Shelley reached out with a hand on her leg to stop her. "Natalie, thank you for coming here. I feel so much better about everything, but I don't want you to think ...well ...I still can't forgive your son. Scott's spirit will not find redemption from me."

Natalie hugged her warmly, clinging for a moment in her own need of comfort. "That is between you and my son. I would never expect that of you. I don't know that I can forgive him either, for what he has done to you both."

Daniel and Natalie left after dark, after hours of enlightening, getting-to- know-you conversation, of drinking bubbly spritzers and snacking on cheese, antipasto with crackers, pickles and olives. She suspected they would never hear from the family of the other man, but she was quite sure this visit would be enough. Though she had initially fought against it, it had been a far more healing experience for all of them than she ever would have thought possible.

"Can we keep in touch?" She asked Shelley with an openness and vulnerability that touched her heart.

"I would like that very much."

Shelley snuggled into bed that night beside Michael with the reassuring feeling that she had made another friend in this new life, albeit the most unlikely one she could have imagined. She could only hope that Fate had different plans for Natalie than she'd had for Marylin.

CHAPTER TWENTY FIVE

"You lost fair and square!" She bellowed as she chased Michael around the couch.

Leaping unexpectedly over the back of it, he grabbed her from behind and gave her a squeeze. His wonderful, deep laughter rumbled against her back. "I don't think I've seen anything as funny as a very, very pregnant woman running 'round and 'round the couch."

Shelley grinned up at him. "Well, somebody has to keep you honest. I won and you gave your word."

He sighed dramatically. "I don't think I'm going to play chess with you anymore."

"Poor sport." Her smile grew even wider. "Have a seat, sweetie pie. I'll go get your new book." She giggled to herself as she searched the library for the perfect book. This was going to be so much fun. He continually ridiculed the books she liked to read, calling them sappy and silly, so now she was definitely going to enjoy making him read one.

His eyes narrowed suspiciously when she handed him her choice. *"The Calling'?"* The cover design was nondescript so he flipped the book over to read the summary on the back. His mouth fell open in horrified disbelief and he tossed the book onto the coffee table. "No way! I'm not reading a romance!"

Shelley actually had to wipe tears from her cheeks she laughed so hard. "Too late," she said cheerily. "You promised."

"You specifically said you wouldn't make me read one of these." His voice was accusing.

"What I said was," she corrected between rounds of laughter, "that I wouldn't make you read one with a tacky cover. No half naked people in compromising positions."

"All right," he grumbled. "Just you wait though. I'll remember this next time when I win." He raised his eyebrows once or twice to emphasize his statement then grabbed the book and opened it in the middle, roughly and deliberately moving it back and forth to crack the spine. Then he crisply turned it to the first page. She guessed that he was trying to be as manly as possible about it.

Shelley wandered into the kitchen to make herself some more ginger tea with blackberry leaf. She made one or two cups a day, for as Natalie had predicted, it helped ease her nausea. Aside from some pains in her lower back and some increasing discomfort in her abdomen today, her health had turned around almost completely in the two weeks since her visit; the headaches had disappeared, she was able to keep her food down and even have a good night's sleep. But the single thing she felt to be most liberating - her thoughts were no longer worrying at her confusion and self contempt like a dog at a bone. She'd been torturing herself with thoughts of what she should and shouldn't be feeling. Talking with Natalie made something just click inside her head and she finally realized she had to focus on the real, honest emotions she was actually having. Sometimes things were so simple you just couldn't see them on your own.

She took her tea and a book of her own to join Michael on the couch, where he was dutifully reading her book. She watched him for a short time. His expression was one of resigned boredom. She even heard a snort or two of disbelief. She tried to think of something else to needle him about, just for the fun of it.

"Hey, Mike?"

"Yeah?"

"You feeling a little stuffed up today?"

"Why?"

She snickered. "Your nose is whistling."

"Shell?" He held up one hand without even looking up from his book and pinched the thumb and forefinger together. "I'm this close to establishing my dominance. My tickle fingers are getting restless."

"I'll be good," she promised, smiling into her own book, but she couldn't concentrate on it. She found herself watching him again instead. As the pages turned and the first hour rolled into the second, his attitude and expression started to change, in turns appearing thoughtful, fascinated, shocked and amused. Another hour passed, seeing him more comfortably settled, reclining into the cushions with his feet up, as she did. Grateful for his change in position, she eased her cold feet into his pant legs to keep them warm and continued to watch him.

It was far more interesting than her book, which still lay on her lap, still open to the first page. She never would have believed she could watch someone read for over three hours and not be bored by it. The book she had given him was one of her favourites. The author had a wonderful ability to make the characters come alive; they were so real and vital, their emotions honest and contagious. It made her laugh and cry every time she read it, which was about four times now. These emotions were reflected on Michael's face, so clearly that she found herself trying to guess what part he was reading. A frown, a slight widening of his eyes, a curl of his lip; all became clues in this new, fascinating game.

He reached a point in the book where his eyes returned, over and over, to the beginning of the page, where he would carefully reread it. Sometimes it looked as though his eyes even stopped moving over the words, fixing instead on a spot and glazing over. He shifted uncomfortably once or twice and Shelley finally began to suspect his problem. Clapping a hand over her mouth to keep the laughter from bubbling out, she continued to observe. When a dull flush appeared on his cheekbones, the urge to laugh was so overwhelming that she almost had to stuff a fist in her mouth to keep quiet. Her face turned red from trying to hold it in and her eyes watered profusely. There was no doubt about it. He was reading a love scene and he was aroused. The thought pushed her over the edge and she exploded with hilarity, long, wheezing bouts of laughter that had her gasping for breath.

It took her some time and much lip-biting effort to control her outburst, yet he never once looked up from his book. Finally achieving a straight face, she nudged his knee with her toe.

He waved her away without looking up.

She nudged it again, more forcefully this time. "Mike?"

"Hmm?"

"What part are you on?"

"Hmm?"

"I haven't heard you turn the page for at least five minutes. I want to know what part you're on."

When he finally looked up from his book, his entire visage was different; his eyes were hot, his mouth relaxed and sensuous, his skin flushed. She recognized that look and it almost set her off again.

"I can't believe it," he stated in amazement. "All these years I thought girls read these because they were sappy and romantic, but no. This is pure sex, Shelley. Hot sex." He shifted the buttons of his jeans uncomfortably. "I've seen you read dozens of these. I had no idea."

Shelley started suddenly as another pain knifed into her belly, sharper than before. "Well, now you know the truth," she said on a gasp. "Mike, all fun aside here, I think I'm going to go to bed. I'm having some cramps and it's getting kind of late anyway."

"All right," he said vaguely, already back into the book. "I'll be up soon."

Although the thought crossed her mind that her labour may have already started, she discarded the idea by the time she crawled into bed. The pains hadn't felt like labour, or at least the labour she imagined, and anyway, she felt fine now.

☙

"Michael!"

The urgent whisper woke him up immediately. The strain in her voice was awful and distantly familiar, stirring panic up inside him. He bolted upright in the bed.

Shelley sat up beside him, clutching her distended stomach, rocking back and forth. "Oh, God," she moaned suddenly, "Mike, I think it's coming. I think it's coming right now!"

"Now?" He echoed stupidly. "It can't! It's the middle of the night! I can't take you to town on a four wheeler when you're in the middle of labour!"

"I know. I know, Mike but it's coming. I'm going to have to have it right here."

His mouth went completely dry in an instant. "I don't know how to deliver a baby!" He exploded, rising to his knees and hovering over her in concern.

She slapped at his hands irritably and pushed him away. "Well, I don't know how to have a baby, so I guess we're even!" Then she grabbed his arm and pulled him back to her, so his cheek rested against hers. "Oh, I'm sorry, Mike. Don't go. I just can't help it - it hurts and I'm so scared."

"I know, I'm not going anywhere," he soothed, trying his best to calm her but it was hard when his own mind was racing a million miles an hour. He took a deep breath and tried to think what he should do. "All right. Let's …um …let's get you out of these pajamas." The first decision always being the hardest, things seemed to come easier for him after that. He helped undress her and slipped a short, roomy nightshirt over her head. Then he stripped the blankets from the bed and shoved absorbent towels under the fitted sheet. He got a basin ready to fill with water, found clean washcloths, towels and sheets for later, even scissors which he disinfected with alcohol. There was nothing left to do but wait and that kind of expectant inactivity stretched his worry and nerves to the limit.

His own gut wrenched in fear when the pains came, writhing in worry with her every contraction. She gasped from the intensity and force of the pain every time, setting her teeth against it, and it seemed to him that her complexion paled more with each new wave of it. Mopping the sweat from her brow, he sat on the bed beside her and read out loud from her favorite book of funny, light hearted poems. She'd had the book since she was a small child and he'd seen her pull it from her night table drawer many times in the months she had been here. It was called 'A Light in the Attic' by Shel Silverstein and he read it from cover to cover for her, to make the time pass. Still, it seemed like many hours before she felt the need to push.

He was more scared than he had ever been in his life. His palms were damp with sweat and his heart was nearly beating out of his chest. His mind kept dredging up birthing horror stories and things that could go wrong. The baby could be too big, or in the wrong position or have the cord wrapped around its neck. Then what the hell was he supposed to do? He couldn't have said how long he waited and watched and worried, or what time he felt the incredible rush of exhilaration as the moment finally came.

"Oh, my God. I can see it! I can actually see it, Shelley!" He shouted, more excited now than scared. The top of the head, dark red and fuzzy, pushed at the opening of her body, then slipped back inside. "No! Push, Shell."

"I am pushing," she snarled, spitting venom at him with her eyes while she mashed the bones of his fingers together in her hand. Again and again she pushed, bringing the baby's head down but it slipped back every time.

Michael felt as though he were watching the most incredible, exciting game of his life. Every time the baby crowned he felt like jumping up and down and cheering with exultation, as though his team finally had the puck, and every time it disappeared back inside her again his heart sank. She was getting tired. With exhaustion painted in mauve streaks under her eyes and drawn in the strain around her mouth, she was pale and sweaty but still spitting mad at the world for doing this to her.

"Push! You're not trying," he accused her, knowing full well it would make her angry.

It did. She screamed at him, every dirty word he'd ever heard came out of her mouth then, some of them twice. But she tucked her full lower lip between her teeth in a grimace of pained determination and leaned forward, scrunching over her knees to push and strain furiously, still grunting swear words and incoherent threats to damage his person. It took only the one extra, mighty push to free the infant at last from the haven of her body.

Michael held the tiny, slippery creature in his hands, not completely sure what to do. "It's a girl," he breathed, in complete awe of her. He was bursting with joy at being able to witness the miracle of this birth, to be able to watch such a wondrous event and especially to be the first to hold her and introduce her to the world. He knew in his heart that he had been right, that this was not the daughter of the man who had so violently altered their lives. It was his, as Shelley was his, and Scott Houseman had nothing to do with this special moment. He cleaned the little mouth out with his finger then cut and tied the cord, severing the final physical connection between mother and daughter.

Shelley flopped back on the bed, panting in exhaustion while he tenderly bathed the baby in the prepared basin of warm water. "Ten little fingers, ten little toes. She's perfect, Shelley. Just perfect." He placed her carefully in the hollow of the chair after swaddling her in a clean, folded flannel sheet. He did his best to be supportive, helpful and efficient after she passed the afterbirth, by helping her wash, then stripping and remaking the bed before tucking her under the clean quilt.

The baby's thin wail rose in volume, burgeoning until it echoed around the room in a full, healthy squall.

"I think she's hungry," he hinted, picking her up and edging toward the bed.

Shelley's head was turned away from him and when he spoke, she shook it vigorously. "No. Don't bring her to me, Michael. I can't look at her. I can't hold her to me. It's not fair to ask that of me when we both know she isn't mine to keep. She was never mine. I can't do it."

"You have to," he insisted quietly, though he understood her resistance. "She needs you."

Her face crumpled and her shoulders began to shake with silent sobs, even as she reached out to take the warm bundle from him. As if pulled by some invisible string, she bent her head to touch the little cheek with her lips, wetting it with her tears. He sat back in the chair by her bed and forced himself to say nothing, giving her this precious time to meet her baby. Or to say good-bye. He had never seen emotions as conflicting as those on her face at that moment and he could hardly bear to see her heartbreak.

It was in her to love it; he could see it shining from her eyes. She was glowing with the same kind of wonder he was feeling, but shadowing those same green eyes was her anguish and grief. Her tears fell freely, even as she raised her nightshirt. The baby butted at her breast for a moment before the little mouth clamped onto a nipple and began to suck greedily. As if unable to help herself, Shelley ran her fingers over the smooth baby cheek, over her tiny ear and the dark fuzz on her scalp. She separated the little fingers of one hand and just held it while she cried. Michael eased himself onto the bed beside her, drawing her into his arms. They laid there for a long time, together, as the sun came up on a new day, silent but for the soft, contented sounds of this new baby girl.

CHAPTER TWENTY SIX

The north wind raced across the bay, leaving sharp little swells in its wake. Broken pieces of ice rode the waves, knocking into each other and filling the air with the sweetest music. The tinkle and chime of the moving ice was magical; as clear and pure as the ring of expensive crystal. It was Break-Up, a special time for northerners that was passionately celebrated. It signaled the eagerly awaited change of season and all the natural wonders that came with it. It meant that the trees, hungry for summer sunshine, would bud soon, blossoming with furry little pussy willows and pin cherry flowers. The hardy crocus and tulip would bloom, adding colour to the black and white palette of faded winter. The bumblebees, bears and snakes would waken from their slumber and the songbirds, seagulls, ducks and butterflies would migrate back home to have their babies. Their world would yawn and stretch and open its eyes to a welcome new summer.

Shelley stuffed her hands into the pockets of her coat, hunching her shoulders against the cold wind. She knew she should go in, but she loved the sound of the ice, and it gave her time to think. A whole month had passed since she'd given birth and she hadn't for one moment regretted her decision. She felt whole and healed and happier than she ever thought possible. As a fresh gust of wind scoured her cheeks, she thought back to that special night and those few hours that she had held her baby close.

She remembered looking down at that little face in the hazy light of dawn and feeling something totally unexpected. It wasn't resentment. Not even close. It wasn't anger or bitterness or even sorrow. It was a rush of incredible, unstoppable triumph and a love so strong and pure that it left her breathless. I forgive you, Scott Houseman, she had thought. I forgive you because I've already won.

All those months she had thought it was all about her saving the baby; first from abortion, then from her own hatred and resentment and finally from her self-enforced detachment. She had never been so wrong. Michael told her those many months ago that the baby would be their salvation and he was right. The child was their saving grace, their ray of light at the end of a long, dark night. She was a living, breathing celebration of the day their lives came together. Michaela Grace Daillant was their daughter in all the ways that counted, and she was the pride and joy of their lives. One journey ends. Another begins.

Sweeping her eyes down the beach, over the small dunes of sand littered with tamarack needles, pine cones and the general clutter of spring melt, she realized she was standing on a footprint. A fresh caribou track. She smiled, remembering her conversation with the sad little girl only weeks before. "Okay, Rosie," she said into the wind, turning in a slow circle with her arms outstretched. "I will walk his path with you, Little Flower. I'm going to claim the caribou. I claim his spirit as my guardian and offer mine in return. We can watch over each other, and together, over you."

With one last look at the ice, Shelley turned up the path to her home. To her family.

I have already won.

ISBN 1412028035